ABOUT THE AUTHOR

Jen DeLuca was born and raised near Richmond, Virginia, but now lives in Arizona with her husband and a houseful of rescue pets. She loves latte-flavored lattes, Hokies football, and the Oxford comma. Her novels, *Well Met*, *Well Played*, and *Well Matched*, were inspired by her time volunteering as a pub wench with her local Renaissance Faire.

Also by Jen DeLuca

WELL MET
WELL PLAYED
WELL MATCHED
WELL TRAVELED

Well Matched

Jen DeLuca

PENGUIN BOOKS

PENGUIN BOOKS

UK | USA | Canada | Ireland | Australia
India | New Zealand | South Africa

Penguin Books is part of the Penguin Random House group of companies
whose addresses can be found at global.penguinrandomhouse.com

First published in the United States of America by Berkley,
an imprint of Penguin Random House LLC 2021
First published in Great Britain by Penguin Books 2022
001

Printed and bound in Great Britain by Clays Ltd, Elcograf S.p.A.

The authorized representative in the EEA is Penguin Random House Ireland,
Morrison Chambers, 32 Nassau Street, Dublin DO2 YH68

A CIP catalogue record for this book is available from the British Library

ISBN: 978-1-405-95653-6

www.greenpenguin.co.uk

For Ian Barnes

Without you there would be no Kilty.

One

T*he card wasn't* addressed to me.

I leaned an elbow on the bar and took a sip of my hard cider. It was happy hour at Jackson's, but I wasn't happy. I wasn't happy at all. And this drink wasn't changing anything. The card still lay there on the bar. It was still addressed to my daughter, Caitlin, and it was still from her father. The man who'd wanted nothing to do with her since the day she was born, or in any of the eighteen years after that. It was hard to believe that even after all this time, his handwriting could strike my heart the way it did. Back in the day, that handwriting had covered pages and pages of love letters. Little notes we'd leave each other on Post-its on the bathroom mirror or near the coffee maker.

Then our birth control had failed, barely a year into our marriage. The marriage itself had failed not long after that. The last time I'd seen Robert's handwriting had been when he'd signed the divorce agreement, terminating his parental rights. Rights that he'd freely, almost eagerly, given up.

Why the hell was he writing to Caitlin now?

Like poking at a bruise, I flipped the card open again.

Caitlin,

*I know I haven't been there for you. But I want you to know how
very proud of you I am. Graduation from high school is an
important milestone in anyone's life. As you move on to greater
things, I want you to know that if you ever need anything from
me, all you have to do is ask.*

With love from your father,
Robert Daugherty

I almost wanted to laugh. *If you ever need anything from me . . .*
How about eighteen years of back child support? That would be a
start. He couldn't even stick a lousy twenty-dollar bill in the card.

Our daughter had turned out great, no thanks to him. Caitlin
was a smart, funny, respectful young woman and I couldn't be
more proud of her. But that had absolutely nothing to do with
Robert, who in the end had been little more than a sperm donor.
What the hell was he thinking, getting in touch now and trying
to do a victory lap as a father? Fuck that. And fuck him.

I stared at his name, wishing my eyes could burn a hole
through this cheap card stock. I'd been April Daugherty once, for
roughly one and a half of my forty years. And if we'd stayed married, my daughter would have been Caitlin Daugherty instead of
Caitlin Parker. I thought, not for the first time, about those two
hypothetical Daugherty women, and the life they might have had.

Would Caitlin Daugherty have had an easier time of things?
Would April D and Caitlin D have worried a little less about af-
fording college, applied for fewer scholarships and grants? I'd sat

up a lot of nights with Caitlin P, our laptops side by side at the
dining room table, filling out forms late into the night. At the
time it had felt very feminist, very "us against the world," the way
most of our lives together had been. But Caitlin Daugherty would
have had a provider for a father. Maybe she would have had to
fight a little less. Maybe—

"What're you drinking?"

Oh. I glanced up and to my right, squinting at the guy in a
gray business suit who'd taken up residence on the barstool next
to mine. He didn't look familiar, and Willow Creek, Maryland,
was the kind of town where everyone at least looked familiar. He
was probably on his way down to DC—he had that Beltway look
about him. Salt-and-pepper hair with a nice expensive-looking
cut, pale eyes, a decent smile. Of course, one strike against him
was that he'd just hit on a strange woman at a bar.

I gave him a friendly-but-not-too-friendly smile. "I'm good,
thank you." There. Pleasant enough, but not encouraging.

He didn't take the hint. "No, I mean it." He moved his stool a
little closer to mine, not quite in my personal space but close
enough. I slipped the card back into the envelope and slid it onto
my other side. He peered at my drink. "Whatcha got there, a
beer? Probably a light beer, huh? I can go for that." He beckoned
at the bartender. I wasn't a person who hung out at bars, but I
came here enough that I knew her name was Nikki, and she
knew I liked the cider on draft.

"It's not a beer," I said.

He wasn't listening. "Another drink for the lady. Light beer.
And I'll have one too." His take-charge voice was grating. Maybe
he'd sound commanding in a government building in DC, but
in a town like this he sounded like a dick.

Nikki raised her eyebrows at me, and I shook my head, covering the top of my glass with the palm of my hand. "I'm good. But he can have whatever he wants." I probably should have been flattered. Not bad for someone who'd recently hit forty, right? But I was itching to be left alone. I wanted to be back down that rabbit hole with my thoughts, not dodging advances from Mr. Wannabe Lobbyist over here.

Nikki brought his drink and he held it up in my direction, expectant. What the hell. I raised mine too, and we clinked glasses in a half-hearted toast.

"So tell me . . ." He leaned in even closer, and it took everything I had to not lean away. I had my best resting-bitch face on, but this guy wasn't taking the hint. "This can't be your typical Friday night. Hanging out all by yourself in a bar like this?"

Engaging him in conversation was a bad idea, I knew, but he wouldn't go away. "Nothing wrong with a bar like this."

"Well yeah, but surely there's something else you'd rather be doing . . . ?" He raised an eyebrow suggestively, and I pressed my lips together. Jesus Christ, this guy was annoying.

"Hey, April, there you are!" Another voice, deep and masculine, boomed from my left, but this time my irritation melted away. I knew this voice. Everyone in Jackson's knew this voice. Mitch Malone was an institution—not only in the bar, but in the whole town. Beloved of the kids of Willow Creek High, where he taught gym and coached damn near everything, and beloved of most adults with a pulse who enjoyed the sight of him in a kilt every summer at the Willow Creek Renaissance Faire. Mitch was good friends with my younger sister, Emily, so by default he'd become a friend of mine too.

"Mitch. Hey . . ." I'd barely turned my head in his direction before Mitch's arm slid around my waist, tugging me half off the stool and against his side.

"What the hell, babe? You didn't order me a beer yet?" He followed up the question with a kiss that landed somewhere between my cheek and my temple, and I had absolutely no idea which to respond to first: the kiss, or being called "babe." I looked up at Mitch with narrowed eyes, about to give him shit for at least one of those things, when his eyes caught mine and one lid dropped halfway in the ghost of a wink. Ah. Okay. I could play along.

"I didn't know when you were getting here, honey." I punctuated that last word with my hand on his cheek, landing a little harder than was strictly necessary. It wasn't a slap, but it was definitely a warning. *Keep your hands where they are, mister.* "Your beer could've gotten warm, and I know how much you hate that."

"You're too good to me, you know that?" Mitch's bright blue eyes laughed down into mine, and the curve of his smile felt good against my palm. A dimple even appeared under my thumb and I snatched my hand back, keeping the movement casual. I'd been a breath away from stroking that dimple with the pad of my thumb, and that was getting a little too into character.

"Much better than you deserve. I know." Our smiles to each other were full of manufactured affection, yet it all felt so . . . comfortable. In a way that talking with Mr. Gray Suit hadn't.

Mitch stepped closer to me, fitting his body against mine, then glanced over at Mr. Gray Suit as though he'd just noticed him. "Hey, man. You need something?" His voice was light, but his arm tightened around my waist in a not-so-subtle message to the guy on the other side of me. *Back off.*

Mr. Gray Suit got the message. "Nope. I was uh . . . yeah. Y'all have a good night." He fumbled for his wallet, then moved down to the end of the bar, where Nikki was waiting to cash him out. She glanced over at us, shaking her head. I could relate. I shook my head a lot when I dealt with Mitch too.

Speaking of . . . now that we were alone, I pulled out of Mitch's embrace. "What was that all about?"

"What?" He picked up my glass, sniffed at it, then put it down with a grimace. "I was helping you out. That guy was practically drooling down your shirt."

I scoffed. "I had it handled. I don't need your help."

"You don't have to." Mitch shrugged. "Needing and wanting are two different things, you know. You can want something and not need it."

"Fine." I tilted my head back, finishing off my cider. "Maybe I don't want it either."

Mitch looked up at me through his lashes, and for a split second I forgot to breathe. Damn. Was this what women saw when he really turned his attention to them? I didn't think of Mitch in that way. I mean, sure the man was gorgeous. Well over six feet tall, his physique spoke of lots of quality time spent with a squat rack, and combined with his golden-blond hair and stunningly blue eyes, he looked like someone who had hit the genetic lottery. He had a smile you wanted to bask in, and a jawline you wanted to run a hand down to see if it felt as sharp as it looked.

Something must have shown on my face, because his expression shifted. He lifted an eyebrow, and this was nothing like when Mr. Gray Suit did it a few minutes ago. I caught my bottom lip between my teeth, worrying the skin, and Mitch's eyes darkened.

"Liar," was all he said, but his voice had a roughness to it that I'd never heard before. The air between us was charged with electricity, and for the space of a few heartbeats I couldn't breathe. Worse, I didn't want to. I bit down on my bottom lip harder so I didn't do anything stupid. Like bite down on his bottom lip.

Then I forced out a laugh, breaking the spell. "Okay, whatever." I picked up my glass, and dammit, it was empty. I put it down again.

"What are you doing here, anyway?" Mitch leaned an elbow on the bar. "You're not a drink-alone-at-the-bar kind of person."

"How do you know what kind of person I am?" But he just looked at me with his eyebrows raised, and I had to admit he was right. I wasn't that kind of person. I put my hand over the card and, after a deep breath, slid it across the bar in his direction. He flipped it open, his face darkening as he read.

"Her father?" He closed the card and handed it back to me. "I didn't realize he was in the picture."

"He's not." I stuck the card in my purse; I'd had enough of Robert for one night.

"But he wants to be, huh?" Mitch gave me a questioning look. "What does Caitlin think about it?"

"I don't know," I said wearily. "She's still deciding. That's one reason she showed me the card. I think she wants my input." He nodded, and I hated the pity in his eyes. I didn't want pity. "Let me get you that beer." I leaned over the bar, catching Nikki's attention to order a beer for him and a second cider for me. "The least I can do for helping me get rid of that creep."

Mitch accepted the beer with a thoughtful look. "You know, if you really want to pay me back, I know a way you can help me out."

"Oh yeah?" I picked up my cider. That first, icy cold sip was always the best. "How's that?"

He didn't meet my eyes. "Be my girlfriend."

I sputtered through my sip of cider. "Be your what?" I waited for his serious expression to break, for him to give me a grin and turn the whole thing into some kind of innuendo.

But instead he grabbed one of the menus on the bar. "Let's get some food. Want a pizza or something? My treat."

My immediate instinct was to say no. I'd been out for an hour or so now, and I was already starting to itch to be home. I'd had enough peopling for one night. But there was something about Mitch that made me want to stay. He didn't seem quite like himself, and I didn't want to leave him on his own.

"Sure," I said. "As long as you leave off the pineapple."

Mitch snorted. "Like I'd do that to a perfectly good pizza."

I smiled and leaned over his shoulder to look at the menu in his hand instead of getting my own. We agreed on one with a lot of meat on it and moved with our drinks to a booth. We sat in silence for a little bit while I waited for Mitch to elaborate on this whole "girlfriend" thing, but he didn't seem inclined to.

"So . . ." I said.

"So . . ." He took a pull off his beer, then cleared his throat. "How's . . . how's your leg?"

"My leg?" That was quite a subject change. My car accident was three years ago—not ancient history, but long enough that it wasn't constantly on my mind. My leg had been all but shattered then. Now it ached a little when it was about to rain. "Fine," I finally said. "I mean, I pretty much had to give up running, but it's fine. So why do you need me to be your girlfriend?" May as well be the one to rip off the Band-Aid, if Mitch wasn't going to do it.

He chuckled around another sip of beer. "I phrased that wrong."

"So you don't want me to be your girlfriend."

"No, I do." He cocked his head to one side and thought for a moment. "It's a long story."

"Well, the pizza isn't here yet, so why don't you get started."

His lips lifted in a smile, but it wasn't Mitch's usual. The guy was ridiculously cheerful on the worst of days, but this smile was different. It was hesitant, not like him at all. And that was what kept me sitting in the booth. "So here's the thing," he finally said. "There's this . . . thing."

I sighed. That cleared it up. "Okay . . . ?"

"My grandparents. This big family party for my grandparents' anniversary."

"Oh!" I barely managed to keep from cooing. "That's adorable! How long have they been married?" It had to be a big milestone for the Malone family to be throwing them a party like this.

But Mitch squinted his eyes and his mouth twisted while he thought. "Fifty . . . seven years? Fifty-six? Something like that. That's not the point."

Oh. So not a milestone, then. "How is that not the point?"

The pizza arrived, and Mitch took over, serving us each a slice before getting back to his story. "The point is, the past couple times I've seen my extended family, I've gotten the 'so when are you going to settle down and get married and pump out kids' thing. It wasn't a huge deal at first, but now that I'm over thirty it's like they're starting to panic. It turns into an interrogation."

"You're over thirty?" The words came out of my mouth before I could check them. I always associated a person's thirties with being settled, maybe even a little boring. But of course I'd had a kid in elementary school and an office job by then, so maybe I was biased. Mitch, however, still acted like a teenager in a ripped man's body, so I'd always thought of him as being somewhere in those amorphous midtwenties.

"Thirty-one." He rolled his eyes. "Ancient, according to them, which is stupid. Guys don't even *have* biological clocks."

"True." I managed not to roll my own eyes. If he was ancient, then I was a withered old crone. Good to know. "Anyway . . . they're starting to panic?"

"Yeah." He nodded emphatically while he chewed a large bite of pizza. "So I thought maybe if I brought a girlfriend that might shut them up. But I don't have a girlfriend."

"Right. Definitely a flaw in that plan, then."

"Yep." He didn't sound bothered by that. "But you'd be perfect." Before I had time for my self-esteem to rise from the compliment, he kept talking. "You know, you're older . . ."

"Hey." I sat back in the booth and crossed my arms.

"No, I mean, you look pretty good for being someone's mom."

I shook my head. "Not any better. So the minute you have a kid you're not hot anymore?"

"That's not what I'm saying. You've heard of MILFs, right? It means Mom I'd Like to—"

I put up my hands. "I know what MILF means."

"Well, you're totally a MILF."

"Um." I had no idea how to process that. Something must have shown on my face, because he sighed.

"That's not what I mean. I mean, you are. But I don't . . ." He huffed in exasperation. "What I mean is . . . You're smart. You're mature. If you went to the party with me like you were my girlfriend, you'd make me look more mature by association, you know? Then maybe they'd get off my back."

"Okay . . ." I could see his point. We'd just pretended to be a couple in front of the whole bar here, so I definitely had the skill set for it. But that had been what, about a minute and a half? This would be a whole evening, with his entire extended family. That was a long time to keep up a pretense.

Then again . . . I stole a glance across the table as Mitch waved down Nikki for the check. He wore his usual tight T-shirt, and his muscles were a great thing to look at. There were certainly worse ways to spend an evening than to be the fake girlfriend of Willow Creek's hottest bachelor. I could waste a few hours hanging on to one of those biceps. And besides, Mitch was a nice guy who'd just saved me from a creep in a gray suit. While we hadn't logged a whole lot of one-on-one time, whenever we'd hung out together we'd had a fun kind of push-and-pull banter between us. Not flirting, exactly, just . . . messing with each other. When it came down to it, Mitch was fun to be around. There wasn't any reason to say no.

But I wasn't quite ready to say yes. *Big family party.* That's what he'd said. That sounded like quite the crowd. And I hated crowds. I took another gulp of cider.

"Can I think about it?"

Mitch's face cleared up as though I'd already agreed to this whole thing. "Yeah! Of course. It's not till next month. Plenty of time."

"Okay," I said. "I'll think about it." I tried to hand Mitch my card to pay for the pizza, but he batted it away with an annoyed look.

"Cut it out, Mama. I got this."

I let him pay, but I sighed at the nickname. Everyone had a nickname when you were with Mitch. "Mama" kind of annoyed me, but it was better than "MILF," at least.

I left Jackson's with my ex-husband's card in my purse and Mitch's words echoing in my head. *Be my girlfriend.* I had a lot to think about.

Two

"S*o, wait." There* was a whir of noise from the espresso machine as my sister, Emily, frothed the milk. "He wants you to do what?"

"You heard me." I dropped into a chair at the table nearest the coffee bar. I'd swung by Read It & Weep, the bookstore that Emily managed, right when it opened. There weren't many people clamoring for books at ten in the morning on a Saturday in May, so I had her all to myself. She'd taken one look at my under-caffeinated face and led me to the coffee bar section to make us some vanilla lattes.

"I did hear you." Emily poured the steamed milk into two mugs with a half-hearted attempt at latte art. She was terrible at it, but the coffee itself was excellent, so who cared. "But I think the machine was too loud and I heard you wrong. Because it sounded an awful lot like Mitch wants you to be his girlfriend."

"Fake girlfriend," I corrected. "I don't think he's proposing an actual relationship here." *Wouldn't that be something.*

Emily came around the counter with the mugs, passing one

to me before sitting across from me at the table. "You're going to need to give me more info than that."

"I don't have much." I blew across the top of the mug. "He needs a date to a family event, and thought I'd be a better candidate than the girls he usually picks up." He hadn't put it in exactly those words, but I'd read between the lines.

"Are you gonna do it?"

"I'm not sure. I mean, it seems harmless, right?" I took a cautious sip of coffee; it was still hot.

"True . . ." Emily tapped her index finger on her bottom lip while she thought. "But you have a lot on your plate right now. Don't want you to overextend yourself."

"It's not that bad. Prom season is over, after all." That had been an ordeal. From finding the right dress, to stressing about her plans, Caitlin had been prom obsessed for the better part of this year so far. Her friend group had decided not to couple up, and instead had chipped in to rent a limo, the six of them piling in together, and from all accounts it had been a success.

"Right." Emily's voice was dry. "So now all that's left is finals and graduation. Oh, and Renaissance Faire tryouts in a couple weeks."

I groaned. "Is it time for that already?"

Emily nodded with the look of a world-weary soldier. "Every year around this time. Caitlin will be there, right? I think Simon's counting on her."

"She wouldn't miss it." That was an understatement. The Renaissance Faire was the town's big fundraiser for the local school system, and it had grown from something held on the high school football field to a multi-weekend event in the woods, including a real live joust with horses and everything. It wasn't my thing, though I'd gone once or twice.

But it was very much my daughter's thing; Caitlin had jumped in right after her freshman year of high school, and had roped in Emily too since she'd needed a chaperone. That was how Emily had met her husband, in fact, since Simon was the one who ran the whole thing. At the time, I'd actually been thankful for my car accident; if I hadn't been laid up, I would have had to volunteer with Caitlin. Or I would have had to tell her she couldn't do the Ren Faire. Both of which had been nightmare scenarios.

"I'm just saying." Emily waved a hand vaguely. "Seems like there's a lot going on at the Parker household. And that's all Cait. We haven't even gotten into your whole to-do list."

I groaned again. "Don't remind me." I should have sounded more excited. After all, I was on the verge of achieving my long-time plan: selling my house and getting the hell out of town.

Cait had been six when I'd bought my three-bedroom house in Willow Creek. I'd told myself then that it was an investment in my future. That by the time she went off to college, I'd have enough equity in the place to sell it, and hopefully get myself moved into a little apartment in the city with the proceeds. It was a dream I'd checked in on with myself every couple of years, and every couple of years I'd told myself yes, that was what I wanted to do. Someday.

But now someday was almost here. With Caitlin starting college in the fall, I was about to be an empty nester. I'd met with a real estate agent not too long ago: the first step on a long road toward achieving that dream.

"Okay, you're right," I finally said to Emily. "There's a lot. But this thing with Mitch is only one evening. How bad can it be?"

"I don't know, but this is Mitch we're talking about." The bell over the door to the shop chimed, and Emily looked up with a sigh.

"Looks like we're starting early," she said, already out of her seat and halfway to the front of the store. "Can you hang out for a little bit? Because we are so not done here."

"Sure." I wrapped my hands around my mug and wandered the bookstore while Emily talked to the customer who had come in to pick up a book she'd ordered. After that a couple more people came in, followed by a family, and a half hour later I was back at our little table, a few pages into a cozy mystery, while the table next to me was occupied by writers with their laptops. Emily was bopping between the front counter, ringing up sales, and back here at the coffee bar serving as barista. This was a tiny indie bookstore that ran on a shoestring budget and a minimum of employees, but even I could see that Em was running ragged here. Her latte had long grown cold, and mine was empty. But I'd come by on enough Saturdays to know that this was a fluke, and I didn't have any other plans so I didn't mind waiting.

My phone dinged and I put the paperback aside to scroll through my notifications. A text from Caitlin, letting me know she was going to the mall with her friends—probably the same ones she'd been out with the night before. I texted back **Sure**, because what else was I going to do? I could count on one finger the number of times she'd missed curfew, and that was when her friend's car had gotten a flat tire. Didn't count.

I stuck my phone in the back pocket of my jeans and brought both my empty mug and Emily's cold one up to the sink behind the coffee counter, right when she appeared again.

"Sorry!" She took them out of my hands quickly, like she was caught doing something wrong. "Don't worry about those, I'll take care of them."

"I can wash a mug, you know."

Her lips quirked up. "Sorry, yeah. Instinct. You know."

I did know. Emily had come to town right after my accident,

and she'd been my caretaker for a few weeks when I was basically immobile. She'd never complained, even when pain combined with narcotics had made me a contender for Snappiest Bitch of the Year. I was twelve years older than she was, but I had a feeling that she still had the need to take care of me. But that was Em. She took care of everyone.

Out loud I said, "No problem. You doing okay here?"

"Oh." She waved a casual hand, but her expression was frazzled. "Yeah. A little Saturday rush, that's all. Did you want to take off? Because I still want to hear about this Mitch thing."

That made me laugh. "There is no Mitch thing. But I can wait. Cait's out with her friends, so nothing going on at home today."

"Okay, I'll be back in a few. With new coffees, because I need caffeine."

As Emily darted up front again to greet new customers and make small talk with everyone who came in the door, I shelved the paperback I'd been reading. It was too obvious that the sweet-faced old grandma was the murderer. Maybe I should read a romance novel instead. I liked happy endings. I moved down the aisles to look through the used books, and I heard the espresso machine start up again. Oooh, was she done already? Because I could use another latte.

I moved back toward our table, paperbacks cradled in one arm, when I spied Emily handing a mug across the counter to one of the writers from earlier, along with a plastic-wrapped lemon square. The store's owner, Chris, had a killer recipe that she'd finally shared with Emily over the winter. Thank God— Chris spent her winters in Florida, and therefore wasn't around to bake for us. Now that Em had the recipe, she'd taken over the baking as well as the bookstore. Hers were almost as good, but not quite. I didn't tell Em that.

I leaned an elbow on the shelf and watched her turn to the other customer waiting for a coffee. My little sister was so in her element, surrounded by books and fresh-ground coffee beans. It was hard to think of my car accident as a good thing, but it had brought her here. Away from a bad situation and into a brand-new life. Now she managed a bookstore, volunteered with the Renaissance Faire, and last summer she'd married the love of her life. Willow Creek had been good to Emily.

"Hazelnut latte." The woman ordering didn't look up from her phone as she placed her cash on the counter. "I'll take it to go." I couldn't even see her face, just dark hair streaked with gray bent over her phone.

"You got it, Carla." Emily kept a sunny smile on her face even though Carla didn't see it. She made the drink and took the money, making change and pushing it back across the counter with the latte in a cardboard cup. "Here you go!" Emily turned away, getting two clean ceramic mugs off a shelf to start making our coffees. Yay.

I was back at our table, skimming the first chapter of one of my chosen paperbacks, when a loud voice startled me.

"What the hell is this?"

I looked up to see Carla, her last customer, slam her coffee back down on the counter with enough force that some liquid spilled out of the sippy-hole.

Emily turned around from the espresso machine, her eyebrows raised. "It's a hazelnut latte. Is something wrong with—"

"I said vanilla. I want a *vanilla* latte. Didn't you listen?"

Emily blinked. "I'm sorry. I could have sworn you said hazelnut. Give me a second, and I'll—" She reached for the to-go cup, and Carla huffed.

"I can't believe you got it wrong." She crossed her arms. "I always order a vanilla latte. Don't you remember that? I come in almost every day." Sheesh, this woman gave lethal stink eye.

"I know you do." Emily's voice was steady, unruffled, as she took the lid off the offending coffee and poured it down the sink. "That's why I thought it was so weird that you'd ordered hazelnut."

Carla folded her arms. "What the hell is wrong with you?"

Okay, that was it. I'd had enough. "You ordered hazelnut." I put down the book.

Carla whirled in my direction, fire in her eyes. "Excuse me?" There was a beat of silence as both of them looked at me.

"I said you ordered hazelnut." My hands shook as I got to my feet. I hated confrontation. I liked keeping to myself. But that whole argument had been ridiculous, and that bitch had been dangerously close to insulting my little sister. I wasn't going to let that happen. "You were on your phone, you probably weren't thinking, but I was right here and I heard you order hazelnut."

"I didn't . . ." Carla stopped speaking, her mouth hanging open for a second, and I saw the moment click when she realized she was in the wrong. A flush climbed the back of her neck, and the fire in her eyes froze. She stared straight at me, and I stared back, the both of us leaving Emily out of the conversation.

"It's fine!" Emily's cheerful voice cut through the tension, and she put a fresh to-go cup on the counter. "Here you go, one vanilla latte. I even upsized it for you, no charge, for the inconvenience."

Carla turned around and looked at the coffee as though she'd never seen one before. She looked at me one more time, then back at the coffee. She sniffed loudly and picked up the cup, not meeting Emily's eyes. Her thank-you was a mumble, and she all but slunk out of the store, leaving Emily and me alone. Finally.

I heaved a long sigh. "Who was that bitch?"

Emily's sigh echoed mine. "Carla owns a shop here in town. Kitschy jewelry. She's head of the Chamber of Commerce. So that's fun."

"Jesus. I bet." I sat back down, and soon Emily joined me with two fresh lattes.

"Don't worry about her. Carla's a cranky old woman and sometimes she likes to take shit out on people."

"And you put up with it?" I shook my head.

Emily sighed. "Head of the Chamber of Commerce," she repeated. "It sucks. *She* sucks. But whatever. I don't listen to her half the time. Thanks for sticking up for me, by the way. The look on her face was priceless."

"Eh." I shrugged. "I stick up for the people I love. You know that."

We shared a smile across the table. Emily and I hadn't always had the best relationship growing up, due more to our age difference than any actual animosity. But since she'd come to Willow Creek we'd gotten closer, and I'd learned what it was like to really have a sister. I loved her, and she knew it. That was leaps and bounds over where we'd both been five years ago.

"So," she said. "Mitch."

I sighed. Crap. Back on topic. "Yeah."

"You're really gonna go there?" She grinned. "You'll have to let me know what's under that kilt."

"Oh, God." I pressed a hand to my forehead. "First of all, I'm not getting under anything."

"Well, that's too bad." Emily snickered into her latte. "I bet he'd be fun."

I shook my head hard. "No, thank you. Himbos are not my type."

"Aw, come on. Give him a little credit. He's more than his looks."

"Seriously?" I stared at Emily. "I seem to remember a certain someone drooling over him when she first came to town."

She put up her hands in a defensive gesture. "Okay, guilty. I thought he'd be a fun distraction. And I stand by that. But then I got to know him, and he's . . ." She shrugged. "He's a good guy. Genuinely nice, and he's not stupid, you know."

"I never said he was." Now it was my turn to be defensive.

Emily narrowed her eyes. "I think 'himbo' implied that."

I clucked my tongue. "Well, look at the guy. His main hobbies are happy hour and hooking up. Pretty sure he encourages people to see him that way."

"Maybe so." She considered that. "But he also helps Simon wrangle those kids every year with the Faire, and performs a complicated fight scene with him. Not to mention teaching full-time and coaching on top of that. I'm just saying there's more to him than his muscles." She took a thoughtful sip of coffee. "They're nice muscles, though."

I tsked at her. "You're married."

"Yeah, but I'm not blind."

I ignored that. "Okay, but the kilt is just a Ren Faire thing, right? That's not till July. This whole fake girlfriend thing will be over long before then."

"Ah. So you *are* going to do it." Emily looked smug as she sipped her latte.

I sighed a long sigh. "Probably."

She shook her head at me. "You're too nice."

That brought me up short. "Me?" That had to be the first time anyone had ever accused me of being nice at all, much less being *too* nice. I liked myself just fine, and I liked a small circle of people. But that was pretty much it.

Emily smiled. "Yeah, you. You know, when I moved here, you hardly talked to anyone. Now you're in two book clubs—"

"Only because the neighborhood one always chooses depressing books," I interjected. "The one here at the store is more fun." Reading two books a month didn't make me nice. Did it?

But Emily kept going like I hadn't spoken. "—and now you're going out of your way to help a friend out. Next thing you know you'll be volunteering for the Renaissance Faire."

I snorted. "I highly doubt that. I don't have the tits for a corset."

"And I do?" She raised her eyebrows, and she had me there. I cast around for another reason. A more obvious one.

"I'm not a joiner, Em. You know that."

Emily nodded sagely. "Two book clubs."

I narrowed my eyes at her as I finished my latte. "Shut up."

To my surprise, Caitlin was home when I got there, sitting at the dining room table, textbooks and laptop open in front of her.

"I thought you were at the mall."

Caitlin barely glanced up from her work. "Yeah, well. Syd couldn't decide on anything, and then her boyfriend showed up, and it wasn't a girls' day anymore, you know? I was the third wheel."

I made a sympathetic noise. "And you'd rather come home and do homework? That's definitely bad."

"Exactly." Her mouth was set in a firm line and she turned a page in her book a little too emphatically. I'd seen that look before, but usually on myself. I didn't like my kid sounding this cynical at not quite eighteen.

That reminded me. I pulled the blue envelope out of my

purse. "Here's this back." I slid the card across the table to Caitlin. "You want to hang on to it, right?"

"I . . . guess?" Caitlin took the card in its envelope like it was plutonium and she didn't have a hazmat suit.

Her tone of voice gave me pause. "Hey. What are you thinking, kiddo?"

"I . . ." She looked at the card in her hand again, then up at me, before closing her laptop and pushing it away. "I mean. Isn't it weird that he's writing to me now? He's never done that before."

"Yeah," I said, keeping my voice as neutral as possible. "It is kind of weird."

"Like . . . does he want something? Am I supposed to see him? Is this going to be a thing now? Does he want to be my dad all of a sudden?"

I blew out a breath at all these questions and sat down at the table next to her. I hated the sad, uncertain look on Caitlin's face, and I wanted to hunt Robert down and kill him for putting it there. How dare he. How dare that bastard do this to our . . . to my kid. "Well," I said carefully, "it's up to you. He sent you that card, and you can respond if you want. If you don't want to, that's fine too. Beyond that, whether he wants to be your dad now, I don't know." I doubted it. But I wasn't going to tell her that. Because there was this sliver of a chance that he meant it. Maybe he had truly looked back on the past eighteen years and wished he'd been a better man. A better father.

Yeah, there was that sliver of a chance. But my cynical heart didn't believe it.

"I . . ." Cait tapped the edge of the card on the table, thinking hard. "I think I'd like to meet him? Maybe get to know him. Would that be okay?"

"Of course—" I started to respond, but Caitlin wasn't done.

"But I don't want to hurt your feelings. You know? I don't want you to think I don't appreciate you, or . . ."

"Oh, honey." I reached over and plucked the card out of her hand, setting it aside before patting her arm. "No. My feelings don't have anything to do with this. You need to understand that, okay? Contact him, don't contact him, you do what feels right to you. Not me."

"Okay . . ." But she still looked uncertain, and it twisted my heart.

"Come on." I squeezed her hand one more time before standing up. "Homework can wait. Let's go find something mindless to stream on TV."

Caitlin tilted her head. "Popcorn for lunch?"

"Sure," I said. "Why not?"

That earned me a smile. Still thin, but genuine. "M&M's in the popcorn?"

I scoffed exaggeratedly. "It's like you don't know me at all." This time her smile put a sparkle in her eyes too, and that made me feel better as I went into the kitchen to get the popcorn going.

I glared at the microwave like it had had something to do with all this mess. *Goddammit, Robert. You left years ago. Couldn't you have stayed away?* There was a tightness in my chest, telling me that things were about to change in a big way. I didn't want to think about my ex-husband anymore, and what he might want out of contacting Caitlin after all this time. Then my mind strayed to Mitch and what he wanted. Much more straightforward, but also much more deceptive.

I sighed again. All these years, it had been Cait and me, not needing to worry about what a man might want. I didn't like this turn of events. I didn't like it one damn bit.

Three

There were *a* lot of things running through my head at once. My ex-husband butting into our lives after years of nothing. Mitch asking me to suddenly be a bigger part of his life, albeit under false pretenses. And, of course, that ever-present list of things I needed to do, according to the real estate agent, to bring the house up to date before selling it.

She'd given me a long list. Refresh the paint on the walls with a neutral color, which I'd expected. New flooring, I'd expected that too. Stain the back deck, which made sense. Update appliances . . . no. What was the point of that? I may as well stay in the house if I was going to drop thousands of dollars on new appliances. The list went on, and I got tired just reading it. I was going to have to hire an army of handymen to help me get it done.

All those things tumbled through my head until two of them collided, halfway through a profit and loss statement at work. I dug my phone out of my purse to send Mitch a text. **You around tonight?**

Baseball practice till 6, he texted back almost right away. **You asking me out, Mama?**

Oh for fuck's sake. **No. I'll drop by the school around 6:15 if that's ok. You know where the practice field is?**

I've lived in this town a long time, I texted back. **I think I can find it.**

A thumbs-up emoji was my only response, and although I waited a few minutes just in case, no other answer was forthcoming. I clicked my phone off and went back to my spreadsheet.

That evening I drove home as usual. But once I hit the city limits I glanced at the clock and turned left toward the high school instead of continuing straight home. The sun had started to dip on the horizon, but there was plenty of daylight left. I'd made good time; it was only a few minutes past six.

When I pulled into the high school parking lot, baseball practice was filtering out. I didn't even need to venture back toward the fields. Kids milled around the parking lot, some heading toward their cars in the senior lot while the younger kids waited for parents to pick them up. Mitch was out front in an intense discussion with one of the kids. Each of them held a baseball, and Mitch demonstrated different ways to grip it, which the boy beside him tried to emulate. His fingers were long and his grip was good from what I could see, and Mitch nodded in satisfaction. He raised his head as I approached.

"Hey, Mama!"

I rolled my eyes and did not take the proffered fist bump. "Seriously? In front of the kids?"

He shrugged. "They're not listening." He was right; even the boy he'd been coaching on his grip had wandered off. Boys scrolled through their phones as they waited for parents and talked to each other in small clumps here and there. "So what's up?"

"Well, I was thinking about your . . . you know, that thing you asked me to do." God, that sounded even worse than just coming out with it.

"Oh, the thing?" His eyes lit up, and joy suffused his face. But joy always suffused his face: Mitch was a joyful guy. "Are you in?"

I sighed. "Yeah. I'm in. But I have a condition."

"A condition?" His brow furrowed. "You mean a medical condition? Like allergies? Or like a food thing? Because I can find out what we're having if that's the—"

I snorted. "No, a condition. As in, if I do this for you, you do something for me."

"Oh." The concern cleared off his face. "Sure. What do you need? Don't worry, I'll be the best boyfriend you ever had." He shot me a wink and I laughed despite myself. I usually tried not to laugh around Mitch; it only encouraged him.

"I'm sure you will." Not a lot to compare to, but I didn't need to go there right now. "I need some help."

His eyebrows shot up, and his gaze turned teasingly appraising. "With what?"

How? How did he turn those two words into an innuendo? "With my house," I said. "I need to get some work done on it before I put it on the market, so—"

"Wait, you're moving?" His face fell, and I felt his frown in my solar plexus. It hadn't occurred to me that someone else might give a shit that I was planning to leave Willow Creek. My own sister had hardly reacted when I'd first told her. Why did Mitch care?

I mentally brushed away the thought. He was probably worried I'd leave before I could help him out with this family dinner thing. "Not for a while. But if you want me to be your fake girlfriend, I need you to come over and help me stain my deck."

He narrowed his eyes at me, and I met his gaze squarely; I wasn't going to lose this staring contest. Finally he nodded.

"Okay. That's fair." He squinted again, this time in thought. "Did you just build it?"

That startled a laugh out of me—the thought of me wielding a hammer and putting this deck together. "No, I had it built a while back."

"Hmm." He tilted his head and looked like he was doing some mental calculations. "You're going to want to clean it before you stain it, then. Do you have a pressure washer?"

I blinked. "Uh. No." Was that something I was supposed to have? "Can I rent one?"

He waved a hand. "Nah. My dad has one. I'll drop it off tomorrow, and then next weekend we can stain it."

"Next weekend . . . wait. Isn't that when Ren Faire tryouts are? Don't you need to be there for that?" The closer it came to Ren Faire time, the more excited Caitlin had become, so it was definitely on my radar. Mitch was another one in town who, like Simon, had been part of the whole thing since the beginning. I couldn't imagine him missing out on it.

But he shrugged. "Eh. Between you and me, I'm kind of a shoo-in. I don't think Simon will mind if I skip tryouts."

I had a feeling that Simon would absolutely mind, but I wasn't going to argue with Mitch about it. "Okay, then. Come by sometime in the morning. Whenever you like, I'm an early riser. We can talk strategy while we work."

"Strategy? What kind of strategy do we need to stain a deck? We get some stain, we put it on the deck. Boom."

I rolled my eyes so hard my head fell back on my neck. "For the dinner."

"Oh." He looked thoughtful. "Good point."

"Don't worry," I said. "I won't keep you at my house all day. You can still go out Saturday night."

He looked blank. "Saturday night? Do I have plans I don't know about?"

I tilted my head. "Isn't Saturday your prime hookup time?"

"Funny." He'd started looking around as we talked, his eyes scanning the kids who were still milling about. It belatedly occurred to me that he was in charge of all these kids, making sure their parents picked them up and they got home without incident. I probably shouldn't have shown up to distract him, but he didn't seem annoyed about it. The man was capable of multi-tasking.

"Funny?" I leaned my back against the wall of the building, indulging in a little stretch. I sat all day, with a fairly long drive both to and from work. My SUV was comfortable, but my days involved a lot of sitting and not a lot of moving. By the end of the day my back was always stiff. My gaze went to the track, a few hundred feet to the right of the main building. Sometimes I missed running.

I shook off that thought too. What was it about Mitch lately that made me thoughtful? "How's it funny? I've seen you at Jackson's plenty of times. Isn't that what you do?"

"Meh." He shrugged, his shoulders massive under his T-shirt. "It's losing its appeal, if you want to know the truth. I end up there a lot of times because there aren't a whole lot of options in this town."

I had to admit he had a point. "Okay, then. We can—"

"Nope." Mitch's voice was harsh, and I jumped at the sound

of it. What did he mean, "nope"? He was the one who'd suggested Saturday. But he wasn't talking to me. He'd reached out to one of the kids walking by, snagging the back of his T-shirt collar. "Say that again," he said to the kid.

The kid flopped in Mitch's grip like a freshly landed fish. "Oh, come on, Coach. I didn't mean—"

"Say. That. Again." Mitch's voice was low and dangerous, and I didn't want to acknowledge the shiver that went up my spine at his tone. I hadn't heard what the kid had said; the small group of boys had been walking by as we'd been talking. But like I said, multitasking.

The boy huffed, blowing his ash-blond bangs out of his eyes. "I was talking about my little brother's birthday party. It was so stupid. Who plays laser tag anymore?" He looked up at Mitch with an *am I right?* expression, but Mitch remained stone-faced. After a ten-second staring contest, the kid huffed again. "I said it was gay," he mumbled.

"Yes," Mitch said, his voice and expression still stone. "You did." He let go of the kid's shirt. "Now go run your laps."

"Aw, come on! We just finished practice, and my mom will be here in like five minutes."

Mitch shrugged. "Not my problem. You know the rules. That's a slur. We don't say stuff like that on my team. So either you run your laps, or you're off the team. Your choice. I'll tell your mom where you are if she gets here before you're done."

"Ugh." He let the backpack fall off his shoulder and tossed it petulantly against the wall. "Don't tell her what I said, okay?"

"Go." Mitch pointed toward the track I'd been looking at wistfully, and the boy trotted off in that direction.

"Wow," I said when the boy was out of earshot and his friends had scurried away. "You're quite the taskmaster."

Mitch shrugged. "I don't like people using that word like that." He leaned against the wall, echoing my casual stance, but tension lined his shoulders. "If I catch them saying it, they run a mile around the track. They know the rules."

"No, that's . . . that's good." The world was nasty enough, and if Mitch could make it that little bit nicer, one small-town boy at a time, more power to him.

"Anyway." His expression cleared, and his shoulders dropped. He rolled his head on his neck, and I heard a faint crack. I'd always thought of Mitch as the kind of guy without a care in the world, but he cared. About a lot of things. Huh. "Next Saturday?"

"Next Saturday." I nodded. "It's a date."

Sure enough, when I came home from work the next night, there was an unfamiliar contraption leaning against my front door. I was genuinely stumped for a full thirty seconds until I remembered that Mitch was loaning me his—or his father's—pressure washer. Cleaning the back deck with it was one of the noisiest but also most satisfying tasks I'd ever undertaken. Once I was done, it looked like it had the day the contractors finished building it, and I considered leaving it that way and not bothering to stain it.

But Mitch shook his head when he got there that next Saturday morning and I broached the subject. "It looks great, but you want to stain it. How long ago did you say this was built?"

I hummed while I tried to remember. "A couple years ago? Something like that?" It was certainly after the accident—this deck had been a present to myself after the settlement from the lawsuit the accident had spawned had come through. The contractor had knocked out the window in the dining room and turned it into a pair of French doors. This deck was my favorite place to linger with a cup of coffee on the weekends.

"A couple years?" Mitch shook his head in disgust. "You're lucky the wood didn't split."

"What do you mean? It's pressure-treated lumber." I stressed "pressure-treated" like I had any idea what that meant. I didn't. But the contractor had specified that he was using it to build the deck, and it sounded suitably impressive to someone like me, who knew nothing about carpentry.

"Pressure-treated means it's not going to rot, but that won't keep it from splitting. You really want to stain it."

"Oh." I studied the planks of the deck, looking for any signs of . . . splitting? Was that what he'd said? I wasn't a handyman, how was I supposed to know this stuff? "But if we stain it now it'll be okay?"

"Absolutely." He nodded vigorously. "It'll look so much better than the bare boards too."

He had a point there. I'd always intended to stain this deck when it had been finished, and then of course like any good homeowner I'd never gotten around to it.

We worked in companionable silence for a little while before I remembered that we were meant to be talking strategy. "So." I reloaded my paintbrush and spread some stain across the railing. "Tell me more about this family dinner situation. You said it's for your grandparents' anniversary? Fiftysomething? Why are you celebrating fiftysomething? Isn't fifty the big milestone?"

He nodded. "We did that too. On their fiftieth, we had a big blowout. Like a family reunion. Malones everywhere."

"Oh, God," I said to the porch railing. Mitch on his own was enough to handle. Malones everywhere? I'd never survive.

Thankfully, Mitch didn't hear me. "It was great. I saw cousins I hadn't talked to since high school. It was a big deal. The whole family got along for probably the first time in history. So now we have to do it every couple of years."

"Oh. Wow." I blinked. That was . . .

Mitch nodded, as if he could read my mind. "It's a lot. But my grandma was so happy. Then she insisted we all get together again the next year, so we did it. And now it's become this annual tradition."

I shook my head. "You can't do Christmas like a normal family?"

He snorted. "Nope, that would be too easy." He moved farther down the stairs with his brush and can of stain. "Besides, someone always misses Christmas, what with in-laws and all. So now, it's this whole anniversary thing at the beginning of June. And if anyone says anything about not coming . . . well, Grandma looks so sad." He shook his head mournfully.

"Oh, God," I said again, but this time I meant it. "That's terrible."

"Exactly," Mitch said. "Grandma's a scammer." That wasn't the response I'd expected and Mitch knew it; he looked up and grinned at my bark of laughter. "You should see it. Total crocodile tears. But you can't say no to her."

"Of course not," I said. "Saying no to grandmas is illegal in some states, I think."

"Exactly." Mitch balanced his paintbrush on his small can of stain before standing up to stretch his back. He'd been hunched over those steps for a while now, and I had to say I enjoyed this little show of weakness from him. It proved he was mortal, or something. Plus, I was getting a pretty nice show here. Hands on his hips, chest practically thrust into the air, those arms with biceps roughly the size of my head. You could see each muscle stand out in relief as he stretched, like an anatomy model covered in warm skin and a tight T-shirt. A shock of blond hair fell over his forehead as he bent forward, and I blew out a long breath.

Then I stood up too, and the cracking of my knees reminded me of who I was, and who he was. All joking about MILFs aside, I was at least a decade older than anyone he'd be attracted to. Cut it out, I told myself. *He's being a nice guy and helping you, and you're ogling him while he does so.*

I was the actual worst.

"How's it going up there?"

I started guiltily. Oh God, had he caught me watching him? But he looked guileless as he tilted his head up and looked at me from where he stood in the backyard.

"Um." I looked at how much I'd gotten done. "Not too bad?" I had a few boards left, but I was almost to the French doors. The plan was for me to stain backwards until I backed myself into the house. But now I saw the flaw in this plan. I looked across the mostly stained deck, down the stained steps to Mitch. "You're kinda trapped, huh?" We'd painted him right down the steps and out of the project entirely.

He waved a hand. "I'll go around to the front and meet you." He popped the lid onto the can of stain, hammering it on with the heel of his hand.

"Sounds good. It's time for a break anyway." I knelt back down (knees cracking all the way) and applied my brush back to the boards, finishing another one as I heard the front door open and close in quick succession. A few moments later I felt his presence in the doorway behind me. I tried to ignore him and concentrate on finishing up, setting the brush and stain aside and wiping my hands on a rag before I stood up to face him. My knees didn't crack this time: small mercies.

"Want something to drink?"

"I'd love it." He gestured, waving me to walk in front of him to the kitchen. I moved to the sink to wash my hands, and behind me the fridge opened, and closed again as he made a disgusted noise.

"No beer, huh?"

"Nope," I shook my head. "You know I'm a cider drinker. Wine sometimes. But beer's never been my thing."

Behind me Mitch let out a long-suffering sigh, but when I glanced over my shoulder I caught his smile that said he wasn't being serious. Of course. Was he ever serious?

"Sorry," I said. "I should have said it was BYOB."

"Next time," he said as he took two bottles of water out of the fridge. He handed me one and we leaned against the counter on opposite ends of the kitchen. I tried not to notice the way his throat worked when he swallowed. But not noticing Mitch, when he was standing right in front of you like that, wasn't easy.

"So the dinner with your family . . ." I said, desperately trying to find something innocuous to talk about. "It's only a dinner? I only have to be your girlfriend for one evening?"

"Gee, thanks. Try not to sound so excited." He made an attempt to look insulted. "I'll have you know I'm a catch."

"Your mama tell you that?" I quirked an eyebrow.

"Every day." He quirked an eyebrow right back, and I had to laugh. He made it so easy to laugh around him. He grinned in response to my laughter, and his smile lasted just a beat too long. Long enough for my blood to spark with heat, and for me to wonder what I needed to do to keep him looking at me like that.

"Anyway, yeah," he continued, as though he hadn't noticed

how something inside me had just shifted. "Sometimes it's an afternoon barbecue situation—Grandpa got a smoker not too long ago, and he loves that thing—but the latest info from my mom is that it's going to be a dinner out somewhere." He shrugged. "So it's only a few hours, really. You're getting off easy." He coughed into a fist, and I was pretty sure the cough sounded like that'swhatshesaid.

I pretended not to hear. "Okay," I said. "That sounds doable." I hoped so, anyway. *Malones everywhere.* I suppressed a shiver. Could anyone be ready for that?

"A little enthusiasm would be nice, you know." He drained the rest of his bottle of water and left it on the counter.

"I know," I said. "I know. You're a catch." I reached for the empty bottle so I could throw it in the recycling, bringing me in close proximity to that chest I'd been ogling outside.

"I am." He didn't move, he just stared down at me, almost in a challenge, while I swallowed hard and forced myself to meet his eyes. Don't show fear. Or anything else that might be heating up this room.

"Thanks for helping with the deck," I finally said, my voice throatier than usual. "This would have been a pain in the ass on my own."

"Sure." He hadn't moved and neither had I, and somehow in these few moments our breaths had syncopated while our gazes locked. His chest rose and fell in time with mine, and good God, how did eyes come in a blue that vivid?

"How soon are you, uh . . ." His voice was hushed, hesitant. "Moving?"

Moving. Right. That was an excellent idea. I stepped back from him. "Not till the fall, at least." I took our bottles to the recycling bin on the other side of the kitchen. "Caitlin's graduating from high school and all, and of course she's volunteering for the Renaissance Faire—"

"She better," he interrupted. "She's a veteran." The way his voice warmed when talking about my kid made a flutter kick up in my heart.

"I know. She looks forward to it every summer. And I don't want to disrupt any of that. I thought I'd get all this stuff done over the summer and put the house on the market in the fall, after she's gone."

"College, yeah?" He nodded, the pleased look draining from his face, replaced with concern. "Gonna be weird for her though, not being able to come home during breaks."

Irritation crawled up my spine. This wasn't any of his business. He was here to help me with a project, not critique my parenting style. "I'll have a guest room in my new place. I'm not abandoning my kid. We'll figure it out." My tone was snappish, more than I wanted it to be.

"Sure, yeah." He waved a placating hand. "You're right. Of course you will." There was a slightly awkward silence until I cleared my throat, trying to salvage something from this conversation.

"At least I'm only asking you to help me with the deck. I still have a shitload of stuff to do on this house before it's ready to sell."

"Like what?" He looked around the kitchen. "Your place is great. A hell of a lot better than mine."

"Paint, for one thing," I said. "Most of the walls in this house."

"What?" He wandered into the living room and I followed, watching him peer around, a frown on his face. "What's wrong with the walls?"

"Wrong color. Everything has to be neutral in order to sell."

We'd painted this room a deep blue, the color of a twilight sky, when we'd first moved in. Caitlin had picked the color; she'd been six at the time, and not very well versed in the ins and outs of home decor. But I'd bought the paint anyway, because this house was ours, and we could paint the living room any god-damn color we pleased. Now, some twelve years later, I barely noticed it.

But the real estate agent had. When she'd done a walk-through of the house, that was the first thing she'd said. Paint the living room walls. Neutral colors only. I loved that blue. Covering it up with beige felt like a sacrilege.

Apparently Mitch felt the same way I did. "Neutral." His face twisted in contempt.

"I couldn't agree more." I turned to the hallway, heading back toward the bedrooms. "Come on. I can show you the rest."

Four

Mitch had spent a lot of time at my house last year. For a few months, my dining room table had been command central for planning both that summer's Renaissance Faire and my sister's wedding. I'd dug out my giant casserole dishes—the ones that didn't get much use when it was just Caitlin and me—and made tons of baked ziti or some other casserole while half-heartedly bitching about all these people in my house. The dining room had buzzed with life and conversation, and Caitlin and I had spent those evenings with our friends around our big table that had never before seen big dinners.

I'd breathed a sigh of relief when the summer came and those planning nights came to an end, glad to get my quiet house back. Yet sometimes over the winter I'd found myself wanting to make a giant shepherd's pie to be devoured by a group in a half hour. I missed the sight of Mitch coming through my front door, balancing a ludicrous number of pizzas in his arms when it was his turn to "cook."

But for all the times he'd been over last year, all Mitch had ever seen of my house was the path from the front door to the dining room table, with occasional stops in the kitchen. So this impromptu tour had seemed like a great idea until we got to my bedroom.

I'd never brought a man into this bedroom. Unless you counted the guys who delivered my king-size four-poster bed, and I didn't count them at all. As I stepped over the threshold I had a mental image of that night in Jackson's, when Mitch had looked up at me through his lashes and my stomach had gone all swimmy. For a second my breath left my body, and I wanted to turn around and push Mitch out of the room. Back into the kitchen where it was safer. But I rallied. *Cut it out, Parker*, I told myself. *He's not here for that.*

"So then this is my room." I tried to sound as casual as possible, which meant I sounded like a nervous wreck. God, I was too old to be this flustered around a boy. Especially a boy who had no interest in me and was almost a decade younger besides. It was fine for older men to date younger women, but it never went the other way around.

I shook my head hard. Dating? Where was my mind *going*? I coughed into my fist. "I don't think it needs a whole lot of work." There. Good. Back on topic.

Mitch shook his head, his gaze roaming over the walls. "You like blue," he said.

"I do?" I looked around the room with new eyes. I hadn't thought about it, but he was right. The living room was blue, and so was my bedroom. In here the soft blue was calming. When I went to sleep at night I felt like I was drifting off in a blue sky, cushioned by clouds.

"Yeah." I sighed. "I guess it's all gotta go, huh?"

"Probably." He nodded absently as he stepped farther into

the room, and I took a panicked look around. But everything was where it should be: no bras lying out on the bed, dirty laundry in the hamper in the closet where it belonged. I wasn't a neat freak by any means, but I was relatively tidy. Which was coming in handy right about now.

"You'll definitely want to paint in here," he said, "but you can probably get away with the carpet the way it is."

"You think? Because that would be nice."

He shrugged. "I mean, I'm not a real estate agent. But I think of it like this: If I'm going to trade in my truck, I'd probably get it detailed, maybe fix up the brakes or something like that. But I'm not going to replace the transmission or put a new stereo system in something I'm about to get rid of anyway. I mean, you might get a slightly better price, but would it be worth what you spent to fix it up?"

That . . . that made a lot of sense. "Okay, so what do you think I should do?"

He leaned against the wall, his arms crossed while he thought, and it was overwhelming how *present* he was in this room. How much space he took up in my space. "Paint everything, definitely," he finally said. "Maybe redo the carpets in the living room and dining room, you know, the high-traffic areas." He'd still been looking idly around my room while he was talking, but now he turned his attention back to me. "Not that this house gets a lot of traffic, huh? You've never been the throwing-parties type."

"Well, no." My jaw clenched with annoyance. What business was it of his if I threw parties or not? I liked my own company just fine; I wasn't going to apologize for that.

Something must have shown in my face, because he put up defensive hands. "Hey, nothing wrong with that," he said. "You want to be antisocial, be my guest."

"Thanks." Acid dripped from my voice, but Mitch kept talking like I hadn't interrupted.

"I mean on the one hand, I think more of the world should get to experience your cooking." A smile quirked on his lips. "On the other hand though, that means more for me."

I couldn't suppress the laughter that burst out of me like a sneeze. "Thanks," I said again, but this time the acid was gone. He had a way of doing that. "Anyway, that's about it." I pushed lightly on his arm, which was a joke; someone like Mitch only moved when he wanted to. But he followed my lead, leaving my bedroom and heading back toward the living room. I breathed easier once he cleared the door; he'd been a very large presence in my room. I hadn't been ready for that.

The timing couldn't have worked out better. Mitch left and I went out into the backyard to clean up the cans of stain and rinse the brushes under the hose. I'd just turned the water on when I heard the familiar sound of Emily's white Jeep pulling into the driveway.

"Back here!" I called once I heard the slam of the car doors. I turned back to the brushes, and I was almost done cleaning them when Caitlin appeared in the backyard, followed closely by Emily.

"How did the sign-ups go?" I addressed the question to both of them, not picky about who answered. I glanced up in time to see Emily about to sit on the steps and dropped my paintbrush, throwing out a hand. "Still wet!"

Startled, Emily windmilled her arms till she regained her balance, then retreated to sit on a patch of grass I hadn't soaked yet. "Good," she said, answering my question.

"Yeah." Caitlin dropped her backpack next to Emily and then

sat down beside her. "Coach Malone wasn't there, so I think they're doing the chess match stuff a different day. But I'm not doing that anyway."

I gave a little start of guilt. Mitch had said he wasn't needed at tryouts; that was why he'd come over here to help me instead. Should he have been there today? I didn't like him missing something on my account.

But when I glanced over at them, Emily shrugged. "The chess match tryouts are a little more involved, since there's all that fighting with weapons and stuff. Mitch said he couldn't make it today, but I think he and Simon are going to get together on it later in the week."

Nope. I still felt guilty. And relieved that Mitch had already left by the time these two got home. I cast around quick for a subject change. "Are you singing again?" Caitlin was somewhat of a dilettante when it came to the Faire. Her first summer she'd been a lady-in-waiting to the Queen. Next she'd helped Emily stage scenes from Shakespeare, and then last summer she'd participated in a five-part girls' singing group called the Gilded Lilies. I all but expected her to announce that she'd be jousting this year. I pictured my kid on horseback with a lance and grinned down at the paintbrushes as I shook the water off them.

"Yep," she said. "Syd wants to do it again, and it was fun last summer. Dahlia didn't come back this year, so Mr. G asked me to help him decide who to cast." Pride filled her voice, and with good reason. She'd gone from that tiny fourteen-year-old lady-in-waiting to being part of the casting committee. Good for her.

"You know, you can call him Simon." Emily leaned over and nudged Caitlin's shoulder with hers. "He's your uncle now."

"Yeah, I know." Caitlin plucked absently at the grass at her feet. "Still feels weird sometimes, though?"

"That's fair," I said. There was no rule book for when a teacher in your high school married your aunt. Nothing wrong with letting her and Simon navigate their relationship in a way that worked for them.

The brushes were clean, so I tapped them against the railing to knock off some extra water before laying them across the top of the closed-up cans. "Here," I said to Caitlin after Emily had gone home for lunch. "Help me pick all this up." I grabbed the two mostly empty cans and brushes, then waved for her to grab the rags and other detritus.

"What's this for anyway?" Caitlin followed me into the garage, where we put everything away.

"Oh, I was getting started on that to-do list from the real estate agent. You know, all the painting and stuff I need to do before I can sell the house."

Silence answered me, and I turned to see Caitlin looking blankly at me, her mouth slack.

"You're selling the house?"

"Honey." I didn't understand why she looked so stricken. "You were there the night the agent came by. We talked about this."

"Yeah, I know, but . . ." She blinked a few times, quickly, and my heart sank. "I thought we were just talking. I didn't know you were really going to do it."

"Well, I am." I didn't know any nicer way to say it. I thought she knew my plans already. "You know that once you're off to college, this house will be too big for me all by myself."

That didn't make her look any happier. "But this is home. And I won't be gone forever. I'll be coming home, you know. Like for Christmas and stuff. Where will you . . . where am I gonna go?"

"Caitlin." I started to reach for her, but the look on her face said that it wouldn't be a great idea. "I'm not vanishing in the night without a forwarding address. You'll know where I'll be. And you'll always have a place wherever I am. But I . . ." *Hate small towns.* I couldn't say that, not to my daughter. I couldn't tell her that the only reason we'd lived here for so long was that she'd been happy here. That was no kind of guilt to put on a kid. "I'd love to live closer to work," I finally said. Better.

Her face darkened. "Whatever. I'm going to have some lunch." She turned away from me and headed inside, leaving me in the semidarkness of the garage, my first home improvement project finished. I should be feeling accomplished: something to check off the list. But my insides felt all jumbled in conflicted directions, and I didn't know what it was going to take to straighten them out.

Caitlin wasn't happy at all.

For almost all of her life it had been the two of us versus the world, which made the whole mother-daughter dynamic a little more casual than it probably should have been. I turned on the authority when I needed to, but for the most part we lived in a harmonious household. Two really good friends, with a significant age, income, and authority gap.

But that wasn't the case now. Now that Caitlin knew I was going through with selling the house, she'd become withdrawn. She didn't act out, she didn't pitch a fit. No, our disagreements took place in loud silence. Homework that used to be done at the dining room table while I did the dishes in the evening was now done in her bedroom with the door closed. Mealtime conversation was kept to a bare minimum without any of Caitlin's usually bubbly commentary on her classmates and things happening at school or in town. After a couple of days I realized I missed her, as though she'd already left for college.

I coped the only way I knew how: I threw myself into this whole home renovation thing. That next Saturday afternoon I went to the family-owned hardware store downtown—those were few and far between these days, and if my little home project could help support Willow Creek's economy, even better. Afterward I swung by the bookstore with a handful of paint chips to enlist the help of my sister.

Emily looked at all the chips spread out on the counter and shook her head. "This is a trick, right? These are all the same color."

"Nope. This one is Eggshell." I tapped a fingernail on the chip on the left. "This one's Ecru, and that one's Vanilla."

She shook her head again. "They all look . . . I dunno, off-white."

"Exactly." I nodded vigorously. "Neutral colors."

"Yeah." Her nod was as listless as mine was energetic. She sighed and looked up at me. "So you're really doing this?"

"What, painting the house?"

"No, dummy. Moving."

"Well, yeah." Irritation tingled through my blood. Was I going to get this shit from Emily too? Why did this seem so hard for everyone to believe? "I've been planning this forever."

"How's Caitlin taking it?"

I didn't like the answer to that question, but Em would see through any lie. "Not great." That was an understatement. I'd gotten the silent treatment most of this week at dinner, and Caitlin had spent the rest of the time in her room.

"I can imagine." Emily sounded sympathetic, but it made my hackles rise. Whose side was she on? And why were there sides in the first place?

I gathered the paint chips and tapped them on the counter,

neatening the stack, giving my hands something to do. "What do you want me to do? Wait for her to graduate from college? The only time she'll be here is during breaks and over the summer if I'm lucky. Am I supposed to sit around this house, this town, on my own for four more years?" The thought was excruciating. I'd put my own life on hold the minute I became a single mother. How much longer was I going to have to wait?

"No. Hey. No." Emily reached across the counter and laid her hand over mine. "You gave up what you wanted to do, and how you wanted to live, to put your kid first. I know that. You deserve to let your own life begin. I'm not saying you shouldn't." She squeezed my hand, and I squeezed back before letting go.

"Well, the first step to doing that is getting the walls painted. Which is going to take forever to do on my own, so I should probably figure out this paint and get started."

"On your own?" Emily tilted her head like a confused puppy. "You're not on your own."

"Yeah, I know that, but Caitlin is barely speaking to me right now. No way am I putting her down for manual labor. I don't want to—"

"I didn't mean Caitlin." Emily pressed her lips together like she was trying to hide a smile. "I mean me. When do you want to do this? Evenings? Weekends?"

"Either? Both?" I shrugged. "I don't think Cait will notice either way. She's spending a lot of time in her room these days."

Emily sighed. "You get the paint, we'll get started tomorrow afternoon. I'll come by after I close up the store."

Relief coursed through me in a wave. My sister was on my side after all. I wasn't alone in all of this. "You're a lifesaver."

"That's what I do," she said with a grin, and I had to laugh.

"Some things never change." Emily was a fixer, and during

the months she'd spent living with Caitlin and me, she'd been in charge of the both of us. It was an essential part of Emily's personality: identifying what people needed to make their lives better, and then doing everything in her power to make that happen.

I looked down at the paint chips, shuffling them in my hands like cards. "I think I like the Eggshell," I said. "It's warmer than the others."

"Then that's the one you get." The bell over the front door chimed, and Emily looked up with a Pavlovian greeting-a-new-customer smile. The customer waved her off with a *just browsing* gesture and Emily turned back to me. "But take it easy on Cait, okay? This is a big year for her—prom, graduating, college, and all that—she's probably feeling a little overwhelmed, and her mom talking about selling the house out from under her is probably stressing her out."

She wasn't wrong. How had she seen this when I hadn't? "Well, *hell*." I scrubbed a hand over my face. "I guess you're a better mom than I am right now."

"Nah." Emily shook her head. "I'm married to a high school teacher. Lots of teenage hormones in our life."

I had to concede that. "You're pretty good at this whole mom thing. You planning on doing it yourself soon?"

"What, kids?" A look of horror came over Emily's face. "God, no."

"Not yet, huh?" That made sense. They hadn't even been married a year yet. Not everyone got pregnant super fast like I had.

"Maybe not ever. Who knows." She shrugged. "We've talked about it once or twice, but I think Simon gets enough kid time with his students. Not to mention all the ones doing the Ren Faire in the summer. I think he likes the quiet at home."

"And you're okay with that?" I didn't want my little sister accommodating Simon's wishes if she didn't agree with them.

But I should have known better. "Oh, God, yes," she said. "Kids are great and all—especially yours—but I don't know if they're necessarily my thing. But we've been talking about adopting a dog later this summer. Maybe after Faire's over? The summer is so busy, I think waiting for fall might be better. But I don't know. I've never had a dog before and—"

"We had a dog." I blinked at her. How had she forgotten?

Emily closed her mouth with a snap, looking confused. "We did?"

"Yeah. Rusty, remember? Our golden retriever?" My childhood had been defined by him. Running around the backyard with Rusty like he was the little brother I never . . . Oh. "Wait. We got him when I was really little, and I was fourteen when he died."

"Yeah. So I was what, two?" She shook her head. "I think I remember seeing pictures but . . ."

"Crap. Sorry." I dropped my elbows to the counter, leaning on them. I'd always thought of our age difference in the abstract, but this was more immediate. My childhood had been filled with a canine companion who had died not long after Emily started talking. Mom had been inconsolable, and Dad had forbidden us to have another pet. Of course she didn't remember. "Sorry," I said again, giving her arm a squeeze.

"It's okay." But she leaned into my comfort anyway. "You could always get a dog too. Someone to keep you company when Caitlin goes to college? Then we can . . . I don't know. Take them to the dog park together or something."

I laughed, not wanting to admit how appealing that idea was. But . . . "I don't know where I'll be living by the fall, much less if

I can bring a pet with me." I ignored the part where Emily seemed to offer this dog-filled life as an alternative to leaving town. "Let me get settled in my new place first."

Emily took my refusal with good grace. "That does seem like the more responsible thing to do." Her ready smile was back. "Anyway, I'm much more excited about the prospect of getting a dog than having kids. How sad is that?"

"Not sad at all." It was very possible that Emily had the right idea. After all, it wasn't like I was the best mother in the world . . . hadn't I just proven that?

One more thing to add to the to-do list. Paint house. Replace carpets. Repair relationship with daughter.

Five

*P*roblem was, I had no idea how to fix things with Caitlin. It was probably a good thing that she was starting to assert her independence—no one wants their kid to be a doormat at almost eighteen. But while we'd always been almost preternaturally close, it had always been very clear that we weren't BFFs here. We were mother and daughter, and she listened to me. Rarely argued back.

But this whole moving-away thing had thrown her for a loop. And that was my fault. I should have broken it to her more gently, maybe found a way for it to make more sense to her. Or I could have apologized and listened to her side of things. But all that was hard to do when she wasn't speaking to me. Her silent treatment continued, and I did my best to stay out of her way when it came to the home improvements I had planned.

Sunday afternoon, my sister showed up as promised, wearing old clothes and carrying a plate of lemon squares in her hand. "Leftovers from work," she said, putting the plate down on my kitchen island. "I think Simon's getting a little sick of them."

"You can bring them here anytime. You know they're Caitlin's favorite."

"I do know that. So what are we doing?" She adjusted her ponytail, and not for the first time I wondered how she could make her hair do that. We grew up with the same curly brown hair, and I'd even passed it on to Caitlin. But while Emily could pile it up on her head and make it look effortless, I chose to tame my curls with the blow-dryer, making my hair smooth.

I passed a hand over my own ponytail—no riot of curls here—before answering. "I figured I'd start with your old room. It gets the least amount of use, so it should be pretty unobtrusive."

"Staying out of Caitlin's way?" Emily craned her neck to look down the hallway before pitching her voice lower. "Is she home?"

I nodded with a sigh. "In her room. As usual." She'd come out for breakfast and later for some snacks, but otherwise had shut herself away.

"Ooof." Emily blew out a long breath. "It's that bad, huh?"

"Yeah. Who knows. Maybe the lemon squares will help."

"Never underestimate the power of baked goods." She followed me back to the guest room, stopping short in the doorway. "Wow," she said. "So weird to be here when it's not my room anymore."

"No kidding." It had taken me a good year to stop thinking of it as Emily's room. When she'd first come here she'd been practically a stranger, but when she'd moved out, first to her tiny apartment and then eventually into the house that she and Simon had bought together a few months ago, not long after their wedding, she'd been . . . well, she'd been Emily. My little sister. Family.

The kind of family who showed up on a Sunday afternoon to

help you with home renovations. "So are we painting?" The eagerness in her voice was refreshing after the one-word answers and stone-faced expressions I'd been living with lately.

"Hopefully," I said. "We need to get everything off the walls and the furniture covered up first." My house was a good size, but there was nowhere to put the bedroom set while we painted, so I hoped that shoving everything into the middle of the room and throwing old sheets over it all would be good enough.

It was. The small double bed and dresser didn't take up a lot of space once they were pushed together, and the framed beach landscape photo I'd taken in the Outer Banks was off the wall and stuck in the closet temporarily. All that was left was my medal rack by the door.

"I don't remember this." Emily tilted her head while she looked at the aluminum rack screwed into the wall. Hanging from it on individual hooks were the handful of medals I'd earned from the footraces I'd participated in over the years. I'd never been an elite runner or anything, but the races had been fun.

"I put it up over the winter." I grabbed three of the medals by their ribbons and took them down, shoving them into the top dresser drawer. Emily unhooked a couple more.

"These are so cute!" She tilted one that looked like a crab. "Since when do you run?"

"Since before I got T-boned in my car." I took the medals back a little more aggressively than necessary.

"And you don't do it anymore? I'd think you'd be healed up well enough by now to—"

"No, I don't do it anymore." I'd tried. Once. A year or so after the accident, I'd laced up my old running shoes and even dug up and charged my GPS watch. But while the spirit had been willing, the flesh was . . . way out of shape. I'd barely made it a mile before I had to turn around and walk home, my breath coming hard in my lungs and my legs feeling like rubber. All that fitness, gone. The logical part of my brain knew that starting over was inevitable, and I'd be able to work my way back to where I'd been before. But the emotional part of me threw my running shoes in the back of my closet and told myself I'd try again later.

Later never came. The medals were pretty though, and I was proud of the reminders of the 10Ks and half marathons I'd completed. Hanging the medals up had seemed like a good idea at the time, but now that Emily was handling them and asking questions, all I wanted to do was hide them away again.

"I'm just saying," Emily said as she applied a screwdriver to the medal rack, taking it down off the wall, "if you wanted to get back into it, I bet Simon would have some advice. He's been running, God, most of his life, I think."

"Really?" How did I not know this? Because I'd never asked, that's how. I liked Simon a lot, he and Emily were great together. But for all the time I'd spent with him, I could probably count the things I knew about him on one hand. And vice versa.

"Yeah. There's a 5K he does every Thanksgiving. Downtown, I think."

"There is." I'd run it once or twice myself, back in the day. It was a fun way to start out a holiday, especially one that involved a food coma later in the afternoon.

"You want me to ask him about it? Like, how to get into it again? I bet he has some kind of training plan that could—"

"That's okay." I took the medal rack from Emily, stashing it in the top drawer of the dresser next to the medals. "Another time, maybe." Of course that was April-speak for not on your life. It was an automatic response. I never wanted to let anyone know my business. Even my sister. Even my brother-in-law.

Emily knew me well enough to know not to push back. "Okay," she said easily. "So is it Eggshell time?"

"It's Eggshell time," I confirmed. "After we sand down these walls and fill in the nail holes."

"Ugh," she said dramatically. "So much work before the fun stuff."

"I'm not sure any of this is the fun stuff." But Emily had to prove me wrong. About ten minutes in, she switched on the clock radio on the bedside table, tuning it to a radio station that crackled out some classic rock. "Oh, God." A smile spread across my face in recognition. "Dad played this album all the time."

"All the time," Emily confirmed, and we grinned at this rarity: a shared childhood memory. Sure, we hadn't grown up together per se, but our parents had remained consistent throughout our upbringing. So we shimmied our shoulders and swung our hips while we worked, turning the tedious chore into an impromptu dance party, something I didn't do often enough.

"Hey, there she is!" Emily said, and I turned to see Caitlin leaning in the doorway, a lemon square in her hand.

"Hey, Em." My daughter didn't say hi to me. "When did you get here?"

"Little bit ago? Come on in and dance with us." Emily stretched out her arms toward her niece.

Caitlin shook her head, laughing around a bite of lemon square. "That's okay."

If Emily caught any of the tension between the two of us, she didn't say. "You sounded good at rehearsal yesterday."

Caitlin groaned. "You heard that? God, we sound terrible. There's so many new girls in the Lilies this year."

"Hey, could be worse. You could still have Dahlia."

Caitlin snorted, sounding like a cross between Emily and me.

"Funny." She popped the last bite of lemon square in her mouth and brushed her hands off on her shorts. "She was supposed to be in charge last summer, and it was the worst."

"Yeah, I remember that day she flaked out and didn't show up . . ."

While their Faire-related gossip continued—nothing to do with me—my phone buzzed in my back pocket. Who on earth was texting? The two people in my life who texted me the most were here in the room with me.

It was Mitch. **How's the home renovation going?**

The girls were still talking, so it was no big deal to tap out a quick response. **Slowly. Working on painting now, tackling the carpets soon.** I was probably going to have to hire someone for that, and I wasn't looking forward to it.

Living room and dining room carpets, right?

Exactly. Wow. Good on him for remembering. **Probably guest room too. It's not looking great.**

If you want to knock them out next weekend I can come by Saturday morning. It'll go quick if we do it together.

"What?" Whoops, I'd said that out loud.

"Everything okay?" Emily turned to me, eyebrows raised.

"Yeah . . ." I looked down at my phone again, then back up at the girls. "You have Ren Faire rehearsals every weekend, right?"

Emily nodded. "From now till we open in July. Why? You finally joining up?"

My laugh was an involuntary bark. "No. I told you, nobody wants to see me in a corset." I glanced over at Caitlin, who was stifling a laugh at my joke. We shared a smile, and in that moment my daughter was more pleasant to me than she'd been for the past couple weeks. I was even more thankful now that Emily had come over. She was an important part of not only my life, but Cait's too. Her acting as a buffer was doing a lot to ease the tension around here.

Their conversation went back to Ren Faire rehearsals, and I turned back to my phone. Because who was I to look a gift handyman in the mouth? **In that case, I'll see you Saturday morning. Around 10?**

You got it.

I clicked off my phone and stuck it back in my pocket. This was a good plan. The more work I could get done with Caitlin out of the house, the better. And the more free assistance I could get, the even better.

On Saturday morning Emily swung by to pick Caitlin up for rehearsals, as usual. I refilled my sister's travel mug of coffee, and after they left I poured a second cup for myself. The knock on the door came at ten on the dot.

"Punctual," I said, ushering Mitch into the house. "Want some coffee?"

"Sure, if you've got some." He paused a few steps into the house, a look of wonder crossing his face. "What smells so good?"

"Oh." I'd put a pork shoulder into the slow cooker late last night, and when I got up this morning I'd drained the fat so it could keep cooking. While it still had a few hours to go before it was ready, the smell of roasting pork permeated the house. I was so used to it that I barely noticed it. But Mitch did. "We're having pulled pork tonight. It takes forever, so I only do it on the weekend, when I can keep an eye on it while it's slow-roasting."

"That's awesome. What time's dinner?" He clapped his hands together, like an invitation was a foregone conclusion.

I snorted. "Long after you leave. Want some coffee?"

He took the rejection with a short laugh and shake of his

head, then he followed me into the kitchen, immediately rummaging around in the cabinets for a coffee mug. I leaned in the doorway and sipped from my own mug, amused. Most people would let their host get everything for them, or at least ask where things were. But Mitch had a way of making himself at home wherever he went.

Coffee acquired, he turned back to me. I'd been admiring the way he filled out his jeans, but now I had a great view of his tight T-shirt, and that was just as good. Did the man buy all his T-shirts a size too small or what? "So," he said. "Carpets?"

I nodded. "Carpets." I took one more fortifying gulp of coffee before putting the mug down on the dining room table. He followed me down the hallway, and we paused outside the bedrooms. "I figured I'd get the guest room done, and then work out toward the living room and dining room." Yikes. That sounded like a lot when I said it out loud. Sure, he'd offered to help, but I didn't want to take advantage. "I'm not saying we have to get it all done today. That'd be too—"

"Nah." He took an unconcerned sip of coffee. "Shouldn't be a problem."

"Are you sure?" I squinted into the guest room. It was still in disarray from Emily's and my painting party that had started the weekend before. She'd come over a couple evenings during the week to help finish painting the room itself, but the bedroom set was still in the middle of the room under drop cloths, lurking like a monster waiting to eat me in my sleep.

Mitch shrugged. "Sure. I mean, we'll be doing some work, but we can get them both done today if you want."

"Oh, I definitely want." I threw a tsk in his direction as he raised his eyebrows at me over his coffee mug. How could he turn everything into a double entendre? "The *carpets*," I said. "I want to get the carpets done." Come to think of it, that didn't sound much better.

"Mmm-hmm." He tilted his head back to finish his coffee and I tried not to be mesmerized by the muscles in his neck as he swallowed. "Anyway . . ." He reached into his back pocket, pulling out two large mat knives. He handed me one, and I took his empty mug in my other hand.

"Easiest way to do this," he said, "is to slice the carpet into strips. We can move the furniture around while we work, instead of moving everything out and back in again."

"Well, that sounds ridiculously sensible." I set his mug down on the dresser in my room and twirled the knife between my fingers. I was glad he'd thought ahead and brought the knives, because all I had was a little box cutter that was about half the size of the one in my hand now.

We fell into an easy rhythm once we got the carpet loosened from the edges of the wall. We pushed the furniture to one side of the room before slicing the carpet into long strips, rolling it up, and getting it out of the room. Then we moved the furniture onto the bare concrete side of the room before doing it all over again.

"You know . . ." I dragged the back of my wrist across my forehead, which did nothing to get rid of the sweat that had started to gather. "All those shows about people remodeling their houses, when they pull up the carpet there's always this perfect original hardwood underneath. I'm feeling a little ripped off here."

Mitch snorted as he handed me a roll of duct tape. "Yeah. That's not going to happen in a house in the suburbs like this. These places were built in the eighties."

"I know." I sighed as I picked at the tape, pulling till I got it started. "But a girl can dream, right?"

"Sure." He held the rolled-up carpet strip together while I wrapped a line of tape around it, then we wrestled it into the contractor's trash bag, laying it out in the hallway with the others. The neighbors were going to think I was cleaning the bodies out from under my crawl space when we started getting rid of all of this.

"Now, my grandma's house, that's a whole different story. That place is something like a hundred and fifty years old."

I gave a low whistle. "I bet you'd find all kinds of stuff under the carpets."

"Oh yeah. And secret passages in the closets."

"Seriously?"

Mitch shrugged. "Someone told me that when I was a kid, and I spent every visit there trying to find them." He paused. "Now that I think about it, maybe they were trying to get me out of their hair. Huh."

"Now, why would they do that?"

"I had a lot of energy as a kid."

"Hmm." I pulled at the last sliced-up strip of carpet, but it wasn't giving. I braced everything and tugged harder. Still nothing. "So not a lot has changed, then, huh?"

"Nope." Suddenly he was down on his knees beside me, grasping the carpet in his much-larger hands, helping me pull. Our hands overlapped each other, and with his shoulder leaned into mine, I tried to ignore the way his breath stirred my ponytailed hair. The carpet came up easily when we were both pulling on it.

"There, see? Easy." His voice in my ear shouldn't be doing things to me. That wasn't what was happening here. But I couldn't ignore the way things inside of me tightened when he was this close.

I didn't want to think about that. "So you're sure it's okay that you blew off rehearsal today? I don't want you getting me in trouble with my brother-in-law."

Mitch shook his head with a smile. "Nothing going on today that I need to be there for. Once we start fight rehearsal . . . that'll be another story."

"Really? Isn't it the same fight you did last year?" Here I was, talking out of my ass again. The Renaissance Faire was in no way my domain.

But Mitch didn't seem to mind me asking such basic questions. "Yeah, for the past few years. But Simon and I want to change it up a little. Pass on the big fight to someone else, you know? Which is great, because then we don't have to work as hard during the summer."

I nodded like I had any idea what he was talking about. "So you've been doing the big fight?"

"Yeah. It's the climax of the whole thing. Simon and I sword fight for a while, then we punch each other around a little. He flips me over his shoulder, and . . ."

"No." I sat back on my heels and shook my head. "There's no way Simon flips you over his shoulder. You're like six inches taller than he is."

Mitch echoed my posture, sitting on his heels and leaning his hands on his knees. "You've never seen our fight?" His voice was wounded.

"Um . . ." It was hard to not cringe. This Ren Faire thing was a part of life for so many people in this town that it was almost embarrassing to be someone who wasn't involved. "Sorry?"

He laughed at my meek attempt at apology. "Here." He reached into his back pocket and pulled out his phone, turning to sit cross-legged on the floor. While he tapped and scrolled, I sat down next to him. It was break time, apparently.

A few moments later he handed me his phone turned sideways. "Here," he said again. "This is the fight we usually do."

I hit Play on the video he'd called up, which unpaused the action of two men mid-tussle on a grassy field. I recognized Mitch immediately, wearing a kilt, knee-high boots, and little else. But it took a moment for me to recognize Simon, wearing leather pants, a loose black shirt, and a red vest. The two fought hand to hand for a few tense moments: punches and backhands, circling each other threateningly. Then Simon caught a punch thrown by Mitch in both hands, turning the larger man's momentum against him, and before I realized what was happening, Mitch was in the air, flipping over Simon's shoulder. I frowned and paused the video.

"I still don't get it. How does that work?"

"Leverage." Mitch reached around me for his phone, taking it out of my hands and rewinding the video about fifteen seconds. "See? He bends like that, gets his shoulder right about there on my chest, and then I basically dive over him. Like a lever, you know?"

"Hmm. I'm very bad at physics." I watched the flip again, but this time my focus was on Mitch's kilt, and the way the fabric flew when he flipped over Simon's shoulder. "Hey." I paused the video again with a frown. "You have shorts on. Under the kilt."

Mitch's laugh was practically a guffaw. "Nice of you to notice."

"I mean . . ." I'd made it pretty obvious where my attention was, hadn't I? Yikes. I rewound the video and watched it again, from the beginning this time. "I know what a stickler Simon is for historical accuracy. I'm surprised he let you get away with that." On the little screen the men circled each other with swords that matched their physiques: Mitch with a massive sword that took both hands to wield, Simon with a slender rapier.

"It's a family Faire." He leaned over my shoulder, watching the video with me. It would have been the most natural thing in the world to lean back against him, but I fought the impulse. Fought it hard. "I understand your disappointment, but that flip alone would make it a very adult show."

"I didn't say I was disappointed." I watched Simon flip Mitch once more, this time concentrating on Mitch's powerful legs, and how the muscles looked when he landed on his feet. Those same muscles were right here next to me, covered up by a pair of jeans. My mouth went dry and I coughed.

"You thirsty? I'm thirsty." That was an understatement, and I shoved the phone back into Mitch's hands before standing up. I needed to get away from him. And while that wasn't possible, I could at least stop sitting practically in his lap.

"Sure." He rose easily to his feet, and even though he was dressed, all I could see were those legs in the video. Powerful. Muscled. Mouthwatering.

Yeah. Definitely needed a drink. Cold, cold water.

Six

S o your grandma," I said on the way to the kitchen. "With the old house? This is the one I'm meeting soon? At the dinner?" I opened the fridge to snag a couple of cans of soda from Caitlin's stash.

"Ugh, seriously?" He looked over my shoulder at the contents of my fridge, close but not crowding me. "Would it kill you to put some beer in here?"

I turned my head, meeting his eyes. I raised an eyebrow and he huffed. Not quite a laugh, not quite annoyed. "Never mind," he said. "I'll bring some next time."

"You said that last time," I reminded him. I handed him a can and bumped the door closed with my hip as he stepped back. "Anyway, your grandma?" I cracked open the soda.

"Yeah. The dinner. About that . . ." I'd never seen anyone look shifty while they drank a can of soda, but Mitch pulled it off.

"What? Is it canceled?" A spark of hope ignited in my chest. There was nothing in the world I liked better than canceled plans.

"No," he said. "No, it's not. It's . . . uh, the opposite, actually."

"The opposite?" I tried to figure out what the opposite of canceled was. Even more dinner? Extreme dinner?

"Yeah. The family group chat went a little crazy this week. My cousin Lulu shared this guacamole recipe she found, and my aunt Cecilia said it was garbage because it had mayo in it . . ."

"Mayonnaise?" I almost choked on my soda. "In guacamole?" I couldn't hide my shudder, and Mitch's lips quirked in response.

"Exactly. So that sparked off a huge argument over what the 'real' recipe for guacamole should be. It got ugly. Lots of harsh words were exchanged."

I shook my head. "I'm not following. What does this have to do with the anniversary dinner?"

"Well, by the end of the night they decided not to do the dinner."

That spark of hope grew to a flame, warming me from the inside out. No dinner. No pretending to be a girlfriend. But . . . "The dinner was canceled because of a fight over guacamole?"

"Oh. No." He took the last swallow from his can of soda and put it down on the counter. "Now they want to do a guacamole-tasting contest, since no one can agree how it should be made. So that's happening on Friday night, and we're all gathering at my grandparents' place down in Virginia."

"Friday night?" I did some quick thinking. "Okay . . . I can probably get the day off, if we need to go down for the day . . ."

"For the weekend."

My brain stalled out. "What?" So much for that flame of hope. Doused in an instant.

"The weekend," Mitch repeated. His voice was elaborately casual, but his eyes were wary as they met mine. "They . . . uh . . . it's a long weekend thing now. Instead of a dinner."

"What?" My stalled-out brain stuttered, tried to come back to life, but failed.

"Yeah. That whole group chat I was talking about . . . it started with the guacamole, and then everyone was all 'oh, it's been so long since we've all been together, we should do more than a dinner' . . . " He shook his head in disgust. "I mean, most of us were together at Christmas, but whatever. And then someone mentioned it to Grandma . . ."

"Oh, no." Understanding washed over me. He'd already told me about his guilt trip of a grandmother. If she got it into her head that a family weekend getaway was necessary, then there'd be no getting out of it.

"Oh, yes." He leaned a hip against my kitchen counter and crossed his arms. "Family dinner is now family three-day weekend."

"Jesus." I pressed a hand to my chest, over my heart that had started thudding with something that felt like panic. I shouldn't have been panicking about this. I wasn't being asked to give a speech. I was being asked to hang out for a weekend. The worst part about it was possibly eating some mayonnaise-tainted guacamole. But this was still a lot.

"Yeah. Dinner with my folks is one thing, but a long weekend out of town is something else. You didn't sign on for that."

"No, I didn't." I barely heard myself say the words, though. I was thinking too hard. How bad could it be? Mitch was fun to be around. He made me laugh, and these couple of times he'd come over to help with the house, we'd worked well together. Besides, he'd offered to help me with these floors out of the blue, the least I could do in exchange was . . .

Wait a minute. I narrowed my eyes. "That's why you're over here, isn't it?"

"Hmm?" He raised his eyebrows, the picture of innocence.

"That's why you offered to help me with the carpets." I pointed an accusatory finger at him. "You're buttering me up. Softening the blow, so I'll go along with the weekend trip."

"Well . . ." He drew the word out, and his shrug was as helpless as his smile. "I figured it couldn't hurt, right?"

A laugh escaped my body from around my pounding heart. My panic was starting to subside under the force of Mitch's smile. I took a breath. "Lucky for you, I have a killer recipe for guacamole."

His smile widened, like the sun coming out after a week of rain. "Yeah?"

"Yeah. And it doesn't have mayonnaise in it, because that sounds like an abomination."

He uncrossed his arms, and I watched the line of tension ease from his shoulders. I hadn't realized how tense he'd been during this conversation until he relaxed. "You really don't mind? Going along with me for the whole weekend? I was sure you'd back out."

"Well, not now that you're helping me get the carpets done." I brushed my hands off on my jeans and took the borrowed mat knife out of my pocket. "But I'm gonna need help with the rest of the painting around here. My bedroom, Caitlin's bedroom . . ." That was a lot of bedroom talk with him, but I was willing to chance it to get things checked off my list.

Mitch chuckled. "Looks like I'll be spending a lot of my free time over here, then."

I shrugged. "If you want a girlfriend, you will be."

"Oh, I want a girlfriend." He took the knife out of my hand and laid it on the counter, and my blood rose at the slight growl in his voice. *Down, girl. It's all fake.* "Let's get rid of the carpet we already pulled up, then we'll get the living room done today too. Just make sure you put avocados on your shopping list."

Sure enough, by the time Caitlin finished with rehearsal, Mitch and I had ripped out the carpet in the guest room, as well as the living room and dining room, and he was gone before she came home. There was a look of shock on my daughter's face when she walked through the front door to see me sweeping the bare concrete living room floor.

"I know," I said. "I know. It looks terrible right now. I promise there will be a real floor in here soon. Sooner than soon." Inside I was cringing. We'd come a long way recently, and things had been almost back to normal around here. Was this blatant show of home renovation going to set us back?

"Okay." To her credit, she swallowed down her shock and her voice was impassive, almost bored sounding. She sniffed the air. "Pulled pork smells good."

"It does. Dinner will be easy tonight." I propped the broom against the wall and sank down onto the sofa. I was exhausted, I was sweaty, and I was already starting to get sore. My plans for the rest of the afternoon involved a nice hot bath, some Epsom salts, and a book. And tacos for dinner. Yum.

"How was rehearsal?" That was a safe question to ask.

"Good." She dropped her backpack by the door, almost directly under the hook it was supposed to hang on, and joined me, flopping down on the other end of the sofa. She echoed my tired stance, our feet propped up on opposite ends of the coffee table. "We didn't do a whole lot today. Mostly introductory stuff. But I think I have a full group of Lilies."

"Well, that's good news." I swallowed my smile. Caitlin sounded like a battle-weary general instead of a teenager. Very in charge. Simon had certainly put her to work.

My tired brain wandered from Simon to Mitch, and I was

glad that he'd already left before Caitlin got home. I didn't know how I was going to explain this weekend trip with him to her. It was bad enough that an English teacher had married into the family, but going away for the weekend with a gym teacher? Caitlin was going to have half the faculty of Willow Creek High in her life at this point.

Not to mention, I didn't know how I was going to handle this. I didn't take weekend trips. Especially sans daughter, and even more especially with a man. I was completely at sea here.

The solution didn't hit me until I was happily submerged in my bath, bath bomb fizzing all around me and turning my bathwater a neon shade of pink. As soon as I was out of the bath, I sent Emily a text. **Going away for the weekend with Mitch. DON'T ASK. Can you watch Caitlin while I'm away?**

Her response came almost immediately, while I was shredding the pork for dinner. **THE WEEKEND??? WTF?????**

I told you not to ask.

Laughing emojis came back in reply. **Your place or mine? (Is that what he said???)**

Cut it out. But I couldn't bite back the laugh at her text. **Let me see what Caitlin would rather do. I'll let you know.**

That was the question, wasn't it? I'd sprung a lot of changes on Caitlin lately, and I wasn't sure how to spring yet one more.

But as the calendar inched closer to the weekend I'd be spending in Virginia with Mitch and the Malone clan, I couldn't hide from the inevitable any longer. "So what would you think," I asked one night over dinner, "if Emily came over to stay for a weekend?"

Caitlin shrugged, but her expression was confused. "Sure, but why? Is something wrong?" Her eyes widened. "Did she and Mr. G have a fight?"

"No, no. Nothing like that." I crunched on a bite of salad. "I have to go out of town next weekend, and I thought she could come stay here with you. You know. Keep an eye on things."

"Keep an eye on me, you mean." Caitlin rolled her eyes and tsked at me in disgust. "I'm practically eighteen, you know. I can take care of myself."

"I know you can." I hated how defensive I sounded to my own daughter. "This is just—"

"I don't need a babysitter." She tossed her fork onto the table and leaned back in her chair, her arms crossed.

"Okay, that's enough." No. I was not going to defend myself. I was still her mother. "If you don't need a babysitter, then don't act like a baby."

She huffed. "I'm not acting like—"

"Yes, you are. You're throwing a tantrum. This isn't about you being able to take care of yourself. It's about me being worried about you while I'm gone." She glared at me, and I glared right back. I hated this. We'd been a team for so long, but it was starting to look like those days were over. I nodded down toward the table. "Now, pick up your fork and finish your salad."

"I'm not hungry." Caitlin pushed back from the table. "I have homework to finish anyway." She took her dishes to the kitchen and then she was gone. I sighed and speared another bite of lettuce. So much for our reconciliation. Another evening of loud silence stretched in front of me like a lonely highway.

That Thursday night, Caroline brought cupcakes to our neighborhood book club.

"Oh, great," Marjorie muttered from where she sat next to me on the couch. "She got laid again."

I snorted into my wine. Marjorie wasn't wrong. Ever since

Caroline's divorce was finalized a year and a half ago, she'd become . . . promiscuous. Word floated around, on the nights that she didn't make book club, that her marriage had been pretty dead for the five years previous, and with it her sex life. So now that she was single again she was making up for lost time. And every time she did, she brought cupcakes to book club to celebrate.

Not that I was judging her for it. It meant free cupcakes for me. And I probably would have done the same thing in her shoes. When I'd actually been in her shoes, roughly seventeen years ago, I'd had an infant, which had been a deterrent against getting any further action in my life. So *get some, Caroline*, was my opinion. Not that anyone ever asked. I was the quiet one in the group, and that was the way I liked it.

After all, I still remembered those early days in Willow Creek, of buying this house and moving in with my young daughter. After some pointed *where's Mr. Parker?* kinds of questions, I'd drawn the curtains. Shut myself into my house. Hidden myself and my daughter away to keep us safe from small-town gossip. Sure, I'd been single for a few years at that point, but the shame, the sting of being rejected by the man who'd promised to always love me, was still there, like it was stamped on my forehead for everyone to see. It was easier to assume the worst in people rather than feel like that again. But then Marjorie had extended the olive branch, inviting me to book club and bringing me into the neighborhood fold. It was nice, for the most part. But sometimes I wondered what they said about me the nights I wasn't there.

"How has everyone's month been?" Caroline put her Tupperware platter of postcoital cupcakes on the coffee table and took off the lid. "Anybody do anything fun?"

"Not as fun as you." I leaned forward and snagged a cupcake

and a napkin from the pile next to them. Red velvet, hell yeah. She caught my eye and we grinned across the table at each other in divorcée solidarity.

"You need to get out there, April," Caroline said. "There's lots of stuff going on. Ladies' nights, meetups. You should come out with me sometime. Earn yourself some cupcakes of your own."

"She's got a point," Marjorie said. She reached for a cupcake even though she'd been disparaging them a minute ago. "Caitlin's off to college soon, right? You can get back to working on yourself then."

"I'm good." I sounded nonchalant as I picked the wrapping off the bottom of the cupcake and licked frosting off my thumb. I always sounded nonchalant, because that was the easiest way to get through life. "Your idea of working on yourself seems to involve going out, crowds. Things that involve putting on pants." I shuddered. "Can't I live vicariously through you and your sex cupcakes?"

Marjorie choked on her mouthful of cake, and Caroline shrugged in an exaggeratedly helpless manner. "I tried. I want to see you happy, that's all."

"Oh, I am. As long as you keep bringing cupcakes to book club." I polished off said cupcake and reached for another. I wasn't getting laid, but I was getting plenty of sugar. Close enough, right?

As Marjorie turned the talk away from my lack of a sex life and back onto the book we'd been reading, I ran my finger around the edge of the second cupcake, scooping up the frosting and depositing it directly into my mouth without needing cake as a vehicle. For a split second, I imagined telling the group about Mitch. About how I'd agreed to pretend to be his girlfriend this weekend. I thought about the girl talk that would ensue, and while there was a part of my soul that craved that kind of connection with other people, I knew I'd shrivel under that kind of spotlight. I didn't want it. Caroline and her cupcakes could have it.

Anyway, this whole thing with Mitch and me didn't count. It wasn't real. A friend helping a friend—nothing that would lead to sex cupcakes. Nothing more than a weekend hanging off of one of Mitch Malone's giant biceps, doing my damnedest to throw enough loving glances his way to fool every member of his family.

Oh God, this was going to be a disaster.

Seven

Caitlin *hardly said* a word to me before school on Friday morning. She glared at Emily's bag in the guest room, huffed a few times at me, and then she was off. I could have made a big deal about it, but my mind was already a few hours ahead, on Mitch's gargantuan red pickup truck pulling into my driveway and getting this weekend started. I already wanted it to be over.

My pulse spiked when he arrived, but I forced some deep breaths as I gathered my things and locked the front door behind me. It was going to be fine. It was all going to be fine.

"All set, *honey?*" Mitch stressed the last word as he hoisted my suitcase without asking, stowing it in the back of his extended cab, next to his leather duffel-shaped overnight bag. Seeing our bags nestled together like that didn't do anything for my anxiety. This wasn't me. I didn't go away for a weekend with a man. What was I doing?

But I forced myself to breathe through the anxiety. I was an adult. I could do this. I made myself smile and roll my eyes at him—the kind of reaction he was used to from me, as opposed to terror. "Let's go, *babe*." I pulled myself up and into the passenger seat.

He flashed me a grin as the engine started with a roar. "Here." He handed me his phone once I'd clicked my seat belt. "Lulu sent me all the info for the hotel when I was at the gym this morning. It's in the calendar. Can you pull it up?"

"Sure." I took the unlocked phone and navigated to today's date. Sure enough, there was an entry for three p.m.—our check-in time—with the address, phone number, and confirmation number for the hotel reservation. I was about to tap on it when an entry from earlier this morning caught my eye: 6:00 a.m.—Fran.

Huh. I glanced over to Mitch, trying hard to not make it a side-eye. "You said you were at the gym this morning?"

"Yep." He glanced over his shoulder as he backed out of the driveway, one long arm across the back of my seat. "Why?"

"Nothing." I glanced down at the phone, then back up at him. "I . . . I figured that's why your hair was still wet." Indeed, his hair was damp, the residual water making it a dark blond color, and he smelled clean, like soap. He'd definitely showered before picking me up, but why was he lying about going to the gym? We weren't a couple. But we were friends. He could tell me if he was having a quickie before going out of town.

"Yep," he said again easily. "You got that address?"

"Oh. Yeah." I pulled it up and plugged the address into the truck's GPS. But I couldn't resist poking through his calendar. I should have, but I couldn't. Every other day this week was dotted with appointments, and I clicked on them. Monday said *Annie*, and Wednesday was *Cindy*. Both at six in the morning, like his rendezvous this morning with Fran. Apparently he was into early morning hookups these days. Good to know.

No. No, it wasn't good to know. I didn't need to know this. I had no right nor reason to know or care who he met up with and when. I plugged in his phone and tucked it into the center console, settling down for the drive to Virginia. Besides, maybe it was good that he'd hooked up before the trip. Maybe he'd keep his flirting with me to a minimum.

The beginning of the trip was tense, as a road trip that went through Washington, DC, always was. But it didn't take long for us to be out of the insane beltway traffic and into the rolling hills of the Shenandoah Valley. By then my nervousness had faded, lulled by the scenery and the classic rock station on satellite radio. Then something he'd said registered, far later than it should have.

"Wait a second. A hotel? What happened to the whole family gathering at your grandparents' homestead?"

"Oh. Yeah." He turned the radio down a few clicks, so this was going to be a conversation, not just a quick answer. "Sorry, I should have told you. There's a lot of people coming this weekend, and there are only so many bedrooms in their house. Lulu emailed me this week to tell me that some of us got put up in a hotel. It's not far from their place—like a ten-minute drive. Not a big deal."

"Sure." I turned back to the window with a frown. The weekend suddenly looked a lot different. It was bad enough when I thought I was navigating a family weekend: three days of social activity, but at least there was a bedroom where I could hide. But now even that had been taken away from me. I hadn't thought this through. What had I expected? He'd told his family we were a couple. Chances were slim that I would have been getting my own room anyway, at either the hotel or the house. No matter what, I was about to share a room with Mitch.

This was bad. But I didn't realize how bad until we got to the hotel. Everything was in Mitch's name, so he checked in while I tried to stretch the kinks out of my back—not to mention my leg—in the parking lot. It had been a relatively short drive, as road trips went, and his truck was so big that it felt like I was sitting on a sofa the whole time. But even a comfortable couch was hard to sit on for hours on end, and as I put my hands on my hips and leaned backwards I heard as well as felt a satisfying pop from somewhere in my lower back. I straightened up just as Mitch came back to the truck and handed me a keycard.

"All set?" He slung the strap of his bag over his shoulder and wheeled my suitcase behind him, again without asking, leaving me to trail after him with my purse and smaller tote. It was weird not schlepping my stuff. Women who had partners in their lives probably had help like this all the time, but I couldn't fathom it. I always carried my own stuff, and at least half of Caitlin's.

"What's in there, anyway?" Mitch nodded at the insulated tote I carried, and I glanced down at it.

"Guacamole supplies. Tonight's the guac-off, right?"

His eyes lit up. "Oh, definitely! I didn't want to put pressure on you, though." The keycard beeped and the light turned green as he unlocked the door to the room.

"No pressure," I said as I followed him into the room. "I emailed my college roommate, Hope, this week. She's from Austin, and if there's one thing Texans know, it's their guacamole. I am in it to win . . ." My voice trailed off as he flipped the lights on and we both came to a stop in front of the bed.

The.

Bed.

As in one.

"Um . . ." I looked up at Mitch, who was staring at the bed as though it were a particularly nasty kind of snake.

As well he should. Said bed was ginormous, and festooned with rose petals, sprinkled across its surface and around the perimeter. A garishly red heart-shaped pillow perched at the head of the bed, on top of the pillows like a vulture of love. A bottle of champagne and a box of chocolates were on the nightstand, honestly the only palatable part of this scenario.

"Hmm?" To his credit, he made an effort to sound unconcerned in the face of this aggressive display of romance.

"Do you . . . do you see this?"

"Yep."

"Any idea what the hell this is?"

Mitch sighed a long sigh. "Lulu was *really* excited when I told her I was bringing a girlfriend."

"So she what, got us the romance package?" I wanted to laugh, but I was too horrified. I wanted to crack open that bottle of champagne and chug it, but showing up drunk at Mitch's grandparents' would probably be a bad idea.

"Yeah, that . . . that looks like exactly what she did." He leaned down and plucked a couple of the rose petals off the bed, which made exactly no difference. I tried to focus on the rest of the room. Two small uncomfortable-looking wingback chairs and a small end table sat near the window, while the wall across from the bed had a desk and a dresser, with a television taking up most of the real estate on the wall itself. It was a nice room, all things considered. Except that I was going to be sharing a rose-petal-covered bed with Mitch Malone for the next two nights.

"Okay." I set my purse and the tote of guac ingredients on the (super-king-size) bed and pinched the bridge of my nose. "Okay," I said again. "Let me call down to the front desk. I can get my own room. Or maybe they can switch this one? Give us a different room with two beds in it?"

"Yeah. Because that's not going to look suspicious for a couple with the romance package." Mitch snorted. "Besides, I don't know who else from the family is staying here. What if someone drops by the room? It would be pretty obvious if your stuff isn't here."

I sighed. While the odds of that happening seemed pretty low, he had a point. Keeping a lie going was a lot of trouble. Probably best to keep things as simple as possible.

"Fine." I reached for my suitcase. We were due at his grandparents' place in a couple hours. That champagne was going to have to wait. "But it's going to cost you."

"Anything you want."

So many places I could go in response to that. But I played it safe. "Well, my living room walls aren't going to paint themselves."

"Deal." We shook on it, and his hand was warm around mine. Odds were good I'd be holding that hand more than once this weekend. I should get used to his touch.

To that end . . . I unzipped my suitcase and got out my makeup bag, along with the outfit I planned to wear tonight. Mitch needed his mature, steady, fake girlfriend. Worrying about sleeping arrangements could wait. It was time to get into character.

Malones everywhere. That phrase had stuck with me ever since Mitch asked me to do this, and it echoed in my head now, over and over, to the rhythm of . . . well, everything. My heartbeat, which grew steadily faster and louder in my ears as we left the hotel and started the drive to his grandparents' house. The music on the radio, which Mitch had kept tuned to the classic rock station because I'd liked one of the songs there about an hour into our trip earlier today. The engine of Mitch's truck, which hummed all around me like I was in a giant cocoon. I felt safe in Mitch's truck. But soon enough we were going to arrive at his grandparents' place, where I'd have to leave that cocoon of safety. Where there were *Malones everywhere*.

My eyes widened and my eyebrows crawled up my forehead when we turned in to a neighborhood lined with what can only be described as mini-mansions. With lush, huge front yards and winding driveways featuring wrought-iron gates, they looked like houses celebrities hid in, where paparazzi hung from the massive oak trees trying to get a million-dollar shot. Mitch didn't seem like a mansion kind of guy. But that didn't mean his family wasn't. My blood pressure shot up a little more until I could hear my heart pound in my temples. I was sitting here in a blouse and slacks that were barely a step up from business casual with a bag of avocados in my lap, and while Mitch had changed into a shirt with an actual collar, I still felt underdressed for houses like this.

But . . . all these houses looked like relatively new construction. I turned to Mitch. "I thought you said they lived in an old house?"

"Hmm?" He glanced over at me for a split second, keeping his eyes on the road for the most part.

"You said it was like a hundred and fifty years old? Secret passages?" I gestured to the houses out the window as we drove past them.

"Oh yeah." He dismissed the scenery outside with a wave. "Don't pay attention to that."

A couple of left turns later, Mitch pulled onto a winding driveway whose gates stood open. We drove through a little wooded area off the street, and while I couldn't see a house right away, I was prepared for something tremendous. How the hell many people were going to be at this gathering if there wasn't room for Mitch at the family home? My chest tightened, and I gripped the oh-shit bar on the door as I tried to take a deep breath. Maybe it was me. Maybe they didn't want me there. Oh God.

But then the trees gave way to a clearing, and the house appeared. And he was right. While it certainly wasn't small—I could probably fit two of my houses in there—the nineteenth-century farmhouse bore little to no resemblance to the huge houses we'd driven past. Obviously well maintained, it was covered in gray clapboard siding and had a wraparound porch dotted with rocking chairs. I couldn't see the backyard from where we were, but trees in the distance showed that it backed onto a forest: the house and the land it stood on seemed snuggled into a semicircle of oak and fir trees. In front of the house there was a carport area of sorts that was mostly gravel, and currently filled with cars.

Mitch maneuvered his truck to a spot in front of the garage and killed the engine. For a few moments we sat in silence. Finally he sighed, and it sounded so unlike him I turned to him in surprise. A muscle jumped in his cheek, and his brow furrowed as he stared at the house.

This was new. I'd never seen Mitch without a smile on his face and a good word for everyone. And I'd certainly never seen him with his forehead creased with worry. My own worry and nervousness waned as I became more focused on his. He hadn't asked me along on this weekend for fun, or to mess with me. There was something he was dreading about this weekend and he'd asked me along because he needed my help. It was time to start helping.

I laid a hand on his arm, and he jumped a little at my touch, obviously brought out of some deep thoughts. "Come on," I said, with a lightness I didn't feel. "Let's go win a guacamole contest."

I held his gaze with mine, and after a few moments some light came back into his eyes. "Yeah," he said. "Let's do this."

Given Mitch's unexpected anxiety, I wasn't sure what to prepare myself for when we walked up the wooden steps onto that broad porch. He didn't knock on the door right away; instead he took a breath, settled his shoulders, then grasped my hand. I wasn't sure if he'd reached for me for reassurance or to illustrate our relationship to his family. But I gave his hand a squeeze as he opened the door, in case he was looking for that reassurance. He squeezed back and led us inside.

A wave of noise hit me once we were in the foyer. Lots of raised voices, and my first instinct was to wince at the sound. It took a moment to realize the voices weren't raised in anger. They were just talking. Loudly. I reminded myself that these were Mitch's people. They were not going to be quiet. I could handle this. Probably.

The inside of the farmhouse was much like the outside. Old. Lived in. Comfortable looking. Not fancy, but tidy. I shook my head and looked up at Mitch. "I don't get it."

"Don't get what?"

"All those houses we drove past on the way here . . . it's like we're not even in the same neighborhood."

"That's because Grandma is stubborn as hell," a new voice said, and we both turned to see a woman had joined us in the foyer. She was roughly our age—well, Mitch's age—and a little taller than my five and a half feet, her strawberry-blonde hair was bound back in a long braid that fell over one shoulder, and she was dressed casually with an apron over her jeans and white blouse. Mitch burst into a grin when he saw her.

"Lulu!" He dropped my hand to embrace her, and I missed his heat. I missed that little bit of connection, and I told myself to get a grip. Instead I folded my hands in front of me, letting him have this moment with his cousin. He would introduce me soon enough.

"How you doing, big guy?" Lulu grinned up at him as she leaned back in his arms, her hands flat on his back, holding him close. "You check into the hotel okay?"

Mitch only hesitated for a fraction of a second. "Oh, yeah. The room's great. Thanks for the, uh . . ." He glanced over at me, and the ridiculousness of the hotel room made me want to burst into nervous laughter. His smile widened before turning back to his cousin. "Thanks for that."

"No problem at all." Her grin was wicked as they broke apart, and then she turned her attention to me. Her smile was like the sun, and that must have been something in the Malone DNA, that bright happy smile that felt like it was just for you. "You must be April." She took a step forward, hand extended, and I returned the gesture.

"I am." I found myself smiling back at her, feeling like we were old friends already.

"It's so great to meet you. Mitch has told me so much about you, and—"

"He has?" I turned alarmed eyes up toward Mitch, who shrugged with a smile.

"Of course," he said easily, slipping an arm around my shoulders like it was something he did all the time. "I'm not gonna tell my favorite cousin about my girl?"

I had to fight to keep a straight face. When was the last time someone had called me their girl? High school? That was a long time ago. "It's great to meet you too," I said. "If only to make you see the absolute wrongness of adding mayonnaise to guacamole."

She burst into a laugh, the kind of honest laugh that had her throwing her head back. "That's right! He said you wanted in on this. Come on, let's get you into the kitchen." Her tug on my hand was firm, and I looked over my shoulder in alarm at Mitch, who shrugged easily and let me be dragged away.

Eight

"Don't worry," *Lulu* said, tucking my hand into the crook of her arm. "I promise we're not scary. And I will convert you to the truth of my guac recipe."

"Not likely," I said, my courage rising. I liked Lulu, and if the rest of Mitch's family was like this I would be okay, boisterousness aside.

The kitchen was full of people, and I was introduced around with a speed that made it impossible to remember who anyone was. But I was handed an apron and directed to a corner of the kitchen island, and before long I was halving the avocados I'd brought. There were four other people, each making a slightly different version of guacamole. The Malone genes were strong, producing almost Nordic-looking specimens: tall, fair-haired, and genial. Next to them I felt short, frizzy-haired, and surly. There was a lot of laughter in this kitchen, though, mostly trash-talking each other's recipes although the resulting bowls of guacamole frankly looked all the same to me. A smile tugged at my lips as I seeded a jalapeño, and Lulu appeared on my right with a frosted glass.

"Margarita?"

"Oooh." I finished with the jalapeño, then washed my hands thoroughly before reaching for the glass. "Thank you."

"There's chips and salsa over there too if you're hungry." She surveyed the rest of the ingredients I'd brought with me: red onion, limes, a few tomatoes, and a small bunch of fresh cilantro. "You know, Grandma made some pico de gallo for hers, and she made way too much. I'm sure she wouldn't mind if you used it in yours."

"No, that's okay . . ." It seemed like a strange offer, especially for a recipe contest, but her ulterior motive became clear as she dragged me across the kitchen, margaritas in hand, to meet Mitch's grandmother: a small, round, elderly woman who looked both fragile and solid at the same time. I wanted to sit her down and bring her some tea, but I also worried that she might kick my ass if I made it wrong.

"Of course, of course!" she said in response to Lulu's request, pushing a small yellow bowl into my hands. There was more than enough pico in there for my needs. But I still hesitated.

"If you're sure you don't need it?"

She shook her head emphatically. "Not at all. Mine's already made and in the refrigerator, see?" She opened the door, indicating a larger bowl in the same yellow as the one I held. "Not that it matters. It's nothing fancy. Something I threw together. I'm sure yours, or maybe Louisa's, will be much better."

Louisa . . . ? Oh, Lulu. Right. "I wouldn't say that necessarily." I gave my margarita a longing glance, but figured it probably wasn't polite to swig alcohol in front of Grandma.

"Do you have a secret ingredient? Everyone else seems to. Some cumin, maybe? Cayenne? I'm sure you know all about Louisa and her mayonnaise." She gave a shudder, but her eyes twinkled at me. They honest to God twinkled. Oh, I liked her a lot.

So I smiled back. A real smile, not a polite one, as I leaned into her, about to impart a secret. "That would be telling, wouldn't it?"

She chuckled and gave me a light pat on the shoulder. "You're going to do fine, April."

I glowed from the compliment as I finished making my guacamole—sans cumin, no thank you—and set my bowl on the counter next to the others, with a saucer in front of each one. Family members started filtering in, snagging chips from big bowls set out nearby, demolishing the dishes of guacamole in record time. We were each armed with a penny, which we used to vote for the guacamole recipe we liked best.

I jumped only a little when Mitch slid his arms around me from behind, cradling me to him. I glanced up at him and he smiled down at me, the picture-perfect boyfriend. As he bent to brush a kiss across my cheek he whispered, "Which one is Grandma's?"

I turned in his arms with a gasp. "You're not voting for mine?" I kept my voice a low murmur. "I worked hard on that shit."

"Listen." His voice was a low rumble in my ear, and to everyone else it looked like a loving embrace, instead of an impending betrayal. "You're great and all, but this is my grandma we're talking about. She's going to win. That's how it goes."

I pressed my lips together, but couldn't hide my smile. "The yellow," I murmured. Sure enough, when I glanced over to the kitchen island, the saucer in front of her yellow bowl had quite a lot of pennies in it. So much for a fair and impartial contest.

"Got it." He nodded, and I tried to not pay attention to the smooth circles his hands made on my back. He was undoubtedly playing up this whole couple thing in front of his family, but that was the point, wasn't it?

The entire dinner was Tex-Mex themed—which had to be in honor of the guac-off, since we were hundreds of miles from both Tex and Mex—with a massive tray of enchiladas in the middle of a large oak table. As dinner wound to a close I nibbled on a tortilla chip and sipped at my second margarita, imagining the many Thanksgiving dinners that had taken place around this table. This was a large, loving family, something I didn't have much experience with, and I could see why they all meant so much to Mitch.

But it was still a lot to take in, and as evening became night, I grew restless. It had been a long day. Beside me I could tell Mitch felt the same. After a few minutes he nudged me. "You ready to head back?"

I nodded, a little too emphatically. I liked these people, but it was exhausting being around them all. And tomorrow was going to be another long day.

It wasn't until we were back in his truck and almost out of the neighborhood that something occurred to me, and I wasn't sure if I wanted to bring it up. Mitch had said that not everyone was staying with the grandparents, and the rest were at the hotel with us. But we were the only ones leaving the house that night. I turned in my seat, looking through the back window at the darkened street behind us.

"Everything okay?" Mitch glanced over at me.

"Yeah." I dropped down to face forward again, thinking hard. Maybe the others were just staying a little longer. Maybe us leaving hadn't broken up the night for everyone else. But I couldn't shake the feeling that we were the only ones in the family staying at the hotel. I wasn't sure what that meant. And until I did, I wasn't going to bring it up with Mitch.

But I forgot all about that potentially awkward conversation when we got back to the hotel and a more awkward, more pressing situation presented itself.

Bedtime.

"So." Mitch cleared his throat and looked around the room, as though surprised that the rose petals hadn't cleared themselves away and the giant bed hadn't split itself in two while we were at dinner. "I can sleep on . . ."

"No, you can't." I didn't let him finish the sentence, because there was no way he could that would make any sense. There wasn't a single piece of furniture that could possibly support him with any kind of comfort. I took out my earrings, laying them on the bureau beside my purse as I surveyed the options. "I could take the . . . chair." But my voice betrayed the uncertainty I felt about that option, and Mitch snorted.

"Which one? The desk chair? Or that one by the window?" He had a point. The mesh-back chair by the desk might be ergonomic for working at a laptop, but not much else. And the two chairs by the window could be pushed together, maybe. But they looked hard and unyielding—obviously purchased for aesthetics as opposed to comfort.

I sighed, which he obviously took for assent. "Look." He rolled his head around the back of his neck. "We're both adults here, I think we can handle this. Right?" His slightly uncertain look belied the statement, but I knew what he meant. This bed was massive. If we each stuck to our sides, the chance of even running into each other between those sheets was minimal. Hopefully.

"Right," I said. I dug my pajamas out from the top bureau

drawer, where I'd stashed them earlier this evening. I'd un-packed and hung up the clothes I was planning to wear this weekend, putting everything else in the bureau. Mitch's clothes remained in his leather duffel in the corner of the room. "I get the bathroom first."

"Be my guest." He brushed his arm in an arc across the bed, dislodging some of the rose petals, before picking up the remote and pointing it at the television.

Through the closed bathroom door I could hear the sounds of a late-night show while I washed my face and brushed my teeth. While I hadn't anticipated sharing a room with Mitch this weekend, I was thankful I'd had the presence of mind to pack real pajamas instead of relying on my standby: an old tank top and whatever underwear I'd worn that day. No reason to scandalize the boy. Besides, he didn't need to see my scarred-up right leg. No one did. The doctor had done a great job, sure. But there was only so much a person could do with an injury like that. I preferred to keep it covered up and out of sight.

I took one last look in the mirror before turning off the light and leaving the bathroom. I wasn't one for wearing a ton of makeup, but the complete absence of it, with serum and night cream massaged into my skin, definitely added years to my face. My gaze fell on my makeup bag, nestled on the counter between the sink and Mitch's Dopp kit. It looked very domestic, yet unfamiliar. Comforting, yet slightly terrifying.

I blew out a long breath and turned out the light, forcing the discomfort from my mind as I strode back into the bedroom. "All yours," I said cheerfully. With any luck I could be under the covers and asleep by the time Mitch came to bed.

Came to bed. Jesus. How on earth was I going to sleep a wink tonight?

I must have slept, but even in sleep I remained tense, because I woke up the next morning practically clinging to the edge of the bed. I carefully rolled on my back, doing my best to move as little as possible, and turned my head to the right. Mitch lay on his stomach, head turned to the side in my direction, sound asleep. I'd still been awake, trying to concentrate on the book on my e-reader, when he'd come to bed, dressed in a T-shirt and basketball shorts. I had a feeling the outfit was a concession to me, as I'd caught him tugging at the shirt a couple of times. He'd been a perfect gentleman, watching television while I read for about a half hour in some kind of farce of domesticity before mutually agreeing to turn out the light. By the looks of things, he'd remained firmly on his side of the bed, and he hadn't even hogged the covers.

He looked so peaceful now, so young, when he was relaxed in sleep, all residual tension drained away. His hair was mussed; a lock fell over his forehead and my fingers itched to brush it back.

I made a fist, punishing those fingers, and then I slipped out of bed and padded as quietly as I could to the bathroom, snicking the door closed behind me. The deep breath I took then felt like the first hit of oxygen I'd had in ages. One night down, one to go. This wasn't so bad.

I'd made a tactical error though, which I hadn't realized till I was already in the shower: I'd been so intent on escaping our bed that I hadn't brought clothes with me into the bathroom. I clearly wasn't used to sharing a hotel room with someone I was pretending to date. After my shower I scrunched my hair and slipped back into my pajamas. I could grab my clothes and get back into the bathroom quickly.

Except when I opened the drawer an alarm blared, and for a

hazy, confused second I looked down at the bureau in confusion, wondering when a booby trap had been set. Then I realized the sound came from the nightstand: Mitch's phone, but Mitch wasn't moving. A split second later he did, rolling over in bed like a wave made of muscle and blankets. He groped for the phone, silencing it, then lay back against the pillows, taking the deep breath of someone waking up to face a new day. I turned quickly back to the bureau, fishing out the jeans and top I'd planned to wear today.

Blankets rustled behind me. "You done in the shower?" His voice was gravelly, barely awake, and I didn't like what that did to my lizard brain.

I stared hard at the clothes in my hand and nodded. "Yep. All yours." I didn't watch him get out of bed. I didn't move a muscle until the bathroom door closed behind him, followed almost immediately by the shower turning on. I blew out a breath and got dressed quickly. After folding my pajamas and leaving them on one of the uncomfortable chairs by the window, I ran my fingers through my still-damp hair and turned back in the direction of the bathroom. On the other side of that closed door was my hair dryer. My styling products. My makeup bag. In my haste to put distance between me and a sleep-rumpled Mitch, I forgot that I hadn't been done in there after all.

"Shit."

Makeup could wait. But my hair . . . oh no. I could feel it frizzing as it air-dried with no product in it. I was supposed to be making a good impression on Mitch's family, and instead I was going to look like a wild-haired forest witch all day. I wasn't upholding my end of the bargain at all.

The bathroom door opened behind me, and I turned eagerly toward it, hoping I could salvage my hair before it was too late.

Mitch emerged, a cloud of steam behind him, dressed casually in jeans and a light blue-gray Henley. Oh thank God, I'd gotten that part of things right.

"Hey," he said as if it was the first time he'd seen me this morning. "You look cute."

I raised my eyebrows. I was standing here with no makeup on and my hair was a certified disaster. "Funny."

"No, I mean it. Your hair's all . . ." He made a twirling gesture with his hand. "You don't usually wear it like that."

I ran a hand over it, trying not to wince too hard. "I need to fix it. Give me a minute." I walked past him to the warm, humid bathroom.

"Nothing to fix," he said, leaning on the doorjamb, eclipsing the room behind him. "I just said it's cute."

I shook my head. "I don't let it do this." I reached for some product, scrunching it in.

"Your sister wears her hair like that all the time."

"Well, my sister's the cute one." My voice was a little snappier than I'd intended, but this line of talk made me cranky, and I hadn't had any coffee yet. I wasn't wrong. Emily was younger, she was cuter, a couple inches shorter. She was made of soft curves and smiles. I was older. Sharper. I hadn't been cute in at least a decade. I looked better when my hair was tamed and calm and straight.

But this morning, I wiped the condensation from the mirror so I could put some makeup on, and looked at my hair critically. It didn't look all that bad. I wouldn't go so far as to call it cute, but . . . I could probably get away without straightening it. So once I finished putting my face on, I dug through my makeup bag for a hair tie and pulled my hair back, securing it in a low ponytail. A few rogue curls escaped to frame my face, and . . . huh. I did look kind of cute.

"You ready?" I said as I came back out of the bathroom. Mitch was sitting on the edge of the unmade bed, scrolling through his phone. I thought about those women in his calendar . . . who had he canceled on this weekend to spend it here?

But he clicked his phone off and stood, stowing it in his pocket. "Yep," he said easily. "I don't know about you, but I'm dying for some coffee. Think they do a breakfast downstairs?"

"Probably. I thought you'd want to get a move on. Get to your grandparents' house."

"Oh, sure. But we could grab breakfast first. See who else is staying here."

A chill swept through me, and I shrugged it off. I was still pretty sure he was the only Malone in this hotel, but I was willing to be wrong. "Sure," I said, shooting for casual and mostly succeeding. "But don't expect me to remember any names."

There were no Malones in the hotel dining room, and after an initial frown Mitch brushed it off in favor of the breakfast buffet. I couldn't blame him there; the omelet station alone made me want to spend the entire weekend in that dining room. But eventually we got to-go cups of coffee and headed back toward his grandparents' house.

"We probably got a late start," he said, taking a sip of coffee before nestling it in the cup holder. "Missed everyone else at breakfast."

I made a soft noise of dubious agreement but otherwise stayed quiet, sipping my coffee until we arrived. Same as the night before, we seemed to be the last arriving, and once inside I noticed the detritus of a family breakfast eaten around that large table: a couple abandoned coffee cups, a single plate that hadn't been cleared. We weren't the last ones arriving. We were the only ones arriving. My worst fear had been realized—Mitch and I had been the only ones shunted off to a hotel.

Mitch's eyes narrowed, and I placed a hand at the small of his back for reassurance. He looked down at me and I watched as he forced the gloom off his face in favor of a smile. *There you go.* I smiled up at him, and with a pat on his arm I gathered up the remaining dishes and brought them into the kitchen, where Mitch's cousin Lulu was up to her elbows in suds.

"Oh, thank you so much! You can dump 'em in here." She jerked her chin down into the sink in front of her, stepping back so I could deposit the dishes. "Dishwasher's already full, so I'm finishing up what didn't fit. Have y'all been here long?"

"No. We . . . uh, we had breakfast at the hotel first." I leaned against the counter and took a quick glance around. We were alone here in the kitchen, and through the window I could see the rest of the family had ventured out into the massive backyard. "So, um . . . I have to ask, Lulu. Are we the only ones at the hotel? Mitch seemed to think that there were more folks staying out there, but we haven't seen anyone."

"Oh. Yeah." She rinsed a plate and stuck it in the dish drainer. I picked up a towel and a clean coffee cup and started drying. "The last time we did a family gathering here was about five years ago. My brothers used to share a room back then, but since they both got married . . . obviously they each needed a room now. We figured Mitch wouldn't mind." Concern clouded her face. "He doesn't, does he?"

"No," I said carefully. "I don't think so. He just didn't know." I stacked the coffee cups as I dried them since I didn't know where anything went. Cups done, I started on the plates.

"It was nothing personal. Besides . . ." Lulu scrubbed at a casserole dish. "He mentioned you're a single mom. I thought you might like a little weekend getaway, you know?" She glanced over at me with a sly smile, and I remembered the rose petals on the bed. There was nothing nefarious about this. She genuinely thought she was giving us a romantic weekend away.

"You're not wrong," I said. That was a lie, of course. Everything about it was wrong. But it didn't bother me nearly as much this morning as it had the day before. I went back to the more important topic. "He told you about me, huh?"

"Oh, yeah!" She pulled the plug in the sink, sending the sudsy water down the drain, and rinsed her hands off before putting away the dishes I'd dried. "I mean, you probably don't need me telling you this, but he really seems into you."

I pressed my lips together to keep from laughing. He was doing a great job of selling this whole thing, so I needed to do the same. I handed her the last of the coffee cups and hung up the towel while she wiped down the counters. Done.

"Come on," she said. "I think the football's about to start."

"The what?" But I followed her out the side door that led off the kitchen to a back deck about twice the size of mine. Roughly half of the adults sat in small groups on the deck, while out in the yard a gaggle of children of all ages and a handful of adults had started to organize into teams. Mitch was out there, and as I watched he picked up one of the smaller children and lifted him over his head, as though the child were a football he was about to throw down the field. The child in the air burst into screaming giggles, but Mitch's grip was solid, and when he put the child down, three more insisted they go next.

"He's popular," I murmured to myself. Lulu had gone over to the other side of the deck, where Mitch's grandfather, with the help of a couple older men—one of whom I was pretty sure was Mitch's father, but I wouldn't swear to it in court—had their heads together over a massive smoker. They were obviously still getting it going: smoke trickled out of the large cylindrical drum, but I couldn't smell any barbecue yet. Which I was thankful for, since I was still full from breakfast.

"It takes them a while," said a voice at my side, and I turned around quickly. Mitch's mother: I remembered her from last night. She'd said hello to me, but otherwise had refrained from any real small talk. I'd decided she didn't like me and had determined to steer clear the rest of the weekend. But now she followed my gaze to the men around the smoker, and when she turned back to me her smile was conspiratorial. "It's new. Mitch's grandfather got that thing for Christmas. I hope you like barbecue, because it's about to be coming out our ears."

"I love barbecue, so that's good news for me." I matched my smile to hers, and she gave me a slow perusal up and down, her smile still in place.

"But yes," she said, turning back toward the yard. "Mitch is very popular with his little cousins. You know he's an only child, right? So no nieces or nephews, but most of his cousins are married with children of their own. He's everyone's honorary uncle."

I let myself chuckle as Mitch ran painfully slowly across the yard, while the four children ran screaming after him. "He really is great with kids." Emily had told me many, many stories of Mitch with the kids at the Ren Faire, and it was nice to see this side of him while we were here with his family.

"He is. He's going to be a wonderful father someday."

"I'm sure he is." But the nape of my neck prickled. This conversation was going somewhere, and I wasn't sure I liked the direction of it.

Sure enough, when I turned back to Mrs. Malone her smile had turned to polite steel. "You have a daughter, right?"

"Yes," I said. "Caitlin's almost eighteen. About to graduate from high school."

"Mmm-hmm." She nodded absently, looking back into the yard. "Empty nester, then?"

A slice of cold slid down my back. There it was. She wasn't even being subtle. Was it a dig at my age? Or the fact that my baby-making days were behind me? Contrasted with Mitch, who still had all the time in the world to become a dad.

The thought of Mitch being a father, holding his own child . . . it did something to my chest. I had Caitlin; I was done with that part of my life. But Mitch hadn't experienced that yet. And maybe he'd want to.

He'd get his chance, I reminded myself. Not with me, of course, which was fine. This was all a charade, and we weren't planning any kind of future past the end of this weekend. It was easy to forget, here in the midst of all this family togetherness, that I didn't really belong here. Mrs. Malone had nothing to worry about; her hypothetical grandchildren remained a possibility.

Nine

I *still hadn't answered* Mrs. Malone, and to be honest I wasn't sure how to. Torn between "that's none of your fucking business" and being that mature fake girlfriend—a little too mature if you asked Mrs. Malone—that Mitch needed me to be. "It hasn't been easy," I finally said. "Raising my daughter on my own. So yes, I'm looking forward to a little me time, you know?" My smile felt as weak as my attempt at a joke.

Before she could respond Lulu was back, two longneck bottles in her hand. "Hey, Aunt Patricia. Can I steal April back? The game's about to start, and I need to teach her how to heckle the family properly."

"Of course." Mrs. Malone—I was never going to call her Patricia—laid a hand on my shoulder. "It was nice to talk to you, dear."

Her nails felt like talons through my blouse, and I had to fight to not wince. I wasn't going to let her win. "Absolutely."

"Come on." Lulu led me to an empty pair of Adirondack

chairs. "Sorry about that. I didn't realize Aunt Patricia was going to swoop in on you that fast. I told Mitch I'd keep an eye on her."

I sank into a chair, still feeling a little shaken. "She really doesn't like me."

"She doesn't like anyone. I don't think she's ever liked any of the girls Mitch has dated. Always something wrong with all of them. Don't hold it against him, okay?" She offered me one of the bottles. "Here you go. It's noon somewhere, right?"

"Damn straight." We clinked the necks of our bottles together and I settled back in the chair with my drink. I looked down, expecting a beer, but was pleasantly surprised to find a craft cider. I took a grateful swig. "Oh, that's good."

"Isn't it? He said you liked cider, so I knew I had to bring some. I'd been saving this stuff for a special occasion, and I couldn't think of a better one."

"He said that?" I looked at the bottle of cider with fresh eyes. The residual coldness from talking to Mrs. Malone melted; it was no match for the thought of Mitch telling his favorite cousin about me.

Out in the backyard, the smaller children were finally starting to tire out from chasing around the adults. I pointed out there with my bottle. "Any of those yours?" I meant the kids but I wasn't specific. Was her husband/wife/significant other out there with the gaggle of adults?

But Lulu shook her head. "None of 'em. Who has time? No, I'm here solo." She didn't elaborate about her personal life, and I didn't ask. It wasn't even remotely my place to pry. We sipped at our ciders and watched the adults form themselves into teams for a touch football game. It was all so . . . upper-middle-class white American. It also seemed incongruous with the ancient house we sat outside. I pictured this kind of thing happening at one of the other houses in the neighborhood—the ones that looked like they belonged in a Ralph Lauren catalog. Which reminded me . . .

"You said something last night about your grandmother being stubborn?" Lulu raised her eyebrows in response, and I continued. "I was asking about the house. This neighborhood?"

"Oh. Yeah." She tipped her head back, finishing her cider. "This neighborhood was mostly farmland back in the day. Our great-grandparents built this house, and Grandpa was born here. Little by little, the land around them was sold off, and then about twenty years ago? Thirty? They started putting this neighborhood in. Someone came knocking for Grandma and Grandpa to sell. I think if it had been Grandpa by himself he would have caved, but Grandma loves this house."

"As well she should." I craned my head to look at the house, where a small patch of paint was starting to peel on the siding. The gray was actually light green up close, giving way to a yellowish color underneath. "It's a great house. Mitch said something about secret passages?"

Lulu snorted and put her bottle on the deck beside her. "My big brother told him that when they were kids. Sent the poor guy on a wild-goose chase when he was seven. Mostly to get Mitch out of his hair. He was . . . an energetic child."

I considered that. "He's an energetic adult." It wasn't until the words were out of my mouth that I realized how they'd sound coming from a girlfriend. My face heated and I swigged the rest of my cider to cool off.

"Yeah. Not touching that." She smirked at me, and the heat in my cheeks became flames. "Anyway. They didn't sell, so now there's a whole neighborhood of McMansions and this little house smack-dab in the middle."

"Little house," I echoed. "Uh-huh." But I liked that. I liked people standing up for what was theirs. I liked that Mitch was cut from that kind of cloth. It made sense.

Morning bled into afternoon. Lulu foisted a second cider on me as the day went on, and the air began to smell like smoked meat, making my mouth water. There was no way to tell what the score was out in the backyard, as the rules they used didn't seem to correlate to anything that any football league would recognize. One attempted touchdown devolved into good-natured shouting and arguing, ending with a teenager jumping on Mitch's back in a poor attempt to take him to the ground. The attempt ended in a piggyback ride that Mitch somehow made look like a victory lap. Lulu caught my eye as we cheered for . . . someone, and we grinned at each other. Maybe it was the cider, but I liked her. I liked his family. I liked this sense of belonging. In the back of my mind I knew that this sense was only going to last the weekend. But I pushed all of those thoughts aside and concentrated on the here and now, something I didn't do very often.

It was nice.

Those warm feelings were still coursing through me when Mitch came up the steps from the backyard. He made a beeline for me, slipping an arm around my waist and pulling me close. Before I could even process it, his mouth brushed over mine as though this was something we did every day. As though this wasn't the first time he'd kissed me.

Which it absolutely was.

As his lips left mine I froze, and so did he. We were both so caught up in this fantasy of being a couple in front of his family that it took our brains a few moments to catch up to what our bodies were instinctively doing. His eyes searched mine, knowing he'd overstepped. Certain I was going to push him away, bring this whole charade tumbling down around our ears.

But that was the last thing I wanted to do. Was it the heat of the day, the slight cider buzz, or the sense of belonging I'd felt around his family? One of those things had made his kiss feel like the most natural thing in the world. One of those things made me curl my hand around the back of his head, pulling him back down for a quick second kiss, punctuating the first one. Something flickered in his eyes—surprise?—but he grinned down at me and tugged me even closer. He was warm, a little sweaty from all the running around in the backyard. But I didn't pull away. Because I was doing my job. Being his girlfriend. Making him look good in front of his family.

Yep. That's all I was doing.

The picnic table on the deck had been filled with snacks, which we'd partaken of all afternoon—veggies and dip, chips, some leftover guacamole—so I had no idea how I was expected to eat dinner. But when the sun started waning in the sky, the main event began. The smoker had eventually yielded racks of ribs and a massive brisket, and the platter of barbecue that resulted made my stomach growl and my mouth water as though I hadn't eaten for a week.

A buffet line had been set up in the kitchen—where had all this food come from?—and I loaded my plate with shredded beef, ribs, and greens before sitting down at the massive dining room table. I slid my water glass to the place next to me, saving it for Mitch, who was farther back in the line. Except for those brief kisses on the back deck we'd hardly spoken all day, which felt a little weird, but as long as he was happy I was doing my job, right?

Once we were all seated, Mitch looked at my plate with a frown. "Wait a sec. You didn't get any of the mac and cheese?"

I shook my head as I forked up some greens. "I've been pigging out all day. I should probably show some restraint."

He made a pfft sound of dismissal. "Restraint doesn't apply when it comes to Grandma's cooking. Here." He tipped his plate, scraping off about half of his macaroni and cheese onto my plate. "You need to try this. Trust me."

I trusted him and took a bite. "Holy shit." I chewed slowly as cheesy goodness flooded my mouth. I'd found nirvana in Grandma Malone's macaroni and cheese, and I wanted to live there for the rest of my life.

Mitch nodded in satisfaction. "Told ya." He took a bite and passed me the squeeze bottle of barbecue sauce. "Here. You need this too. Grandpa is a master at barbecue sauce."

I didn't even question it this time, I just slathered sauce on the brisket before taking a bite. The moan that escaped me was indecent. I was a fan of Virginia barbecue—tomatoey, a little garlicky, a little vinegary. But Grandpa Malone knew his shit, and took it to a whole other level. "Do you cook like this?" I asked. "Because you've been holding out on me."

He laughed and shook his head. "You know my specialty is ordering pizza."

"Still can't cook, huh, Mitch?" One of Mitch's cousins laughed from across the table. I couldn't remember his name, but he was one of the ones playing touch football in the backyard.

"Nope," Mitch said cheerfully, his attention still on his plate. "But I still do okay." He draped an arm around my shoulders. "You should try April's shepherd's pie sometime. It's amazing." His hand on my shoulder felt a little heavy, and his grip was tighter than it needed to be. I looked up at him, and when he met my eyes, his smile was tight before he let go. I didn't like that.

"I have to say, April, I'm glad to see you here." His cousin kept talking. "We were starting to worry that Mitch might not meet anyone worthwhile. It's not like he's that much of a catch, you know?"

"Bryce, stop." The woman next to him—Cousin Douchebag's wife maybe?—batted him on the arm, but her giggle was insipid, belying any kind of rebuke she was making.

I blinked. "What do you mean?"

Cousin Douche looked abashed for a moment. "Oh, I'm not belittling your taste or anything. But you know . . ." He shrugged. "It's not like he's applied himself, ever. I told him he should go for an advanced degree, but . . ."

"But I didn't want to," Mitch said. He didn't sound angry. His voice was almost aggressively cheerful. This was an old argument, and he didn't want to be having it again, so he was going to grin his way out of it.

"So what do you do?" I put down my fork and leaned forward, elaborately interested in what Bryce was about to say. I wouldn't normally be so bold in front of people I'd just met, but that sense of belonging had fooled me. That, and I was pretty pissed off.

"Oh, I'm a hedge fund manager. I got my MBA from Cornell, and I've spent the past ten years building a massive portfolio of clients." He pointed with his fork down the table. "Craig is a child psychologist, and Lulu is about to make partner at her law firm."

"Oh." I looked down the length of the table. Craig had been one of the quarterbacks in the touch football game, and despite the rules Mitch had tackled him to the ground more than once. And if Lulu was working to make partner then her "who has time" comment about relationships suddenly made more sense. "Good for them."

Mitch snorted. "Yeah, good for them. I still say I came out ahead. Do they get to play dodgeball at work? I don't think so." He took a swig of beer and set the bottle down a little too hard on the table. "I win."

"I'm just saying, you could have gone into sports medicine, like we talked about. You—"

"Like you talked about," Mitch interrupted firmly. "You talked about it, I told you it's not my thing. I'm good."

"Good," Bryce repeated. "Come on, dude, you're a gym *teacher*." Those last two words came out with a derision that made me clench my teeth.

"Now, wait a second." I threw down my napkin. "What's wrong with being a gym teacher?" Oh, no. What the hell was I doing? This wasn't like me at all. But my blood had hit the boiling point, and it was either launch myself across the table at the guy or talk back. Talking back seemed like the lesser of two confrontations.

Mitch covered my hand—and half of my wrist—with his. "April, it's okay."

If he'd sounded convincing, I would have backed off. I really would have. But he didn't. He sounded defeated. Mitch Malone, the most confident person I'd ever met, a guy who'd happily spend an evening failing to pick up a woman at Jackson's, shrugging good-naturedly without a wound to his ego, was now reduced to someone with resignation in his eyes. Brought low by his own family.

Nope. Not on my watch. "Do you know what being a gym teacher involves? Do you have any clue what your cousin does all day?" My hand shook under Mitch's, and my voice shook even more, but I didn't back down. "You think all he does is run around in shorts and a whistle, playing dodgeball with a bunch of kids?" It was a good visual, but I didn't let myself focus on that right now.

"Pretty much." But Cousin Douche's chuckle was thin; he obviously wasn't used to being challenged. He looked around the table for backup, but none was coming. A few family members, Mitch's mom included, had their attention trained on me, their expressions blank, almost stunned. Lulu met my eyes, but then turned her attention to her plate. Was I the first person to ever stick up for Mitch? What the hell?

"Then you don't know him at all," I said. "He coaches football in the fall and baseball in the spring. Do you know how much organization that takes?" Personally, I had no idea, but it seemed like a lot of work. And Mitch never complained about it. "He took the baseball team to State last year, you know, and—"

"This year too," Mitch said in a low murmur beside me.

"—this year too," I said without missing a beat.

"Yeah, but our football team sucks." Mitch shrugged when I turned incredulous eyes on him. "I'm sorry, but I don't have a single kid who can throw. It's hopeless."

"Not the point," I said. We were getting off topic. "And I haven't even brought up all the stuff he does with the Renaissance Faire."

"The what?" Grandma said from the other end of the table, a puzzled expression on her face.

"The Renaissance Faire," I repeated, a little louder and clearer, but a beat later I realized she hadn't had any trouble hearing me. She just didn't know what I was talking about. I turned back to Mitch. "They don't know about the Ren Faire?"

"Well, Mom and Dad do." He gestured toward them, and they nodded.

"Of course we do," Mrs. Malone snapped. "I volunteered with them for two summers myself."

"You did?" I tried to imagine her in medieval garb and failed miserably.

"Mom sold tickets," Mitch supplied.

"Ah." So she wore the red volunteer T-shirt, not a tavern wench outfit. That made a lot more sense. "Well, do they know what all you do for it?"

"Probably," he said, while his mother answered over him.

"We know he's still involved with it, dressing up and all that, is that what you're getting at?" She pursed her lips into a frown. "We live in Willow Creek too, of course we know what our son is up to."

"Dressing up . . . You don't . . ." I turned in my chair to Mitch. "They don't know . . ." His eyes were wide as he met mine, and he shrugged. If he'd told me to hush at any moment I probably would have, but otherwise I was too far into my rant now.

I turned back to his family, ready to deliver a TED talk on Mitch's kilted assets. "Y'all don't know what he does. Okay. He's been involved in the school's major annual fundraiser every year since it started."

"Second year," he corrected in a mutter beside me, but was I listening? I was not.

"He practically runs the thing himself now." I crossed my fingers under the table. *Sorry, Simon.* "They do this huge chess match fight thing with . . ." I started flagging here, because all I had to go on when it came to the Faire was my daughter's incomplete reports from her weekly rehearsals, that video on Mitch's phone I'd watched too many times, and that one time I'd gone to the Faire with my sister. But the hell if I was going to admit any of that right now. "Well, there's swords and stuff. He wears

a kilt, and I mean . . . I don't have to tell you what he looks like."
I waved my hand at him in illustration. "He's practically the
main draw all by himself. And he does all of this as a volunteer.
Out of the goodness of his heart. You volunteer a lot for your
community, Bryce?"

Lulu laughed then, a thin bubble of amusement, while across
the table from me the hedge fund douche turned bright red. I
looked down the table at Lulu and she shot me a grin and a
subtle thumbs-up. She still liked me, at least. But as my tirade
came to an end an awkward silence fell over the table until
Mitch cleared his throat.

"Well, I need more mac and cheese." He stood up with his
plate and took mine too. "And so do you. You've earned it, babe."

Mitch was silent the entire drive back to the hotel. I sat in the
passenger seat, a leftover container of macaroni and cheese that
Grandma Malone had pushed into my hands gently warming my
thighs. I still felt shaky as the adrenaline of ripping an entire
table of Malones a new asshole drained away. Tears prickled in
my eyes; some girlfriend I was. I'd completely fucked this up for
him. It wasn't about our agreement anymore. It didn't matter
what I'd been pretending to be. I'd been out of line, and I absolutely deserved the silent treatment he was giving me now.

I busied myself with my phone, sending Emily a text. **Everything okay there?** I couldn't believe it had taken me until now to
check on my daughter, but it had been a busy evening, yelling at
Mitch's family and all.

All good, came the reply as we pulled into the hotel parking
lot. **We went to the mall today and bought her a dress for graduation.
She's really excited about it, so ask to see it when you get home,
okay? That might help.**

God bless my sister. Will do, thanks.

Also, we were talking about her working at the bookstore this summer. You ok with that?

I raised my eyebrows as I texted back. **Of course! Does she want to?** We'd discussed Caitlin getting a summer job, to save up for the fall when she was in school. But volunteering for the Ren Faire was important to her, and I wasn't about to ask her to give that up.

Definitely! She's excited about it.

Then I'm on board too. That's perfect. Sure, the bookstore wouldn't pay a lot, but it was a good solution. More time with her aunt, some money for college . . . there was no bad here.

How's it going there? Everything okay?

All good. My fingers were good at lying. **See you tomorrow. Thanks again!** I clicked my phone off and stowed it in my bag. The next twenty-four hours were going to be brutal, as we were stuck together until he dropped me off at home tomorrow afternoon. But I had to woman up and take it. I'd been through worse, right? I'd divorced the love of my life, my daughter's father, when I was in my early twenties, and that'd almost killed me. I could handle this one night, as awful as it was going to be.

Inside the hotel room, Mitch tossed his keys onto the bureau and strode across the room to the window, staring out into the night with his hands on his hips. I blew out a long breath and slid the leftover container into the room's mini-fridge. I wished he would say something. Anything. Start yelling at me so we could get this over with.

As the silence stretched out, I couldn't take it anymore. "I'm sorry." My voice shook, and I hated how small I sounded. But I pushed on. "I'm really sorry. I shouldn't have—"

"You didn't need to do that." The sound of my voice seemed

to have woken him up, as he spoke over me. His voice was low, even. Giving nothing away. That was worse than yelling.

I nodded, though his back was still to me and he couldn't see. "I know," I said. The tears returned and I blinked hard against them. "I don't know what I was thinking. I'm so sorry." I probably shouldn't have apologized so much, but I didn't know what else to say. "I'll skip brunch tomorrow, obviously. You can swing back here and pick me up on the way out of—"

"Wait, what?" He turned around, an incredulous look on his face. "Why the hell would you skip brunch?" He peered at my face and frowned. "Hey. Are you crying?"

"No," I lied, but he was across the room in an instant, taking my face in his hands and dashing away my tears with his thumbs.

"Shhhh," he said. "No, no, stop. Stop. There's no reason for you to be upset. This is all my fault."

"How?" I tried to focus on his words when all I wanted to do was lean into his touch. How was being here with him like this so comfortable? Until now, our friendship was mostly based on mutual antagonism and snark. It didn't stretch to casual kisses in the backyard and wiping away my tears. "I'm the one that screwed up. It was my job to make you look good this weekend, not yell at your grandma."

"Eh." He waved a hand. "She's tough, she can take it. Besides, you weren't yelling at her so much as Bryce. And he deserved it; he was being a douche." I gave a watery laugh—at least I'd gotten that part right. "No, I mean I should have filled you in better. But I thought . . ." He let go of me and strode back to the window with a deep sigh. "I thought they'd take me seriously this time."

"This time . . . ?" The pieces all fell into place with a click. This hadn't been about him being single at all. "You mean they always treat you like this?"

"Yeah." He didn't look at me; instead he leaned his hands on the window and looked out into the night. "I guess it shouldn't be a big deal, huh? Getting that shit from them."

"Of course it's a big deal," I insisted. "He shouldn't . . . they shouldn't . . ."

"Probably not," he sighed. "But I'm pretty used to it. I'm nobody special in this family."

"Nobody *special*?" That was the absolute last thing I'd ever expected Mitch to say about himself.

"Sure. I mean, look. I'm not the oldest grandchild. I'm not the baby. I'm not the first grandson, or the last. I'm somewhere in the middle, one of a million grandkids running around, who cares. And then we all grew up, and everyone else started getting all these fancy degrees and doing all these important things, and when I didn't they . . ."

"Stopped respecting you completely?" The outrage I'd felt at dinner had become a banked fire, and now it roared to life all over again as I blinked away the rest of my tears. "That's bullshit and you know it."

"Yeah. It is." He turned around then, leaning against the wall, his arms crossed. "Remember when I asked you to come with me? I thought if you were here, and they could see that I'd managed to snag this . . . I mean, you're smart, April. And you're gorgeous, and you have your shit together . . ."

I snorted at that last bit, even though my brain skidded at that "gorgeous" comment. "I really don't."

But he wasn't done. "I thought that maybe they'd take me seriously for once. Stop acting like I don't matter." His gaze had traveled down to his shoes, and he kicked his heel into the floor.

"Fuck them," I said fiercely. I joined him at the window, grasping his arm. "You matter," I said. "You know that, right?"

"Yeah." But his smile looked forced. "I should have filled you in on my cousin the asshole. But I . . ." He broke eye contact and his gaze traveled up to the ceiling. "What was I supposed to say, 'By the way, I'm the family meatball and they all think I'm a loser'?" The laugh he gave was hollow, and it hurt to hear. This wasn't the Mitch I knew. For all that he said his self-esteem was fine, it was still something that could be broken. And I wasn't going to let that happen.

"You're not a meatball." I shook his arm to get his attention, making him look at me again. But when he did, I wasn't prepared. His eyes, so freaking blue. I'd seen his eyes countless times since we'd started hanging out, but right now, right here, they were mesmerizing. I wanted to crawl inside of them. I wanted to drown in that ocean of blue.

"Yeah," he said again. He blew out a long breath and scrubbed a hand through his hair, shaking off the rest of those bad feelings. "Seriously, I see these people once, maybe twice a year. I don't lose a lot of sleep worrying if they like me." Now his smile was more genuine; the Mitch I knew was coming back to the surface. "I like me, and that's what matters, right?"

I had to smile at that. Mitch's favorite person had always been Mitch, but that self-confidence was armor, something he pasted over some deep hurt. Deeper than I'd realized. Maybe even deeper than he'd realized. "I like you too." My voice was low, throaty.

"I know." He stepped closer to me, crowding me a little, but in the best possible way. "And thanks. No one's ever stuck up for me before. I usually have to stand up for myself."

"Well, get used to it. I stand up for the people I—" I barely managed to close my mouth before I finished that dangerous sentence. This wasn't a conversation I was used to having. I kept to myself. I was all I needed. Hell, it was only three years ago that my own sister and I had started building a relationship. And now I was here in a strange town, in a strange hotel room with . . . let's face it, the most attractive man I could possibly be stuck in a strange hotel room with, about to tell him how I really felt about him. I was way, way out of my depth here.

"I know. Hey . . ." His voice was low, and there was a rasp to it that I'd never heard before. He moved his arm, letting my hand slide down his forearm, over his wrist, until he caught my hand in his. "I know."

He looked at our joined hands, then back up at me. The air between us had become charged, and I knew what was about to happen. I could stop it. I should stop it. I should drop his hand, step back, and make a snarky joke. I shouldn't want this.

But I did. So when his other hand came up to cup my cheek I moved even closer, into his space this time. He caught his breath when I did. "You're not skipping brunch tomorrow." The rasp in his voice became gravel, and it sent a prickle of heat down my spine.

"Are you sure?" I wasn't even paying attention to what I was saying. All my senses were caught up in Mitch, in how close he was. How solid. How warm.

He nodded and leaned into me, his eyebrows rising in a silent question. I nodded back, answering, and we weren't talking about brunch anymore. We weren't talking at all. My name was a whisper of breath a moment before his mouth closed over mine. Tentative, gentle. Warm. Confident, but not aggressive. He was testing me. Letting me make the decision. I knew that even now, if I changed my mind, said no, he would have backed off without complaint.

But I had no intention of saying no. Time didn't exist here in this hotel room. Real life wouldn't be back until tomorrow afternoon. For now, I didn't have to be a mom. I didn't have to be anyone, or anywhere but in this man's arms.

I rose onto my toes and plunged my fingers into his hair, deepening our kiss. My decision was made.

Ten

I thought I was used to Mitch. We'd spent time together since he and Emily had become friends. He was a tactile guy, and I'd become accustomed to his touch: his arm thrown around me at Jackson's when he chased off that guy in the gray suit. That brief press of his fingertips at the small of my back when we were in a crowd.

I thought I was ready for Mitch. He'd kissed me before. Hell, he'd kissed me that *day*, in the backyard after the touch football game. He was a good kisser, that was for sure. So when I reached for him, blatantly asking for more, I thought I knew what I was getting into.

I was wrong. He'd been holding back. And I was about to find out how much.

He made a startled sound in his throat as I pressed closer, harder, nipping at his top lip with my teeth. But he recovered fast: he cupped my head in one large hand, steering the kiss, drinking me in. His other arm slid around my back, pulling me into his body. He was so tall, so broad, so present, that it didn't take long to feel completely consumed by him. Dominated.

My whole world had spiraled down to nothingness, a place that only contained him and me and this room. He spun us, pressing me against the wall next to the window. His growl of frustration rumbled against my chest, a shiver breaking across my skin. Before I could react he'd lifted me against him; my back hit the wall and my legs wrapped around his hips like it was something we did all the time. How could someone that much taller, that much bigger, fit against me so well?

He rocked against me, using the wall as leverage, and I broke our kiss with a moan. I squirmed against him, the heat between my legs pulsing, seeking out the hardness between his. God, it had been so long. So. Damn. Long.

"April." My name was a groan, and he pressed a hand flat on the wall next to my head. "We . . . are you sure you want to do this?"

I'd never heard my laugh the way it sounded now. Rough. Desperate. "Are you kidding me? I'm not exactly playing coy here."

He laughed too, and God, he was gorgeous when he did. A smile like noontime sunshine and eyes crinkling at the edges. "I'm just saying . . ." He leaned in and kissed me again, slowly now and leisurely, his tongue lingering and thorough like we had all the time in the world to do nothing but this. "This is kind of above and beyond our agreement."

"That's okay . . ." My smile turned into a gasp as his mouth moved across my jaw and to my throat. "Weekend's not over yet. You still need a girlfriend."

"I really do." His mouth against my skin muffled his voice, and I shivered when his tongue found that place at the side of my neck that melted me. I'd forgotten all about that spot. "Hmmm. You like that?" He did it again, tongue stroking, teeth nipping, and I let my head fall back to thud against the wall.

"I like all kinds of stuff," I managed. My breath shuddered in my lungs. "I haven't . . . it's been a while, you know? So it's all . . ."

"Wait, what?" He pulled back to look me in the eye. *No. Get back to kissing me.* "How long, exactly?"

I didn't want to think about that. The worst part was that I couldn't rattle off an answer right away, and his eyes became more alarmed the longer I took to think. "Four years? Five? Maybe?" Certainly before my accident, and a little before that. Derek had worked in my building; we'd run into each other at the elevator or the lobby coffee cart enough times that he'd finally asked me out to dinner. It hadn't lasted, but it had been fun while it had.

"Five years?" Mitch looked appalled. "That's ridiculous, are you kidding me? Five years without an orgasm? That's—"

"What? No!" It was my turn to be appalled. "You think I don't know how to take care of myself? My vibrator collection begs to differ. The top drawer of my nightstand is my happy place."

Mitch laughed, a sharp crack of sound. "That's my girl." His grin was infectious, and I tried to ignore the thrill that went through me at his words. I wasn't his girl. I shouldn't want to be his girl. But none of that seemed to matter right now.

"So." His hands on the backs of my thighs tightened, hitching me a little higher up his body, and my hands tightened instinctively on the back of his neck as sparks flew through me. "What say we move this party about ten feet that way?" He jerked his head backwards in a nod, indicating that massive bed in the middle of the room.

Yes. Every single part of me started rejoicing, but I couldn't speak, my throat clogged with a combination of emotion and desire. So I nodded and he hitched me up even higher, turning to walk across the room with me still wrapped around him. Each step moved me against his body in ways that made my blood go nuclear.

"God, you're strong." He was carrying me around the way I'd carried that bag of avocados last night. Like I weighed nothing. Like I was something he was going to make into something delicious. I tightened my thighs around his hips and he took in a sharp breath.

"CrossFit, babe." His voice shook a little and he stole another quick kiss. "It works everything."

"Everything, huh?" I cast around for some kind of innuendo, but with him hard against me like this, the time for innuendo had passed. Innuendo was meant to lead to something, and we were already there.

"Good thing too. Five years of solo orgasms . . . I feel like I have some work to do here." He sank down to sit on the edge of the bed, and now I straddled his lap. His lap was a great place to be, and I squirmed, getting a little more comfortable, making my blood a little hotter. His too, from the way he hissed in a breath as I moved against him. He leaned in to kiss me again, his mouth devouring, claiming, and his hands went to the front of my shirt, unbuttoning with nimble fingers. No piece of battery-operated silicone could compare to the backs of his fingers skimming the sensitive skin between my breasts. He pushed my blouse off my shoulders, and I tugged at his shirt until he helped me pull it over his head.

"You don't have to feel sorry for me." My turn to let my hands wander, over those broad shoulders, down the curve of his biceps, and up again. "I've got a pretty nice collection in that drawer. Different textures, sizes. Some are waterproof . . ." I cupped his jaw in both hands, stealing another kiss, then trailed my fingers down the line of his sternum, all that solid muscle under warm skin. I lost the thread of what I was saying, because damn, there wasn't anything in my bedside drawer that could replicate the feel of his skin under my fingertips. I let my mouth follow my hands, relishing the gasp he made when I licked my way back up his chest to his throat. "Some are rechargeable." I leaned in to whisper in his ear, indulging in a nibble on his earlobe as I did so. "And one has *attachments*."

He choked out a laugh, fisting his hands in my hair, holding me to him as I took my time with his throat. "Listen, there's nothing wrong with, um, attachments or whatever. But there's something to be said for the real thing." He popped the button on my jeans, and I sucked in a breath as one hand slipped in, down. I wanted to reach for him, unbuckle his belt, but all I could do was cling to him and tremble as he stroked me with a featherlight touch. "See?" His voice was a low rumble in my ear, his teeth closing gently on my earlobe. I rocked up, my fingernails digging into his shoulders, giving him more and better access. He knew what he was doing; it only took a few strokes for an orgasm to flash through me, quick and sudden and intense as summer lightning. I wasn't prepared, so all I could do was cling to him and shudder, any sound I might have made canceled out by the breath I sucked in.

"Jesus." I fought to regain both my breath and control of my body as he eased his hand out of my jeans. "I guess it has been a while. I don't usually—"

"That was nothing." He reached around, unsnapping my bra with practiced fingers. "Letting off steam. You needed it. Five years. What the fuck." He shook his head. "What the hell is wrong with the men in our town."

"I'm a single mom," I reminded him. "Men aren't exactly . . . lining up . . ." I forgot how to speak as my bra fluttered to the floor and he took my breasts in his hands. My nipples tightened fast, almost painfully, against the pads of his thumbs as he stroked in slow, maddening circles. Oh, the hell with it. Who needed talking right now? The quick orgasm had cleared my mind, so while his large hands moved to map the curve of my waist and the swell of my hip, I got to work on his belt, getting that buckle the hell out of my way so I could unbutton his jeans. Then the worst thought swept through me, chilling everything.

"Wait." I put my hands over his where they now lay on my hips, anchoring me to him. "Protection. I don't have . . . I'm not on . . ." I hadn't needed to think about birth control in years; I was out of practice here. Regret dashed cold water over the fire he'd stoked in me, which was a shame, because damn, was he good at this.

"It's okay." His mouth was busy on my neck as he spoke, not missing a beat. "I've got some. In my bag. In the bathroom."

"But that's so far away." I couldn't believe how annoyed I sounded despite the relief that coursed through me. But now that this was really happening, getting condoms out of the bath-room meant there'd be a minute or so that his hands wouldn't be on me, and that was, frankly, bullshit.

"Don't worry." He lay back in the bed, taking me with him, his arms closing around me like I was all he wanted in the world. "I'm not gonna need 'em for a while." He pulled the tie out of my already loosened hair and spread it over my shoulders so the ends of it brushed across his skin.

"But you already made me . . . I mean, I already . . ." I used to be better at talking than this. But it didn't seem important as he rolled me under him, his hands and mouth everywhere.

"I told you, that was nothing. We're just getting started here." He lifted his head to catch my eyes, and his crooked, slightly cocky smile reminded me that I was in bed with *Kilty*. The endless innuendo machine that I spent most of my time rolling my eyes at. Years of snark had led us here and now I was under him with my jeans open. With his jeans open. Holy shit, how did we get here?

But all I could do now was smile up at him. "Promise?" I wasn't sure what I was asking for. For this to be the beginning of what could be the best night of my life, or for this to be the start of something more?

"Promise." His voice was solemn, but humor still danced in those blue, blue eyes. "Don't worry. I've trained for this. If nothing else, I gotta show you that there's more to life than battery-powered orgasms."

"But . . ." I couldn't keep the giggle out of my voice as his mouth worked its way down my neck, to the base of my throat and then the swell of my breast. He was thorough. "But I *like* my toys. And the attachments."

"Those goddamn attachments." His lips closed over a nipple, his tongue teasing, flicking over the sensitive skin. My laugh turned to a helpless moan and I arched up to him, offering myself, offering more. Offering everything. I was so distracted by the progress of his mouth, the brush of his hair against my skin as he kissed his way down my body, that I didn't realize he was easing my jeans off until they were halfway down my legs, and I froze, anxiety pricking through the pleasure.

"Don't you think we should . . . turn off the light?" I slapped blindly for the bedside table, but I was too far away to reach anything, and there was no way I could get out from under Mitch. There was no way I wanted to even try.

"What?" He raised his head from my stomach—no, *get back down there, kiss me some more*—his expression incredulous. "No way. I don't work out six days a week to do this in the dark."

I gave a ghost of a laugh over my discomfort. "Point taken. But . . ."

He went back to tugging at my jeans, pulling them the rest of the way off. I told myself it was fine, no big deal, but all the desire that had been building in me fled with the sound of my jeans hitting the floor. "I like to see what I'm doing . . ." His voice broke off when I flinched away, rolling to my right side, doing my best to hide my leg and the scar that marred my skin. I couldn't hide it forever, but I sure could try. "Hey. April. Hey. What is it?"

God, I was making a mess of this. No wonder I didn't date. No wonder all my orgasms were self-inflicted these days. I didn't know what to say, but I let him gently pull me over to face him again. My hand went to my leg, covering the worst of it while I took a shuddering breath and let him be the first man to see me like this.

"Is this . . ." He swallowed hard and I searched his eyes for the pity that I was sure I'd find. But his gaze moved over the puckered skin, then back up to my face. "Is this what you're worried about? Me seeing this?"

"Well, yeah." Lying here naked in front of him was one thing, but letting him see my scar felt like a dealbreaker. "It's not exactly sexy."

"Are you kidding me?" He laid his hand over mine, over my leg, and threaded our fingers together. He lifted our joined hands to his mouth and kissed each of my knuckles, one by one. Then he bent over me, his mouth on my calf a few inches below my knee where the scar began. "Look how strong you are." He laid a kiss there, then another an inch farther up, his tongue starting a trail that followed the length of my scar, up over my knee and to my thigh. "Look what you survived. You kick ass. You have no idea."

His words wormed into me, as warm and welcome as his mouth on my skin. He worked his way up, parting my thighs with his hands, and I fell back to the bed, all inhibitions gone. "Fine." I don't know how I managed to sound cranky when Mitch's head was between my legs, but I did. "Just . . . fine."

His chuckle was a buzz against my sensitive skin, and I shuddered. "Oh, you're about to be more than fine." He gave me a long, slow lick, nearly sending me into orbit, before his mouth got to work in earnest. He was right. It didn't take long for my blood to catch fire and my vocabulary to devolve into an endless chant of *please, please, please.* He murmured encouragement as he brought me closer and closer, the flat of his tongue and his long, strong fingers finally sending me over the edge, and all I could do was shudder under him.

As I came back to myself I faintly heard the soft clink of his belt buckle as his jeans hit the floor, followed by a rip of foil. Then he was back, crawling up my body, his mouth lingering. I kissed him greedily, reaching for him, opening for him, my legs going back around his hips where they belonged. His hands were on the backs of my thighs, pushing them up, spreading me wider for him. I reached down to help him, to guide him, my hand curling around him, hot and hard and oh shit, *big.*

"Go slow," I gasped. "Long time, remember?" Toys in my bedside drawer were one thing but this was real, this was him, and thank God I was already relaxed from two orgasms so I could take him inside.

"You got it." But his voice was strained, that jovial tone

rougher, his breath coming harder in his chest than I'd ever heard him. He brushed against my entrance and then he was inside, dipping in slowly, pulsing into me gently, inch by precious inch, and it wasn't enough.

"God," I said. "Fuck. The hell with slow." I grabbed at him, my hands on his hips, greedily pulling him closer.

"April." My name was a plea, a moan as he sank into me, and I arched up, bringing him in deeper, welcoming him in as his hips came flush with mine. He was huge, he was everywhere, his breath hot in my ear. I'd never felt completely a part of someone else, and I welcomed it even while I knew I shouldn't. This was a one-night-only thing, and never having this again was going to hurt.

But I wasn't going there. Not now. Not yet. Instead I turned my head, seeking his mouth, devouring him as much as he devoured me. As he pushed into me harder, losing control, beginning that last desperate shiver as he let go, I clung to him with everything I had. Tomorrow was so far off. It didn't have any place here.

Much, much later, after some talking, some laughing, and a desperate dig through Mitch's Dopp kit to find the second condom he swore was in there somewhere, we sat up together in bed, wrapped in the hotel sheets. We ate the last of his grandmother's macaroni and cheese and washed it down with the cheap hotel champagne. It was the best late-night snack I'd ever had.

"Told you," he said. His arm was around me and I nestled into his chest, high on carbs, alcohol, and the best sex of my life. I turned his words over in my head and looked up at him with a frown.

"Told me what?"

His lips twitched as he downed the last of the champagne in his plastic glass. "You're a MILF."

I snorted, which was painful when you had a mouthful of champagne. I sputtered and whacked him on the arm at the same time. His smirk turned into a laugh as he wrestled my glass out of my hand. I pretended to fight him, but who was I kidding, I didn't want to. He leaned away from me to put the glasses on the bedside table, and when he turned back to me, I got his full attention—something I was still getting used to. The full force of Mitch's attention was a lot, but thankfully he seemed to be about as tired as I was. We eased down under the sheets together over the course of a few long, lingering kisses, and he tucked the blankets around the both of us. He looped a lock of my hair behind my ear, his fingertips lingering on my cheekbone, and I studied the sleepy satisfaction in his blue eyes.

As we both began to drift off to sleep, I remembered how I'd woken up that morning. At the very edge of the bed, every muscle tense with fear that I'd move too close to Mitch as we slept. Now our pillows were piled together in the middle, our heads nestled close. He fell asleep with a long sigh, one arm slung over me, cradling me to him. I felt warm. I felt safe. Sleeping in Mitch's arms was like being under a warm weighted blanket.

Weighted Blanket I'd Like to . . .

I wanted to laugh at the ridiculous thought as it floated through my head. I wanted to tell Mitch, because I knew he'd laugh too. But I was more asleep than awake at that point, and it was easier to close my eyes and slide into a dream. But with the night I'd just had, dreams had a lot to live up to.

"April." Mitch's voice was very far away, but his hand was right there, warm on my shoulder, shaking gently.

"Mmmf." I turned to bury my head in the pillow, not at all ready for it to be morning.

"Come on." His mouth replaced his hand, placing lingering kisses on my bare shoulder. "Gotta get up. Brunch time."

I groaned. "How are you so chipper? I didn't get nearly enough sleep last night. And neither did you." But I grinned into my pillow, because what a way to lose sleep. It beat insomnia any day of the week. I turned to peer at him over my shoulder. "Are you always this much of a morning person?"

"Pretty much." He tugged at the blankets, and I half-heartedly tugged back, trying to burrow under them and capture some of the warmth we'd shared last night. I wasn't ready for morning. Morning meant our night together was over. "I told you, I've trained for this. Now, come on."

"Nope." I pulled the sheet over my head, and he tugged it down again.

"See?" His arms went around me under the blankets, tucking me into his embrace. I gave a little hum of pleasure at being his little spoon. Yes. Let's stay here all day. "I told you the real thing is better than the battery-operated stuff."

I snorted at that, but also moved lazily against him as his hands began to wander. I wasn't ready to renounce the contents of my bedside table, but he did have a point. "The battery-operated stuff is less demanding, you know. And lets me get more sleep." I yawned extravagantly. "Give my regrets to your family, but I'm pretty sure you killed me last night."

His chuckle was a low rumble against my back. "Sure. No problem. I'll tell Grandma that you're too tired to come to brunch from all the banging we did last night."

"Hey, it'll help sell the whole fake girlfriend thing."

I expected another laugh, but instead he was silent, his hands pausing on my body. I turned in his arms, and when I caught his eyes he smiled, but it wasn't a full smile. It was a smile like he'd had yesterday with his family—the kind you threw at someone when you were supposed to but didn't feel it. The sight of that insincere smile made my chest throb. I didn't like that I'd put that smile there, and I didn't like that I didn't like it.

"Fine." I threw the blankets aside and levered myself up, groaning and trying to ignore all the cracks my joints made. That had been quite a workout last night. "I'm up. But you have to soap me down in the shower."

Now a real smile was back on his face, and that made me happier than I'd expected. "Gladly."

I gave him my hand and let him pull me out of bed. I wasn't kidding; I could barely walk. My thighs were stretched and sore, like that one summer in college that I'd learned horseback riding. Which made sense—I'd done a little riding last night. Would anyone notice at brunch? Would it be obvious that something had changed between Mitch and me the night before?

And how was I supposed to forget all of this when I got home later today, and my fake girlfriend job came to an end?

I pushed those thoughts away as I let Mitch pull me into the shower and draw me into a soapy embrace. The weekend wasn't over yet. We still had a few hours.

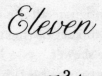

Eleven

*N*o one noticed. Which was probably a testament to how well Mitch and I had been faking it all weekend. But me? I noticed everything. I was hyperaware of his hand at the small of my back as we walked in the front door at his grandparents' house, and the way he absentmindedly trailed his knuckles up and down my spine while we talked to Lulu on the back deck after the meal was over. We stood a little closer to each other, leaned into each other a little more than we had the day before. But if anyone noticed, no one said a word.

The beginning of the ride home was filled with the classic rock station on his satellite radio. Which meant, of course, it was also filled with bad singing along. I won't say who was doing the bad singing, because what happens in Mitch's truck stays in Mitch's truck. As we closed in on the city limits of Willow Creek, Mitch turned down the radio.

"Thanks for this weekend."

I wanted to snort in response, my mind immediately going to last night's acrobatics, but he was using his rare Serious Voice, so I refrained. Instead I shrugged, casual. "I got free barbecue out of the deal, so I came out ahead."

He considered that, then nodded. "That's fair. Not to mention the mac and cheese. Best part of every get-together, I'm telling you."

I stole a glance at him, my cheeks heating up as I remembered finishing off the rest of it in bed with him last night. But he didn't seem to be alluding to anything. Sometimes, macaroni and cheese was just macaroni and cheese. This whole ride home, I'd been wondering if we were going to discuss what had happened the night before. Was it time for an awkward conversation about what this meant for our friendship going forward?

But he didn't say anything about it and neither did I. I reminded myself of his early morning appointments in his phone, each with a different woman. His mind was probably back on them already, and I was in the rearview. *Been there, done her.*

So when he pulled into the driveway and handed me my bag after I got out of the truck, I just said, "Thanks." There was an awkward beat where we didn't look at each other; instead we both glanced toward my house, and out to my front yard that needed mowing.

"No, thank you," he said. When he finally looked at me it was like a switch had been flipped and he was the old Mitch I'd always known. Same smile, same cheerful personality. "I'll see you, right?"

"Right." Okay. That's how this was going to go. Back to being friends, like the last couple days had never happened. Like we hadn't done those very more-than-friend-like things together in the dark last night. I could handle that.

I waved as he hopped in his truck and drove off, and then turned back to the house. Emily's Jeep wasn't in the driveway, so maybe she and Caitlin were at the bookstore. Having the house to myself for a bit might not be a bad thing. My brain was still a little wobbly from the events of the past forty-eight hours.

But the television was on when I opened the front door, and Caitlin was sprawled across the couch, scrolling through her phone. So much for alone time. She glanced up as I came inside, and I braced myself for another ten rounds of passive-aggression from my daughter. Instead she gave me a tentative smile.

"Hey."

"Hey yourself." I left my suitcase and purse by the door and went to the couch, picking up Caitlin's feet, dropping down onto the cushion, and replacing her feet in my lap. "What happened to your aunt?"

"She went home this morning." Caitlin clicked her screen off. "She said that I could probably behave myself until you came home."

"Good job on that. I knew you could be trusted." I patted her ankles and she huffed out a laugh. Then she gave a pointed look toward the front window, then back at me.

"Are you dating Coach Malone?"

"What?" A tingle spread through me at the thought, and I didn't want to take the time to analyze what that tingle meant. The important thing was to shut down this line of questioning. "Where did you get that from?"

She scoffed. "That was his truck dropping you off, Mom. I'm not stupid. Besides, Emily told me that you went away for the weekend with him."

"Did she." It wasn't a question. It was a statement that said, *I'm gonna kill my little sister.* I didn't like gossip. Never had. It brought me back to those final days of my marriage: the pointed looks at the grocery store, the conversations between friends that hushed to a halt when I showed up. The whispers here in Willow Creek when the single mother and her little girl had moved to town.

"Yeah. Which was more than you told me," she said pointedly.

"What? I told you where I was going."

"No, you didn't. All you said was that you were going away for the weekend and I wasn't mature enough to be trusted without a babysitter."

"Okay. That's not exactly what I said." I took a deep breath. This wasn't gossip, I reminded myself. This was family. "You're right. I was with Coach Malone this weekend. But we're not dating. It was . . ." I thought hard. "You know how you and your friends did a group thing for prom? Instead of going as couples?"

Caitlin nodded. "Because none of us were dating anyone. And the girl that Toby liked had turned him down. So we went as one big group that all stuck together, instead of coupling up, so Toby wouldn't feel bad."

"So you were each other's dates but at the same time just friends, right?" I nodded while Caitlin did the same. "It was sort of like that. He had this family thing over the weekend that most people brought dates or spouses to, but since he didn't have either of those things I went with him instead." That was close enough. I didn't need to tell her about the fake girlfriend part and I sure as hell wasn't going to tell her about last night. "And I'm sorry if I hurt your feelings, having Emily stay with you." I patted her ankles again. "I trust you. It's just that . . . I'm your mom, and moms worry about stuff. You're my favorite kid, you know?" That was a low blow, and I knew it. But it was an old joke, stemming from when she'd called me her "favorite mom" when she was about five. We were always each other's favorites. She came first. Maybe I needed to remind myself every so often.

"Yeah. No, I get it." She rolled her head on the arm of the sofa to look at the television. "I'm sorry too." Her voice was almost impossible to hear, and maybe if I'd been a better disciplinarian I would have asked her to repeat herself, but the hell with it.

"Hey," I said. "Emily told me you two went dress shopping. Can I see?"

"Oh. Yeah!" She swung her legs off my lap and bounced up from the couch. While she went to her room to change I propped my feet on the coffee table. A cup of coffee would be nice, but that involved moving, so I decided not to bother. This was not going to be a productive Sunday, but that was okay. As long as Cait and I had something clean to wear to work and school tomorrow, we could order a pizza for dinner and call it a day. If you couldn't be lazy on a Sunday, when could you?

"What do you think?" Caitlin appeared in the doorway to the living room, and when I looked over at her my heart stopped.

"Oh, honey." I sat up straight on the couch and pressed a hand to my mouth, tears flooding my vision. I wasn't an emotional person, at least I hadn't been for a couple decades. What was happening to me lately?

Caitlin shuffled her weight from one foot to the other, her expression dubious. "Is that a good 'oh, honey' or a bad 'oh, honey'?"

My laugh was watery, and I ran my fingertips under my eyes as I stood up. "It's a great 'oh, honey.'" As I walked over to my daughter, flashes of memory came into my head, unbidden: middle-of-the-night feedings, those first tentative steps, all those times I had to bend down to hold her tiny hand. Staying up late reading books together. Dance parties in the kitchen. All those little moments culminating in the young woman standing in front of me now. My little girl. Not so little anymore.

"I love it. Do you love it?"

She nodded, plucking at the full skirt. "I mean, I guess it's silly to have a nice dress for graduation, since we have to wear that stupid gown over it. But Emily said—"

"No. I think it's perfect." And it was. She'd brought her cap and gown home the week before, pale yellow and made from flimsy polyester. What a terrible thing to put on a bunch of kids and then make them sit outside in the June heat. Who planned these things?

But Caitlin (and Emily, probably) had picked out the perfect dress to go underneath. Willow Creek High's colors were green and yellow, and she wore a light green sundress with little white heeled sandals. With her hair pulled back from her face she looked innocent and all grown up at the same time. Far too young to be going off to college on her own, yet her own independent woman. I wasn't sure how to handle it.

"It's perfect," I said again, and Caitlin smiled at the praise. Things were starting to feel normal between us again. I made a mental note to text Emily tonight and thank her for . . . whatever she'd done to thaw things between my daughter and me. "You should wear it Friday night too. Get at least one more wear out of it, since it'll be hidden under the gown at graduation."

She blinked, startled. "Friday night?"

"Yeah. Friday. The reception party thing at the high school? That's the night before graduation, right?" A faint alarm bell rang in the back of my head. I'd written it down in my planner, but had I gotten the date wrong?

"Yeah. It's on Friday night. I just . . ." She shrugged. "I didn't think you were going."

"What? What are you talking about, of course I'm going."

"Oh." She chewed on the inside of her cheek for a moment, then brightened. "Cool. No, that's good! I just didn't realize."

That wasn't it. I'd known Caitlin for every moment of her life, and I knew when her smile was hiding something. But I was tired and my brain was full, so I let myself be fooled and didn't question it.

But I should have questioned it. If I had, maybe Friday night wouldn't have bitten me in the ass the way it did.

"Um . . . Mom?"

"Yeah, honey?" Single moms were good at multitasking, so I could both answer my daughter and refresh my makeup at the same time. I'd left work an hour early, but Friday afternoon traffic had been a bitch, so I didn't have a lot of time to get changed and ready for this reception thing. The details of this evening were sketchy, but maybe that was my fault for not volunteering for a single school event over the years. I was able to glean from Emily that it was set up as a faculty-parent mixer; a way for the parents to socialize with the teachers who'd guided their children through the past four years of high school, getting them prepared for the future. Some crap like that. Most parents had formed relationships with these teachers, I supposed, through volunteering, Friday night football games, and multiple parent-teacher conferences. As for me, well, Emily was going to be there, since she was a teacher's wife. And Simon would be there, as said teacher. And Mitch, probably—we hadn't talked since he'd dropped me off on Sunday, but it seemed like something he'd attend. So there. I would know three whole people.

God, I should have been more involved when my kid was growing up.

Caitlin appeared in my bedroom and perched on the end of my bed where she could see me at the bathroom mirror. "I need to . . . um." She threw her gaze to her feet, tapping the toe of one shoe against the floor. "I need to talk to you about something."

I blotted my lipstick and considered my reflection one more time before declaring it good enough. "Sure, but can we talk in the car? I'm running a little late." I slipped past her into the bedroom, grabbing my dress from its hanger on the back of the closet door.

"Yeah." She watched me with large eyes, reminding me of a guilty puppy, and a tingle of dread crept across my skin.

"Everything okay?" I narrowed my eyes as I stepped into the dress. "Are you worried that one of your teachers might tell me something? If you're not graduating tomorrow, you better tell me now." I was joking, but was I really? Something was up.

"Oh, God, Mom! No! It's not that. It's . . ." But she bit at the inside of her cheek again, screwing her face up in a partial scowl. "No, you're right. We can talk in the car."

She fled the room as I settled the dress into place and stepped into my shoes. A frown creased my forehead as I tucked my lipstick into my bag and grabbed my keys. Caitlin should be in a much better mood. She was finished with high school; only the reception tonight and the graduation ceremony tomorrow to go. She had the Ren Faire to look forward to over the summer and college in the fall. Everything was going her way. What was the problem?

She was silent in the car, and about halfway to the community center on the other side of town, I got impatient. "Okay, out with it. What's up?"

"It's . . ." She took a deep breath and pressed a hand to her chest. "Okay, I should have told you before now, and I'm really sorry I didn't. But I didn't know what to say, or how to tell you that—"

"Caitlin." My voice carried a hint of warning. Stalling time was over.

"Okay." Another deep breath. "So. Um. I may have invited . . . um . . . my father to graduation."

I gripped the steering wheel as my vision went white around the edges. I concentrated on taking a slow breath. In through the nose. Out through the mouth. "Okay." I'd known this was going to be a possibility, ever since he'd sent Caitlin that card. Ever since she'd said she might contact him. "Okay," I said again. "Did he say if he was going to come?"

"I think so?" Her voice went high-pitched, uncertain. "I mean, he emailed back and said he was looking forward to it, so I guess he is."

"That's fine." I was pleasantly surprised at how even my voice was. I sounded like I wasn't thrown for a loop at all. Go, me. "I mean, I wish you'd given me a little more notice than the night before, but that's—"

"Oh. No. I mean I invited him to the thing tonight too."

"You *what?*" My grip on the steering wheel tightened, and I was surprised it didn't snap in half. I wanted to turn and glare at my daughter, but I couldn't look at her right now. I was driving. And I was about to have a panic attack.

"Look, I was mad at you, okay?" Caitlin's voice was shrill now, and I could hear tears in her voice. "You went off for the weekend without telling me where you were going, you stuck me with Emily like I was some kind of baby that needed supervision. And he said in his card that he was proud of me, and I thought . . ."

She kept talking, but I couldn't hear anything over the sound of the blood pounding in my temples. I didn't know what to do. I wanted to slam on the brakes. I wanted to make a quick U-turn and drive home. Or bypass home completely, drive past the city limits, and keep driving until I was in another state. Another time zone. I hadn't been in a room with Robert Daugherty in almost two decades, and I wasn't ready for that to change.

But this wasn't about me, was it? This was about Caitlin. As her words sank in, I realized I'd upset my daughter so much that she'd turned to a man she'd never met because he offered her a single bread crumb of support. She'd thought she couldn't count on me. There were a lot of things I could say at this moment, but they were all terrible. Vindictive. And that wasn't something I wanted to pile on Caitlin's head. She'd set all this in motion, but none of it was her fault. It was mine.

So I didn't say anything. I went back to that breathing thing: in through the nose, out through the mouth. I did that until we were safely parked at the community center and I'd killed the engine.

"I'm sorry, Mom." Caitlin sounded miserable. "Please. I'm sorry. I didn't think you were going to come tonight. You never come to school stuff. So I didn't think it would be a big deal. You'd said before that it would be okay if I contacted him."

"You're right. I did." I nodded and stared straight ahead. I needed to get a grip. I needed to be Mom of Happy High School Graduate tonight, not Abandoned Ex-Wife. So I pushed down everything I was feeling and focused on Caitlin. My default setting since the day she was born. "Hey." I reached across the console and grasped her wrist. Her skin was cold, and mine probably was too. We were both beyond anxious. "It's okay." Her eyes when they met mine were frantic, so I did my best to telegraph calm. "I'm not mad at you. And it's fine that you contacted him. I'm glad you did, and I'm glad he's coming." Okay, that was a lie, but it wouldn't be the first one I'd told my daughter. "Where did he say he was meeting you?"

She shrugged, looking toward the entrance of the building. "He didn't say?"

My heart sank. I didn't want to see him, but if he stood her up after all this . . . "Come on. Let's go inside and see if we can find him." Would I recognize him after all this time? Would he recognize me?

"No." She squared her shoulders, and when she turned to me she looked like that young woman again. Not a frightened child. "No, I'll go. I can do this."

"You can do this," I echoed as I watched her disappear into the building. I didn't care what this night did to me emotionally. I'd stopped caring about Robert Daugherty a very long time ago; seeing him would suck, but he couldn't hurt me. He could hurt my daughter though, and I wouldn't stand for that.

After spending an extra few minutes in the parking lot, gathering both my thoughts and my nerve, I followed Caitlin into the community center. Just inside the door, long tables were set against one wall, their surfaces covered in name tags that had been largely picked over. We'd gotten there late. As I scanned them, looking for my name, I remembered the RSVP I'd sent in. Had Robert RSVP'd too? Or would he have to scrawl his name on a blank name tag with a Sharpie?

The moment I spotted my name, neatly printed on a name tag in the center of one of the tables, a voice to my right jolted me out of my thoughts. "Did you find your name okay?"

"Sure did." I scooped it up, peeling off the backing and sticking it to the left side of my dress. It wasn't going to last; I could tell right away that it would start curling on the edges in about a minute and a half. Name tags never lasted, and we wore them anyway.

"Oh, are you Mrs. Parker? Caitlin's mother?"

"That's me. Not a Mrs., though." My voice was snappy with nerves, so I turned with what I hoped was a friendly smile to the woman who'd materialized next to me. She was older than me, and about an inch taller. Early grandma age, she looked like someone who would be absolutely stoked to make cookies for grandchildren. She wore a navy pantsuit, and her gray hair had that style that seemed to be handed out to women of a certain age—the kind achieved by going to a salon once a week to have it "set." Her name tag read AMELIA HOWE, and it was an engraved one, with a pin back and everything. She must be faculty— someone who attended functions like this often enough to warrant the investment in a permanent name tag.

She looked dismayed by her faux pas, and probably by my bitchy tone. "I'm so sorry! I saw Caitlin here with her father, and I thought . . ." She bent to the table, straightening one or two of the already perfectly straight name tags, not noticing how I gripped the edge of the table, relief mixed with dread sweeping through me. Robert hadn't stood up our daughter, and that was good. But he was here. That was bad.

I didn't like people who assumed things, like Ms. Howe just had. But embarrassment pinked her cheeks, and that made me want to reassure her. Probably because some of this was my fault. If I'd been more involved with the school all these years, maybe she would have known me better. "It's okay," I said. I gave my name tag a reassuring pat since it was already curling at one edge. See? Just like I'd said. "Did you teach Caitlin?"

"Not technically." She seized on the change in topic, her smile coming back to her face. "I teach music here. But I also advise the organizers of the Renaissance Faire, and I believe Caitlin is going to be a Lily again this year? I'm helping those girls rehearse for this summer."

"Oh, that's great." Did everyone in town do this Renaissance Faire thing? Did Ms. Howe squeeze herself into a corset every summer? Now I pictured her less baking cookies and more belting out bawdy songs in the tavern that Emily had worked in her first summer. I pressed my lips together to hide the smile that mental image prompted. "She's excited for this summer. She's excited for every summer since she started volunteering at the Faire, honestly."

Ms. Howe chuckled. "That's what happens. A lot of volunteers do it for a summer or two and move on with their lives, but then there's always a few that get hooked, and they come back every year. I wouldn't be surprised if your Caitlin kept on volunteering when she's home for the summers from college."

"I bet." But I said it absently, because Caitlin wouldn't be coming here during the summers, would she? This time next year, the house would be sold and Caitlin would be coming "home" to wherever I'd moved. This was going to be Caitlin's last summer at the Willow Creek Renaissance Faire. I hadn't thought of that.

"Well, I won't keep you." Ms. Howe patted me on the shoulder, indifferent to the direction my thoughts had taken. "I'm out here doing greeting duty, but you should go on inside and catch up with your daughter."

"Thanks. That's the plan." But was it? Was I supposed to stand next to Robert all night, like we were some kind of pretend family? No. That wasn't the plan at all. Tonight's plan was simply to survive.

Inside, I made a beeline for the refreshments. Despite my anxiety, I was starving, and Emily had promised there would be snacks at this thing. I loaded a plate with vegetables and spinach dip, as well as some promising-looking stuffed mushrooms. Then I tried to eat them like a human being and not shove them all in my face at once. While I did so, I scanned the reception hall. It was cavernous, full of people in little groups milling around, mingling like people who were good at social gatherings. Everything and everyone blurred together in a haze of color and sound, and my heart pounded faster. But I willed my mom instinct to kick in, and soon I spotted my daughter. A baby carrot almost stuck in my throat when I saw the man beside her.

God.

It really was him.

I coughed, swallowing the carrot, and when I looked down I wondered why the plate was blurry. I gripped the plate harder, but my hands were shaking too badly to hold it. I'd lost my appetite anyway. So I ditched it in the nearest trash can, then melted backwards till I was practically hugging the wall. If I pressed my shoulder blades hard enough against it, I could probably manage to stay upright. And while I was upright I could watch Caitlin with her father. This was a good thing.

Across the hall, Caitlin looked a little uncertain as she talked, introducing Robert to a woman that might have been Caitlin's history teacher. But Caitlin didn't look unhappy, and Robert looked . . .

Well, he looked good. Which sucked, frankly. I wanted him to have aged horribly so I'd feel better about all this. But he wore a well-tailored dark blue suit and a smile that I'd almost managed to forget. Sure, his face was more lined, and that dark hair was threaded with silver now, but it only managed to make him look distinguished. So unfair. When that much gray appeared in my own hair, I knew it was time for another trip to the salon.

Caitlin didn't look like she needed me, so I stayed pressed against the wall, watching my ex-husband work the room. He said something to the history teacher that had her throwing her head back. I could hear her giggle from here. Robert smiled at her, indulgent. Winning her over. By the end of the night he would win them all over. He'd know all these teachers better than I ever had, and I'd be even more of an outsider in my own town.

That had always been his superpower: being at ease in a crowd of strangers, turning them into immediate friends. Meanwhile, my tongue grew three sizes and I struggled with the smallest of small talk at these kinds of things. No wonder we hadn't lasted. Who wanted an antisocial walking panic attack for a wife?

I forced my attention back to Caitlin again, studying her expression. Because if she didn't look okay with any of this, I would be on my way over there, anxiety be damned. Her hands were clasped in front of her, one of her signs of nervousness, but her smile was genuine, and she looked almost relaxed in his company. She was fine.

This was good. I could let her have this night. Let him have this night. Whatever, right? I'd had all the other nights with her. The important ones. Maybe I could just slip out the way I'd come, go to Jackson's for a drink, and pick up Cait when this was all over. Maybe—

A hand seized my upper arm, pinching it. "Ow!" I jerked my arm out of Emily's grip and glared at her.

My sister pinned me with her gaze, her eyes looking like fire. "What the hell is going on here? Who's that guy walking around with Caitlin?"

"Who do you think?" I crossed my arms over my chest and raised my eyebrows. Emily squinted at them, then back to me again.

"Tell me that's not . . ."

"Yep."

"Caitlin's *father?*"

"Well, he's a little old to be her date."

Emily snorted at that, but when she looked out into the room again she heaved a big sigh. "Shit."

"Yep."

"Are you okay?"

"Nope." My breath shuddered in my lungs. "Don't ask me that again." I was barely holding it together here, telling myself it was only one evening. Admitting out loud that I was not okay with any of this made it worse. It made the tears come. I didn't want the tears to come.

"Okay. Come on, let me get you something to drink." She took my arm, more gently this time, and steered me back toward the refreshment table. "And when I say 'drink,' I don't mean the good stuff, sadly. The punch is that sherbet and ginger ale bullshit, but it's better than nothing. Here." She pushed a paper cup into my hands, and I took a sip of the overly sugary confection. She was right: it was better than nothing, but just barely.

"You look nice," I said.

"Thanks." Emily smoothed her hands down her skirt. She wore a yellow sundress with a halter neck, a white lacy cardigan over it, and her hair was bundled up in a riot of curls on top of her head. She looked like springtime. Like a teacher's wife in a small town.

I took another sip of the sherbet punch; the sugar was helping. A sugar rush was better than adrenaline any day. "I'm okay, Em. Honestly."

"Are you sure?" She looked skeptical, and I didn't blame her. But she had a job to do. She wasn't here to babysit me. She was here to be Mrs. English Teacher, to charm parents and students alike.

"I'm sure. Go. Simon's probably lost without you." While he was most likely in his element here, he was as social as I was.

"I don't know about that." But her gaze went across the hall, and it was easy to spot her husband. He was in a light green shirt with a dark brown tie that matched his vest, in conversation with a handful of parents. He looked perfectly at ease, but he spotted us with a casual turn of his head, and his eyes turned desperate. He didn't exactly mouth, *Help me*, but Emily got the message anyway.

"Go." I nudged her, and she sighed.

"Yeah, I probably should go rescue him. But . . ." She turned back to me. "I know you said not to ask, but are you sure . . . ?"

"Yes. I'm fine." I lifted my punch cup. "I'm pretending this is vodka."

She nodded, but before she left she threw her arms around me in an unexpected hug. "I love you, you know," she murmured. "And I've got your back if you need it. *We've* got your back."

"I know." I blinked away those threatening tears again and patted her arm. I was terrible at this whole PDA thing. "Now, get out of here. Go be Mrs. Graham. He needs you."

She sketched a little salute before darting back into the crowd to rescue her husband, and I finished off my punch. As I refilled my paper cup, I took another look around the hall, needing to have eyes on the man I was doing my best to avoid. Oh shit. They weren't far away. And they were coming closer to the refreshment table. But Robert hadn't seen me yet.

My courage failed me, not that there had been much to begin with. But all my senses said, *Nope*, in unison, and before I could process it I'd taken a big step backwards, then a second. Then I turned tail and ran out of there like the giant chickenshit I was. Past Ms. Howe and her tables of name tags and out the double doors into the night. I stopped on the landing and tried to re-member how to breathe.

Tears mingled with my heaving breaths, and I turned back toward the entrance, ready to take one last look at my failure. But my view was obscured entirely by a brick wall. A brick wall wear-ing jeans and a button-down shirt, who'd followed me outside.

"Whatcha doing hiding out here?" Mitch asked.

Twelve

U m . . ." *I stared* up at him and tried to formulate an answer. It was next to impossible, as Mitch appearing in front of me out of nowhere had scrambled what was left of my brain cells.

I hadn't seen Mitch since he'd dropped me off in my driveway on Sunday, and somehow I'd managed to forget how blue his eyes were. We both had blue eyes, sure, but mine were dark, almost inky, while his were bright. Alive. And set off now to great effect by the royal-blue tie he wore with his button-down shirt and jeans. He had one of those little pin-back name tags too. This was the most dressed up I'd ever seen him, and so instead of saying something snarky I just gaped up at him.

"Oh, God, are you drinking that shit? All that sugar will kill you." He took the cup out of my hand—because in my panic I'd apparently brought my sherbet punch with me—and tossed back the rest of it before pitching the cup into a trash can about ten feet away.

"Show-off," I said weakly.

"You know it." He leaned an arm on the wall over my head, caging me in, cutting me off from the rest of the world. With anyone else this would be a threatening move, but when he looked down at me I didn't feel threatened. I felt protected. I wanted to throw my arms around him in gratitude. I wanted to climb him like a tree.

But I did neither one of those things, because we were in public. Anyone could walk by.

"So what are you doing out here?" He nodded his head back toward the door we'd both just come through. "You know the party's in there, right?"

"Yeah, but I . . . I can't . . ." There was too much happening in my head right now and I couldn't articulate any of it. I shook my head hard and dug in my purse for my keys. "I have to go." But I fumbled my keys and they jangled to the ground.

"Okay." Mitch scooped them up. "Come on. I'll take you home."

"No . . ." But he'd already taken my hand, leading me into the parking lot to my SUV. "You don't need to . . . aren't you supposed to be working this thing?"

He shook his head. "The only people who want to talk to me are the sports parents, and they grabbed me early. I'm just scenery at this point." He clicked my key fob, and my SUV chirped in response. I wanted to protest, but instead I chose the path of least resistance and let Mitch bundle me into the passenger seat of my own vehicle.

"Was that him?" Mitch's voice was casual and he didn't look at me as he navigated into the Friday evening traffic. "The one who sent the card. Caitlin's dad?"

"Yeah." The word was a long exhale. I didn't want to talk about it. The farther away we got, the more my panic faded, and now I felt exhausted. Boneless. All I wanted was to be home in my pajamas. I should have let Caitlin go to this thing by herself after all.

Caitlin. "Wait." I bolted upright and looked behind us at the back windshield. "I can't just run out of there like that. I need to make sure Caitlin's . . ."

"She's fine." Mitch didn't take his eyes off the road. "I texted Emily. She'll keep an eye on Cait, get her home."

"Oh." I sagged back into the seat again. "Good. That's good." Then understanding dawned. "Emily sent you after me, didn't she?"

"Yep." He tossed the word down absently as he turned in to my neighborhood. "But if I'd known what was up I would have been there sooner. You should let me know these things next time."

"Got it." I nodded firmly. "Next time my daughter ambushes me by inviting her long-absent father to a high school function you'll be the first person I call."

"Smart-ass." He reached over, giving my hand a squeeze. "Did you meet any of the teachers before you bailed?"

"No. Oh, wait. I talked to Ms. Howe out front. The music teacher?"

"Ahh." A smile quirked his lips. "My old girlfriend."

"Your *what*?" I turned in my seat, panic forgotten.

"Taught me everything I know." His smile became a grin as he glanced at me. "Hey, I was young. It was a big scandal, but we've both grown a lot as people since then."

I blinked helplessly at him as he pulled into my driveway. "You're kidding."

"I'm kidding," he confirmed. "But seriously, she's great. One of those people who remembers every kid she's ever had in a class."

"She remembered Caitlin," I said. "And she didn't even have her in a class. Just the Ren Faire stuff."

"See? She's great. And she really did teach me everything I know." He let the pause stretch out before adding, "About being a teacher. I know where your mind went. Pervert."

I was almost able to laugh at that. I unclicked my seat belt. "You didn't think this through. How are you getting back to the party?"

He waved his phone at me as he followed me into the house. "Uber's a wonderful thing."

"Point taken." I went straight to the kitchen, and to the bottle of vodka that lived hidden away in an upper cabinet. Cider wasn't going to touch the way I was feeling tonight. I splashed some vodka into a glass and offered the bottle to Mitch, who waved it off.

"That doesn't look like tequila."

"That's because it's not." I tossed back the shot and poured another. I was home. I was safe. I could drink as much as I wanted to. And tonight I deserved it.

After my third shot Mitch opened the fridge, passing a can of Sprite to me across the kitchen island. "Here. Put that in there."

"Fine." I struggled with the pull tab on the soda can. Wow, that vodka was hitting fast. "Buzzkill," I muttered, either to the can or to Mitch.

"Have you eaten anything tonight?" He took the can from me and cracked it open before passing it back. "Or did you go straight to that sugar punch shit?"

"Mostly the sugar punch shit." I added more vodka to the soda I'd managed to pour into my glass. "No, wait. They had some little mushrooms, those were good. And some carrot sticks."

"So that's a no, then." He started rummaging around in my fridge, and I peered at him.

"You're not cooking for me."

"Sure I am." He put butter and cheese on the counter before pulling my loaf of bread off the top of the fridge. "I make excellent grilled cheese sandwiches."

"That . . . that sounds amazing, actually." It was probably the vodka talking, but honestly when was a grilled cheese sandwich a bad idea?

"Do you want to talk about it?" His voice was casual as he made himself at home in my kitchen, finding a skillet and putting it on to heat.

"No." I slurped at my vodka and Sprite and wondered how this had become my life. Getting drunk in my kitchen on a Friday night while a gorgeous man who was way too young for me made me a grilled cheese sandwich. "No," I said again. Yet I kept talking. "We were married for what, three years? Not even? I shouldn't be that rattled seeing him again."

"You loved him." Mitch's shrug was casual, belying the conversation we were having. "Marriage is supposed to be forever, right? You had Caitlin with him."

"True." My turn to shrug. "He didn't want kids. I mean, to be honest, I didn't either. Not right away, at least. But . . ."

"Accidents happen?" He glanced over his shoulder at me, brow raised. I nodded.

"A good accident, though. The best." I took a long drink and added more soda to dilute the vodka. My tongue was loose enough, no need to make it worse. "But he didn't think so, and that was that." Understatement. Seeing Robert again, just from across a room like that, brought old feelings, old memories surging back. That cautious joy when I'd realized I was pregnant. The cold sting of betrayal when Robert rejected me. Rejected us. Giving birth while getting a divorce had done a number on me. It had built a brick wall around my heart so effortlessly, so quietly, that I hadn't noticed it was happening until it was done. There were lots of reasons I hadn't dated much as a single mom, but that was the biggest one. How was I supposed to trust someone with my heart again? Better to keep it hidden. Safe.

"He missed out." Mitch put a plate of sandwiches on the island between us. "Your kid is great."

"She is." I took a sandwich—hot and crispy and slightly greasy with butter—and tugged it apart, watching the hot cheese stretch before I took a bite. I groaned in pleasure and Mitch smirked as he picked up a sandwich of his own.

"Gotta say, I love when I can put that look on your face."

I almost dropped the sandwich. This was the first time either one of us had alluded to what had happened in that hotel room, and if I'd been sober I probably would have said something snippy and shut him down. But my limbs felt loose from the vodka and my smile came much more easily than it usually did. So what the hell. "You're pretty good at putting that look on my face," I said. I held his gaze with a courage I would've never had sober, and for once he was the first to look away, clearing his throat and going back to the fridge.

"Still no beer." The refrain was a familiar one by now, and there was hardly any heat behind it.

"Sorry."

"No, you're not." He returned to the island with a bottle of water and another can of soda, which he passed to me. I never drank this much soda, but it meant I could put more vodka into my glass too, so I was all for it. We stood in silence on opposite sides of the island, braced on our elbows, eating grilled cheese sandwiches, and it was one of the best nights I'd had in a long time.

"Thank you," I said quietly. "For getting me out of there. I thought I could handle it, but . . ."

"Anytime." His voice was uncharacteristically serious, and when I locked eyes with him this time he looked like he had in that hotel room. Sincere. Open. That look made me catch my breath and wish that I hadn't had so much vodka. Something was happening here, and I wasn't sober enough to catch on. "I wish . . ." He sighed. "I wish I could have helped."

"What are you talking about?" I shook my head. "You saved my ass tonight."

Mitch shrugged. "No, I mean back then. When he left. I think about you going through all that alone and I . . ." A thundercloud passed over his face and he shook his head, his gaze going to the countertop.

"Back then?" I thought about those days, some eighteen years ago, when I'd tried to hold on to my marriage with both hands before realizing that what I was trying to preserve didn't even exist anymore. The helplessness I'd felt. "It's okay." I reached across the island. I couldn't quite reach him, but I laid my hand flat on the counter between us. "You're here now, right?"

He reached across the counter too, laying his hand over mine. "Yeah." My hand disappeared, warm and safe under his, and there was that feeling again, that I was protected. Also the feeling of wanting to climb him like a tree, which was only encouraged by the vodka swirling through my bloodstream.

I forced my swimmy brain back on topic. "Besides, I wasn't alone back then. My parents helped me get back on my feet, and Emily was a kick-ass babysitter when she was a kid." That made me do some quick math in my head. "Wait. You would have been what, twelve? How would you have helped out, exactly?" The thought of Mitch being a tween while I was divorced with an infant splashed a little cold water on the memory of that hotel room. For a minute there I'd forgotten about the cradle-robbing aspect of our relationship.

"Hey, you never know. My lawn-mowing skills back then were life changing." His chuckle was a low rumble, reminding me that he wasn't a boy anymore, warming up that splash of cold water. All I could do was smile back and resist the urge to turn my hand under his and thread our fingers together. Instead I leaned back, reclaiming my hand, and picked up another sandwich.

By the time we finished demolishing the plate of sandwiches, I'd mostly sobered up, though my blood was still humming from all the sugar I'd consumed. Mitch scheduled an Uber while I washed the minimal dishes. When his ride swung into the driveway, I got a text from Emily, saying she was bringing Cait home and that my ex-husband was a dick.

"Thanks again," I said at the front door. There was a beat of awkwardness where I wasn't sure what to do. Hug him? We weren't a couple, so a kiss goodbye seemed like a little much. I settled for squeezing his arm, hoping he'd understand it for the affectionate gesture it was.

He caught my hand in his, giving a reassuring squeeze back. "See you tomorrow."

Tomorrow. I closed the door and let my forehead thunk against it. God, I still had graduation day to get through too. This wasn't over.

I woke up the next morning about ten minutes before the alarm, snuggled up against my daughter. She'd done this a lot as a kid: running into my room in the middle of the night after a bad dream or when a thunderstorm got especially boomy. I'd throw back the covers and she would crawl underneath with me. She'd be my little spoon, and we'd be our little family of two united against whatever scary thing was out there in the night.

She'd outgrown that phase years ago. But this was a special day.

For a few moments I just watched her breathe. She'd been quiet when she'd gotten home from the reception last night. It was a lot to process, seeing—no, *meeting*—her father, and I hadn't wanted to push her. But sometime in the night she'd crept into my room and curled herself around my shoulder. Now I was the little spoon. She'd shot up around fifteen to be an inch or two taller than me, and now that I was reacquainted with Robert's height it made more sense.

The alarm blared on my nightstand, and I groped for my phone, hitting the snooze as Caitlin came awake beside me.

"Good morning, graduate," I teased. She groaned, hiding her face in her hands before stretching and scrubbing her hands over her face, waking herself up. She blinked sleepily at me.

"I don't like this."

Uh-oh. "Don't like what?" I'd expected her to be excited this morning, giddy even. But as she came fully awake her face crumpled and she snuggled into me. I put my arms around her while my senses went on high alert. What had Robert said to her last night?

"This," she said again, her voice quivering. "Graduating. It's all ending. Changing. I don't think I'm ready for this."

Ah. This was rite-of-passage graduation stress, not dealing-with-her-father stress. "Here's the thing." I held her closer, rubbing my palm up and down her arm. "No one's ever ready. For any of those big changes that life throws at you. You just have to meet them head-on and do your best. It's okay to be scared a little. If we all waited till we were ready, we'd never do anything."

"Yeah?"

"Yeah." I nodded emphatically, punctuating it with a kiss on top of her head.

"Okay." She sighed and snuggled in closer, more like the little girl she used to be, and that was okay. It was nice to see she still needed her mom.

"You're going to do great," I whispered against her hair.

"I hope so." Her voice was still small but stronger now. "I'm sorry about last night. About the whole thing with . . . with him."

"It's okay." I loosened my grip and rolled to my back, staring up at the ceiling. "Did you have a good time? Meeting him and all that?"

"I guess?" She rolled to her back too, echoing my movement. "I'm glad I got to meet him." She sighed. "I kind of wish he wasn't coming today. But I don't know how to uninvite him."

"You can't," I agreed. "But see, there you go. That's part of being an adult. Sometimes you make choices and you wish you could take them back, but you can't. You just gotta plow through them." I probably wasn't phrasing this advice very well, but I'd had a fair amount of vodka last night.

"Yeah." Another long sigh. "I'm sure it'll be fine. It's just . . . I thought I'd feel something. Like he'd be family, right? But he was just this guy. And he made you leave last night, and . . ."

"You saw that, huh?"

"Yeah. I don't want him to do that to you today. You belong there. He shouldn't make you feel like you don't."

"Oh, he won't," I said. "Don't worry." Sure, I'd fled from the reception last night at the sight of him, but now I was prepared.

And the hell if I was going to let that ghost from my past ruin the biggest day of my kid's life.

At least, that was the plan. There was a little ping of anxiety in the back of my mind, ready to turn into panic at any moment. But I wasn't going to let Caitlin see that. Even if I had to throw up in my purse later or something, I wasn't going to miss this day.

Speaking of which, it was time to get the day started. "Come on, graduate." I nudged her shoulder. "We've got time for eggs and pancakes before we have to get ready, if you want to help."

"Of course I want to help." She threw off the covers on her side of the bed. "You know I make better pancakes."

"Oh, you do not." But I grinned as I followed her out of the bedroom. Caitlin made terrible pancakes, but hope sprang eternal with that kid. And far be it from me to quash that kind of optimism.

Thirteen

I *wasn't a sundress* kind of person. Emily looked great in them, and our friend Stacey was a big proponent of them. But I was always more the trousers-and-twinset type at work, and on weekends lived mostly in jeans. Sundresses were twirly. Sundresses could show my scar.

But graduation was outside at the football field where there was no shade to speak of, and midmorning in June was just too hot for jeans or twinsets or any of it. So when I slipped into the end of a row of bleachers, off to the side where I could stay unobtrusive, I was wearing a flowered dress and heeled sandals, my hair blown out and up in a twist. I spotted Emily down in front, her head bent toward Simon's. He had some papers in his hands, so he was probably one of the ones giving a speech at commencement.

I sat quietly, waiting for the ceremony to start, while all around me families buzzed with life and laughter. Dads held bouquets of flowers for their graduating daughters—shit, I should have done that—and younger siblings bounced fearlessly on the bleachers and squinted into the sun, pointing out their graduating brother or sister in the crowd below. My heart thudded when I spotted Robert, a few rows down and to my right, toward the front like he had every right to be there. And here I was skulking in the back. My shoulders rolled forward as I tried to make myself smaller. I didn't want him to turn around and see me. See how much I wasn't part of this community.

Just then, Emily turned and through some kind of weird family psychic power spotted me. She made an exaggerated face of impatience and waved me toward her, pointing at the bleacher behind her, which was still empty. I shook my head, but that only made her frown more and wave harder, so I grabbed my bag and made my way down there before she sprained something.

"What the hell, April," she said once I'd picked my way down the rows and slipped in to sit behind her. "I was saving you this spot. Why were you sitting up there all alone?"

I shrugged; I didn't have a good answer for her. I also didn't want to draw too much attention to myself. This new seat put me almost directly into Robert's sight line—we were in the same row now, and he was just a few feet to my right. Too close. I turned my head a little to the left so I couldn't see him. So he couldn't see me.

"Hey, there you are." Mitch slid onto the bleacher beside me, bumping my left shoulder with his right one. "I was looking for you."

"Here I am," I repeated, trying for a brusque tone, but all the tension inside of me eased now that he was next to me. He was dressed much like he had been last night: jeans and a button-down shirt—light blue this time—his tie already loosened.

Mitch leaned forward, his elbows on his knees, but still looking at me. "How you feeling?" His voice was pitched low, just for me. "Headache?"

That forced a laugh out of me and I shook my head. "A couple glasses of water and some aspirin before bed. All good. Besides." I gave him a small smile. "I had plenty of bread and cheese in my stomach to soak up the alcohol."

His smile widened, lighting up his eyes. "You're welcome." I rolled my eyes in response, an automatic gesture, but his smile was infectious.

The ceremony began with a speech from the principal, and I leaned toward Mitch. "Are you giving a speech too?"

He snorted, which made Emily glance over her shoulder at us. She took one look at how close our heads were and raised her eyebrows with a small smile. I made a face at her and she turned back around. "Hell, no," Mitch said, as though he hadn't noticed Emily. "They leave that to the smart guys like Simon."

"Hey." My protest was low but vehement. "You're a smart guy." This was too much like that night in the hotel room, with Mitch confessing that his family thought he was nothing more than a mindless jock. I didn't like that.

"Shhhh," he said through his smile. "Don't tell anyone. You have to do more when they think you're smart." He nodded down at Simon, shuffling the papers in his hands, clearly preparing for his turn to speak.

"Good point." We shared a conspiratorial smirk before turning our attention back to the principal, who was still talking. Oh God, this was going to take forever.

Speech finally over, awards were given out next, and to my surprise, when Simon got up to speak, it was because he was presenting an English department award to Caitlin. He'd refused to have her in his Advanced Placement class, for fear of any appearance of favoritism, so it was nice for him to make this gesture now. "I didn't have the pleasure of having her in my class," he said, "but nonetheless I couldn't be more proud to present this award to Caitlin Parker." Polite applause covered her walk to the podium, and while he presented her with a small plaque the two of them spoke in low tones I couldn't hear. They shared a smile and then a hug, and I dashed some tears from my cheeks. She spotted us in the audience when she headed back to her seat and grinned in our direction. I waved, Emily clapped, and Mitch sent out a piercing whistle that made me start.

"What?" He grinned at me when I turned to him. "She's a good kid. I'm proud of her. This is about celebrating the graduates, right?"

"True." I cupped my hands around my mouth and shouted, "Great job, Cait!" A few families around us chuckled, and I tingled all over with adrenaline from yelling in a crowd like that. Instinctively my eyes darted to my right, and just like I suspected, Robert was looking my way. No, he was glaring my way. I hadn't been on the receiving end of that glare in a long time, but there was still a part of me that shrank at the sight of it.

"That's him over there, isn't it?" Mitch kept his smile on his face, like we weren't talking about my estranged ex.

I nodded. "And he's pissed. Not only did I make a spectacle of myself just now, but I called her Cait. He hates nicknames." I hated that I remembered that about him. That brain cell would have been put to better use remembering my high school locker combination.

"Wow. He sounds like more and more fun the more you tell me about him. Have you talked to him yet?" Mitch's voice was casual, but his eyes were intent, studying my face. When I shook my head, he relaxed a fraction. "Good." He wrapped an arm around me like it was something he did every day.

"What are you doing?"

"Quid pro quo, babe. You were my girlfriend last weekend. Now it's my turn."

"To be my girlfriend?"

"Funny." His fingers tightened on my shoulder.

"Okay, but . . ." I gave up on trying to get free; honestly I wasn't trying that hard. Something about his arm around me softened all my sharp edges. He was just so damn comfortable to be around.

But I still tried to protest. "We can't do this here."

"Sure we can. We've had practice."

The words were innocent, but my mind went straight to that hotel room. Probably not the practice he meant. But it flustered me all the same. "That was different. This is in front of the whole town. You're a teacher at my daughter's high school," I reminded him.

That only made him take my hand with his free one. "One: Your daughter doesn't go here anymore. That's what this whole graduation thing is about. Two: Who cares?"

That was probably the most simplistic argument I'd ever heard, but I couldn't refute it. Not when his arm around me felt so good and my hand in his made me feel like I could face anything. Or anyone.

The rest of the commencement ceremony passed uneventfully, if slowly, under a June sun that only got hotter as the morning went on. When it was Caitlin's turn to get her diploma Mitch and I both cheered like fans at a football stadium; all that was missing was face paint and those giant foam fingers. Simon turned in his seat toward us with a raised eyebrow while Emily quaked with laughter, though she clapped as loudly as she could too. She tossed a grin at us over her shoulder once we settled down. I grinned back, amazed at how much fun it was to be loud once in a while.

Once the ceremony was over, parents and children mingled on the football field along with the faculty, no one quite wanting the morning to end. My original plan had been to stay in my seat, maybe find Emily if I was feeling outgoing, but otherwise wait for Caitlin to be ready to go home. She had an afternoon of graduation-party hopping with her friends planned, so my job today was almost done.

But of course my plan had changed. I was with Mitch now, and he wasn't going to let me lurk in the back of anything. Instead he stuck by my side as we wove our way through the crowd to my daughter. On the way, though, I apparently needed to meet every teacher who had ever taught Caitlin at Willow Creek High. The weird guilty feeling I had, meeting these important people in her life so late in the proceedings, faded relatively quickly. I wasn't the only working mother they'd encountered, each of them assured me. And all of them seemed to give me bonus points for raising Caitlin as a single mother. This . . . surprised me. Hadn't Robert gotten to them first, last night? I'd expected him to have won them all over.

Eventually I caught up with Caitlin. Emily and Simon had gotten to her first, and her face was animated as she talked to them. Then she saw me, and her smile got even wider.

"Mom!" She waved enthusiastically, and my heart swelled.

"Congratulations, honey!" I caught her up in a hug. I couldn't put into words how proud I was. I loved every little thing about this moment: the way my hands slipped on the cheap polyester fabric of her graduation gown, the way she was taller than me now so I had to lift a little onto my toes to hug her. Her hair was down, hanging in long, dark curls that were going slightly frizzy in the heat, and I'm sure my blowout was starting to suffer the same way.

I adjusted her mortarboard, because that was something that

moms did, and I caught her eyes widening just slightly as she looked over my right shoulder.

"Oh! Hi!" Her voice was full of false cheer bordering on manic. Her eyes darted back to me, and at first I didn't look. I didn't need to. I didn't want to.

But I had to, didn't I?

So it was with a sense of resignation that I turned around and found myself face-to-face with Robert. To his credit he looked like I felt: prepared for this eventual encounter, but still startled when the moment arrived.

"April?" A tentative smile lifted his face, and rage swept through me. *No. You don't get to smile at me like that after all these years.* I took a step backwards and Mitch's hand was there, warm and strong at the small of my back. Where had he come from? Didn't matter. He was here now, and if I'd leaned back more, he would have held me up.

"Robert. Hi." I sounded . . . normal. My voice only shook a little as my eyes cataloged all the ways the man in front of me had aged. Just like when I'd seen him last night from a distance, those changes had been mostly good. But looking at him made me feel the passage of time acutely. We'd both grown older, but not together. Like we'd thought we would.

"You look great." He moved infinitesimally toward me, almost a twitch, like he was going in for a hug. I wasn't ready for that and so rocked back, shifting my weight, and would you look at that, I was right. Mitch held me up. His hand pressed harder into my back, then slid to rest around my waist. Giving me a united front to present.

"Thanks," I said with a confidence I didn't feel. "So do you." It killed me to give him that compliment, but what the hell.

"Thanks. Been a long time." Robert slid his left hand down his tie, smoothing it, and a gold band glinted on his wedding finger. So he'd remarried. Well, of course he had; we'd split up so long ago. Had he changed his mind about kids over the years? Did he have another family after he'd thrown Cait and me over? My breathing grew deeper, labored in my chest. Panic was starting to take over again, that same panic that had sent me out of the reception hall last night. I couldn't let Caitlin see me like this.

But a quick glance over my shoulder showed me that she'd moved away, walking down the football field, with Emily and Simon. Giving Robert and me a little privacy for this auspicious meeting. I wasn't sure if that made my whole panic situation better or worse.

But Mitch had no such intentions of giving me privacy. He shifted closer, his arm tightening around me, until Robert was all but forced to acknowledge him. "Oh. Sorry." Robert extended his hand. "Robert Daugherty."

Mitch met his handshake firmly, tucking me even closer as he did so, like I was in need of defending. Maybe I was. "Mitch Malone. Nice to meet you, Bob." My lips twitched at Mitch's use of a nickname, and I fought to keep a neutral expression. Also, Mitch's voice had gone very deep. Very masculine. He was playing this up, and I couldn't help but feel grateful. This encounter would have sent me sinking into the forty-yard line of this football field if I'd had to do it alone.

Robert pressed his lips together, but apparently decided against correcting Mitch. "I was just going to say hi to Caitlin, if that's all right. Congratulate her on winning an award; that's pretty great, isn't it?"

"It is." This was ridiculous; the two of us making awkward small talk about the child we'd created together. But what else did we have to talk about? "I'm very proud of her."

"You should be." His gaze lingered in our daughter's direction. "You did an amazing job with her, April. Everyone I've met here has said that."

"They did?" I tried to hide the surprise in my voice. I couldn't pick out most of her teachers in a lineup, and I'd just talked to most of them. I had to have been one of the least involved moms here.

"They did," he confirmed. He smoothed down his tie again. "Look. I'm sorry that I—"

"Don't." I held up a hand, surprised that it didn't shake. It was like my body was drawing strength from Mitch's when I needed it most. "You don't get to do that. Caitlin invited you because she wanted you here for this. It's not about us and what you may be sorry about."

"Yeah." He put his hands in his pockets, looking around idly. All around us were people who loved Caitlin, and who appreciated what I had done to raise her. It was just occurring to him that he'd had nothing to do with any of it. He may have come here to take a victory lap, try to gain some credit for the daughter he hadn't helped raise, but when it came down to it, Willow Creek—this town that I was planning to leave—had sided with me. I hadn't expected that at all.

"Are you heading home today?" This was good neutral ground. Logistics were always easier to discuss than emotions.

"Yes. I was planning to start the drive back after this." He turned that sentence into a question, like he was angling for something else, an invitation for him to join us in whatever celebration we'd planned.

Nope. "Where's home? Are you still in Indiana?" I hoped not, for his sake. That was a long-ass drive.

"Pennsylvania. A little north of Philly."

"Oh." That was closer than I'd expected. Closer than I wanted, honestly. All this time he'd lived a couple states—a couple *hours*—away and had never . . . I cut off that train of thought.

"That's not bad," Mitch said, clearly just as eager to shove Robert out of town as I was. I pressed my lips together to hide my smile. "That's what, two or three hours? Even if you hit a drive-through on the way out of town you can be home before dark."

"Yeah. Getting home before dark is good." Robert was floundering in the conversation, and I had no desire to rescue him.

"Great." Mitch was deliciously dismissive, and then an awkward silence fell, because we'd run out of small talk and there was no way to segue into anything else we could possibly discuss. *What's your second family like? Do you have kids with your new wife? Does she know where you are this weekend?*

I decided to have mercy on him. "Go talk to Caitlin," I said. "I'm sure she'd love to spend a little more time with you before you go."

Robert seemed surprised by the suggestion, and his smile was grateful. "Thanks. I'll do that. I . . . I appreciate you being okay with this, April. Honestly. I know I don't deserve—"

"It's fine." I cut him off, because this line of conversation was just like the one I'd had with Emily recently. I wasn't fine with it. Not at all, and if I talked about it any more the tears were going to come. And I was not going to cry in front of him. Never in front of him.

"If you wanted to take off, I can drop her by your . . ."

"No." The audacity of this guy. Trying to drive me off, when he was the interloper? All of my goodwill was almost burned away, but I managed to say one last thing. "Tell her to come find me when she's ready to go."

"Smart," Mitch said as we watched Robert walk away.

"Hmm?" I turned to him, eyebrows raised.

"Not letting him stick around. Or take Caitlin anywhere. I'm sure he's trustworthy and all, but . . ."

"Oh, I'm not sure of that. Not at all. And hell if I'm letting him know where I live."

"See?" Mitch dropped his arm from my waist, but before I could miss the heat he draped it back around my shoulders instead, giving me a one-armed hug. More casual. Less loverly. Probably for the best. "Like I said. Smart."

"That's me," I said absently. My attention was across the field as Robert reached Caitlin where she still stood with Simon and Emily. He spoke to Caitlin, and she instantly looked around until her gaze caught mine. I waved, and she waved back, the smile on her face genuine, if not huge. She was going to be okay. I could relax.

Mitch must have felt some of the tension leave my shoulders, and he tightened his grip. "You did great, babe."

"Don't call me that." I tried to resist him, but something inside me melted when he brushed a kiss on my temple. Oh, the hell with it. He was right: Caitlin wasn't a student here anymore.

Families had started filtering out now that everything was over, and Emily found me again a little while later.

"You okay?"

"I told you to quit asking me that." But my rebuke had no teeth. I kept my eyes on Caitlin, where she and her father sat together on one of the bleachers, talking. Their phones were out, scrolling through photos, passing them back and forth. Seeing them together like that, I could see the parts of Robert that were in Caitlin. The shape of her jaw, the line of her shoulders. I'd never noticed that before. "I'm good," I said, my eyes still on my daughter.

"Yeah. You are." Emily smirked. "You and Mitch looked great, by the way."

"Ha." Mitch had taken off a few minutes before, after asking roughly five hundred times if I could make it through the rest of the day without him. I brushed off his innuendo with a laugh and sent him on his way, sternly quelling the butterflies in my stomach.

"No, I mean it. When I talked to him last night he said he'd help you out, but he went above and beyond, right? He looked really convincing, pretending to be your boyfriend."

"Right." *Pretending.* The butterflies in my stomach thudded to their deaths. It had all been fake. For a few minutes there I had completely forgotten. And in those few minutes I'd felt better than I had in . . . well, probably ever.

"Hey, Mom."

I looked up from my phone. Caitlin stood in front of me, a disheveled graduate. The heat of the day had set in, and it was definitely getting to her. She'd shucked the cheap polyester gown and carried it over one arm, the mortarboard dangling from the same hand.

"Hey, baby," I said. "Need a hair tie?" Not even waiting for an answer, I started digging in my purse. Since our house had two long-haired women in it, there was always a handful of hair ties at the bottom of my bag.

"Please." She took the thin elastic band, dropping her graduation cap and gown to the bleacher next to me before catching her hair back in a ponytail. I glanced around while she did so.

"Where's . . . did your father take off?" I almost winced at the way I phrased the question. That was all her father did, her whole life. Take off.

But Caitlin just nodded. "Yeah, he said he needed to get on the road. Going home, I guess." Her voice was carefully neutral, and I tried hard to parse how she was feeling.

"Do you want to call him? If you want to spend a little more time, we can . . ." I had no idea how to finish that sentence. We can what, exactly? Have an excruciating lunch together? But this was Caitlin's day. If that was what she wanted, I would make it happen.

She waved a hand. "Nah." She picked up her stuff as I got to my feet, and we started the long walk to the parking lot. "I'm glad he came, though. It was good to talk to him. He said we'll stay in touch." She shrugged. "He's nice, I guess. But he's not family. I already have plenty of that here. You. Emily and Mr. G. And . . . you know, Coach Malone." She slipped a side-eye in my direction, and I groaned and let my head fall back on my neck.

"Not you too! I told you, there's nothing going on . . ."

She held up her hands. "I'm just saying! You went out of town with him last weekend. Not to mention, Toby told me last night that he saw you talking to Coach Malone a few weeks ago, after baseball practice. Was that when you started not dating him?" Her eyebrow went up, and I resented that she could do that. Something else she must have picked up from her father.

"Okay. I'll tell you again. I'm not dating Coach Malone." I drew in a deep breath. "But—and this is petty, so don't ever do this—it's possible that I pretended like I was today when I saw your father."

Caitlin smirked. "Smart."

I had no response for that, at least not one I wanted to share with my daughter. "Your teachers are great," I said, desperate for a subject change. "I'm sorry I wasn't like the other moms. You know, the ones that volunteered and did stuff like that."

She waved it off. "It's okay. It's not your thing. I know that. Like with the Ren Faire, remember? When I first started, I needed a chaperone?"

"Yeah, but . . ." My SUV was in sight, and I pushed the remote on my keychain, unlocking the doors. "We'd just been in the accident. I couldn't even walk. Emily handled that for me."

"She did. But, Mom." She dumped her stuff in the back seat and then climbed into the passenger seat. "Were you really going to volunteer?"

"Well, I'm sure I . . ." But it was my turn to trail off, because my kid knew me well. I didn't volunteer. I didn't get involved.

All these years I thought I'd been a good mom, had done a good job raising Caitlin on my own. But keeping to myself had meant missing a lot. And it was too late now.

"Yeah." Caitlin's voice was gentle, understanding even, and it was weird to be handled this way by my own kid. "But hey," she said. "Don't worry about it. Everything worked out, right? Emily did the Ren Faire with me, and she met Mr. G. So that's a happy ending."

"Good point." I smiled as I clicked my seat belt. "Things work out the way they're supposed to, I guess." I didn't want to follow that train of thought too far, because what other awful things in my life would turn out to be blessings in disguise? My car accident? My divorce? Everything in my life—good and bad—led to me being the person I was now. The life I had now.

And on days like this, that life didn't seem so bad.

Fourteen

For years, I'd looked forward to Caitlin's graduation day as an ending. The culmination of my job as a full-time mother, signaling the beginning of me regaining time for myself. With the date circled in red in the calendar of my mind, I thought that things would somehow be calmer, easier, once that day was behind us. After all, I'd successfully raised a daughter. She was poised to take her first steps out into the world, and I would be that proverbial empty nester.

It didn't work out that way, though. Instead of being an ending, graduation was just the starting bell on the summer, and I watched that next Saturday morning as Caitlin's friends picked her up and they headed down to Virginia for Beach Week. Recent high school graduates spending a few days unsupervised at the beach . . . what could go wrong?

"They're gonna be fine," I said to myself, not for the first time that morning. Hell, not for the first time in those five minutes. Kids went out of town for Beach Week all the time, and I was pretty sure none of them went with their mothers. Caitlin was responsible, and I was ninety-eight percent sure she wouldn't get arrested. This was good. This was practice for her leaving for college and being on her own.

Besides, I should be relishing the quiet. I'd taken this next week off too, to focus on home renovation projects. My to-do list was prepped, takeout menus were ready to go for the nights I didn't feel like cooking, I could even play as much bad hair metal as I wanted without my kid complaining. This was bliss.

That was what I told myself, anyway. But as I got ready that morning, I couldn't shake the feeling that the house felt empty. No Caitlin running out the door to Ren Faire rehearsal, no movie night to plan when she got home. There really was too much space in this house for just me.

My phone chirped on the kitchen counter with a text. Caitlin had left early that morning—had she forgotten something? But to my surprise it was Mitch. **Hey, where's your kid? I don't see her at rehearsal.**

Beach Week, I typed back. **Special dispensation from Simon to skip the next couple rehearsals.**

Ahhhh he's going soft. I call nepotism.

I snorted. But before I could respond he sent another text. **So when are we painting your living room?**

Oh my God. I'd forgotten all about that: the price I'd charged him for sharing that king-size bed in Virginia. Our weekend away seemed like so long ago now, and it wasn't like sharing that bed with him had been much of a hardship. Mitch had certainly made the experience worth my while. My cheeks heated in memory and I couldn't keep the smile off my face as I typed. **What a coincidence! That's what I'm starting on today. You're off the hook, though. I'm not holding you to that.**

No way. I don't break a deal.

Don't you have fight rehearsal right now?

Yep. These kids are hopeless. But we're done at 1, and I'll be over after that.

Well. I wasn't going to say no. The vaulted ceilings in my living room made it a bitch to do all by myself.

I had just finished taping out the baseboards when my doorbell rang a little before two. "Thank God you're here," I said as I opened the front door. "I severely overestimated what I could get done myself."

"So what color are we going with?" he asked. "Or do I even need to ask? It's some boring beige, right?"

I nodded with a long sigh and hefted one of the cans of paint. "Eggshell. It's . . ." I looked down at the little splotch of paint on the lid and tried to find a positive word to describe it. Something that would make me feel better about covering up these gorgeous blue walls. "Fine," I finally said. "It's fine."

Mitch snorted. "I can see you're stoked about it. Well, come on. Let's get it done."

"This first, though." I put down the paint can and reached for the white primer. "God, this is going to take forever."

"Well, it is if you're gonna spend all day bitching about it." But his grin took the sting out of the words. He took the primer out of my hand, opening the can and pouring the white paint out into a tray. As he loaded a roller with the primer he squinted up toward the ceiling. "I'm not going to be able to reach all the way up there, and I know you sure as hell aren't. You have a ladder?"

I nodded. "In the garage. I'll go get it."

"No, you won't." He handed me the roller as he shook his head in mock disgust. "You get started and I'll get it."

I tsked as I moved to the front wall by the window. "You know, I got along just fine without you for the past forty years," I called after him. "I can get my own ladder."

"Yeah, but you got me now, and I'm like a foot taller than you. Let me help."

"I'm not that short!" But if he heard me, he didn't react, and I huffed out a sigh. I'd lived most of my adult life on my own, and hadn't relied on a man for much of anything. I could change a tire, I relocated my own spiders, and I hired a handyman if there was a problem I couldn't tackle on my own. I felt like a proud feminist every time I did any of those things. But I had to admit that it was nice to have help. Not from someone I'd hired, but from a friend. Someone who helped out because he wanted to, not because I was paying him.

With Mitch's help, the work went smoothly. After a couple hours I took a break for some water and to check my phone. Caitlin had texted that they'd arrived safely at the vacation rental and were all checked in. I texted back the usual mom stuff: be careful, wear sunscreen, don't trash the place and make me lose my deposit. Next I did a quick spin through my email. I'd gotten on the local hardware store's mailing list, and they sent a newsletter out every weekend with sales and home renovation tips. I was looking over their latest installment when Mitch came into the kitchen, peering over my shoulder.

"Those bookshelves would look great in the living room."

I glanced up at him. "I'm moving out, remember? Why would I be putting bookshelves in?"

"Because they would look great," he said again. He took the phone out of my hand and scrolled through the instructions and schematics. "These look super simple too. We could knock them out in, like, a weekend."

"Maybe." I took my phone back. There was no maybe. My job was to make this house ready to sell. Not make it better or more comfortable. This house was no longer about me.

"I bet your place looks great," I said a little while later as I rolled another stripe of white primer, talking to distract myself from the pain of covering up the blue paint.

"What do you mean?" Mitch asked from where he stood at the top of the ladder. He'd almost finished cutting in the edges up near the ceiling.

"It's just, you've done so much to help me fix up my place. You do a lot of work on your own house?"

He snorted and shook his head. "I rent. It's nothing special. I'm not home all that much anyway. Between work and sports after school, and then the Ren Faire stuff in the summer . . ." His voice trailed off and I looked up to see him frowning at the paint he'd just laid down. Then he shook his head, clearing his thoughts. "My place is just my place. Lease gets renewed every February because why not, you know?"

"Oh." I squinted up the ladder at him. "You stick around here for your parents, then?"

"What's that?" He threw a glance down in my direction, and I wondered what I was doing. His personal life was none of my business. But that didn't stop me from asking.

"Just . . . you don't seem to be putting down roots here or anything."

He huffed out a laugh. "Nothing to put down. My roots have been here my whole life. You'd rather I lived with my parents?" He gave an exaggerated shudder, and it was my turn to give a weak laugh.

"Not necessarily. But you know. You're renting, you don't have any serious relationships here . . ." Come with me, I suddenly wanted to say. *Let's leave this small town together. Live somewhere else. Start over together.* But it was a crazy thought, and I squashed it immediately.

"I've known everyone in this town my whole life. If I haven't dated them by now, I'm not gonna. You know . . ." Up at the top of the ladder, Mitch put down his paintbrush and turned his full attention to me. "You're awfully interested in my personal life all of a sudden, Mama." That old nickname suddenly felt like a wall between us—I thought we'd moved past that kind of thing. There was a teasing spark in his eye, but his quirked eyebrow was clearly asking me what was up.

"No, I'm not." I loaded up my roller with more primer and turned my attention back to my living room wall and away from Mitch's personal life, something I had no right to. "Just making conversation."

"Uh-huh." But Mitch's attention was still on me. "No reason," he said.

"Huh?"

"No reason," he said again. "No reason to leave, you know? Things are good here. I like the kids."

That wasn't what I'd expected him to say. "The kids?"

"Yeah." He turned back to the wall, starting to paint again. "At first it was kinda funny, coaching my friends' little brothers, watching them grow up, knowing I'm having a part in making them better people. Same with the Ren Faire, you know? Kids who were in middle school when I started, getting older and becoming adults. I don't know, some crap about helping along the next generation. But bottom line, the kids are fun. This life is fun, you know?" He glanced down at me while reloading his paintbrush. "Why leave?"

I couldn't help but stiffen at the question—it was like he'd directed it at me. But it was plenty obvious that Mitch had a lot more fun in his life than I did. And a lot more reason to stay in Willow Creek than I did. "Sure," I said, making an attempt at agreement.

"Doesn't mean I want a mortgage, though," he said, the cheer in his voice telling me that our serious conversation was over.

I didn't push it. Instead I got back to work. "Still not doing those bookshelves," I muttered, just to be contrary and to see if I could get him to laugh.

It worked. A chuckle floated down from the top of the ladder. "We'll see about that."

By the time the sun had started to dip in the sky, we'd put a coat of primer over the entire living room, and all there was to do was wait for it to dry. My stomach rumbled obscenely while we cleaned up, and I realized I hadn't even thought about dinner. Thank God for my takeout menu collection.

I tilted my head at Mitch. "Do you like Thai?" It was my secret favorite, something I treated myself to for lunch at work because Caitlin's palate hadn't developed past that neon-orange sweet and sour chicken from our local Chinese place. But she wasn't here, so I could indulge at home.

I expected Mitch to have a similar reaction to Cait, but he considered it and nodded. "Not my first choice, but I could go for that. If you want to finish up here, I'll go pick it up."

"You don't have to—" But I bit my tongue. This was going to be the ladder argument all over again. "Thanks, that would be great."

I knew it would take him at least a half hour to pick up dinner, so I used that time to take a long, hot shower. My mind wandered as I shampooed my hair. Today had gone so much better with Mitch here. Just the primer would have taken me the entire weekend. Of course, thinking about Mitch while I was in the shower brought back memories of when Mitch was in the shower with me. My hands started to wander along with my mind, pretending my hands were his, remembering the way he'd touched me. The way he'd made me feel.

I shouldn't think like this. That had been a one-weekend thing, brought on by heightened emotion and being in an enclosed space with a man who looked like that. It certainly wasn't going to happen again. He had a revolving list of women on his calendar and I was too old to give him those kids he liked and would certainly want someday. But even those thoughts didn't cool me down, so instead I indulged myself, retreating into the memory of his hands, his mouth on my skin while the hot water beat down on my body in time with my fingers between my legs. The orgasm that rushed through me shook me so hard I leaned against the cool shower wall for support, and I turned the shower to cold to calm myself down. Mitch would be back soon. I needed to get a grip.

When Mitch arrived with the food I was significantly more relaxed, wearing my comfiest sweats and with my hair piled on my head in the messiest bun known to man. I was ready to eat takeout and do absolutely nothing else with my evening. When he came inside he had the takeout bag in one hand and a six-pack of beer in the other. He made a show of moving some of my ciders out of the way to make room for his beer in my fridge.

"Finally." He handed me a cider and took one of his beers out before closing the door. "Something decent to drink around here."

I shrugged and cracked open my cider, handing him the bottle opener. "You don't know what you're missing."

"Apple juice, that's what I'm missing. And believe me, I'm not missing a thing."

"Your loss." I took a swig and started unpacking the food. "God, this smells so good." I opened my container of noodles and my stomach rumbled in response to the scent of the savory brown sauce, obviously agreeing.

We sat together at one end of the dining room table and at first there wasn't a lot of talking as we both inhaled an obscene amount of noodles. I was starving, since I'd been working most of the day without a break. Mitch had done the same, plus he'd come here straight from rehearsal.

"How is rehearsal going?" I asked. "Did you and Simon end up changing that fight thing you were talking about?"

Mitch lit up, as though he was pleasantly surprised that I remembered. "Oh, yeah! We did. Decided to let a couple of the younger kids throw each other around for a change."

I laughed, digging in my carton for another bite of noodles and a stray piece of broccoli. "Smart. And it's going okay? You said the kids are hopeless."

"Oh, they are," he said cheerfully. "But it's a good kind of hopeless. They'll get it. We've still got a few more weeks to practice before Faire starts."

That reminded me . . . "Is it too late to volunteer for this whole Ren Faire thing?"

Mitch had just taken a bite of his super-spicy pad Thai and he froze, his eyes going wide and his jaw stopping mid-chew. "Are you serious?" The words were muffled by the mouthful of noodles, and he coughed and took a swig of his beer. "I didn't think volunteering was your thing."

"It's not. But . . ." I wasn't sure how to express it, but Caitlin's words had stayed with me. Maybe it was too little, too late to get more involved in my daughter's life, but I had to try.

"No, this is great." He put down his chopsticks and rubbed

his hands together like a gleeful mad scientist. "Let's call Simon. Do you sing? I bet we can get you in a corset by next weekend, and—"

"Wait. What? No." I held up a hand. "I didn't mean like that." God, no. The thought of being in costume? Playing a character? Spending the day speaking in a questionable accent? I fought against a shudder. "I mean like your mother said she did. Taking tickets or something."

"Oh." He deflated slightly but rallied quick. "Okay, that's less fun, but sure. I think Chris coordinates all that stuff. You know Chris, Emily's boss at the bookstore?" He didn't wait for my nod before continuing. "She's back from Florida for the summer now, so you should drop by the bookstore and talk to her about it."

"Hmmm." I crunched into a spring roll. "Yeah, I'll do that." The thought of working a ticket booth shouldn't make me nervous, but it did. Everything made me nervous. Frankly, I was getting tired of being nervous all the damn time.

The best thing about takeout was that there were hardly any dishes to do, so after I washed the chopsticks and recycled the containers, the kitchen was just as clean as it had been this morning. I folded the kitchen towel and hung it up while Mitch leaned in the doorway between the kitchen and the dining room.

"I was gonna ask if you wanted to go out to Jackson's tonight, but . . ." He gestured to my hair and my outfit, neither of which telegraphed a going-out vibe.

I shook my head with a smile, ignoring the little flutter that flared up in my chest. "No, thanks. You'll have to pick up girls all on your own tonight."

He rolled his eyes and crossed his arms over his chest. "You know that's not the only reason I go to Jackson's, right?"

"Sure, but I bet it's top five." I echoed his stance, leaning one hip against the kitchen counter.

He opened his mouth to object, but instead he just laughed. "Okay, maybe. Only when I have to go alone, though." He raised his eyebrows meaningfully, and the flutter in my chest grew uncomfortable. I didn't want to think of him picking up someone else. But I didn't want to go out with him either. Sure, we'd hung out there together before. But the energy between us felt different now. What if someone saw us standing a little too close to each other? What if someone said something?

So I made a disgusted noise in the back of my throat and started herding Mitch toward the front door. "You're on your own tonight, I'm afraid. I have very important plans with my bed." Whoops. That came out wrong.

"Now, wait a second." He turned to me when we got to the front door. "Maybe I spoke too soon. Your plans sound a lot more fun. Tell me more." His voice went all rumbly, and this close, that massive chest of his was *right there*. I knew what was under that T-shirt and I wanted more. Taking care of myself in the shower earlier hadn't been enough, apparently. Now my mind was on the drawer in my nightstand, and the box of condoms I'd tucked in there recently. Just in case.

For a long moment silence hung between us, and I was aware of every breath we took, practically in unison, while his bright blue eyes darkened with promise. It was just the two of us here. It would be so easy. So goddamn easy to reach for him. To ask him to stay. I could practically taste his skin, feel the heat of him over me, and every part of me ached for it. Ached for him.

This was a bad idea, I knew that. This was a line that I shouldn't cross. Not a second time.

But I was too caught in the blue of his eyes and the brilliance of his smile, so instead of pushing him out the door like I should, I nodded back toward the kitchen. "There's a couple beers left, you know. If you wanted to stick around and . . . finish them."

His eyes never left mine as he stepped closer, one hand curling around my waist. "You know, I think I'd like that."

"Good." I leaned around him to throw the bolt on the front door, which shifted my body so that I was flush against him. He sucked in a breath and his hand slid to the small of my back, pulling me closer.

This didn't change anything, I told myself as I led him to my bedroom. We were still just friends. Just friends, I reminded myself as his mouth was hot on my skin, as I pulled his T-shirt over his head, as he laid me back on my bed. This was all meaningless, I thought as his fingertips trailed across my skin, cupping my breasts while his tongue licked up inside me.

As I dissolved under his hands and his mouth, as he groaned out my name while pushing inside me, as I dug my nails into his back to pull him closer, harder into me, I took comfort in knowing that wall around my heart was still intact.

This didn't change anything.

We were still just friends.

After our impromptu sleepover and leisurely breakfast on Sunday, we finished the living room, painting over the primer with the acceptable-but-boring Eggshell. Monday morning I took all the painter's tape off the edges of the wall, waiting for Mitch to come by to help me move the furniture back. When he got there he didn't even knock, just came right in the front door. Making himself at home.

"So what are we working on today . . ." His voice trailed off and I heard his footsteps come toward me in the kitchen. I glanced over my shoulder to see a puzzled expression on his face. He took an exaggerated sniff of the air. "What's that . . . is that . . . ?"

I shrugged. "Nothing exciting. Pork shoulder in the slow cooker again."

"Yeah, but . . ." A grin crawled up his face. "You made this for me?"

"I did not," I said a little too quickly. "I made it for me. I can't afford takeout every night, you know." It'd seemed like a good idea when I'd started it last night, making a big slab of meat for us to devour at the end of the day, but not if he was going to be all smug about it.

He nodded firmly, moving to the coffeepot to pour himself some coffee, which of course I had also made extra of, in case he'd want some. "It's for me."

His conviction was maddening, but when he was like this it was easier to just not argue with him. While he sipped his coffee I went back to what I was doing when he got there: staring at the kitchen with a critical eye.

"You sure I shouldn't do anything in here?"

He shrugged. "Like what?"

"I don't know. But now that the rest of the house is starting to look better, it looks kind of dingy in here, don't you think?"

"I don't know that I'd say that." He leaned his elbows on the kitchen island and studied the room with me. "Your appliances aren't all that old, and the floor's in good shape. But it's up to you."

"Yeah." I decided to table the thought for now. One room at a time, one project at a time. "Let's get the living room put back together."

The living room was so much brighter now that it wasn't blue anymore. The Eggshell wasn't quite as soulless as I'd feared, and once we'd put the furniture back the way I liked it, the whole room looked larger and sunnier. It wasn't bad, but I wasn't sure if it was me. But it didn't have to be. I wasn't making these changes for myself. I was making them for whoever owned this place next.

We prepped the dining room on Monday afternoon and it was painted by Wednesday evening. Mitch brought over a second six-pack of beer, so my fridge remained stocked. I gave him shit for it, more because he expected it from me than because I wanted to.

Wednesday night we ordered a pizza and demolished it sitting on the floor in the living room while watching a superhero movie. Then we had sex on my living room floor because Mitch's arms reminded me of Captain America's. He didn't seem to mind.

We took Thursday off from home renovations; Mitch said he had errands to run, and I had book club that night anyway, so I spent the day lazing on the couch, finishing the book just in time. I'd been busy that week, what with doing all the work on the house and doing the guy helping me out. Who had time to read?

It was Caroline's night to host, and when I walked into her house, there was a mountain of cupcakes on her dining room table.

"My God, woman." I reached for one and accepted the glass of wine she handed me. "Did you go to an orgy or something? This is a lot of cupcakes." But I wasn't complaining, because she'd made red velvet again. My favorite.

"Oh, these aren't mine," Caroline said, mischief sparking in her eyes. "These cupcakes are all yours, April."

I froze, the cupcake halfway to my mouth. "Excuse me?"

She scoffed. "Oh, come on. You think I haven't noticed a certain red pickup truck in your driveway since, oh, the minute your daughter left for Beach Week?"

"Wait. Red pickup?" Marjorie turned to me with a grin. "That wouldn't be a certain baseball coach I saw you with at graduation, would it?"

"Oh, *really?*" Caroline's smile was wider than Marjorie's, and the combined force of their gazes was like a spotlight.

Marjorie nodded emphatically at Caroline. "You should have seen them, they looked so cute together. Screw the book, I'm going to need to hear more about you and Mitch Malone."

I'd heard the phrase "blood running cold" before, but I'd never experienced it firsthand. "I . . ." I put the uneaten cupcake on the table, barely having the presence of mind to put a napkin down first. "It wasn't . . ."

But the conversation about me had, oddly, moved on without me. "You know, I always say it's the quiet ones that you have to look out for," Caroline practically sang. "They're the freakiest."

"Who's the freakiest?" Oh good. Everyone was here now: the last two stragglers had just shown up and Caroline made a beeline to the living room to meet them, where they were going to get a recap of my love life. Except it wasn't my love life. It was an elaborate lie with a side of friends with benefits, and I'd been caught.

I spun for the hallway, looking for the bathroom. I needed to hide. Possibly for the rest of the night. The rest of my life.

"Hey." Marjorie hooked her hand around my arm, stopping me. The smile had fallen from her face as she caught what had to be a wild look in my eyes. "I'm sorry. I was just teasing. I'm happy for you if—"

"It's not," I blurted out. "I mean, *we're* not. He's a friend. I don't know what you think you saw at graduation, but it wasn't that." I was lying. She saw exactly what she thought she did. But right now some light gaslighting was preferable to explaining the weird tangle of subterfuge that had become my relationship with Mitch.

A peal of laughter came from the living room, and I winced. "I can't do this," I whispered. I didn't realize I'd said the words out loud, but Marjorie's grip on my arm relaxed and turned into a pat on my shoulder.

"Go to the bathroom." Her voice was low and urgent. "Take some deep breaths and a few sips of water. I'll shut them up out here, okay? Give me five minutes."

I nodded dumbly and fled to the back of the house. Once I was safely locked in the bathroom I leaned against the door, breathing deeply, trying to slow my heart rate before it pounded all the way out of my chest. I barely recognized the woman in the mirror. She looked wild; she looked miserable. God, the irony. This had been one of the best weeks of my life, because Mitch had been in it. But now all I wanted was to erase the last few days. Scrub out the evidence of the red truck in my driveway.

My phone chimed in my purse, and speak of the devil. I unlocked my phone to see a picture taken at a big-box home improvement store. **If you're still worried about your kitchen, we can replace your cabinet fronts with something like these. What do you think? I can pick them up tomorrow and bring them by.**

The cabinet doors looked nice, and Mitch was right. They'd look perfect in my kitchen, and it would achieve exactly what I was looking for: maximum effect with minimum effort. It was perfect. He was perfect.

But I knew what I had to do, and a sob erupted from my throat as I started typing. **I'll think about it, thanks. But I don't need any more help. You've done enough.** Boy, had he ever. It wasn't his fault that the whole neighborhood had clued in to what was going on. I should have seen it coming. But I couldn't let it continue.

My phone chimed in my hand. **You sure? Because it's been fun. I don't mind.**

I'm good, I typed back. **See you at the Faire in a few weeks.** The start of Faire was almost a month away. Maybe by the time I saw him again I'd have my head on straight. Mitch wasn't for me, and never had been. Really, I should have been thanking my neighbors for waking me up from this fantasy I'd been lost in these past few days.

I turned off my phone, not waiting for any response, and shoved it back into my purse. The giggling out in the living room had stopped, so I washed my hands and pressed them, cold and wet, to my overheated cheeks. Then I smoothed out my hair and unlocked the door. It was all going to be okay. Time to stop being distracted by Mitch and his tight T-shirts and the amazing way he kissed me.

My heart only hurt a little as I scooped up a glass of wine on the way to the living room. I left the cupcake where it was.

Fifteen

On the edge of town—not toward the highway, where Jackson's was located, but the other side, where the back roads snaked out toward wine country—there was a grassy field of undeveloped land. It backed onto some woods, and the only remarkable thing about it was that the entire acreage, woods included, was fenced in, with a padlocked gate. Eleven months out of the year you wouldn't give it a second look if you drove past it.

But for four incredible weeks, that field transformed and became something completely new. The padlocked gate stood wide open, and the fence around the perimeter of the field was festooned with banners. But it wasn't the field that was special. No, the field itself was just the parking lot. The real magic lay on the far side of the field, the part that backed up to the woods. Wide paths led into the trees where, for four weeks of the year, it was home to the Willow Creek Renaissance Faire.

Magic wasn't my thing. I wasn't someone who had a lot of time or energy to devote to make-believe. So I was the first to admit that I didn't get it. I didn't understand how or why my sister had fallen in love with these woods and this event. I figured it was just something that she did because it was important to her husband. Simon had helped start the thing, after all, and it had grown into a big responsibility that gave back to the community.

I could understand it on those terms, and that was what had me donning a red volunteer's T-shirt and showing up for duty on opening day. I reported to my station selling tickets at the box office: a plywood booth painted by high school kids to look like a gray stone castle. There was a crude countertop built inside with a cashbox and two high-backed stools for the volunteers.

"It's pretty simple. One price across the board for the tickets, and kids under five get in free." My booth-mate, a woman named Nancy, waved me to the empty stool and I perched on it. Nancy was seventy if she was a day. Her hair was bright and red and there was no way it was natural. I liked her already.

I stretched my bad leg in front of me, massaging the muscle just above my knee through my jeans. I'd stopped wearing shorts after the accident, but the day was already warm, on the way to even hotter. I may have miscalculated here.

Clearly, Nancy thought so too. She looked pointedly at my jeans. "Honey, you're going to get heatstroke in those."

I waved a hand, trying to look unconcerned. "Probably. I'll be okay." My attention went to the parking lot, which was quickly filling up with cars. I checked the time on my phone. "We don't open till ten, right?" That was a half hour from now. Why were all these people here already? And why were they just hanging out in the parking lot instead of coming up to buy tickets?

Nancy nodded. "That's right. The early folks are here though, and they're getting ready. Watch." She leaned back on her stool. "I'm telling you, we have the most fun job of everyone. The people-watching here at the front makes it all worthwhile."

"Really?" I shifted a little uncomfortably. This may have been a mistake. Volunteering to man the front gate wasn't exactly getting involved in my daughter's activities. My sister and brother-in-law practically ran this whole thing, and I hadn't seen either one of them. Nancy was obviously enthused, but for what? To sell tickets to people? Where was the people-watching fun in that?

It didn't take long to understand what she meant. Because it wasn't a normal crowd of people lining up to buy tickets. Well, sure, there were normal people. Families with little kids, or married or dating couples, all dressed in cool summer clothes for a day in the sun—those kinds of people lined up in droves. But just as often, the families or couples or groups of friends were in costume. I'd spent those last few minutes before the gate opened spying on the people in the parking lot, who threw the doors of their cars or SUVs or minivans wide, taking out hoopskirts and wide leather belts and elaborate headdresses. These attendees spent a good fifteen minutes to a half hour assembling a costume. I watched one woman get out from behind the wheel of her minivan wearing what looked like a calf-length nightgown that came dangerously close to sliding off her shoulders. By the time she was done she looked like royalty.

I watched all these people get dressed out in the open, building layer upon layer of their outfits, with something between amusement and wonder. For all the years I'd lived here in Willow Creek, the closest I'd come to being part of the Renaissance Faire was on the furthest fringes. I'd run Caitlin's costumes to the dry cleaner's and done some extra laundry consisting of chemises and long stockings. I remembered Emily going to and from the Faire wearing basically the same nightgown-looking thing that the woman in the minivan had worn. Now from my high-backed stool in this little box office I was still on the fringes, but as we started selling tickets to grown men dressed as pirates and women dressed as queens (and women dressed as pirates and men dressed as queens) their excitement was palpable. They'd come to play. And I couldn't help but smile back as their excitement became infectious.

Before I knew it there was a tap on my shoulder, and I turned my head to see a man I didn't know, but he was wearing a red volunteer shirt like I was.

"April, right? I'm Mike. Your replacement."

"What? It's one already?" I checked my phone in confusion. How had I already been here four hours?

"Yep." He jerked a thumb over his shoulder. "You're free."

I relinquished my seat and Nancy waved goodbye. "You should walk around a little before you go," she said. "Take in the festival."

"You sure you don't need a break?" It seemed odd that I had a four-hour shift while Nancy was here for the entire day. She was easily my mother's age—wouldn't this wear her out? But she waved me off with a laugh.

"I've been doing this since the start. Best part of my year, seeing everyone come in. You go on now."

I wasn't going to argue. Besides, now that I'd gotten up my stomach growled, and there was plenty of unhealthy Faire food inside. I followed the other attendees who had arrived down the path under a canopy of trees festooned with colored banners. I caught a flash of yellow out of the corner of my eye, so I turned in that direction, heading for a small stage set up in an alcove. A group of girls in yellow dresses were on the stage, singing in beautiful a cappella harmony, and my heart swelled because there in the middle of the group was my girl. Caitlin was easily the tallest so she was in the back of the group, but my mother's ears could pick out her voice in the harmonies. I leaned against a tree, not too close. I didn't want her to see me. The last thing I wanted to do was distract her.

Once they'd finished singing and hopped down from the stage, her eyes caught mine and flew wide. She said something to the girl beside her before taking off toward me, skirts flying, enthusiasm making her seem so much younger.

"Mom!" She shut her mouth with a giggle, and when she spoke again it was in an exaggerated English accent. "Honored Mother! I did not expect you! What a pleasure it is to see you on this fine day!" She gave me a deep curtsy, her mannerisms that of a woman instead of that giggling girl, but when she stood up again her eyes still danced with merriment.

Oh, God. I was not doing this. I was not doing the whole accent thing. And I didn't have to, since I wasn't in costume. "Oh yeah," I said, as nonchalantly as I could. "I'm helping out this summer. I must have forgotten to tell you."

She raised her eyebrows. "I think not," she said, accent still in place. She was good. "I believe you failed to tell me on purpose, so that you might surprise me."

"You're probably right." I gave her some unenthusiastic jazz hands. "Surprise." Having a conversation like this was unsettling, like I was speaking one language and she was speaking another. But the hell with it.

Caitlin laughed again, and even her laugh was in character. I was impressed. "It's a wonderful surprise. Do Captain Blackthorne and Emma know that you are here? You should find them as well."

"Captain . . ." I shook my head but then the penny dropped. Simon and Emily. Of course. I knew he was a pirate, but I'd forgotten his character name. "Do you know where they are?"

She shook her head. "Emma is often at the Chaucer Stage, where the Shakespeare scenes are acted. And of course the Captain participates in the human chess match at two of the clock. She often cheers him on then. But at this moment I know not where they are."

"Great, okay." I looked down the path that went through the middle of the Faire. I could probably just walk around for a bit, find something to eat, and catch my sister at the chess match thing. I turned back to Caitlin. "Would it be too out of character to give your mom a hug?"

Caitlin blinked quickly, shaking her head. My arms closed around her and she squeezed me tight. "You sounded great," I whispered.

"Thanks, Mom," she whispered back in her normal voice. "I'm so glad you came."

"I'm here all four weekends," I said as we parted. "I'll see you around."

Caitlin dipped into another curtsy, back in character. "Enjoy your day, madam!"

I wasn't going to curtsy back in jeans, so I just waved as I set off down the path.

"Never again in jeans," I said to myself a few minutes later. Maryland in the middle of July was hot as hell, and wearing jeans outside all day was probably the definition of insanity. The heavy, confining denim stuck to my thighs, and I was starting not to care about the scar on my leg. Vanity was one thing, but there was also the very real possibility of dying of heatstroke here. I would never doubt Nancy again.

I distracted myself with a frozen lemonade purchased from a fellow volunteer at a small kiosk, and while I fought the brain freeze I wandered the lanes of the Faire, admiring handmade jewelry and leather goods. Before long I heard the thumping sound of a hand drum in the distance, and I followed the sound. I knew that drum and the music it accompanied.

Before long I'd arrived at the Marlowe Stage, where a show had just begun. A trio of kilted musicians were playing a set of slightly naughty drinking songs and Irish standards. I tossed my empty lemonade cup in a nearby trash can and entered the glade where the Dueling Kilts were about midway through their set. But I didn't take a seat at one of the long benches meant for the audience. Instead I skirted around the back of the crowd, to a tall, slender man wearing black jeans and a black T-shirt, his red hair mostly eclipsed by a backwards-facing baseball cap (black, natch). His face lit up when he saw me.

"April, hey."

"Daniel." Daniel MacLean was the band's manager and he traveled with them. I'd only met him a couple of times, but I liked him. He was a quiet, steady man, very organized and business oriented. Friendly without being effusive. He didn't offer a hug or a handshake when he saw me; a friendly nod was enough for the both of us.

The same could not be said of his girlfriend.

As the set came to a close Daniel leaned toward me. "She's at the merch table. I'll send her over." He threaded his way through the crowd while musicians onstage collected tips and chatted with the audience. I tried following Daniel's progress, but he was quickly swallowed up by the crowd and the trees. As a result, the only warning I had was a high-pitched squeal before I was almost bowled over by a tackle-hug from a blond woman wearing voluminous skirts.

"Oh my *God*! April! What are you doing here?"

"Hi to you too, Stace." I laughed as I steadied myself, hugging her back. "It's been a while."

"I was just home at Christmas." Stacey adjusted her bodice as we broke apart, tugging at the chemise underneath it and making sure everything was covered. She was much more well-endowed than I was—Stacey was the kind of woman who could really fill out a corset. Between her outfit and her blond hair, curled and held back from her face, she was soft curves everywhere. A native of Willow Creek and one of Emily's best friends, Stacey had run off last summer with the two loves of her life: the Renaissance Faire and Daniel MacLean.

I nodded. "That was seven months ago, that qualifies as a while."

Stacey crinkled her nose at me and stuck out her tongue. "Whatever." She took in my red T-shirt. "So you're a volunteer now? Who talked you into that? Simon or Emily?"

"Maybe I just wanted to get involved in my community," I said primly.

She studied me carefully for a moment, then burst into laughter. "Yeah, that's not it. So are you done for the day? Want to get a drink?"

"Yes, and absolutely. And one of those funnel cake things before we go see the human chess match, what do you think?"

"Oh, that sounds perfect." She waved at Daniel across the way. She pointed at me and then toward the path, and he waved us off. "Let's go." She took my arm and together we headed down the lane.

"So that seems to be going well." I nodded back toward the Marlowe Stage and Stacey's smile lit up her whole body.

"It really is." She sighed and hugged my arm closer, and I patted her hand. I'd seen her at her worst, and Mitch and I had taken her to the Maryland Renaissance Festival last summer so she could make up with Daniel. It was good to see her so happy.

Shit. Mitch.

I'd done my best to not think about him lately, with varying degrees of success. I'd seen him briefly across the bar at Jackson's when we'd all gone out for Emily's birthday the weekend before, but we hadn't spoken. Not talking to him felt more and more like a breakup, which was wrong since we'd never been together. Things had gone back to normal, to the way they'd been before that night he saved me from that annoying guy in the gray suit at Jackson's. He was back to the bevy of women he rotated through, and I was back to my extensive vibrator collection.

See? Normal.

Normal kind of sucked.

"Are you all right, love?" We'd run into Emily on the way to the chess match, and concern creased her brow when my steps faltered on the path.

"Yeah," I said. "Fine." I was not fine. I'd caught sight of Mitch at the edge of the chess field. Kilt. Boots. Very long sword. Lots and lots of muscled, golden skin. It had become hard to breathe when faced with a sight like that. But I was stubborn. I was going to play this off. "Just tripped on . . . on a twig."

Stacey nodded knowingly. "One does need to watch one's step around here." She'd slipped back into an accent that matched her ensemble, much like Emily. I was the only one in our little group dressed like a civilian, and next to these two my jeans and T-shirt was the outfit that stood out.

We reached the benches that ringed the chess match, and I got a good look at the field—a roped-off patch of land painted in alternating white and grass-colored squares. For all that Mitch had talked about rehearsing this year's show that took place here, and for all that Emily had told me about what it was like to watch it, I'd never actually seen it in action, and while part of me was fascinated, the rest of me tried not to look at Mitch and wished I were anywhere but here.

Emily ran ahead to the chess field itself, and a man dressed in red and black, wearing a hat with a huge red feather, went to greet her. It took me a second to recognize Simon, and then only because I'd seen pictures of him in costume on social media and that one video on Mitch's phone. Emily's mind-mannered English teacher husband was transformed into a roguish pirate. It wasn't just the outfit, though photos didn't do justice to how good he looked in leather pants. His smile, the way he moved, everything about him was different. I watched him bow over Emily's hand before drawing her in for a kiss and I couldn't keep from smiling.

"God, those two." Stacey blew a lock of hair off her forehead and led me to one of the benches toward the back, away from the tourist crowd. "Just obnoxious, don't you think?" She'd dispensed with the accent; it was something that came and went with her. Must come with living this life on the road.

"Ahh. It's kind of cute." I followed her to sit on the end of the bench, brushing the surface with my hand before sitting down. "About as cute as you and Daniel, I bet."

"Guilty." She grinned at me and flapped her skirts around her knees in an attempt to cool off. "I mean, we try to keep it to a minimum, but you've seen him. I can't keep my hands off him."

"Hmm." I frowned as I looked at Stacey. Sweat beaded her hairline and her cheeks were flushed. I was hot too, and sweating like crazy, of course. But I wasn't wearing a million skirts and a restrictive bodice like she was. "You okay?"

"Oh, sure. Just a little warm. But you know, it's July and all that."

"How long till the show starts?" I checked my phone: five minutes to two. "I'll be right back, okay?"

The tavern was just across the way, and it didn't take long for me to duck under its canopy. They were doing brisk business, but the red-shirted volunteer caught my eye almost immediately.

"Water?" He was a mind reader, bless him.

"Please." I held up three fingers, and he passed three icy cold plastic bottles of water across the bar to me. When I dug into my pocket for cash to pay, he scoffed.

"Nope. Volunteers get free water, you kidding me?"

"Eh, I'm feeling generous." I stuck a five into the giant tip jar, and another volunteer rang an obnoxiously loud bell.

"Huzzah to the generous tipper!" Her voice was as loud as the bell, and I tried not to swear. Talk about no good deed going unpunished.

I jogged back to the chess field and slipped into my seat next to Stacey, passing one of the bottles to her.

"Oh, you are the best!" She uncapped the bottle and drank three long swallows, then screwed the lid back on. "Thanks for that. I keep forgetting to get water."

"In this heat? It's a wonder you're still alive." That came out harsher than I'd intended; the heat was making me cranky. But Stacey was used to me, so she just batted me on the shoulder while I took a gulp of my own water.

"Good morrow, ladies."

Of course. Of course Mitch would choose that moment to approach us. Of course he would wait until I had a mouthful of water before he came over here, all shirtless and kilted and golden-haired and Scottish accented. Was he trying to drown me here?

But Mitch wasn't looking at me. While I struggled to swallow my water, wishing desperately for gills, Stacey bounced to her feet and gave him a deep curtsy, and he turned his smile to her.

"Good morrow, sir!" Stacey trilled as she offered him her hand. "I cannot tell you how good it is to see you again, Marcus MacGregor. It has been too long."

"It has indeed." He took her hand and bowed over it, his lips brushing the top of her hand. I felt an answering jolt of heat even though he wasn't touching me. I knew what those lips felt like. I wanted a refresher.

Nope. No lips. Stop thinking about his lips.

"Come to see the fighting, eh? I do hope you have a strong stomach!" Mitch—or Marcus, I guess—spoke in a deep, rumbling accent, the r's rolling to amazing effect. I squirmed in my seat while trying to not be obvious about it. And he was full of crap. Strong stomach? Pretty sure Simon wasn't letting him perform a ritual disemboweling twice a day on Faire weekends.

I must have made some noise—a scoff, probably—because Mitch turned to me. "And how are you enjoying the day, milady?"

I'd just swallowed a ton of water, yet my throat went dry. There was just too much to take in. Mitch's green-and-blue-plaid kilt, brushing just below his knees. His surprisingly good Scottish accent, which did flippy things to my stomach. Those blue eyes turned to me, reminding me that beneath this brash and bold character he played at this Faire, he was just as brash and bold in person. When he gave you his attention it was worth basking in. I hated how much I'd missed that.

I had no idea how to put any of that into words that weren't "take me home and to bed right this second," so instead I sloshed my icy cold water bottle at him. "Hot." The word came out sharper than I'd intended, but it was hot as hell out here and I didn't feel like dealing with Mitch. Or Marcus. Or whoever the hell he was right now.

His eyebrows went up, and I knew he was bursting to turn it into an innuendo, but maybe it was out of character for him to do so, because he refrained. He stepped closer to me, taking the bottle from my hand. "That's because you're not cooling off properly."

"Oh, really?" I crossed my arms and attempted a glare, but God, he looked too good. You couldn't glare at abs like that.

"Really." There were at least fourteen r's in the word. "If you'll allow me?" I nodded, even though I had no idea what I was agreeing to. I tried not to flinch away as he reached for me, his fingers skimming the back of my neck as he brushed my hair over one shoulder. A shiver went across my skin that had nothing to do with hot or cold and everything to do with Mitch touching me. Before I could say anything he laid the still-icy bottle across the back of my neck, and the sudden cold was a shock of relief.

"Oh, God," I moaned. My gaze flew up to his and the cold I felt was almost burned away by the fire I saw in his eyes. He'd heard me moan like that before, and I could see in his expression that he was remembering it too.

"Good?" His voice was a low rumble, meant just for me, and all I could do was nod dumbly. "Good," he said again, and this time the word promised something so intimate I didn't want to contemplate it.

Thankfully, just then a man in royal dress announced the

beginning of the chess match, calling the cast to their places. I reached up to grasp the bottle, brushing his fingers with mine as I did so. Once I had a good grip on it, he let go, stepped back, and quirked a small smile. Then he placed his hand over his heart and bowed. "Milady."

And then he was off, taking his place on the board for the match to begin.

Stacey nudged me. "What was that all about?"

"Nothing." I took the bottle off my neck and uncapped it again, taking a gulp. My neck was cold but the rest of me burned.

"Oh, 'tisn't nothing," Emily piped up from the bench behind us. Where the hell had she come from? She leaned between the two of us and grinned at Stacey. "You've missed a lot around here lately."

"I have? Like what?"

"Like April and Mitch, that's what."

"*What?*" Stacey's squeal was drowned out by the fighting that had started on the chess field. Fighting that none of us were paying attention to. Good thing we were sitting in the back.

"Shhhh," I said. "Show's started." I pointed out toward the field, where teenage costumed actors took swings at each other with a staff and a sword.

But the girls didn't care. "You should see them together, Beatrice." Emily was back in her accent, using Stacey's in-character name. "They make quite a pair."

"Do they?" Stacey's smile was wide as she turned her interested gaze back to me. I scowled. It was getting annoying, being the only person not playacting here. It was either that or being gossiped about. Teased about something that wasn't real. Book club all over again.

But this wasn't book club. Emily threw her arms around my

shoulders, hugging me from behind. Reminding me that she was on my side through everything, and this was sisterly teasing, not gossip. I shook my head hard. "We were just doing each other a favor," I said. "That's all, honestly. Nothing going on there."

Stacey sighed. "Well, that's too bad. Because I can see it. I bet you look good together."

"They do," Emily confirmed, and I batted her on the arm while she tried to look innocent. "I am telling the truth, on my soul!" She was loving this way too much.

I turned back to the chess match, where Mitch blocked an attack with that massive sword of his, and there I was, with no choice but to watch the way his back muscles worked under his skin as he pushed his attacker backwards. He went through the steps of the choreographed fight, and I tried. I tried so hard to not remember how those powerful legs felt tangled up with my own. I tried to block the memory of the feel of his skin against mine, the way those same back muscles rippled in the same way under my hands when engaged in more intimate activities.

I tried. But unfortunately, I had a really good memory. I was going to need a lot more water.

Sixteen

I *barely survived the* human chess match, and fled not long after that, leaving my costumed friends behind. I'd been there long enough anyway. I was supposed to have gone home hours ago. As it was, I barely got home in time to take a long shower and order Chinese food for dinner—our Saturday-during-Faire tradition—before Caitlin got home.

"Did you catch up with everyone at the chess match?" Caitlin was wrapped up in a bathrobe, her wet hair combed down her back, as she scooped sweet and sour chicken into a bowl of rice, spooning neon-orange sauce on top of it all.

"I did." I didn't elaborate. I didn't want to. What was I going to say? *Remember how I'm not dating Coach Malone? Well, that's still true. However, there may have been some drooling today. And some slightly dirty things involving a water bottle. That man should come with some kind of advisory.*

But something about the day felt wrong. I felt it in those moments when Emily and Stacey conversed in character, like it was a language I didn't know, or a club I didn't belong to. Something about how all of my friends and family in their bright costumes made me feel like they were on the other side of a chasm I couldn't cross. They weren't mean about it or mocking. But it was clear that their experience here was much different from mine. I wasn't used to that. And I wasn't used to caring about it. I'd always kept to myself—wanting to belong wasn't exactly in my DNA.

So the next morning I reported for my shift at the ticket office, stayed my requisite four hours, and went the hell home. I didn't want to run into Mitch again. I didn't even want to run into my daughter or my sister while they were in costume. All of them with their characters and their accents just made me feel like an outsider.

There was little point in getting involved, anyway. I'd only be getting attached to something I was about to leave behind. I should be focusing on my future. On selling the house and leaving Willow Creek. I didn't need to be putting down more roots.

From now on I was going to do my volunteer shifts and no more. I would ignore the seductive thumping of the hand drums and the clash of steel on steel from the various stages while I sat in the box office. Who needed the distant sounds of bagpipes floating on the breeze and the faint smell of horses coming from the jousting field?

I sure as hell didn't.

Yeah. That resolution got me through that first weekend and no more. But in my defense, what happened next wasn't my fault.

I got to the Faire early in the morning on my second weekend as a box office volunteer with a to-do list in my head. After I was done here, I was going to hit the grocery store on the way home so I could relax that evening. Get my shower before Caitlin came home so she could clean up after a long day of Faire. Then I'd go to bed early, maybe read a book before going to sleep and doing it all again on Sunday.

It was a good plan. And it was shot to hell by about ten thirty.

Nancy was right—working the box office was probably the best people-watching spot at the whole Faire. Everyone was bright-eyed and energetic when they first arrived. Costumes were fresh and perfect, not yet marred by the dust of the lanes of the Faire and the sweat that came from the inevitable heat of the day. Patrons were excited to be there, and went through the gates like kids on Christmas morning. People met up in front of our booth and greeted one another with hugs and cheers. There were lots and lots of cries of *Huzzah!* to the point that I now understood those times that Emily or Caitlin slipped the word into a regular conversation.

But there was that weird feeling of separation again. For all the "thank you, miladys" that I was given when I collected their admission fees or scanned their tickets, it was like speaking to someone from another world. A world I had no desire to be part of, so why was this bothering me?

The next group was a family: a mom and dad with two almost school-age children. The boy was dressed as a pirate with a big black hat and a plastic sword, while his younger sister was a princess. Meanwhile, Mom wore a comfortable-looking sundress and Dad wore a camera around his neck over his polo shirt. The miniature pirate insisted on paying, waving the bills that his father had handed him. I slid off my stool and came around to the front of our makeshift building, squatting down to the diminutive pirate's level.

"Thank you, kind sir." I didn't put on an accent, but I figured this little guy deserved some playacting in return. I handed him his change and the tickets for his family, and he turned back to his dad in triumph. I smiled up at the family. "Enjoy your day." I'd said that about a bazillion times so far this weekend, and I'd be saying it three bazillion times more.

"April?"

The voice was unfamiliar, and as I straightened up from my crouch I wondered if it was me they were talking to. Probably not. April wasn't that uncommon a name, after all . . .

"April! Hey!"

Then I focused on the next group in line to buy tickets.

"Lulu." My voice was weak with surprise. Because in front of me was Mitch's cousin Lulu. Even worse, with her were two elderly people, smiling at me in recognition. Mitch's grandparents.

"Mr. and Mrs. Malone," I said. "Hi."

Shit.

Lulu was a hugger; I'd forgotten that about her. But the memory came back as she threw her arms around me like I was a long-lost friend, instead of the pretend girlfriend of her cousin that she'd met one time a few weeks ago. I was a little startled but I went with it, patting her on the back before she let go.

"This is great! I didn't know you'd be here too!" Lulu was the picture of cool casualness. Her hair was caught back in a ponytail, poking out the back of a tie-dyed trucker hat that would look absurd on anyone who wasn't her. She made it work along with a summery sundress and high-top sneakers. Practical for this kind of day: sandals were hell out here in the woods, according to both Emily and Stacey.

"It's so good to see you," I lied, directing my attention to both Lulu and her grandparents, people I had never expected to see again.

"Well, that's convenient, since we're here because of you," Lulu said with a smile.

"What?" I had no idea how to respond to that, so I settled for blinking dumbly.

Grandma Malone's smile was probably warmer than I deserved. "You said we should see Mitch in action, didn't you?"

"Oh. I did, didn't I? That's . . . that's great!" I tried to inject some enthusiasm into my voice, but my mind was whirling too fast to settle on anything coherent. "I'm sure Mitch left tickets for you here to pick up, right?" I darted back to the safety of my little booth, trying to put as much distance between us as I could. As if that would help to calm my racing heart.

"Oh. No," Grandma Malone said as Grandpa Malone took out his wallet. "He doesn't know we're here." She leaned forward conspiratorially, and my responding lean was involuntary. "We thought we'd surprise him."

"That's great," I said again, because my conversation skills had gone entirely to shit. But I rallied enough to wave at the money Mitch's grandfather extended toward me. "Put that away. I'm sure Mitch has comp tickets left. And if he doesn't, I do." I reached for the stapled stack of papers that listed all of the cast and volunteers along with the free tickets that had been issued in their name.

"What do you mean, you're not sure?" Grandma asked. "Is your boyfriend giving out tickets behind your back?"

I turned alarmed eyes to her, but she was chuckling at her own joke, and while I tried to relax I was thinking too fast, too hard. Was that something a girlfriend would know? Especially a girlfriend who was volunteering alongside her boyfriend at the same Renaissance Faire? I'd been prepared the first time Mitch and I had done this. And when Mitch had returned the favor at graduation it had just been a quick thing to help me save face in front of my ex-husband. I wasn't prepared to slide back into this role a third time.

Still, I managed to force a low-key laugh. "You know your grandson," I said. "I don't know half of the things he gets up to."

Lulu snickered. "Yeah, that sounds like Mitch."

Beside me, Nancy had finally caught wind of the conversation. "Are these Mitch's grandparents?" She clasped her hands together, delighted. "Oh, it's so wonderful to meet you! Mitch is such a darling boy. You should be so proud." I tried to not snort. There were lots of adjectives to describe Mitch; "darling" wasn't one of them as far as I was concerned.

But when I looked over at Grandma Malone, she was practically twinkling at the praise. There was nothing better to a grandma than to hear flattering things about her grandchildren. "Thank you," she said, practically preening. "We're all so very proud of him."

My eyes flew to Lulu's, and she met my wide-eyed gaze with a shrug. This was the opposite of the way his family had talked about him—to his face even!—when I'd seen them last, but whatever. They'd come to see him, and that was the important thing.

I ushered them toward the main gate, and Lulu grasped my arm in farewell. "So good to see you," she said. "Maybe I'll run into you again before we go?"

"Sure." I shrugged with a smile. I wasn't sure how that was going to happen, but it was better than saying "not likely," right?

But as they went through the main gate and I returned to my spot at the ticket booth, Nancy turned to me with a wide smile. "You sneaky girl," she said. "You never said a thing."

All I could do was blink at her. I had roughly three working brain cells left at this point, and nothing made sense. "About what?"

"About that." She nodded toward the main gate. "You and Mitch Malone? You've been more discreet than I would be if I were in your shoes, that's for sure." She fanned herself with a hand.

"Oh . . . that . . ." Oh *no*. Now what? Re-spin the elaborate lie of our make-believe relationship for the benefit of this whole goddamn Renaissance Faire? And for how long? Just because his family had shown up today?

My brain slammed shut on that last thought. His family was *here*. And Mitch didn't know. I checked the time on my phone; I had an hour until I was done here and could warn him. But that would be too late. Surely they'd find him before then, and he'd be thrown into the same position that I'd just been in: having to think on my feet. It had shaken me up to the point that I was ready to lie down in a dark room for the rest of the day. Mitch had to perform an elaborate fight with swords and shit. He didn't need this kind of distraction.

But I still had to deal with the more immediate problem, as Nancy was still looking at me speculatively. I stuck my phone in my pocket and gave her a weak smile. "I'm a private person. I don't like to brag."

Apparently that was the right thing to say, because Nancy practically doubled over in giggles, which . . . looked good on someone her age. "Go on." She pushed lightly on my shoulder. "Go catch up with them, show them around. I can handle things till Michael gets here."

"Are you sure?" The last thing I wanted to do was go anywhere near anyone named Malone right now. But the crowd here at the ticket booth had thinned to a trickle, something more than manageable to a pro like Nancy.

"Sure." She pushed again. "I hereby release you for the day. Go have fun."

I wanted to laugh at that. Hanging out with Mitch's family, living this lie yet again, was hardly what I considered fun.

I almost chickened out. I made it all the way to my car, whipping off my volunteer T-shirt, which today I had knotted over a long sundress—much cooler than jeans—and tossing it into the passenger seat. I looked longingly at the steering wheel, imagining sliding behind it and getting the hell out of here. Then I looked back toward the Faire. Toward the faint music and laughter, the muffled calls of *Huzzah!* Mitch was about to be ambushed by his family. Nancy had looked so gleeful about the prospect of Mitch and me being together that I was sure word was already spreading across the Faire about us. He was going to be ambushed by that too. And he'd have to face all of it alone, while I fled for home like a chickenshit. He'd have to explain why his girlfriend had ditched them all instead of being social.

But going back there . . . I'd have to be his girlfriend. Again. And this wasn't out of town, where I was with strangers and didn't care what they thought. Or a quick performance so I'd look good in front of my ex. This was in my hometown. My sister was here. My daughter was here—oh God, my *daughter*. Plus, I had to volunteer with these people for two more weekends. They would all be talking about this. They might be talking about this with Caitlin. They'd be looking at me. Talking about me. It made me want to shrink down until I was nothing.

I blinked back panicked tears, gripping my keys so hard that they hurt, digging into the soft skin of my palm. I couldn't do this.

But I had to do this.

"Goddammit!" The word was a growl, and I punctuated it by

slamming the car door. I didn't so much walk as stomp back toward the front gate.

And that's how I became the grumpiest person to ever walk through the front gates of a Renaissance Faire.

At least I knew my way around this time. I threaded my way through the crowd, my eyes focused straight ahead. I refused to let myself be distracted by all the shiny things on either side of the lanes. I wasn't here to shop. I wasn't here to take in any of the shows. I was here on a mission: to intercept my fake boyfriend and tell him that I was his fake girlfriend. Again.

"Last time," I muttered under my breath as I walked faster, past the Marlowe Stage, where I glimpsed Stacey and Daniel, their band in the middle of a set. "He's gonna have to tell them we broke up sooner or later. May as well be sooner." Who was I talking to? Did it matter?

"Beloved sister! Good morrow!" Emily emerged, smiling, from the tavern right in front of me, and not for the first time I wondered how she could breathe in that getup. Last weekend she'd been in blue, but today she was dressed in colors to match her husband: dark wine and black, and a red rose was threaded through the updo she'd made of her curls. Even despite my low-level panic I could appreciate how right she looked here.

I couldn't just blow past her like I hadn't seen her. "Hey. Yeah. Good morrow and all that." I'd stopped walking, but my eyes darted ahead, behind, around. Looking for a tie-dyed trucker hat ushering a couple octogenarians through the Faire.

Her brow furrowed, but since there were a lot of people around us, she stayed more or less in character. "Is everything all right, sister? You seem troubled."

"Yeah. Just . . ." I didn't see them, which wasn't necessarily a good thing. They could have already found Mitch. Which wouldn't be an utter disaster, but I needed to get over there. Emily was still waiting for my answer, so what the hell. Might as well fill her in. "Mitch's family is here. His grandparents. His cousin."

Emily's eyes went wide and she tugged my arm, pulling me off the path and to a quiet copse of trees so she could drop the accent. "The douchey one?"

"No, no." Thank God for small favors. "Lulu."

Emily made a face. "Who names their kid Lulu?"

"It's short for something. Louisa, I think?" I shook my head; not the point. "Anyway, she's the nice one."

"Oh. Well, that's not so bad."

"It is when he doesn't know they're here. And they're going to be all 'where's your girlfriend?' and he won't have an answer for them."

"Ahhh." Emily blew out a breath, and honestly, how could she do something like that in a corset? It was a mystery.

"Yeah." I pointed toward the chess field, where a small crowd had started to gather, but not enough to signify that a show was starting. "Is he over there? I wanted to try and talk to him before—"

"Yes, of course. I understand." Emily slipped back into her accent as she put her hands on her corseted hips, following my gaze. "I do not see him, but he cannot have gone far. Their first show begins soon, after all."

More importantly, I still didn't see any other Malones, so that was promising. "Okay. I need to find him."

"Of course," she said again. Then she grinned at me, dropping the accent once more. "He's gonna owe you a new roof at this rate."

I snorted. "No kidding." If it were earlier in the summer, I would have absolutely leveraged this into more work on my house. But that was the last thing on my mind now. Besides, having him anywhere near my house was a bad idea. Not with my nosy neighbors. Not to mention, spending time with Mitch had stopped being a transaction long before now. I hadn't talked to him—really talked to him—for a few weeks now, and I missed that. Missed him.

The revelation was startling. It was unwelcome. And it was something that I absolutely did not have time to contemplate right now. Because I'd spotted the tie-dyed trucker hat, not too far from the chess field. I swore under my breath.

"I gotta get over there," I muttered, either to myself or to Emily. She gave me a small smile and pushed on my shoulder.

"Go."

I went, skipping the lane entirely and cutting through the grouping of trees between the tavern and the chess field, emerging behind the benches that ringed the field. And oh, thank God—Mitch was right there, his back to me, in conversation with one of the other cast members. His sword lay on the bench beside him. A match was imminent, like Emily said; the rest of the fighting cast had begun to gather.

I was a polite person; I didn't like to interrupt people when they were talking. But I was also desperate, and the other Malones were on their way. So I reached out, laying a hand on Mitch's arm, trying to ignore how warm and solid his flesh was, and how that warmth seemed to radiate up my arm. That wasn't what I was here for.

He turned immediately at my touch, his eyes registering surprise. He gave a dismissive nod to the person he'd been talking to, then turned his full attention to me.

"Good morrow, milady." He didn't look particularly happy to

see me. In fact he looked guarded, not like a boyfriend at all. That was my fault, pushing him away the way I had. And while this wasn't the time to fix it, I had to do something.

"Look happy to see me," I hissed before stepping closer, a too-wide smile on my face. Instead of doing what he was told, Mitch looked down at me like I'd had a stroke. "Your grandparents are here," I said through my manic grin, trying to remember how to look like a girlfriend.

"Are they?" His voice was still in character but his eyes widened. They flicked over my head, glancing around before pausing. "Ah. I see them." When he looked back down at me he'd managed to arrange his face into a pleased expression, not quite boyfriend-like but getting there. We could do this. Hopefully.

"Yep. So we gotta . . ." I touched his arm again, because it was right there and how could I not? I even indulged myself, sliding my palm up his sun-warmed skin, enjoying the way his muscles flexed under my hand. God, he felt good, and for a moment I forgot why I was there. I was touching his skin and his breath had quickened; I knew if I looked up into his electric blue eyes I'd see them dark and wanting. My mind was back in that Virginia hotel room from a while back—hell, my living room floor from a few weeks ago—and I knew that his mind was there too.

"Hey." He'd dropped the accent, but his voice was so soft that no one else could hear him except me. I didn't look at him; I stayed focused on my hand on his arm, until his fingertips were under my chin, tilting my head up to meet his eyes. I caught my breath, because there it was. There was that look, the one I'd been expecting. The one I'd been dreading. Now he looked like a boyfriend. "It's okay." His voice was little more than breath, and the smile that played around his mouth wasn't playacting at all. Before I could think about it, he leaned down, brushing a ghost of a kiss across my mouth. "Thanks for coming to save me," he whispered into my mouth.

"Of course," I breathed back, fighting the impulse to rise onto my toes to get another kiss. A real kiss. "Quid pro quo, remember?"

"Oh, yeah?" He smiled against my lips. "What do I owe you this time?"

I grinned as we parted. "Consider this one a freebie."

That made him laugh, a rumbling sound that was for more than just the two of us as he slid back into character. Both as the Scotsman with a sword and as my fake boyfriend. "Too right, my love," he said, chucking me under the chin, his eyes alight with merriment. "Now, if you'll excuse me, I have a fight to win." He picked up the sword and bowed in my direction before turning back to the chess field and his castmates. He walked directly over to Simon, who was buckling on his sword belt. The two men had a quiet, serious conversation, ending with Simon nodding emphatically and Mitch clapping him on the shoulder with a relieved expression before coming back to his side of the field.

My job was done, technically. We'd performed in front of his family, and now I could get the hell out of there. Mitch wouldn't be caught off guard when they found him after the show. He was prepared now, and could give them some bullshit excuse for me leaving.

But my legs didn't want to work. They still shook from the force of that barely-there kiss, so instead I sank down onto the bench where his sword had been. My heart fluttered as he got into position, and my breath came short in my chest. Maybe I should just sit here for a few minutes. I could do that. Then I could go home.

"Oh. Em. Gee." Stacey slid onto the bench behind me, her face suffused with joy. "You two are the cutest!"

I turned to her with a scowl, even though all my nerve endings were still buzzing happily from the feel of Mitch's skin against mine. "Don't you have an actual job here? Shouldn't you be doing that instead of harassing me?"

Stacey shrugged, completely unconcerned in the face of my ire. "We're between shows. Prime walking-around time. And I'm so glad I did, because I got to see that!" She hugged herself with glee.

"It was nothing," I insisted, but I didn't sound as certain as I wanted to. "Nothing," I repeated. "Just doing him a favor."

"A favor?" She shook her head. "How so?"

"April! There you are!"

My head whipped around in time to see Mitch's cousin Lulu, waving at me, shepherding her grandparents in my direction. Because of course she was. I stood up instinctively, ushering Grandma and Grandpa Malone to sit on my front-row bench, while Lulu and I took seats next to Stacey on the bench behind. I made quick introductions, glaring at Stacey from behind Lulu's back as I did so.

"I met them when I went with Mitch to a family gathering a little while back." I infused the words with as much meaning as I could, mentally begging Stacey to read between the lines.

"Oh, how nice!" Stacey said, playing along. Thank God for Stacey.

Grandpa Malone turned to look back at me. "I have to say, April, you were right."

I blinked at him. "I was?" Right about what? I'd hardly spoken two words to him that whole weekend, except to praise his barbecue, which wouldn't be news to him.

Grandma Malone nodded, joining the conversation. "I had no idea what Mitch does here. I knew that he did this Faire, of course, but I didn't know what that meant. And I decided that needed to change."

Grandpa Malone nodded in agreement. "That's why we came today."

"Oh." I didn't know what to say to them. My whole rant at their dining room table had been an embarrassment as far as I was concerned. I'd expected the main takeaway to be that I was unstable.

"Yep." Lulu nudged my shoulder with hers. "And when they told me they were going to come up, I insisted on coming with. I had to see this whole kilt thing for myself. Between you and me, kilts aren't really my thing, but . . ." She looked across the field at her cousin with a grin. "You're right. I bet he's very popular here."

"Oh, he is," I said before I could think about it. Should I sound jealous? What the hell was girlfriend protocol for that kind of conversation? I decided that as Mitch's girlfriend I would be confident. Willing to share him with the masses. Because honestly, would anyone be able to stop Mitch from being Mitch?

"I don't understand what we're watching." Grandpa Malone shook his head. "What exactly is happening here?" He directed the question to me, which was a terrible idea. Because my answer was "human chess match" with absolutely no clarification.

But thank God for Stacey—she knew this Faire like the back of her hand. "In human chess, that whole field is the board—see the squares? And the people are the pieces." She pointed. "See, pawns in front, the rest of the pieces in the back. They get directed on where to move, and when a piece takes another piece, it's a whole fight. Like with swords."

"Ah. Okay." He shifted on the bench, and I frowned.

"Are you all right? I know these benches aren't the most comfortable." I didn't like his grandparents sitting out here in the summer sun. Especially since it was on my account that they were here in the first place. Mitch wasn't going to thank me if his grandparents keeled over while they were here.

But he waved me off. "I'm fine. Don't worry about me."

Meanwhile, Stacey was still explaining the whole chess match deal to Grandma Malone and Lulu. "Mitch is on the white side, so he's the white knight."

"Of course he is," Lulu murmured, and I snickered in response. She caught my eye and her smile was wide like Mitch's— there was that Malone DNA. I liked her. Part of me wished I could confess everything to her. She might understand. But no. Mitch had asked me to do this whole girlfriend thing in the first place to make him look good. Telling his family it was an elaborate lie would be the exact opposite.

So instead Stacey and I sat with Mitch's family as they watched him go through the steps of the chess match. It didn't take long for me to see that it looked different than the week before. They'd gone back to the original choreography for this one, where he and Simon faced off as the final battle of the show. That must have been what he'd gone to talk to Simon about. This fight was more intricate, and more importantly Mitch won this one. Of course he wanted to show off for his grandparents.

This was the same choreography I'd seen on his phone, more than once, but it was another thing entirely to see it in person. Mitch's enormous sword clashed with Simon's more slender pirate's rapier. Before long they'd disarmed each other and had resorted to hand-to-hand fighting. Then Simon flipped Mitch over his shoulder, and that kilt flying was an amazing thing to behold, even with the shorts underneath. When Mitch landed on his feet, dropping into a crouch before spinning back to Simon again, Grandma Malone clapped in delight, and her pure enjoyment did something to me. A sweet spark inside my chest that both filled me with happiness and made my heart ache. His family really did love him. How could he think otherwise?

The fight ended with Simon on his knees in the grass while Mitch held a dagger to his throat. Grandpa Malone let out a piercing whistle as he joined the rest of the crowd in applause.

"Wait a second." Lulu turned to me, eyes narrowed. "Where did he get the knife from?"

"You don't want to know," I deadpanned. Grandma Malone snorted.

"His boot," Stacey said, whacking me on the shoulder with a giggle. "That cousin of yours is very crafty."

"Huh," she said. "I missed that part." She clapped harder, yelling, "Do it again!"

Mitch had just helped Simon up from the ground, both men breaking character for a moment, and he turned at the sound of his cousin's voice. The force of his smile was blinding, and I lost my breath. He was breathing hard, chest heaving with exertion from performing in the sun, and sweat glistened on his golden skin. I tried hard to not look. It wasn't going well.

The show ended shortly after that, and Mitch scooped his sword from the ground before joining us. "Grrrandparents!" His voice was booming and very Scottish, and Lulu practically doubled over in laughter at the sound of it.

Grandma Malone got to her feet, grinning at Mitch's arrival. "Mitch, that was—" Before she could finish her sentence he'd scooped her up, lifting her off the ground in an exuberant yet careful hug, making her squeal. "What are you . . . put me down!" But she was giggling like a little girl when he set her back on her feet. She poked him in the chest, pretending to scold him. "You are all sweaty."

Stacey tsked at him while trying not to laugh herself. "Hauling your grandmother around like a sack of potatoes, what is wrong with you?"

"Yeah," Lulu said around a wide smile. "Rude."

"Ach, I'm sure you're right." He wasn't letting up with the accent. "Respect me elders and all that." But when Lulu went in for a hug he gave her the same treatment, this time spinning her around a couple times. He was showing off. I loved it.

Lulu squawked in delight, clapping a hand to her head to adjust her hat as he put her down. "Knock that off!" She batted at his arm. "I'm your elder too."

He scoffed. "Five years. Doesna count."

I held up a hand as he turned to me. "Don't you dare."

"Wouldn't think of it." His smile was warm and his arm around me was warmer. He didn't pick me up and swing me around. Instead he hugged me against his side and planted a kiss on my temple. It wasn't a showing-off kiss, trying to prove something. It was simpler than that, yet more profound: a comfortable declaration that we were together. And even though we were in a crowd, it felt intimate. It felt real.

I'd missed this. I'd missed feeling like Mitch and I were a united front against . . . well, against anything. Every time we did it, we got a little better at it. And every time we did it, it was harder to remember that it was all based on a lie. That at the end of the day, even though Mitch and I looked like a couple that was perfect for each other, we'd soon be going back to normal. And I'd be going home alone.

Being alone used to be the dream, but with Mitch's arm around me I found myself preferring the lie.

Seventeen

Being *left alone,* however, was off the menu today.

Mitch stayed with us for a few minutes, but it wasn't long before Simon called him away. No rest for pirates or Scotsmen around here, apparently. There were a few moments of awkward silence after he left, as I wondered how I could get the hell out of here now that my job was done.

But Grandma Malone turned to me. To *me.* Why? "What's next?"

"Next?" I raised alarmed eyebrows to Stacey, who was absolutely loving this.

"Next . . ." She pulled her phone out of a pouch on her belt, checking the time. "Well, if you thought Mitch's kilt was something, you should come with me. Our next show is about to start, and it's nice and shady over there. We can get some water on the way."

"Good idea." Lulu linked her arm through mine. "Let's go."

God. I was never going home.

We made our way down the lane, stopping at the tavern for

some cold ciders for Lulu and me, an even colder beer for Grandpa Malone, some sweet mead for Grandma, and icy bottles of water to go for all of us. Emily served us, giving wench's banter the whole time, while we sat at one of the tables at the tavern to cool off in the shade, Stacey leaving us to head to the Marlowe Stage. By the time we caught up, she had the Dueling Kilts merchandise table set up and was settled behind it, shooting us a little wave as I ushered the grandparents Malone to seats in a shady spot under some trees and made sure they were supplied with water. No grandparents would be dehydrated on my watch.

Watching the Dueling Kilts' show had been a good call. I hadn't seen their full set in a while, and I'd forgotten how much fun it was. Honestly, their show was worth the price of admission— it had nothing to do with their association with Stacey, a little bit to do with their talent, and a lot to do with how they all looked in those kilts. Mitch's family seemed to have a great time, but a low level of panic bubbled up as the show drew to a close. What was I going to do with them now? And why was I in charge of their fun?

As most of the audience filed out, Grandma Malone turned to me. "It's much cooler here. Do you think they'd mind if we just stayed here for a little while?"

I shrugged. "I can't imagine it being an issue. Are you sure?" Sitting here was fine with me. It was a good ten degrees cooler in the shade, and—

"Good," Grandma Malone said. "Then you and Lulu go off and have fun. You can come find us later."

"Oh." I blinked and glanced over at Lulu. "Um . . ." There was no polite way out of this, was there?

"Are you sure?" Lulu's eyes were concerned as she leaned toward them. "It's hot today. We can go back to the hotel if you want."

"Not yet." Grandma Malone sipped her water. "I thought I could sit here and look pathetic, and maybe those kilted boys will come out."

I choked on my sip of water, but Lulu just rolled her eyes and Grandpa Malone tsked. "I'm sitting right here, you know," he said.

"I know." Grandma Malone spoke to him but looked at me, dropping a wink, and I fought to keep a straight face.

"Come on." Lulu pulled me to my feet, and I forced a smile. "Show me the joust."

Okay, that sounded like fun. I hadn't been over that way yet this year. "You're on."

On our way out we stopped by the merch table to say goodbye to Stacey. She was talking to some patrons, and while we waited I noticed a rustle at her feet. Her black-and-white cat, Benedick, wearing a harness with little dragon's wings attached, was leashed to a leg of the table and he rolled in the dirt, batting at a leaf with murderous intent. Everyone was enjoying their day at the Faire. Except maybe that leaf.

Finally alone, Stacey beamed at us. "Good show, right?"

"Definitely." Lulu shook her head in awe. "You travel with those guys? Damn, girl."

Stacey sighed dramatically. "I know. It's a hardship. I'm still working on getting Daniel into a kilt. He won't do it."

"Wait, which one's that?" Lulu tilted her head. "They're all in kilts."

"Oh, *those* guys, yeah." She waved a dismissive hand. "I'm with their manager, though. Daniel. He's not a kilt kind of guy."

"There's more to life than kilts," I said. Which felt like blasphemy at a place like this, but oh well.

"You are so right," Stacey said. "Believe me, he makes up for it in other ways." Her smile turned wicked, and I didn't want to know. There were things about my friends that I didn't want to picture.

I cleared my throat. "I'm taking Lulu over to the joust. Is it okay if they stick around?"

Stacey followed my gaze over to the grandparents. "Of course. We have a break for a couple hours, but I can keep an eye on them. They okay?"

"Oh, yeah," Lulu said. "I think they got a little overheated during the chess match."

Stacey nodded in sympathy. "It gets hot over there. Full sun and all that."

Lulu looked over her shoulder at her grandparents. "I'm gonna take them back to the hotel in a little bit. I don't want them out here in this too much longer."

"Sure." Stacey waved a hand. "I'll text April if I need to get hold of you, okay?"

"Sounds good." But as we watched her grandparents, the men of the Dueling Kilts strolled back onto the stage, then hopped off to the ground, clearly on a break. Soon they were grouped around Grandma Malone, who looked positively delighted. Grandpa Malone looked . . . tolerant. Good man.

"Yeah." Lulu rolled her eyes again. "They're gonna be fine. Let's go find some fried food on a stick or something."

"You got it."

But a few steps down the lane Lulu glanced over her shoulder, as if to verify her grandparents had stayed put. Then her smile faded, and her shoulders sagged with a sigh.

"You okay?"

"Yeah." She pulled her phone out of her pocket. "Sorry. Grandma goes nuts if we're looking at our phones when we're hanging out with her. Like I'm playing *Candy Crush* or something, not getting seventy-five texts from work."

"On a Saturday?" My eyebrows crawled up my forehead.

"Saturday, Sunday. Eleven o'clock on a Wednesday." Lulu shrugged. "No rest for the wicked. Or lawyers." She scrolled through her phone, frowned, and tapped out a few replies. "Sorry," she said again as she pocketed her phone. "I probably shouldn't have come today. But Grandma was determined to see this, and I was worried about them being here all day in this heat. There was no way to talk her out of it, so here I am." She glanced around, and I imagined her sizing up the whole Faire, wondering if it was worth her while.

"Hey." I tried not to sound defensive on behalf of the Faire, on behalf of Mitch, but as a representative of both I had to say something. "I think it meant a lot to Mitch that they came. And that you're here too. This is important to him."

"Oh, I know!" Her expression was chastened as she looked back at me. "I didn't mean . . . no, this is a great thing he's doing, and I see what you mean about him being such a draw." A small smile touched her lips. "He seems happy. I'm proud of him, that he's found that." She nudged my shoulder. "I bet you have something to do with it."

"Me? No." I shook my head. "He's been doing this Faire thing longer than I've known him."

"Not that. I mean about him being happy."

"Oh." A wave of guilt washed through me, and all I could do was shrug and slip back into the grand lie. "I . . . I suppose?"

"Don't sell yourself short. He looks so happy with you. With his whole life. I'm glad he's got it figured out. More than the rest of us, I think." Her sigh was wistful, almost jealous. Which seemed strange for someone who was about to make partner at her law firm. The frown crept back on my face. There was something going on here. Lulu wasn't as happy, didn't have it all together, the way Mitch—and probably the rest of her family—seemed to think. And we were just close enough to being friends that I hated that for her. I wanted to help.

If I couldn't help, I could do the next best thing: take her mind off it. "Come on." I hooked my arm through hers, the way she'd done for me earlier. "Another cider on the way to the joust. And feel free to check your phone if it makes you feel better. Turn it off if it doesn't."

Lulu's smile was stronger this time, on its way back to the patented sunny Malone expression. "Sounds perfect."

I wasn't an expert at being a Ren Faire patron, but I'd been Ren Faire adjacent for long enough that I knew the highlights that we needed to hit. Consulting the map showed us that we had almost an hour before the joust started. Plenty of time to swing by the tavern again. Emily passed us two more ciders across the bar.

I slipped a couple of bills into the tip jar and pointed a finger at Emily in warning. "Don't you dare."

Her smile grew wide as she reached for the bell, ringing it aggressively loudly while maintaining eye contact the whole time. "Huzzah to the generous tipper!"

"Jesus Christ." I covered my eyes with one hand while the volunteers chorused, "Huzzah!" and Lulu's laugh pealed behind me. She'd obviously shaken off her ennui, and all it had cost me was a little embarrassment.

We finished our ciders at the tavern before moving on, and halfway to the joust I introduced her to the frozen lemonade stand—the icy sweetness was perfect for this late-July day. Since I wasn't wearing my volunteer shirt anymore, I felt incognito, which was nice. I was just out for an afternoon with a friend. Whose friendship was entirely based on a sham. Hmm. Maybe that wasn't the best way to think about it.

"Ooh, flower crowns!" Lulu darted ahead to a table set up on the right side of the lane, and I followed in her wake. Wreaths of flowers hung from hooks, their ribbons floating in the slight breeze like lazy live things. I reached out and let the ribbons trail between my fingers. I'd gotten one of these the first time Emily and I had come to this Faire. So much had changed since that day, three years ago now. That day had been a bit of a sham too, come to think of it; all I knew at the time was that Caitlin had told me that I had to help her talk Emily into going to the Faire with me that particular day and then get her over near the jousting field. It had been an elaborate scheme planned by Simon to get her back into his life, and it had ended perfectly for the both of them. Something about these flower crowns, these ribbons, reminded me of that day.

I had no idea where that flower crown I'd bought that day had ended up. Caitlin had borrowed it at one point, and I hadn't thought about it since then. So what the hell; I could use a new one.

Lulu took off her hat, shaking out her ponytail and resecuring it low on her neck. "What do you think?" She held up two different crowns, raising and lowering each in turn like Lady Justice with her scales.

I pointed to the one in her right hand. "With your hair? Green. Definitely green." I chose a crown made mostly of daisies with yellow ribbons, which stood out well against my dark hair. We both looked very wood nymphy now, but that was the point of flower crowns, wasn't it? We paid the vendor and secured our new headgear. I hazarded a glance into a mirror set up at the table, adjusting the way it sat on my head. My cheeks were pink from the heat of the day, and my hair had frizzed a little, but the thing that took me aback was how happy I looked. I practically glowed, which wasn't a look I was used to seeing in the mirror. But I was having fun, and my expression certainly matched.

At the other end of the table, the flower crown vendor had struck up a conversation with an older gentleman. There was a whole display of crowns between us, so I had to bend around the flowers and ribbons to see him clearly. He had to be part of the Faire circuit, with his long beard and weatherworn face. He was dressed in a longer kilt and high leather boots with large buttons down the side. His outfit didn't look like a costume, like the clothes that Simon and Mitch wore. More like Stacey's getup: everyday clothes that were lived in, just from a different century.

"Going well?" His voice was a low rasp, and the flower crown seller nodded vigorously.

"It's a good souvenir, you know? They always sell well. How about you, are you moving any of the leather?"

He gave a harrumph. "Not a lot, but that's to be expected. Small place like this. Don't exactly see anyone around here shelling out for anything big."

She snickered. "Hey, they could surprise you. Maybe there's a mundane just waiting to buy a new vest."

He laughed along with her joke, but I was missing something. What was funny? "Yeah, no shit. Or boots, right? Nah, I bring a lot of the smaller stuff to this show. Journals, little bags. Goes over a lot better with the mundanes."

"Sure, makes sense." They kept talking, but Lulu appeared at my left elbow.

"You ready? What time is that joust thing?"

"Oh." I turned away from the table, and as I did I saw the two vendors looking over at me, startled. They hadn't seen me. "Joust is this way," I said. "Toward the back." As I led her away the leatherworker's startled face was burned in my brain. I couldn't help but feel like I'd overheard something I wasn't supposed to hear.

That conversation with the leatherworker echoed in my head the whole next week. *Mundane.* I'd never heard the word before, and certainly not in that context. It reminded me of when Caitlin had been in her Harry Potter phase, calling people muggles when she didn't like them. The word had been dismissive, derisive. I didn't like it.

The worst thing about it was that it put into words—well, word—that vague sense of dissatisfaction I'd been feeling this whole time, hanging out with Emily and Stacey at Faire. The sense that I didn't belong, because I didn't wear a costume or pretend to be someone else. Did they look at me and think "mundane" too?

I tried to put it out of my mind and focus on the positive. I'd had such a good time on that Saturday afternoon with Mitch's family. Lulu had given me her number, and I'd plugged it into my phone a little guiltily, knowing that my relationship with Mitch wasn't going to lead to long-term friendship with his cousin. Sunday at Faire had been uneventful; a few volunteers had teased me about "dating" Mitch, but it had mostly been of the "how on earth did you keep it quiet and not brag to the whole county about that" variety. If there'd been any real gossip about a middle-aged volunteer robbing a kilted cradle, I didn't hear anything about it.

So I was feeling pretty good about things for the most part when I got up the next Saturday morning, except for that one word, like a black spot on my psyche.

Mundane.

Great. It wasn't even eight a.m. on Saturday and I was already getting a headache.

"Hey, Mom?" Caitlin's voice floated down the hall from her room.

"Yeah?" I called back, turning to look at myself sideways in the mirror. I'd gotten some new knee-length shorts that weren't doing a damn thing to make me not look like a middle-aged mom, but they were long enough that they covered the worst of my scar, so I could live with that. Because no matter what, I was a middle-aged mom. No point in trying to hide that.

Mundane.

Shut up. "Yeah, Cait?" I said again, going out into the hallway, where my daughter met me. She was wearing her long under-dress and her boots, which was all she wore on the ride over to the Faire site. Her hair was already braided into two plaits on either side of her head. Once on the grounds she would lace into the long yellow overdress, put on a little lip gloss, and she'd be ready to go.

"I forgot to ask, but Nina invited me to her house tonight, is that okay?"

"Oh." I shouldn't have been surprised. Caitlin and Nina had been friends since they were in elementary school. They even volunteered for this Faire together. And in a few short weeks they'd be off to different colleges, meeting entirely new people. That had to be scary. It was tough to face the future without your best friend by your side.

But it wasn't time to think about Caitlin going off to college yet. It was just the first weekend of August; we still had some time. I crossed my arms and leaned in the doorway. "I guess that means more Chinese takeout for me."

"Just save me some sweet and sour." She flashed me a grin and darted back into her room to finish getting ready.

"What makes you think I'm going to order sweet and sour if you're not here to eat it?"

"You know you like it!" There was a giggle in her voice and I shook my head, not even trying to hide my smile.

"Do not."

I drove her to Faire that morning, with the understanding that Nina would drive them both back to her place. We pulled into the parking lot a few cars over from Nina's so Caitlin could throw her overnight bag inside. As I reported to my post forty-five minutes before gate opened, ready for my volunteer shift, I was already mentally planning the rest of my day. Long, hot bath instead of a quick shower before Cait came home. Dinner from the Thai place instead of Chinese . . . though maybe I should pick up some sweet and sour for Caitlin to have tomorrow night. There was a documentary streaming that I'd been meaning to watch but had never taken the time to. Maybe tonight would be perfect for that.

A picture came to my mind, unbidden: another evening alone on the couch with the remote in my hand. The thought made me want to burst into frustrated tears right there in front of a scantily clad female pirate and the wizard on her arm. I was a woman who kissed men in kilts at a Renaissance Faire, for God's sake. Was an evening of takeout and television my best option? Surely I could do better than that.

Oh, God. Now I knew why the leatherworker's words had hurt so much. Because they'd described me to a T: I was mundane as hell. All these years not getting involved. Eyes straight ahead. Raising my daughter on my own. The most excitement I had in my life were my fucking book clubs.

Even now, when my sister and my daughter and my friends were all a part of this magical, whimsical event, all I did was sell tickets. Not committing enough to wear a costume or have any actual damn fun. No, I stayed on the outside looking in, sticking to my same old routine. Routines were safe. Routines were reliable.

But routines were boring. And so was I. And I couldn't stand it for one more minute.

I had to, though, so I bit hard on my lip and kept selling tickets. Smiled and joked with Nancy until my shift was over. But instead of going straight to my car, I left my keys in my pocket and headed for the front gates of the Faire.

Emily wasn't at the tavern, so I doubled back to the Marlowe Stage, hopping impatiently from one foot to the other, waiting for the Dueling Kilts' set to be over.

"Hey, you okay?" Daniel touched my elbow, and I was wired so tightly I almost flew out of my skin. He looked down at me, his brow furrowed. "You seem . . ."

"A mess?" My laugh was almost frantic, and I didn't understand why. What was happening to me?

Daniel studied my face. "I was going to say 'over-caffeinated.' Everything all right?"

"Sure." I forced a deep breath, then another. "I just need to talk to Stacey, that's all."

"Well, let's go get her. I can man the merch table for her." He ushered me ahead of him and we skirted the audience toward the merchandise table. I hung back while he talked to Stacey, and she turned a concerned face toward me. I tried to look cool, but cool had left the premises a while back.

"Hey, what's up?" Stacey's voice was elaborately casual.

"Stace . . ." I wasn't sure what I wanted to ask, or how to put it into words. So I did the best thing I could: take a deep breath and plunge on ahead. "Am I mundane?"

Her eyebrows flew up and she blinked. "Well. You're not in garb, so . . . yeah? I mean, it's not like it's a bad thing. It's just a . . ." She shrugged. "A thing."

"Well, I'm sick of it. I want . . ." I wasn't sure how to articulate what exactly I wanted, or how to get it. But I wanted to belong. I wanted to be on the other side of that chasm, with the people I loved. I wanted to have fun. Hell, I wanted to *be* fun.

I took a deep breath. "Stacey, will you help me?" I wasn't even sure what I was asking for. But I trusted her. I wanted to put myself into her hands and let her transform me. Make me not mundane anymore.

Stacey's smile got wider and wider as though she was going to levitate. She gripped my hands with hers, squeezing tight.

"April," she said. "It would be my absolute pleasure. Let's go shopping."

Eighteen

S tacey *didn't give* me a chance to change my mind, which proved how well she knew me. Before I knew it, she'd practically dragged me bodily to a costume vendor's tent, and I was wrestled and tugged and laced into a dress.

"Oooh boy." I tried to take a deep breath but quickly discovered that wasn't something I'd be doing for the rest of the day. "I don't know about this."

"I do." Stacey walked behind me, examining the back of my outfit while I turned this way and that in the mirror. "You look amazing. Red is your color."

"I doubt that." I ran my hands down the tightly laced brocade bodice, over the unfamiliar shape that this corset had made of my body. All I could see was red. Lipstick red. Pick-you-out-in-a-crowd red. Not a color I wore ever. Not by choice. I looked like a stoplight, albeit a fancy one with a long swishy skirt.

I ran a mental tab on all the layers I was currently wearing: A white off-the-shoulder nightgown of my very own that fell to my knees, with a petticoat under that to give the outfit some fullness. Over that was a forest-green underskirt, followed by the red brocade, which was both bodice and overskirt in one, cinched in at my waist and laced up my torso.

"Yeah, but what about this green?" I tilted my head and scowled at my reflection in the mirror. "You don't think I look like Christmas?"

"Here we are! Accessories!" Emily's voice sang out, still in her Faire accent. She'd shown up not long into this whole makeover event, serving as Stacey's assistant. Now she appeared from the other side of the tent, her arms full. First she tied a length of blue-and-green-tartan fabric around my waist like a sash. Over that she buckled a brown leather belt, on which she'd threaded multiple things, so it took a little finessing to get everything in the right place.

"Okay, so I got you a little bag, that's here . . ." She patted the leather drawstring pouch that rested against my right hip. "You can put your phone, keys, cards, and whatever else in there. Then you don't have to worry about a purse, see?" She barely waited for my nod before she continued. "Now, these are skirt hikes, there's one on each side. You can pull up the sides of the overskirt, and then the skirt underneath shows too. Plus it gives everything some fullness. See?"

"I do see." Because while Emily was talking she and Stacey were working, drawing up the sides of the overskirt and running them through the skirt hikes, like hooking curtains out of the way in a window. But they weren't done yet. I stood still, letting them move me around like a giant doll they were playing dress-up with, while they adjusted fabric, pulled a little harder at my bodice strings until I thought I might fall over at a badly timed tug.

"Hold up! I'm going to need to breathe at some point, right?"

Emily waved a hand. "Eh, that's what nighttime is for."

Stacey giggled. "You say that now." She caught my eye and shook her head. "You should have heard her complain the first time I put her in her outfit."

I remembered those days, and I laughed at the memory. "Oh, she complained plenty at home too."

"It just takes some getting used to, that's all." Emily tugged at the neckline of my underdress, making it fall in a pretty, ruffled line across my suddenly enhanced cleavage. Wow. This was not a Monday–Friday look.

"Am I done yet?" I was already weeping internally on behalf of my credit card, but screw it. It had been a long, long time since I'd indulged myself, and I was due. Part of being not mundane, I decided, was spending an irresponsible amount of money and enjoying every second of it. And, lack of breathing and slight squashing of internal organs aside, I was enjoying the hell out of this. I turned back to the mirror; from the neck down I didn't recognize myself. My body wasn't shaped like this. My breasts were pushed together and up, mounding nicely over the white ruffle of my underdress. My waist was nipped in, and hadn't looked this small since I'd given birth. With the red skirts pulled up and the plaid sash around my waist, the stoplight effect had been muted nicely. The blue in the plaid had made me look a lot less like Christmas and a lot more like . . .

"Wait a second." I narrowed my eyes in the mirror, my focus on the two behind me. "Why are you trying to make me match?"

"Match what?" Emily's eyes were wide blue innocence, but when I shook the plaid sash at her she melted into a grin. "Okay, look, that was a complete accident. I was trying to tone down the red some and punch up the green. And it looks good, so hush up."

Stacey nodded. "She did a good job, so I agree."

"You agree with what? That I need to hush up?"

Now Stacey's smile matched Emily's, and if I didn't love them both so much I'd hate them. "Pretty much."

"Fine." I dropped the sash and looked in the mirror again. They were right; I did look good. "What about my hair, though? This ponytail kind of spoils the look." I pulled my hair tie out and ran my hands through my hair as it tumbled down. The daily frizzing had already begun, and if I left it down it was going to just get worse. Not to mention all this hair was already getting hot on the back of my neck.

But they had a solution for that too. It didn't take long for them to drag me down the lane to where some women were set up, braiding hair for patrons.

"What is this, the grown-up equivalent of face painting?" It seemed like an extravagance to have my hair all done up for the last three hours of the day.

"We could do that too," Stacey said. "The face painters are over by the jousting ring. We could put a little unicorn on your—"

"No thank you." I cut her off because I didn't need a unicorn anywhere on my body. But I let them push me down onto a stool—sitting was out of the question in this outfit, as my body didn't bend the way it should. But I could perch just fine, so I balanced myself on the edge of the stool, my torso perfectly upright as the woman behind me took my hair in her hands.

Stacey and Emily perched on adjacent stools, watching me get my hair braided like it was the best show in town.

"Mitch is going to flip his shit." Emily wasn't even trying to use a Faire accent anymore.

Stacey nodded vigorously. "I can't wait to see his face. He's gonna—"

"This isn't . . ." I narrowed my eyes at them, and they didn't even try to look guilty. "I'm not doing this for him." Okay, maybe a very little part of me was, but the hell if I was going to admit that out loud. "I'm not," I insisted.

Emily put up defensive hands. "I'm not saying you are. Nothing wrong with dressing up for yourself. I was just making an observation."

I tried to shake my head, but the hair-braiding lady had too tight a grip, so I had about an inch and a half of space to move. "Well, your observation sucks. I told you, there's nothing going on between us."

Emily gave a singsong hum. "So you keep saying. And yet I keep seeing you two together."

"And you're super cute," Stacey chimed in, not helping in the least.

I huffed, which was about all I could do under the circumstances. "First of all, I'm sure that's not true. I'm like a decade older than he is, so I'm sure it looks ridiculous. Second—" I held up a hand, cutting off Emily, who was about to interrupt. "Secondly, I don't need to be one in that long line of women he dates. That won't do a thing for my self-esteem."

"I don't know about that." Stacey shook her head. "The long line, I mean."

I clucked my tongue at her. "You've seen him at Jackson's. You know his modus operandi. He's always on the prowl." I didn't tell them about the list of women in his phone calendar. That wasn't my business, and it sure as hell wasn't theirs.

"No. I mean, yeah, I know that. But . . ." Stacey's face scrunched up as she thought. "Daniel and I went out with Mitch last weekend after Faire, and it wasn't like that. Like, you know how he'll hang out with you, but wander off every so often when someone catches his eye? He stayed at the table with us the whole time. I don't think he even looked around." She shook her head hard, dismissing the memory. "I didn't think anything of it till just now. Huh."

"Huh," I echoed. She was right: that was weird. But then again, he'd been trawling Jackson's for years now, hadn't he? Hadn't he said something lately about running out of people to date in this small town? That probably had something to do with it.

Meanwhile, the hair braider finished her work and offered me a hand mirror.

"Oh my God." I couldn't say anything more than that. I looked . . . well, I didn't look like myself. My hair was pulled back from my face in small, intricate twists that fed to the back of my head. I put up one hand, tentatively patting at where it had all been braided in a spiral. It felt like I was wearing a crown made by my own hair. My fingertips skidded over little plastic pearls that had been tucked in here and there. This wasn't a hasty updo. This was a work of art. How long could I go before I'd have to take this down? A week? Two? Dry shampoo could work wonders, after all.

As I handed over my credit card to pay for my hair makeover, a familiar voice came from behind us. "Tired of me so soon, my good lady?"

I glanced over my shoulder to see Simon—no, I couldn't think of him as my brother-in-law right now. Because my mild-mannered, buttoned-down brother-in-law would never saunter around in leather pants, a half-open shirt under a black leather vest, a ridiculously feathered hat, and a wide smile. No, this wasn't Simon. This was his Renaissance Faire alter ego, Captain Blackthorne the pirate.

While the hair braider and I shared a conspiratorial smile, Emily turned to her husband with a bob of a curtsy. "Not at all, my good sir. I pray you, why would you say such a thing?"

He folded his arms across his chest and made a valiant attempt to glower. But these two had been married for barely a year, and there was no way that Simon-as-pirate could frown at his wife. "It is well past three of the clock, wife, and you were nowhere in sight when I was fighting just now."

"Oh!" She clapped her hands over her mouth and looked around as though trying to find a clock. But of course no one was wearing a watch, and all three of us had missed the chess match. "I apologize, my love. Truly, I do. But as you can see, my friend Beatrice and I were otherwise occupied." By the time she'd finished speaking I'd tucked my credit card back into my new leather pouch and turned around. There was this long, delicious beat as Simon realized it was me in this outfit, and his hazel eyes flew wide, his jaw dropping into an openmouthed smile.

"Why. My. Lady!" He strode forward and held out his hand, and I took it without thinking. He bowed extravagantly over our joined hands, and the little flutter my heart gave in response made a lot of things clear. Namely, why Emily had given him the time of day three years ago when he'd been a pain in her ass. Put a man in leather pants and eyeliner and a lot of sins could be forgiven.

I smiled at him as he straightened up again. "I'm not doing an accent," I said.

His laughter was an involuntary sound that warmed my heart. Why didn't he laugh like that year-round? He was so handsome when he did. "Wouldn't dream of putting you out, milady." He patted my hand with his other one, but when I thought he was going to release me, he instead tucked my hand in the crook of his arm. "Come along. There's someone who needs to see this."

This was inevitable, wasn't it?

As Simon dragged me away I looked over my shoulder at Emily and Stacey, trying to telegraph a plea for help. But they were useless. Those traitors practically skipped along behind us as we made our way past patrons, most of whom gave me second and third looks. Anxiety made my blood thrum in my temples, not helped by the blazing sunshine and all these damn layers I had on.

"How do you do this all day? I'm already sweating."

"Welcome to Faire life, darling," Simon said under his breath but still in character, and I choked on a laugh.

"Thanks, I hate it."

It didn't take long for us to reach the chess field, and Simon was right: the match had just ended. A few patrons were milling around with some of the cast, asking questions and taking photos.

And . . . I tried to take a deep breath before I forgot that I couldn't. So the air stalled in my lungs when I saw Mitch across the way. I was never going to get used to him looking like that, and I wiped my suddenly sweaty palms on the plaid sash around my waist. The sash that, now that I looked from it to the kilt that Mitch was wearing, didn't quite match. But it was damn close. Emily knew what she was doing.

I waited to feel that usual defensive surge of embarrassment, of denial. All the feelings that flowed through me whenever Emily gave me shit about whatever had been going on between Mitch and me for the past few weeks. But it wasn't there. Something about being in this dress made things between Mitch and me very clear. And very right. Suddenly all I wanted was for him to see me like this. I wanted to be someone who belonged in this part of his life.

So I nodded to Simon and lifted my skirts, weaving around the audience benches and two children dressed as knights facing off with wooden swords, until I reached my target. I got there just as the patrons Mitch was talking to left, and he turned as though sensing my presence. Then he froze. His eyes became enormous.

"Holy shit." He'd dropped the accent, as well as all pretense at character.

I tried to cross my arms, but it didn't work too well with my boobs all hiked up, so I settled for putting my hands on my hips. "I don't think that language is period appropriate."

"It is now." He looked me up and down, and if his gaze lingered on my cleavage a little too long, I didn't mind a bit. Payback for all the back-muscle ogling I'd been doing. He held out a hand, and after I took it, he raised our arms and encouraged me to do a slow twirl under them. "You look incredible, milady." The accent was back, and those r's rolled right down my spine.

"Thanks, kind sir." I raised my eyebrows at him. "I'm not doing an accent." The more people I told, hopefully the more acceptable it would be.

"Not required." Was he using words with lots of r's in them on purpose? Because that seemed mean. "May I ask what brought about this . . . transformation?"

I shrugged. "Thought it might be fun."

"And? Is it?"

"Well, I never knew how much I took breathing for granted, but other than that . . ." For once, I let myself smile the way I wanted to. "Yeah, it's kind of nice."

"Good." His gaze roamed over me again, and it was worth not being able to take a good deep breath if he would keep looking at me like that.

"Sorry I missed your show."

He shrugged, his smile matching mine. "Ye've seen it. But I have good news."

"Oh yeah? What's that?"

"No more shows today."

"Really? You're done for the day?" Disappointment pricked my good mood. I'd spent a lot of time—and not a little money—getting dressed up like this. How was him being done for the day good news? Dammit.

"I didnae say that." He cleared his throat and switched back to his normal voice since there weren't any patrons around. "I said I'm done here. Now I walk the grounds, take pictures with patrons—"

"Of course." I wanted to roll my eyes, but my usual annoyance with Mitch didn't seem to be there. Huh.

He continued talking like I hadn't spoken. "—check on the volunteers—especially the kids. Make sure everyone's where they're supposed to be." He shook his head. "You don't know how many times I've caught kids sneaking out to the woods to check their phones. Or worse." He wiggled his eyebrows and I got his meaning.

"You're actually busy. Got it. Then what's the good news, exactly?"

"The good news is that my job is to walk around. And I'd love some company. You know, if you're free."

He held out his hand again and I didn't hesitate to take it.

"Why yes, good sir," I said in my accentless voice. "I'm free."

As we stepped onto the lane, arm in arm, he glanced down at

my feet when I twitched my skirts up a couple inches. "Nice sneakers," he said sotto voce.

I dropped my skirts so they covered up my battered Converse. "I ran out of money," I muttered. "This shit is expensive." Plus I didn't want to give any money to that leatherworker who sold the boots. He could kiss my no-longer-mundane ass.

Mitch snorted, putting the accent back on. "I can relate."

I gave him a side-eye. "Seriously? You have on like half an outfit."

"You think kilts are cheap? And these boots?" He hiked up a leg, and while I tried to ignore the way the fabric of his kilt slid up his thigh, I glanced down at the boots strapped to his calves. They looked similar to the leatherworker's: sturdy black leather with pewter buttons the size of a silver dollar studded up one side.

"They're nice," I said.

"They're expensive as hell," he said. "But they last. This is my third year with these."

"Hmm." Okay, maybe that dickhead of a leather guy knew his craft. I still wasn't buying anything from him.

Mitch wasn't kidding. Even though his job right now was "walk around and look good" he was still busy. Patrons stopped him for photos, and I found myself dragged into a few of them myself. "Try and look happy about it," Mitch murmured in my ear, but he couldn't see how I was already smiling. It felt so right to be here with him, doing nothing in particular. Just existing next to him. I'd made it to the other side of the chasm, and I loved it here.

We stopped for my now-traditional frozen lemonade, which I forced myself to eat instead of dumping directly down my dress. He checked in on the volunteers up front, making sure they were staying hydrated and weren't screwing around on their phones when they should be handing out maps or otherwise interacting with the guests. We lingered in the back of the crowd when the Gilded Lilies sang, and I enjoyed watching Caitlin's eyes pop out of their sockets when she caught sight of me. I bobbed an awkward curtsy in her direction before the set ended and we moved on. We took the circuitous route to the back of the grounds, where the last joust of the day was in full swing.

It wasn't far from there that Emily flagged us down. "Oh, thank God. I need your help."

"What's the matter?" Mitch's attention snapped to her with a concerned expression.

"Oh, no. I'm fine. I just need warm bodies." She tugged on the both of us, pulling us toward the Chaucer Stage. "The crowd's thinning out, since everyone's heading up front for pub sing. But the kids have one more show, and there's like three people in the audience. Just come sit and pretend to enjoy their performance, okay?"

That didn't seem like much of an inconvenience. "I don't mind sitting for a little bit. What's the show?"

"It's theatre," Emily explained. "It's a few scenes of *Much Ado About Nothing* with some of Simon's honors kids. They get extra credit next fall for surviving the whole experience."

I smirked. "That seems fair."

But Mitch groaned at Emily. "Aw, come on, Park. You know I don't like all that Shakespeare stuff."

"Well, I do." I led the way into the clearing of trees where the Chaucer Stage was set up. Behind me Mitch grumbled out another protest but he followed me to one of the benches in the back. I picked a bench that was under a tree, and the shade was pure cool bliss. Emily was right; the audience was sparse for this last show of the day, so it was fortunate that between my skirts and Mitch's sheer size we took up a good amount of space.

Caitlin had never been too interested in theatre. She'd done Shakespeare scenes with Emily one summer of Ren Faire but otherwise had steered clear. I didn't realize until now just how I lucky I was, because high school students mostly murdering Shakespeare was painful.

"Are we gonna have to sit through this whole thing?" Mitch's voice was low in my ear and just for me.

I elbowed him in the ribs and tried to deny the rush of heat I felt from his voice in my ear. "Hush. This is art."

"This is crap." That earned him another elbow and he caught my arm with a snort, capturing it while he wrapped his other arm around my shoulders, keeping me from injuring him any further. I grinned and relaxed into him, even going so far as to rest my head in the hollow of his shoulder.

I got it now. I understood why Emily did this every summer, and how it had become such a part of my friends' lives. Dressed like this, with my hair braided and my skirts hiding my sneakers, wrapped in the arms of a strapping-looking, kilted faux Highlander, I didn't feel like a fortysomething single mother. I wasn't introverted me at all. I was someone who got to do this. Who got to stroll through the trees with the guy she liked, subsist on frozen lemonade and funnel cakes, and live in a world where swords and kilts and knights on horseback were an everyday thing. No nosy neighbors or judgy mothers. No lists of women in his phone. No decade of years between us. No leaving town.

I was someone who got to sit here in the shade, nestled against Mitch's side, his heart beating under my ear and the rise and fall of his chest against my cheek. Yes, I could see the appeal of this. In being someone else. Because in this moment, all I wanted to be was this woman in his arms.

Onstage, the teenage Beatrice and Benedick had stopped their bickering and had fallen in love. The girl was sitting on a rough-hewn bench, the boy kneeling at her feet, his voice earnest. "I do love nothing in the world so much as you: is that not strange?"

The words hit me full in the chest, where I felt something shift. That wall around my heart had never felt so precarious. "Is that not strange?" I repeated in a whisper, dashing away a tear that had sprung to the corner of my eye.

"Hmm?" Mitch glanced down at me, his face softening as he took in whatever expression was on my face.

I shook my head and patted his thigh, enjoying the way the muscle felt beneath the kilt despite those infuriating bike shorts he wore. "Nothing." I left my hand where it was. His arm tightened around me and I remembered the most wonderful thing: Caitlin wasn't going to be home tonight.

"What are you doing after this?" I whispered, still looking ahead at the stage.

"Going out, like always," he said with a general lack of enthusiasm. Or maybe he was just being polite and staying quiet because the show was still going on. "Why?"

"Oh, no reason. It's just that I'm home alone tonight."

He froze, muscles tensing. I continued talking like I didn't notice. "So I was wondering if you . . ." I let the sentence trail off while my heart pounded in my throat. Was I really going to do this? But it wasn't me inviting Mitch over, was it? It was the woman who wore this dress. And she was a lot more fun than I was.

"Oh," he said. Then his eyes went wide. "Oh. Well." He cleared his throat quietly and shifted a little on the bench. His fingertips had found the slice of skin between my drop-shouldered under-dress and bodice, and he drew little circles there. "I mean, going out isn't all it's cracked up to be. Especially if staying in with you is an option."

My shrug was a slight twitch of my shoulders, an excuse to snuggle more into him. "I don't have anything exciting planned. Maybe just order some takeout and . . ."

"I bet we can think of something." He was still murmuring in my ear, but his voice had dropped an octave, going a little grav-elly, and I felt it all the way down in my bones. "Maybe some-thing involving attachments?"

I snorted a laugh that tried to be scandalized, but that was an emotion for someone else, not the woman in this dress. Instead I gave his thigh a squeeze. "I think I can guarantee that."

Onstage, the girl was saying to the boy, "I love you with so much of my heart that none is left to protest," and I felt that down in my bones too.

Nineteen

The magic of being the woman in this dress ran out about halfway home. Probably because I had to unlace the bodice before I could comfortably sit behind the wheel to drive, and the magic drained out that way. Whatever it was, by the time I pulled into my neighborhood I was practically vibrating with tension. I could picture Marjorie, Caroline, everyone from book club and everyone who'd ever gossiped about the single mother who lived on the block, all of them looking out their windows. Clucking their tongues over how I was dressed, raising their eyebrows when that bright red truck showed up again in my driveway. And, if everything went well tonight, when it was there the next morning.

This may have been a terrible idea.

I turned onto my street and weighed the lesser of two evils. Decision made, I opened the garage door but parked on the far left side of my driveway, risking the thirty-second walk of shame in a fairy-tale gown from the car to the front door. Once inside I dug out my phone and texted Mitch.

I'll leave the garage door open for you, if you can park in there.

The message was marked Read almost right away, but it was a couple minutes before he texted back.

Okay. But do me a favor. Don't order dinner yet.

As requests went, that was pretty innocuous. **Sure. Still deciding what you want?**

I know what I want. Food can wait. Even through the screen his innuendo was clear, and I felt my blood heat up in response. I dropped my phone to the counter like it had burned me.

A few minutes later I heard the rumble of a truck engine, loud in my garage. As the engine cut off I slipped through the door in the kitchen, hitting the button to close the garage door as Mitch got out of his truck. The garage door rattled down, and we were sealed in the semidarkness, safe from prying eyes.

Mitch's eyes met mine across the hood of his truck in the dim light of the garage, and I caught my breath. He looked . . . predatory, and with each step he took toward me I stepped back, until we were both in the kitchen and he'd closed the door behind us. His approach continued; I was backed up against the kitchen island and his eyes darkened as he closed the space between us. He reached out and traced his fingertips down my loosened bodice.

"You unlaced this." His voice flowed, low and warm between us, with a slight rumble that made my chest grow tight. "I've been thinking about doing that all afternoon."

Untying my bodice hadn't helped; I could barely breathe with how much I wanted him. "Sorry. Couldn't drive otherwise." My voice was a mere rush of breath. His touch was hot, even through the layers of fabric I still wore, and when he stroked back up my chest to the neckline of my underdress I braced myself against the island to hold myself upright.

But two could play at this. I reached out, bunching the wool of his kilt between two fingers and twitching it upward, slipping my hand underneath to flirt with the hem. My fingers skidded against a well-toned thigh, solid and warm and very, very bare. "Hold up," I said. "You had bike shorts under this today."

"I did. Stopped by home on the way here." He dug in his sporran as he talked, and he produced a fistful of condoms, slapping them down on the counter beside me like a winning hand of poker.

"Ah. Someone's got plans for tonight." Even though my heart pounded in my throat, I tried to keep my voice, my touch teasing. But I made my intentions clear as I stroked up his thigh, over painfully defined quadriceps to his hip. I itched to move those few inches inward, to touch him, to curl my fist around him, but this anticipation was delicious torture, and I couldn't let it end quite yet.

But Mitch was done with teasing. With waiting. "Fuck yeah I do," he growled. That growl was the only warning I had before his mouth was on mine and oh, I'd forgotten how good it felt to kiss him. To be claimed by him. He lifted me like I was nothing, sitting me on the kitchen island before he got to work unlacing my dress the rest of the way. Freed from its confines, the chemise underneath slipped down over one shoulder, and his mouth was there, kissing the bared skin in a trail up to my throat. I clutched at his shoulders, trying to pull him closer, and our kisses grew more and more frantic. Layers of fabric between us were moved aside as we tried to get to each other. He shoved my skirts up, over my knees and higher, stepping between my legs while he spread them with his large hands. He peeled my underwear down my legs to the floor while I groped blindly for a condom, ripping it open before my hands were back under his kilt, getting it the hell out of my way. He wasn't gentle as he pulled my hips to the edge of the counter, and I wasn't gentle as I dug my fingernails into his shoulders when he pushed into me.

There was nothing slow about this. Nothing sweet. It was hard, quick, intense. With every thrust we pulled at each other, trying to get closer, deeper, trying to consume each other.

"God, I've missed this." He hitched one of my legs higher, driving deeper, and the change in sensation sent a shiver through me.

"You feel . . . I need you . . ." Closer. I needed him closer. I needed more.

"I've missed this," he said again. "I've missed you, April. Missed you so much." Then his mouth was on mine and one hand was pushing under my skirts, finding where we were joined, stroking hard, and I felt the sparks everywhere. I chased them, rode him, shuddered under his touch when my climax shook me, and swallowed his shout when it was his turn to shudder hard into me.

It took long, long moments for our bodies to calm. Mitch pressed his forehead to mine and our breaths mingled as our heartbeats slowed, syncopated. This close, I studied his face, ran a hand down his cheek, traced the shell of his ear. "I've missed you too." My confession hung between us in the quiet of my kitchen, and Mitch's smile lit up everything inside me as he moved that fraction forward to kiss me again.

"Now?" I asked when he'd disposed of the condom and I could speak again. "Now can I order dinner?"

"Nope," he said cheerfully. He reached out a hand, helping me down off the island, and I tried to stand on legs that shook. "Now it's time for that important Ren Faire tradition. The post-Faire shower."

My laugh was a huff as I let him lead me into my bedroom and to the master bathroom. "I've done that before, you know. I always take a shower when I get back from my volunteer shifts."

"Ahhh, this is different. You walked the lanes with me today. You don't realize it, but you're covered in dirt. Probably in places you haven't thought about in years." He turned on my shower like he'd been there a million times before coming back into the bedroom to unhook his boots. Boots were followed by socks, and I sat on the edge of my bed, enjoying the show as he unbuckled his kilt.

"You could charge tickets for this, you know," I said as the plaid fabric fell to the floor.

He snorted. "Nah. Let's keep this a private show." Unselfconsciously naked, he held out a hand and I took it, letting him pull me to my feet before peeling away the layers of my now-disheveled costume.

I stepped under the spray, letting the hot water pound between my shoulder blades, loosening muscles I didn't realize were tense. But a different, happier tension crept into my body as Mitch joined me in the shower. He reached for my body wash and a loofah, turning me this way and that as he rubbed me down with suds-covered hands. I returned the favor, covering his skin in swirls of soap, urging him to turn so I could explore those back muscles one by one.

"God." I glanced at my feet, where water swirled down the drain. It was dark at first as the evidence of the day spent in the woods sloughed off our bodies. "We're disgusting."

His laugh was a rumble. "We're authentic. Or something." He reclaimed the loofah and scrubbed my back gently. "One of the kids said to me a couple years ago, if your boogers aren't black you're doing Faire wrong."

My laugh bounced around the shower tiles and his chuckle joined it. "Charming."

"Teenagers are smooth." His arms closed around me, cuddling me to his body as we let the spray rinse us off, and there was that tight feeling in my chest again. But this time it wasn't about lust. There was nothing about this time in the shower that signaled sex. His arms stroked down mine till he reached my hands, threading our fingers together and holding on tight. I felt safe in his arms. I felt sheltered. Like nothing was going to hurt me ever again.

He felt so good I could cry. In fact, I was crying: silent tears that streamed down my cheeks and were thankfully washed away unnoticed by the shower. Being with him like this was dangerous. It was temporary. It was fake, just like everything else between us. But it felt real, and that was why it was so dangerous.

What if I said something? What if I said the words, told him I didn't want to pretend anymore? What if I made a hole in this wall around my heart and showed him the way in? He might not want it. He would be so kind as he let me down easy, making sure I understood this was just a friends-with-benefits thing. I should be thankful, really, that someone like him would give someone like me just a little bit of his time . . .

I fought to breathe against the sob in my chest as I willed these feelings away. They were inconvenient. They were unwanted. Especially right now, while I still had him. Plenty of time to cry later.

But I should have known better. Mitch noticed everything when it came to me, and the hitch in my breathing was too obvious, especially with my back pressed to his front like this. "Hey."

He turned me around and tipped my face up to his, cradled in his hands. "What is it?"

I shook my head hard. I couldn't do this. Not with his eyes so blue and open and staring down at me like I could hold his heart in my hands. But to my horror the words spilled out before I could stop them. "I know this isn't real. But I don't care." I reached up, holding his face in my hands the way he held mine, as though this could anchor us together. As though reality couldn't intrude on what we shared right here and now. "I don't care," I said again. "I just want . . ."

"Are you kidding?" He kissed me deeply, thoroughly, his tongue laying claim to my mouth while his hands laid claim to my body. "What about this feels fake to you?" He turned us carefully, moving us in a slow, intimate dance until my back was against the porcelain shower wall. "Do you feel this?" He took my hand and curled it around his cock, hot, hard, and growing harder as I touched him. "Does this feel real to you?" He encouraged me to stroke him as his hand delved between my legs, doing some stroking of his own.

"Yes," I gasped, moving against his hand, unable to think.

"I'm not sure." I could barely hear his voice over the spray of the water and the haze of pleasure that had taken over my senses. "Maybe I'm not doing a good enough job of convincing you here." He took his hand away, but before I could protest he'd lowered himself to his knees in front of me, hands stroking up my legs to grasp my hips, and my hands went flat to the shower wall as he let me know with his mouth, his tongue, and some very well-placed fingers just how real this all was. I shattered into a million pieces in that shower, doubts spiraling out of control and away, more tears mixing with water that was starting to grow cool. Something in my heart broke as well, taking a sledge-hammer to that wall that had encased it, kept it safe for all these years, leaving nothing but dust in its wake.

How was I going to put it back together?

Much, much later, I was curled up on the couch in my favorite yoga pants. Right before dinner had been delivered Mitch had pulled on a pair of gray sweats that he'd taken from the duffel bag he'd optimistically tossed in the back of his truck. I recognized that duffel from our weekend away and that knowledge warmed me, made me feel like we had a shared history that we were building together. Condoms, an overnight bag . . . he'd definitely come prepared tonight.

But now, full of spicy Thai noodles and with every muscle in my body relaxed, I indulged in a full-body stretch while Mitch channel surfed, looking for a movie we could pretend to watch. A yawn slipped out of me, long and languid and completely unexpected. I slapped a hand over my mouth, embarrassment heating my cheeks. But Mitch just tugged me closer against him, kissing the top of my head and encouraging me to rest against his chest. One hand stroked through my long-since-unbraided hair, over and over in a hypnotic rhythm.

"Long day." I felt his voice against my ear as much as I heard it, and I nodded.

"You don't have to stay if you need to get home." I blinked heavily, embarrassed that I was practically dozing in his arms. God, give me a couple of orgasms in quick succession, followed by carbs, and I was out for the night. Some exciting date I was.

"What?" He looked down at me, brushing a lock of hair off my forehead. "You don't want me to stay?"

"No, I do. Just . . ." I didn't know how to put this. How was I supposed to ask when he was meeting someone next? What woman's name was in his phone for tomorrow morning? For Monday? I had no right to ask, but it was all I could think about. "No early morning appointments tomorrow?" There, that was as obvious as I dared.

He made a negative sound as his fingers made lazy circles on my arm. "No, tomorrow's Sunday. It's a Faire day. I don't work out on the weekends during the summer. Those chess matches are enough of a workout, believe me."

"Is that what they're calling it these days? A workout?" I tried to sound light, unconcerned. The words were supposed to be a joke but they were coated with bile as they came out of my mouth. I couldn't help it. I pictured my name going into his phone on today's date. Did he enter names retroactively?

When I chanced a look up at him he was blinking at me in confusion. "What else would I call it?"

Oh, the hell with this. Sleepiness gone, I scrubbed a hand over my face and sat up. He frowned at the loss, but I held up a hand. "Look, I saw your phone. When we went to Virginia."

He looked nonplussed. "Okay . . . ? I think I remember that. Getting the address of the hotel, right?"

"Yeah. But I saw the names."

"The names," he repeated blankly.

"The names." Now I was getting mad. Was he being deliberately obtuse? "In your phone." I reached for it on the coffee table and waved it at him. "All the women you're with. Early in the morning."

His brow was a knot of confusion as he took the phone out of my hand, and I kept talking, my voice getting higher and my words becoming suspiciously close to a babble. "It's none of my business, I know it's not, but I don't want you to think you have to stay here with me if you have . . . you know . . . another engagement." *Engagement?* I sounded like a Jane Austen heroine. What the fuck.

He scrolled through his phone with a perplexed expression while I was talking, then stopped. "Wait." Some more taps, some more scrolling. "You mean like Fran, Cindy, Annie?"

"Maybe?" *Definitely.* I shouldn't have remembered them, but they were burned into my brain and onto my heart. Reminding me that the guy paying attention to me paid attention to a lot of other women too. I was nothing special.

"Angie, Diane . . . ?"

I put my hands over my ears. "I don't need to hear all their names."

He tugged my hands down. "Come here. Please." I wanted to resist, but I sighed and let him pull me back down against him. His arms went around me, and he held his phone in front of us both. "Look. They're workouts."

"Yeah." I didn't look at his phone. "You said that already. And it frankly sounds a little misogynistic if you ask me. To refer to banging someone as . . ."

"CrossFit workouts." He spoke over me. "Look . . ." He pulled up the web browser on his phone, then navigated to a page for an industrial-looking gym that seemed to be a glorified garage. The kind of place that blasted hardcore metal music twenty-four hours a day. "Here's where I work out, see?" He tapped again, bringing up the schedule. "Six in the morning, so I can get it done and get to work during the school year. I remember now, right around when we went to my grandparents', we were doing a bunch of the girls."

I shook my head. "Not sounding any better."

He sighed in frustration, tapping a little more. "Okay. Here. Here's a list. See how they're all girls' names? They're benchmark workouts, so you can track your progress as you repeat them. Here's Cindy." He scrolled to the name, in big red letters on the site, and read off the list below it. "That's five pull-ups, ten push-ups, and fifteen squats."

"That . . . that doesn't seem too bad." I leaned forward, intent on the phone.

"As many times as you can for twenty minutes."

"Oh." I sat back. "Never mind. That sucks."

He snorted. "Especially at six in the morning. Fran's different: that one's timed, so the point is to beat your time from last time. If you'd actually clicked on the calendar entries, I was keeping track of numbers of reps, time, stuff like that for the different workouts."

"Huh." I was quiet for a moment as I reordered my thinking. I imagined clicking on Fran, picturing him timing himself while he . . . nope. I wasn't going there.

"Wait." He leaned forward, leaned us both forward, to drop his phone back on the coffee table. "You really thought . . ." He grasped my shoulders, turning me to face him. "April." The intensity in his voice and the seriousness in his expression were jarring. This was not a guy who looked like this. Not often. "There's been no one. Not since Virginia. God, before that even. Since that night at Jackson's, when I chased that guy off. There's just been you. You know that, right?"

"I . . ." This was too much, and I couldn't respond. All I could do was shake my head, eyes wide. I couldn't even blink when he was looking at me like this.

"Look. I know this shit is hard for you." He tucked my hair behind my ears while he talked. "I know you've done everything on your own all this time. You don't like letting people in. But . . . I'm here, okay? Whatever you need. *Whenever* you need."

"I need . . ." But I couldn't say it. I couldn't tell him about my secret heart, the one that had just begun to beat for the first time in so long. The one that wanted to let him in. I didn't have the words. Not yet. I needed time. I needed him to understand.

So instead I kissed him, hoping I could say it this way. And from the way he kissed me back, pulling me into his lap and holding me close, he got the message.

That night was the first time my king-size bed had ever felt cozy. I loved the way he tucked me against him as we fell asleep, one arm around my chest. Copping a feel even in his sleep, I thought as I started to fall asleep myself. Typical.

It wasn't until that last second of consciousness before sleep took me that I realized. He wasn't groping me. His hand was placed flat on my chest. Over my heart.

Twenty

I *woke up the* next morning alone. My heart sank, and I closed my eyes against the swell of disappointment that surged through me. For one barely awake moment I wondered if I'd dreamed last night. But no: even though the pillow on the other side of the bed was cold, it had clearly been slept on, and the blankets on that side were pushed toward the middle of the bed. I rolled to my back and heaved a long sigh.

Then I smelled coffee.

The surge of disappointment became a swell of happiness, and not just because I didn't have to make my own coffee this morning. I climbed out of bed and, after putting on the shorts-and-tank pajamas I'd never bothered to wear last night, I padded toward the kitchen. I didn't speak at first, I just leaned in the doorway and watched Mitch, his back to me, wearing nothing but the gray sweats he'd worn last night, pouring coffee into two mugs. He moved to the fridge, getting the carton of creamer out of the door and pouring a good dollop into one of the mugs, and the swell of happiness became a little glow in my chest. He remembered how I took my coffee.

I scuffed one foot along the floor, making my presence known as I walked the rest of the way into the kitchen, and he turned.

"Hey, you're up." He passed me the mug of coffee he'd put cream in. He didn't ask if he'd gotten it right; he just knew. On anyone else that confidence would be irritating. On Mitch it was just . . . him.

So I said thank you and took that blissful first sip of coffee, letting the caffeine soak into my system and chase away the rest of the cobwebs in the corners of my brain. Mitch leaned one hip against the counter, sipping from his own mug, and the whole thing felt so domestic. So right. I could get used to this.

What? No. I pushed that thought right the hell out of my brain. We weren't there yet.

"You want breakfast?" he asked, as though I were the guest. He really did make himself at home, didn't he? "I usually grab something on the way to Faire, but . . ."

I shook my head and hoisted my mug. "Coffee's fine. But help yourself." I nodded toward the fridge. "There's eggs in there if you need some protein. I mean, I'm no Cindy, but I definitely feel like I had a workout last night."

Mitch's laugh was loud and long, something that didn't happen often in this house, and his laugh made my smile widen. "Believe me, you're a lot more fun than Cindy." His good-morning kiss was coffee flavored and I leaned into it, even though black coffee wasn't usually my thing. "You should come with me to CrossFit sometime," he said when he straightened up again. "You might like it."

"Nah, that's okay." I finger-combed his sleep-rumpled hair off his forehead, softening my dismissal of his suggestion. "I'm more of a runner." The admission surprised me even as I said it, because I hadn't thought of myself as a runner in a long time.

"Oh, yeah?" Interest lit his eyes, which, of course. He was interested in all things sports and fitness, and I hated to disappoint him.

"Well, I was. I used to be, before . . ." I gestured down to my bad leg, and his eyes followed my hand, glancing down for a moment, then back up, bewildered.

"Was there lasting damage?" His brows knit together in concern. "Did the doctors say you can't?"

"No." But my voice was uncertain. Because that was true. I remembered that last visit to physical therapy, that last follow-up with the surgeon. Both times, I was told that everything was a go. I should be good as new. But I hadn't been.

"It's been what, about three years? You should be able to pick it up again."

I shook my head, looking away as I put my coffee mug down on the counter. "I tried once, but . . ." Frustration clogged my chest, just like it had that time that I'd gone out on that abortive run. My body had betrayed me and I'd never gotten over it.

"Have you tried lately?" He took a step toward me, his voice gentle like I might spook and run away. "Working back up to previous levels of fitness can be hard to do, but it's not impossible. Start slow." His hand stroked up and down my arm, and I found myself leaning into the comfort his touch offered.

"Yeah?"

His smile was intimate and encouraging. "Yeah. You need to ease back into things when it's been a while. Don't push yourself too hard or you'll give up."

"Good advice." I had a feeling we weren't just talking about running anymore, but I also didn't have the nerve to clarify.

That would definitely be pushing myself too hard. So instead I turned back to my coffee while he did the same.

"Hey." Mitch looked around the kitchen like he was just seeing it for the first time. "You never did the cabinets."

"Hmm?"

"The cabinets. Remember? You were going to change out the fronts. I sent you that picture."

"I said I'd think about it." At least I hoped that's what I said; I'd completely forgotten his text until just now. That had been that horrifying night at book club, with the cupcakes, and . . . thank God I'd had him park in the garage last night. I studied the cabinets. "It's not a bad idea, though. I'll go look soon."

"Or I can do it. I'm not all that busy this week. I can text you some pics while you're at work."

"That . . . that would be great. Thank you." A warm feeling bloomed in my chest. I'd missed having Mitch over, helping me with the house. Maybe it would be worth a little neighborhood gossip to have him come over again.

Or maybe I could talk him into continuing to park in the garage. Less ammunition for the neighbors that way.

"I'm going to swing by my place real quick, but do you need a ride to Faire this morning?" Mitch took my mug when I was done, putting them both in the dishwasher. See? Domestic. But my eyes flew wide at the question, and tension washed away all those tender domestic feelings.

"What? No. No . . . I can drive myself." Gossip at Faire had been bad enough last weekend. It had already died down, in favor of newer scandals involving one of the traveling acrobats and a guy from the mud show. I didn't need to be back on the front page, as it were, by showing up in the passenger seat of Mitch's bright red truck.

Thankfully, Mitch wasn't a mind reader and couldn't see my inner turmoil. "Okay. Come by and say hi later if you want." He went through to the dining room to pick up his overnight bag that he'd left on the table.

"Come by?" I couldn't keep the alarm out of my voice. Come by where? His place? I'd never been there before.

"Yeah. The chess field. For the two o'clock? You know, if you're hanging out when you're done at the box office."

"Oh. Right." I shook my head. "I think I'm gonna go straight home today. Someone kept me up kind of late last night." I forced a yawn, which frankly wasn't too hard. I wasn't kidding about him giving me a workout. Maybe I should take up CrossFit after all.

Mitch grinned at my innuendo and pulled me close. "Then I'll call you later, okay?" His goodbye kiss was short but still toe-curling. It was a confident kiss that said this was just the beginning.

The beginning of what? That thought echoed through my head as I closed the garage door after he left. I was absolutely out of my depth here, and had no idea what to do. How to act. It had been almost two decades since I'd been a wife, even longer since I'd been a girlfriend. Faking it for Mitch's family or for my ex-husband was one thing. It was low stakes and finite. But this no longer felt like a performance, and I had no blueprint on how to move forward. Were we going to be out in public together for real, where everyone could see us? Where everyone could comment on Mitch and his much-older girlfriend? I wasn't ready for that.

Or was I jumping the gun? Sure, last night had been great, but in the brightness of the morning the things we'd said to each other seemed like something out of a dream. Yesterday I'd been in a Ren Faire costume with flowing skirts and elaborately braided hair. Today I was throwing on my volunteer T-shirt, tying my hair in a ponytail, and going back to selling tickets. I was back to being just me.

Back to being mundane.

And if there was one thing I knew for sure, it was that Mitch wasn't a mundane kind of guy.

The next week went relatively smoothly. I went to work, then I had dinner with Caitlin when I got home. She'd been working extra hours at the bookstore lately; Emily'd had the sudden urge to inventory the books, and Cait was enlisted to help her out. I had a feeling it was less to do with inventory and more to do with throwing a little extra money my daughter's way, now that the summer was coming to an end and she was starting to pack for college.

During the week Mitch, as promised, texted me photos of cabinet doors, and we both agreed on a pale green set that wasn't obnoxious enough to be considered bright, but was different enough to not be another damn neutral color. I placed the order, and Mitch offered to pick them up for me on Friday.

Leave the garage open, he texted, **and we can unload them in there.**

I heaved a sigh of relief. His truck in the garage meant fewer neighbors talking about my business. Win-win.

I parked out front when I got home on Friday and left the garage door open while I changed out of my business casual clothes from work and into jeans and a T-shirt. I made it back to the garage, throwing my hair up into a ponytail, just as Mitch arrived. He backed into the garage, which was an act of bravery given how much junk I had in there.

"Is this them?" I stretched up onto my tiptoes to peek into the bed of the truck.

"No." The slam of the driver's side door punctuated his state-ment. "These belong to someone else. I'm making deliveries." He greeted me with an eye roll and a smile, and I punched him lightly on the arm.

"Funny." I waited while he unlatched the lift gate, hopping from one foot to the other like a kid on Christmas, then reached for one of the shrink-wrapped packages and tugged. "Oh. These are heavy."

Mitch hefted one of the packages like it was nothing. Figured. "See, this is why you need me." His voice was teasing, so I tried not to make too much of that statement. He directed me to the smaller packages, and I wrangled those into the house while he unloaded the larger ones. Soon my kitchen was full of cabinet doors, stacked along the wall like firewood.

"Not bad." But I was breathing hard; I hadn't expected a work-out this soon after work.

"Not bad at all," he agreed. "We can get these changed out pretty quick. One more weekend of Faire, but then after that? Make a weekend out of it?"

I shook my head. "We'll be in full-on college prep mode for the next couple weeks after that."

"Ahhhh, right. Is she excited?"

"That's an understatement."

"And how about you, Mama? Are you excited?" But he seemed to know the answer to that, wrapping an arm around me and kissing my temple before I could formulate an answer.

"Not sure if 'excited' is the word." I accepted his embrace, even leaned into it as I slipped an arm around his back. "Is there a word for full of dread yet proud yet worried, and feeling like I won't get a good night's sleep till I see her again at Thanksgiving?"

"Probably one of those really long German words." He released me to open the fridge in the kitchen while my phone buzzed on the kitchen island. "Aw, man! Am I out of beer?"

"Hey, you know the rules," I said lightly as I scooped up my phone. "BYOB around here."

"Fine," he sighed elaborately, grabbing a soda instead and nudging the door shut. He reached for his phone in his back pocket, and we both looked at the text we'd simultaneously received from Emily.

Beer and pizza at Jackson's in an hour? Let's give Stacey and Daniel a send-off before they go!

"Is Stacey leaving already?" I glanced up at Mitch, who shook his head in confusion.

"She shouldn't be. One more weekend of Faire and all." He shrugged. "But it'll be a busy weekend, and then they're off to the next festival, right? Getting the goodbyes out of the way early, maybe."

I considered that. "Okay, then. What do you think? Want to go?"

"Yeah," he said. "May as well." He looked down at the soda in his hand. "At least they have beer at Jackson's."

I bumped his arm with my shoulder and he chuckled in response. We bent over our phones, and while I sent a quick text to Caitlin at the bookstore (**You okay if I go out tonight? No wild parties while I'm gone**), Mitch's response to the group text came through. **We're in. See you in a bit.** A chill prickled my skin.

"We?" I looked up at Mitch with alarmed eyes. It felt like he'd announced something without checking with me first.

"Yeah. Wait, you said you were going, right?"

"I did." But I looked back down at my phone, where the words "We're in" seemed to be blinking at me in red.

Beside me, Mitch didn't notice my discomfort. "You want me to drive?"

"No," I said quickly. His text was bad enough: answering for both of us like we were a couple. If we rode over together that would pretty much seal the deal in a town like this. "No," I said again. "I haven't heard back from Cait yet. I'll drive myself over in case she needs me."

He scoffed. "She's eighteen and it's Friday night. I can guarantee that she doesn't need you."

"Almost eighteen." I gave him a thin smile. "Humor me, okay?" I needed some distance while I got myself together. I needed to keep my cool and not hang all over him at Jackson's like . . . like a girlfriend or something. In my secret heart I hoped we were heading in that direction, but it was all still too new. He hadn't made any real declaration, and neither had I. Those words were impossible to take back once they were said. I wasn't ready to make that leap, and I certainly wasn't ready to take this public. Not even to the people I felt closest to. No matter how natural it felt to have his arm around me, his lips in my hair.

No, I needed to get a grip. On myself. Not on Mitch.

Twenty-One

On nights that I went to Jackson's with my sister we usually grabbed a booth in the back, so we could talk quietly while the bad karaoke happened toward the front. But there were six of us tonight, and with Mitch's huge shoulders and Daniel's long legs, there was no way we'd all fit in a booth. By the time I got there Simon and Daniel had pushed two tables together, and I helped Emily grab the chairs to put around them. Mitch and Stacey came back from where they had gone to get menus, as though we all didn't have it memorized. After some good-natured fighting over pizza toppings (Stacey and Emily were pro-pineapple, Mitch and I were solidly against, while Daniel and Simon wisely stayed neutral), we placed our orders for a couple pizzas, far too many mozzarella sticks, and a round of drinks.

"I can't believe you're leaving already," Emily said, grabbing Stacey in a one-armed side-hug. "Didn't you just get here?"

"Sure feels like it," she said. "But we're not going anywhere, you know."

"You're not?" I asked. "This is the last weekend of the Faire, right? Isn't Maryland Ren Fest next, down by the coast?"

"Sure," Daniel said. "But it's not that far away. Stacey's parents offered to let us stay, so we don't have to worry about hotels or camping or any of that."

"Wait," Simon said. "'Us'? You don't mean . . ."

"I do." Daniel's eyebrows arched in a smile as he picked up his pint of Guinness that had just been delivered. While he took a sip, Stacey finished his thought.

"The whole band is staying at my house," she said, almost with a straight face. "The guys are in the spare bedrooms, and Daniel and I are in my old place over the garage. Mom offered, and then she wouldn't take no for an answer. I think she was mesmerized by their kilts."

"God. Please." Daniel grimaced and closed his eyes. "These are my cousins you're talking about. I don't want to think about your mom looking at them in any way."

"Anyway," Stacey giggled. "Lucky for Dex, my parents got rid of my pink canopy bed, and I spent this week cleaning out my old bedroom of any incriminating teenage evidence."

I snorted and took a sip of cider. "So that means you're here till when? October?"

Daniel nodded. "And we've already been here a month. So Willow Creek is going to be home base for a while. That's, what . . ." He glanced over at Stacey. "Almost four months in one place? For us that's practically putting down roots."

"Okay, fine. I guess this isn't much of a send-off, then." Emily pretended to grumble, but the mozzarella sticks had arrived to cheer her up.

I raised my glass. "It's a plain old Friday night out, then. Nothing wrong with that."

"Yeah . . ." She looked around the table and a grin crawled over her face. "Look at all of us! It's like a triple date!"

I choked on my cider as my heart thudded in my chest. I kept my eyes on the baskets of mozzarella sticks and pointedly didn't look across the table at Mitch. I couldn't.

"Speaking of . . ." Stacey propped her chin on her hand, twinkling her smile in my direction. "You two have looked awfully cute at Faire lately."

Goddammit, Stacey. I bit down on my bottom lip to keep from scowling. Mitch laughed, but before he could answer her, I cut in. "Thanks," I said with a laugh of my own that came out a little too loudly. "I think your grandparents bought it, right?" I looked across the table at Mitch, whose smile faltered a little, but he rallied.

"Oh, I know they did. They were a little put out you didn't join us for dinner that night, you know."

"Oh no!" My eyes went wide. "I didn't know I was supposed to . . ."

He waved a hand, cutting me off. "I told them you had plans with Caitlin. Don't worry about it."

"What was all that about, anyway?" Stacey asked. "Were you just pretending for their benefit, or what? I was definitely missing something there."

I took a deep breath, and my eyes met Mitch's. He shrugged, as if to say, *Go ahead.*

"Long story short," I said, "Mitch helped me out at Caitlin's graduation when my ex showed up . . ."

"*Nooo.*" Stacey's eyes went wide, and she looked at Emily, who nodded in confirmation.

"Yep. And Mitch had mentioned to me once that his folks

were giving him trouble for still being single. So when his grand-parents came to Faire, I returned the favor. That's it." I ended the truncated story with a firm nod, not inviting questions. I'd left out as many details as I could about the original event, because Mitch bringing me to his family's place wasn't my story to tell. Hopefully he'd appreciate that. My glance across the table was inconclusive; Mitch was looking at me with a furrowed brow that cleared up when he saw me looking at him.

"Yep," he said. "That's it." There was a hollowness to his tone that gave me pause, but no one else seemed to notice. The pizza came then, and topics changed as plates were passed around and filled. Thankfully, with five other people here I stopped being a topic of conversation, and I could eat pizza, drink cider, and steal the occasional mozzarella stick off Emily's plate when she wasn't looking.

But of course it didn't last.

"April, how's your house coming along?" Simon asked, right when I popped a mozzarella stick in my mouth, of course.

"Good." I crunched down on the fried cheese, feeling my arteries hardening but not able to bring myself to care. I chewed and swallowed quick. "I'm about to switch out the cabinet doors in the kitchen, and then I think I'll be about done." Across the table, Mitch's face went stony for a split second before his usual pleasant expression went back on like a mask. I raised my eyebrows at him in a question, but he didn't meet my eyes.

"I'm impressed," Emily said. "You've gotten so much done."

I shrugged. "Not just me. I had some help." I didn't elaborate, and no one asked me to. My phone buzzed just then with a text from Caitlin—she'd gone out with her friends but was home now, and I smiled with relief.

"All good?" Mitch asked from across the table, and I extended my smile to him.

"Yep." I waved my phone in illustration. "Cait's in for the night." He nodded in understanding, and Emily looked from him to me and back again, that wide, nosy smile on her face.

"So, uh, what else is going on there, sis?" Her voice was pitched so low that I had to lean over to hear her. "You get under that kilt yet?"

"Em!" My voice was louder than I'd intended, and she dissolved into giggles. Mitch's eyes narrowed and a frown crossed his face for a moment before he turned to Daniel, his expression cheerful again.

"So you're seriously going to drive two hours a day till October? You sure your piece-of-shit truck can handle that?"

"Hey!" Stacey's laugh belied the offended tone she tried to take, but Daniel just smiled, unflustered.

"That truck may be about the same age as me, but she's never let me down."

Stacey sighed, her smile big. "His best friend, that truck."

"Not my best friend, I'd say." He slid an arm around Stacey and kissed her hair, and the look they shared made my heart swell. I loved how happy they were. Emily met my eyes and I could tell she was thinking the same thing.

So why was I tearing up? I blinked hard and cleared my throat. "I need to get home."

Simon checked the time on his phone. "Us too. Tomorrow morning is going to come fast."

Emily rolled her eyes. "It's barely nine." But she kissed her husband on the cheek as he stood to find our server to get the check. I hugged the girls goodbye and waved to Mitch in an elaborately casual way before slipping out the door.

I was hoping to make a clean getaway, but Mitch caught up to me in the parking lot.

"What the hell was that?"

"What the hell was what?" My heart trembled as I turned around, but I wasn't going to let him see that. I kept my expression as neutral as possible, but it was no match for Mitch, whose face was made of stone.

"That." He waved over his shoulder toward the building we'd both left. "That load of bullshit in there."

"I don't know what you're talking about." But I had a sinking feeling that I did. I didn't want to go into it. Not now. I hunted through my purse for my keys until Mitch stepped closer, putting a hand over mine, stopping my movements.

"You're hiding me, April. Acting like I didn't help you with your house. You're still telling people it's . . ." His voice faltered, and I looked up in alarm. The stone of his expression had started to crack, and disappointment and hurt peeked through. "You know it's not fake between us anymore, right? I stopped pretending a long time ago."

"I . . ." My mind went blank. I wasn't ready for this.

He threaded his fingers through mine and brought our joined hands to his mouth, brushing a kiss across my knuckles. "You want me to come over later?" There was that voice again, the one that sent heat surging through me and made me want to promise him anything.

"Not tonight." My voice was a whisper as my apprehension melted. "Caitlin's home."

"Right." He nodded, his eyes still on mine. "But once she's off to college? What do you think? I could come over at night? On the weekends?"

His voice was hypnotic, and what he promised was delicious. I swallowed hard and nodded, unable to look away from those bluer-than-blue eyes.

"Should I park in the garage? So people don't know?"

I nodded again, a wave of relief sweeping through me. He got it. He got *me*. God, I was so lucky. I—

"No." He dropped my hand and stepped back, and the sudden loss of his heat felt like a slap. The stony expression was back on his face. "You really do want to hide this, don't you? Hide us? Why?"

"Because . . ." So many reasons. They all whirled through my head, competing for attention, but none of them would make rational sense if I said them out loud. I seized on the last one. Probably the least significant one, which only made me angrier. "Because your truck is fucking ridiculous! It's like a beacon. I may as well hang a banner outside my house that says I'm banging the gym teacher." I cringed inwardly as the words flew out of my mouth. That wasn't what I meant. Worse, it was exactly what I meant.

"Well, you *are* banging the gym teacher!" He fell back another step, spreading his arms wide, his face twisted. "Sorry, babe. That's all I am. I thought my family made that clear." His voice was dripping acid, and it hurt to hear him like this. His family made him feel like shit, even though he never let it show. And now I was doing the same thing. He didn't deserve that. Not from me. Not from anyone.

"Fuck." I pinched the bridge of my nose. "That's not what I meant."

"No, it's exactly what you meant." He paced away a step, raking a hand through his hair. "Look, April. I know you don't need me. You're the strongest woman I've ever met. You don't need anyone, do you? But I thought . . ." He turned back to me, his lips pressed together in a thin, hard line. I wanted to cry at the look on his face, knowing I'd put it there. "I thought you wanted me. But you don't, do you?"

"I do. That's not . . ." But my voice wasn't working. I didn't know what I wanted to say, much less how to say it.

"Not enough. Not enough to say it out loud, in front of your sister." He shoved his hands in the front pockets of his jeans and sighed. "Pretending to love you was the easiest thing I've ever done. But I can't pretend anymore. And I can't sneak around like this. I can't lie to our friends. I'm not going to be someone's dirty little secret. Not even for you."

"I'm not asking you to . . ." But it was exactly what I was asking for, wasn't it?

"Do you love me, April?"

The force of his question hit me in the chest, knocking all the air from my lungs. *No. Don't ask me that.* I put out a hand, steadying myself on the side of my SUV. "Mitch . . ." My voice was a ghost. "Don't . . ."

"Do you?" He took a step toward me, then another. All I could see were his eyes, wide open and honest. His whole heart was in his eyes, and I was breaking it in real time. "It's a simple question, April. Because I love you. You may not want to hear it, but you have to know by now."

I shook my head, frantic. He'd done it; he'd made the leap and said the words. But I didn't know how to follow him and make the leap myself. Instead something inside of me crumpled. He couldn't be saying this. Not now. Not to me. "It's not that simple." My voice shook so hard the words barely made it out. God, this was the most important conversation of my life, and I was having it in the parking lot of a dive bar. Worse, I was getting it all wrong.

"It is," he insisted. "Either you love me or you don't. Either we're together or we're not."

Rage overtook me then. If he truly loved me he wouldn't push me like this. He would give me the time I needed. He would understand. But he didn't. And I didn't know how to explain it to him. "Fine," I snapped. "Then we're not." There it was. There I was, getting it all wrong.

He wasn't expecting that. His mouth closed with a snap and his face went blank. "What?"

"We're not together." The words hurt as I said them, shredding my heart that I'd protected for so long. "If those are my two choices, then that's what I choose." I took a breath that shuddered in my throat. "I think maybe . . . all the times we pretended to be together . . . we let ourselves get mixed up." My next breath was a little steadier. "This is for the best," I said, convincing myself as much as I tried to convince Mitch. "The house is about done anyway. Thank you for everything. I couldn't have done it without you." I was thanking him for the house, but I was really thanking him for so many other things. For getting me through Caitlin's graduation. For making me feel like part of his family. For making me feel like someone who deserved love. It had been a nice change. But we'd never been meant to last. I knew that now.

He looked at me blankly. "You're still leaving?"

That brought me up short. "Of course I am. I'm putting the house on the market in September. My plans haven't changed." My plans were all I had left.

"Right." Mitch's laugh was bitter as he shook his head, his eyes fixed on his shoes. "Your plans." One more sigh aimed at the ground and he looked up at me again. His blue eyes shimmered in the lights of the parking lot, and I caught my breath, tears threatening in my own eyes. This was all wrong. I didn't want what we'd had to end like this.

But I didn't know what to say, so after a long moment of silence Mitch broke it, rapping his knuckles twice on the hood of my SUV. "Take care of yourself, April."

As he walked away from me, I knew that I'd probably made the biggest mistake of my life. But I couldn't find the words to call him back. To promise to be the person he wanted me to be. The person he probably deserved.

He deserved better than me anyway. He deserved someone younger, more vital. Someone who could give him a family someday. Not a middle-aged empty nester.

"This is for the best," I whispered again as I watched him get into his truck.

I almost believed it.

There was no magic for me the last weekend of Faire. Both days I showed up for my shift, I sold tickets, and I went home as soon as I was done. I didn't venture through the gate. I'd had enough. No more magic. No more kilts or kisses or curtsies.

The next week I took the outfit I'd bought to the dry cleaner's with all of Cait's costume pieces, and when I picked it up I shoved it to the back of my closet, still covered in its plastic bag. The woman in that dress didn't exist anymore. She'd faded like a half-remembered dream that night in the parking lot at Jackson's, and I had a feeling she wouldn't be back.

Twenty-Two

I knew it wouldn't be easy to forget Mitch, and that part of me never would. But the end of the Renaissance Faire also meant the end of the summer was nigh, and I had a kid about to go to college who deserved my full attention. My days and nights were full: last-minute shopping trips after work, packing, more last-minute trips planned for the weekend. The more checklists Caitlin and I made, the more things we realized we'd left off said lists. Those last two weeks before it was time to take her across the state to begin her college career were chaotic to say the least. Missing a man who'd never really been mine should have been as far in the back of my mind as possible.

However, adding to the chaos was that damn pile of cabinet doors. They'd started off in my kitchen, but I'd moved them—slowly—to my dining room. And every time I saw them I re-membered Mitch in my kitchen. Passing me a perfect mug of coffee. Complaining good-naturedly about the lack of beer in my fridge. Shoving my skirts up and out of the way, kissing me deeply while he fucked me on my kitchen island. I shivered at that last memory and did my best to push it out of my mind. Push him out of my mind.

It was a project I'd been putting off till September, but the third time I stubbed my toe on those damn cabinet doors, I knew I had to do something.

Swapping them out was definitely a two-person job, and as much as I wanted to enlist Caitlin, she had enough to do. When she wasn't packing she was engrossed in final nights out with her high school friends, and I didn't want to deprive her of those last childhood memories. So one night after work I texted my sister, asking her to come over on Saturday with a toolbox. She did one better and brought her husband and his cordless screw gun.

"I can't tell you how much I appreciate this." I climbed up on my kitchen counter, holding the cabinet door steady while Simon went to work on the hinges. "I don't even have any power tools."

"Don't mention it." His eyes were intent on his work, but he tossed a smile up in my direction. "We missed you last weekend, by the way."

"What?" I asked, at the same time Emily made a hissing noise from the dining room, and we both turned to her, where she was holding one of the cabinet doors and shaking her head frantically at Simon.

"What?" Simon asked her, then he blinked as something seemed to register. "Oh," he said, glancing at me. "Crap."

"What's going on?" I asked again, and Emily sighed elaborately.

"Last weekend," she explained. "We had a thing. At Jackson's."

"Oh." I took a second to absorb that and tried to decide if I was sad to have not been invited. Plans were the worst, honestly, and I loved when I could decline them. But to not have been invited in the first place still hurt. That made no sense, but I had no explanation.

"Yeah, it was . . ." Emily looked down at the floor, over to the side, down at the cabinet door in her hands.

Now it was Simon's turn to sigh. "It was Mitch's birthday." He looked right up at me as he spoke, and I appreciated his forthrightness. "A bunch of us got together."

"Oh," I said again. I hadn't even known when Mitch's birthday was, or that I'd missed it. Would I have texted him, wished him a happy birthday even though we weren't friends anymore? Would I have gone out with the group, nursed a drink at the bar while gazing at him across the room, wishing I still had the right to be in his orbit? I couldn't even be upset with him; it wasn't like he'd cast me out of his life. I'd done that all on my own. "Well, I hope y'all had fun." The last screw came free, and I tugged the door from the cabinet, handing it down to Emily as she passed up the new one.

Simon shrugged as we wrestled the door into place. "It was Jackson's on a weekend. You know." He and I shared a look, because I did know. He liked going out about as much as I did, but he was with Emily, so sometimes he had no choice.

"Yeah," Emily said. "It was fine. The karaoke got a little out of hand, though."

"Oh, God," I said. "Worse than usual?"

"Ohhh, yeah," Simon replied. One eyebrow went up, though he kept his attention on the work. "Unless you've seen Mitch sing karaoke before."

A horrified laugh bubbled out of me before I could check it. "I . . . have not." But I had listened to his singing on our trip to Virginia. That had been bad enough. The idea of him joyfully leaping onstage and subjecting a crowd to it was . . . well, it was very Mitch. I couldn't decide if the thought made me want to laugh or cry.

"'Mr. Brightside,'" Emily confirmed, her voice making an attempt at solemnity. "But kind of angry."

Oh. Scratch the "joyfully leaping onstage" part, then. "That's an angry song, though."

"Okay, angry and a little bit teary at the same time." Emily shuddered with the memory. "It was not great."

"Yeah, he was definitely working something out up there," Simon added.

All I could offer in response was a wince. I didn't want to think about Mitch and what he may or may not have been going through on his angry-sad karaoke birthday. He was no longer my concern, remember?

I scrambled to change the subject, because I didn't want to think about Mitch anymore, period. "How goes the dog search? That's still happening, right?" Emily had said a while back that they were planning to adopt a dog in the fall, but hadn't mentioned it since. Maybe they'd changed their minds?

"Good," Emily said, while Simon said, "Terrible," at the same time. They both sighed. "We keep looking at rescues online, but this one"—Simon nodded his head toward his wife—"wants to apply for all of them. Our place isn't that big."

"Plus I think technically we can only have so many dogs in one house. Some stupid local ordinance or something," Emily said. "But we'll narrow it down soon."

"Either that or you can just get a bigger place." I hopped down off the counter as Emily looked at me, horrified.

"Oh, hell no. We just moved. I don't want to go through that ever again."

"Agreed." Simon tightened the last hinge screws with a loud rattle of the screw gun. "Packing is a pain in the ass."

I groaned as I got a glimpse of my future. My future had a lot of boxes in it. "I haven't even thought about that yet."

"Don't worry. We can help with that too." Simon joined us in the dining room and we all looked into the kitchen at our progress.

"Thanks," I said. The new cabinet doors were a perfect match for my kitchen, but looking at them brought me no joy. I thought having them installed would make me feel better. But they just made me think of Mitch. Everything did these days.

I needed to sell this house and get the hell out of here.

Everything Caitlin wanted to bring to college fit into my SUV, but just barely. Emily and her Jeep were on standby, but my daughter and I were able to make the trip with just the two of us. The way we'd done almost everything else in her life. It seemed fitting.

A whirlwind of registration forms, key collecting, and endless trips up and down two flights of stairs later, I had done my cardio for the month, and my daughter was moved into her new dorm room.

"Mom?" Caitlin had been checking out the view from her window, but now she turned to me, her voice small. "Thanks."

"Of course. Did you think I was going to let you move into your dorm alone?" I put my hands on my hips and surveyed our progress. She was about ninety percent unpacked; we'd put most of her clothes away, and her bed was made up with those special extra-long dorm room sheets. Something that hadn't changed since my own college days. Books and snacks were piled on her desk to be dealt with later. Her pillows had been plumped, and her faithful stuffed rabbit lounged in the middle of them.

It was the rabbit that did it. I couldn't count the number of times that she'd thrown Mr. Ears out of the stroller when she was a toddler. The road trips we'd taken with him on her lap. His fur was worn thin and he hadn't been fluffy in years, but he was still her favorite thing. Caitlin was all grown up now, but my little girl was still in there somewhere. And I was just leaving her here, on her own. It didn't feel right. I wanted to throw her in the SUV and drive the hell away from here.

"No, I don't mean that. Well, I do mean that, and thank you. But . . ." She tugged on her ponytail, tightening it. "I mean for everything. Just . . . just everything." She walked across the room and her arms wrapped around me in a hug so tight that it squeezed those threatening tears from my eyes.

"Hey." I held her close, one last big hug from Mom before she started college. She could do this. I could do this. "I'm so proud of you, sweetheart. You know that."

She nodded against my shoulder but didn't let go yet. "You're my favorite mom."

My laugh was watery but, goddammit, I was not going to cry in front of my daughter. She didn't need that. Not when her life was about to begin. "You're my favorite kid. My all-time favorite."

I kissed her twice on the cheek and she let me go, running her fingertips under her eyes to catch the tears.

"Hey," I said again. "Don't worry, okay? You're going to do great."

She nodded, sniffed, and smiled. "You are too."

"Me?" I shook my head. "You know me. Not a lot going on."

"Maybe there should be. I want you to be happy, okay, Mom?"

"Oh, honey. I am." But that was an automatic response, and my kid wasn't a kid anymore.

Caitlin huffed. "I know. But . . . I mean really happy. I'm not stupid, you know. I know you gave up a lot for me. All my life."

"That's what moms do, you know." I reached out and tweaked her ponytail, tried to sound teasing. "Put their kids first. It's part of the job."

But she wouldn't be distracted. "Mom. I want you to put you first now. And if that's selling the house and moving to the city, then that's good. But . . ." She took a deep breath, her expression uncertain. "But I know you've been happy lately. Happier than I've seen you in, like, ever. Just . . . maybe think about that, okay?"

I didn't want to think about that. In fact, thinking about that was the last thing I wanted to do. Because she was right. I had been happy. And then I'd thrown it away because I'd gotten too scared to let it be real. But I forced a smile, made it look casual. "I will, baby. I promise."

One last hug goodbye and I left her to it. I made it all the way back to the car before the tears started to fall, and I swiped at them as I fired up the engine and pulled out of the parking lot. No one needed to see this. I needed to hold it together until I was home.

The house was empty, and when I turned off the engine, safe in the garage, I laid my head on the steering wheel and cried. And it was a good one—one of those long, hard cries that left you with eye makeup all over your face, a headache, and dehydration. When it was done I picked up my phone. My thumb automatically scrolled to Mitch's name, but my brain kicked in before I could tap on it. The greatest comfort I could think of was his arms around me. It had only been a couple of weeks, but I already missed the way he made me feel whole.

But I didn't have the right to that anymore. It didn't matter how much I missed him; I shouldn't look backwards. Caitlin was starting the next chapter of her life and now it was time for me to do the same.

Instead I flicked to Emily's name and hit the Call button.

"Hey!" Her voice was cheerful, when I wondered if I would ever smile again. "Everything go okay with Caitlin?"

"Yeah. I just got home." I cleared my throat hard, but my voice was rough and there was no fooling my younger sister.

"Hey. Don't worry, she's gonna do great. She's eighteen—all grown up now."

"Not till next week." A fresh sob escaped from my throat. "I'm going to miss her birthday. I'm going to miss all her birthdays from here on out, aren't I?" That revelation was a fresh stab to my heart. This whole empty nest thing was overrated as hell.

"Okay. Stay right there. I'm ordering a pizza now, and I've been saving a bottle of wine for this very occasion. I'll be over in a few minutes."

"You don't have to—"

"Shut the hell up. Of course I do. Do you want me to invite Stacey over too? She should be getting home from Faire right about now."

"No . . ." But I regretted the word as soon as I said it. I was used to saying no, to not wanting to get people involved in my business, in my emotions. But Stacey wasn't just "people." She was a friend. A good one. She was optimism personified, and a hug from her was like serotonin.

Besides, hiding my feelings from my friends had become overrated too. That was how I'd lost Mitch, wasn't it? Maybe it was a habit I should let go.

So I took a deep, shaking breath. "Yeah. See if Stacey wants to come."

"You got it. Now, sit tight." She hung up before I could protest further. I stared straight ahead through my windshield at the back wall of my garage. All my emotions had been cried away and all I felt was numb. All those years of my life I'd put aside to raise Caitlin, and now I was alone. The kind of alone that wine and pizza and girl time wasn't going to fix. But it was nice of Emily to try.

Eventually, I dragged myself into the house, taking the remains of my makeup off before Emily saw the ridiculous mascara tracks on my cheeks. I'd wallow with her and Stacey tonight. But tomorrow I needed to get back to work. I had a project to finish, and a house to get on the market.

I was busy for a few weekends, but before I knew it, the day had arrived. The day I'd been working toward all summer, not to mention the better part of my adult life.

My nest was empty.

The house was done.

I sat at the dining room table on a Saturday morning in late September, sipping from a mug of coffee in my empty house. Everything was so quiet. Even when Caitlin had been out of the house, her presence had still been here, in a backpack she left on the couch or some books on the table. But now even that was gone, and for the first time in my life I truly lived alone. Something I'd craved for years.

I hated it.

It was the house, I told myself. All this time spent painting the walls in neutral colors, replacing carpets and cabinet fronts, had transformed the inside to a place that I barely recognized. All those memories my daughter and I had made in this house, gone. Which had been the point, after all—paint over the memories, paint over the personality, make the whole place a blank slate for the next family to move in. They could make new memories here, while I started over somewhere else.

But this blank slate already had new memories imprinted on it. The living room walls reminded me of that week in June when Mitch and I had done all that painting together. *You've got me now*, he'd said as he'd fetched the ladder from the garage early in the day, and dinner from the Thai place that night. Superhero movies and sex on my living room floor. The Eggshell paint made me remember how I'd justified it to Mitch: *fine*, I'd said. *It's fine.* I'd sounded so defeated then. But now when I looked at these walls, I saw myself looking up that ladder, watching Mitch cut in the top edges near the ceiling. He was laughing at something he'd said—he always laughed the loudest at his own jokes—and his merriment had made me laugh more than the joke itself.

I picked up my mug of coffee and strolled to the back of the house. Past Caitlin's room, where the rest of her childhood was neatly put away. The guest room was anonymous again—I'd thought of it as Emily's room for so long, but now it could be anyone's. My running medals had stayed packed away.

But that room, that hallway . . . when I closed my eyes I saw Mitch helping me heft lengths of rolled-up carpet into giant garbage bags. I remembered waiting for someone in the neighborhood to call the HOA to report me for being a serial killer. I smiled now at the memory and went back to the kitchen to refill my coffee.

I wasn't intending to text Mitch just then. But this house was so quiet and so empty, and I missed the way he took up space in my life. Before I could think about it my phone was in my hand and I was tapping out a text. **Hi. Thank you again for helping me paint.**

The place really does look great. I'd been so caught up in memories of the summer that my brain had been back there, and it wasn't until I hit Send that I remembered that this wasn't something I got to do. He wasn't a part of my life anymore, and I wasn't a part of his.

A few minutes later, after I'd put my coffee mug in the dishwasher and wiped down the counters, my phone buzzed. I grabbed for it a little too eagerly, and my heart beat a little too quickly when I saw Mitch had texted back. **No problem.**

Okay, that wasn't much to go on. But maybe it was a start? Maybe we could start talking again? Worth a try. **How's your football team this year? Less hopeless? Got anyone who can throw?** The questions brought me back to that evening at his grandparents' house, when I'd been by his side, defending him to the entire Malone clan. I missed them all. Hell, even that douchey cousin of his.

Another text came back. While my heart soared at the chime of the follow-up text, a few moments later it came crashing right back down again at the response. **Yeah. They're fine.** He'd answered me, sure. But barely. This wasn't a text chain from someone who was reestablishing a connection. This was dismissal.

Dismissal that I totally deserved. I'd broken his heart that night in the parking lot at Jackson's—hell, I'd broken mine too—and texting him out of the blue like nothing had happened wasn't the way to get him back.

Get him back? I shook my head, my scoff loud in my empty kitchen. No. It was time to move forward. Not look back. The real estate agent's business card was on the kitchen island and I picked it up, tapping its edge against the counter. It was time to call her. Time to list the house and get on with my life.

I picked up my phone and the screen came to life with that

last text from Mitch. Part of me hoped he would send another
text and keep our conversation going, but he hadn't. He wasn't
going to. My heart sank so low that the spark had gone out of
calling the agent. I tossed the card back to the counter. Maybe it
wasn't quite time yet.

"What's the matter?" Emily passed me a vanilla latte and shooed
me over to one of the small tables by the window. Her boss,
Chris, had taken one look at my face when I'd arrived at Read It
& Weep and told Emily to take a break to talk to me.

"Nothing." I stared down into my mug. Emily's latte art was
still pretty bad, but it was getting better. I could almost tell that
was supposed to be a leaf. Almost. I sighed. "Everything."

"Okay." Her voice was neutral. Pleasant. She sipped her coffee
and looked out the window as though she had all afternoon to
sit with me until I figured my shit out. I didn't have the heart to
warn her that she'd be sitting there forever.

"It's just . . ." I sighed. "It's time to list the house." I couldn't
sound less enthusiastic about it if I'd tried.

"But that's good, right?" Emily said gently. "It's what you've
been working toward all this time."

"Yeah. But now that it's time . . . I don't want to go through
with it."

"Okay," she said again. "So what do you want instead?"

Mitch. Nope. I couldn't say that. Besides, it wasn't just Mitch,
was it? "I think I realized something." I watched my sister, wishing she could jump in and help me out here, but she just raised
her eyebrows. Waiting.

Fine. I had to do this myself. "I think that Willow Creek is
my home. It always has been." I sounded miserable as I said it
out loud.

"Okay . . ." The neutral tone was still there. "So why do you sound like that's a bad thing?"

"It's just . . . I've been planning to leave this place since the day I moved in. I didn't get involved. With the neighborhood, with Caitlin's school. All I could think about was raising Cait, you know? Getting her grown up and out of here. And now that she is, it's time to go, and . . ."

"And now you don't want to?" Emily asked carefully.

"I mean, I have all these book clubs, you know?" My laugh was as thin as my joke, but Emily gave me a sympathetic smile, humoring me. "And . . . when Robert showed up for Cait's graduation, it was like the whole town had my back. People I didn't even know. And there's you and Simon. You're my family, and that means something. And there's . . ." My throat closed, and Emily reached across the table, laying a hand over mine.

"There's Mitch." Her steady quiet voice was getting me through this whole conversation, and I clung to it like a rope, navigating me out of this maze of emotions.

"God, yeah. Mitch is . . ." I drew in a shaking breath and blinked hard. How could I explain what he meant to me? What he'd done for me? But this was Emily I was talking to. I had a feeling she already knew. "Well, he's Mitch, isn't he?"

Emily's lips quirked in a smile. "Best one I know."

My laugh was a little more robust this time. I swiped at the tears on my cheeks that I didn't realize had fallen. "Shit," I said. "He really does love me." A terrible thought came to me then. "Or he did."

Emily squeezed my hand. "He doesn't seem like the kind of guy that changes his mind that fast. You love him, right?"

"Yeah." Suddenly it was the easiest thing in the world to admit.

What the hell had taken me so long? "But what about my plans?" It was the worst argument, and I knew it as soon as I said it.

"Hmm." Emily thought about that, or at least pretended to. "You list the house yet?"

I shook my head. "I was about to, but . . ."

"Yeah." She took another sip of coffee. "You started looking for a new place? Near work you said, right?"

"Right. And no." I'd always meant to start looking, but I'd never gotten around to it.

"That's what I thought. Okay." She set her mug down. "I think those plans were great for Ten Years Ago April. Maybe even Five Years Ago April. But plans can change. People can change." When she smiled at me now her eyes were bright with tears. "You taught me that, you know."

God, she was right. I'd given her the same advice three years ago. And here she was, throwing it back in my face. Some sister she was. The best.

"I fucked up with him, you know."

She shrugged, unconcerned. "I bet you can fix it." She seemed so sure that I almost believed her.

As I took a fortifying sip of coffee her eyes lit up. "Hey, if you're sticking around for a bit, can you do me a favor?"

"Sure." But I narrowed my eyes, wondering what I was getting myself into.

She pulled out her phone and woke it up. "I got an email from one of the rescue organizations. You know, about adopting a dog? They just got some puppies in, and Simon and I want to go see them tomorrow. Would you mind coming with? I think having a tiebreaking vote could come in handy." She passed me the phone, and I swiped through the puppy photos, each cuter than the last. Everything seemed better when you were looking at pictures of puppies.

"As long as the tiebreaker agrees with you, right?" I raised my eyebrows as I gave her the phone back, and she snorted.

"That would certainly help. You are my sister. You should be on my side."

As she put her phone away, mine buzzed on the table between us and I turned it over. With Cait at school now, I kept my phone with me like a lifeline, just in case she needed me. She hadn't yet. I didn't dare hope it was Mitch.

It wasn't either of them, just some new email notifications. I bit back a sigh and clicked it open anyway.

"Something up?"

"No." I scrolled through, swiping and deleting. "Junk mail." My finger lingered on the newsletter from the little downtown hardware store. I'd gotten hooked on that particular one, each of their suggested projects filling me with inspiration while Mitch and I had transformed my house. We never did build those bookshelves. I squinted at the subject header. "Huh," I said. "There's a sale on paint."

Emily huffed a laugh and picked up her coffee mug. "That's the last thing you need right now."

"Yeah." But my mind churned as I clicked off my phone and put it back down. Because an idea had taken hold. A way to show Mitch how much I wanted him in my life. For real this time. And paint might actually be the way to get there.

Twenty-Three

I**t took a** couple weekends to get everything the way I wanted it, especially since I was on my own this time, but eventually I got it done. After a quick stop on the way home one Friday evening, I pulled into the garage and tapped out a text to Mitch. **Can you come over? I need you.** My breath froze in my chest at the truth in those last three words, and I hoped he could tell through the magic of text messaging how much I meant it. Before I could wuss out I hit Send.

I had no idea how long I'd have to wait for an answer. Our last text conversation hadn't gone that well, after all. He could have blocked my number by now, and I wouldn't have blamed him. I clutched my phone as I went into the house, and when it buzzed I felt the vibration all the way up my arm. **I can't do this, April. I told you. I'm not sneaking around with you.**

There was that magic of text messaging: the hurt I'd caused pulsed through each word on the screen. God, I'd really fucked this up. All I could do was hope he'd let me try to make it right.

I put my purchases in the fridge, then leaned against the

kitchen island to answer his text. **No sneaking. I'm parked in the garage so you can take the driveway. Please? It won't take long. Just need your opinion on something.**

He didn't answer right away, and my heart sank. I stared at the words I'd just typed. Too desperate? Did the "please" sound like I was begging? Ugh. When staring a hole in my phone didn't make him text back I let it clatter to the counter and pressed my palms against my eyes. I had my answer. And I didn't blame him.

Oh, well. It had been worth a try.

I got a cider out of the fridge, popping it open before wandering into the living room, where my new roommate snored lightly on a pile of blankets on the couch. I sat down next to him and touched his head lightly, hoping I wouldn't startle him. His hearing wasn't the best, and he was still getting used to living with me.

"Did Emily already take you out, Murray?" He nuzzled into my hand and thumped his tail in response. I'd gone to the shelter with Emily and Simon as promised. While they both fell in love with a wriggly black Lab puppy—no tiebreaker needed—my attention was drawn to an elderly black-and-white Jack Russell terrier snoozing in a nearby kennel. He was almost ten, the shelter person had said, and he was here because his elderly master had died. She shook her head in sympathy, because who was going to adopt a dog that old?

Me, apparently. I adopted a dog that old. Emily was thrilled, and promised to come by in the afternoons to take him out while I was at work. I'd named him after our grandfather— another old man who was a little hard of hearing and preferred naps—and we'd settled into a happy coexistence. He liked lots of blankets on his side of the couch, carrots, and snuggling against my hip while I read or watched television. We took slow, meditative walks in the evenings and on weekends, where I did a lot of thinking and he did a lot of sniffing. It was a promising beginning to a relationship, and the house didn't feel as empty with Murray in it with me.

Now I scratched his head and leaned back against the couch, sipping my cider and looking at the freshly painted walls. Had this been a good idea? The more time that went by, the more I doubted myself.

All my senses went on high alert when, somewhere between ten minutes and three years later, headlights shone through my living room window as a gargantuan red pickup truck swung into my driveway. Every muscle I had tensed up as the engine cut off, and the headlights went out a heartbeat later.

"Here we go, Murray," I whispered, but he was already asleep again. He was a terrible wingman.

My heart pounded and the cider suddenly tasted sour in my mouth, but I forced myself to swallow it. The slam of the truck door was loud, but I could barely hear it over the blood rushing in my ears, and when the doorbell rang I jumped.

This was it. Mitch was giving me my chance. All I had to do was not screw it up. I took a deep, cleansing breath as I opened the front door.

"Hey." His hands were shoved in the front pockets of his jeans, and he met my eyes briefly before casting his gaze away, studying the doorjamb, then the porch light.

"Hi." For a long moment I didn't move. I was so glad to see him again that I'd forgotten why I'd texted him. I just wanted to look at him there in my doorway. I wanted to look at him every day.

He cleared his throat and brought his eyes back to mine again. "So. What did you need?"

"Oh. Right." I stepped back and gestured him inside, closing the front door behind him. God, I'd forgotten how much space he took up. His presence should be crowding me, this person who always wanted to be left alone. But now that was the last thing I wanted. And it was time to let him know that.

I took a deep breath. "Like I said. I wanted to get your opinion on something."

"Okay." He raised his eyebrows. "What's that?"

"Come see." I led him into the living room, but he stopped short in the doorway.

"You got a dog."

"I did." I watched while Mitch and Murray looked at each other for a long moment, sizing each other up. Murray quickly determined that Mitch hadn't brought him a carrot, and put his head back down with a long sigh.

"That's not why I asked you over, though. I redid the paint in here. What do you think?" I took a step more into the center of the room, waiting for him to follow.

He did. "Let me guess, you changed your mind on the Eggshell." I didn't answer, I just waited for him to see what I'd done. "Seriously, as long as it's some boring neutral color they're not gonna care . . ." His voice stopped abruptly, and I turned to look at him. His eyes were huge in his face, and his jaw had gone slack. "April." His voice was hushed.

"What do you think?" I moved to stand beside him, my arms crossed over my chest. We both studied the accent wall that I'd spent this week painting blue. Not-even-close-to-neutral blue. It wasn't the bright blue of his eyes, or the dark blue of mine. It was somewhere in between. A perfect mix of the two. Just like I wanted us to be.

"What . . ." He cleared his throat. "Why the hell did you do that?" He swung his gaze down to me, and I bit down hard on my lip. He wasn't getting it. I really should have rehearsed something to say here.

"Because . . ." But my voice failed me. There was so much I wanted to say, and I didn't know how to say any of it. But I had something else to show him besides the wall. Maybe that would do the trick. "Here. Do you want a drink?" I reached for his hand but thought better of it. He might not want me touching him. I wouldn't blame him. But he followed me into the kitchen. He was still here. I still had a chance.

"Hey, you did the cabinets! They look great." He huffed out a laugh. "I guess you didn't need me after all." He was trying to make the words a joke, but his voice was laced with hurt.

That was a good place to start. "Maybe not," I said carefully. "You were right, what you said. That I don't need anyone. I think that's what happens when you raise a kid on your own. You get used to not relying on anybody else. But you know, someone told me, not too long ago, that you can want something without needing it."

A ghost of a smile lit up his eyes. "I remember that."

"But this isn't easy for me. I need you to know that." I took a deep breath, steadying my nerves. "Do you know how long it's been? Since someone's said they . . . they loved me?" The tears came out with the words, but I couldn't hold them in anymore. Maybe I didn't need to. Not with him.

"Yeah." His voice was a little hoarse. "A couple months ago. In the parking lot outside of Jackson's." He spread his arms in a *here I am* gesture. A smile teased at his mouth, and my responding laugh was little more than a sigh.

"Before that, then. Almost twenty years." I pressed a hand to my forehead, which suddenly felt hot. My pulse was racing, and

I could feel the blood throbbing in my temples. "I'm not even sure I know how to say it anymore. It's been my daughter and me against the world for so long. And there are so many reasons why you shouldn't want me."

"Name one." His eyes, those perfect blue eyes that I wanted to spend forever lost in, stayed fixed on mine, and that gave me courage.

"I'm too old for you, you know. I know you're going to say it doesn't matter, but—"

"You're right. It doesn't matter. I—"

"But it's going to. It'll matter a lot in five years or so when you decide you want children. You're barely out of your twenties. I'm forty." I waved a hand in the vicinity of my abdomen. "Factory's closed. Been there, done that, sent her to college."

He looked at me, incredulous. "I don't give a damn about kids."

"But you like kids."

"Sure I like kids. The ones I teach. The ones I coach. The ones my cousins have, that I can feed sugar to and give back to their parents." He shrugged. "Doesn't mean I want kids of my own."

My argument faltered; I hadn't expected him to say that. "But your mother," I said. "She's looking forward to you having kids. She told me—"

"My mom's full of shit." He put his hands on his hips and paced away from me, around the kitchen, then back toward me. "She wants grandchildren like the rest of the family. I keep telling her it's not going to happen. Jesus, April, I spend five days a week with kids, and more on Ren Faire weekends. That's enough for me. Besides, you were there with my family. You saw all those kids running around. There's plenty of Malone DNA out there in the world without me contributing to the gene pool."

He seemed so certain that my lips quirked in an almost-smile. But my insides still churned like I was on a roller coaster. "I don't know how to do this," I finally confessed.

"Do what? Love someone? Be in a relationship?"

I nodded. "Yes. All of the above. But I've never been happier than I was this past summer with you. And I'm sorry it took you walking away from me that night for me to realize it." I waved a hand toward the living room. "I painted that wall because this house is my home. Willow Creek is my home. I'm not going any-where." My breath shook as I sucked it in, and those tears I thought I'd gotten under control started to obscure my vision, but I didn't care. I couldn't care. I had this one chance to make it right. I needed him to understand. "You are my home."

He sucked in a sharp breath, and he shut his mouth with a snap.

"Here," I said. "Let me get you that drink." I turned to the fridge.

A small laugh stuttered out of him. "Still not drinking that apple juice that you like so . . ." Now it was his turn for his voice to fail as the refrigerator door creaked open. There, nestled next to the milk, were six green glass bottles. The six-pack of his fa-vorite beer that I'd picked up on the way home.

I took one out and pressed it into his hand. "No more sneak-ing around," I said. "No more pretending. I want you to . . ." God, I really should have thought this out beforehand, because all I could think to say now was . . . "I want your beer in my fridge. I want you in my life. With me. For real this time."

He blinked down at the beer in his hand as though he'd never seen one before. But when he looked up at me, his expression was unsure. Unexpectedly vulnerable. "You say that now. When you're by yourself, and Caitlin isn't home. What about in November, when she comes home for Thanksgiving? Are you gonna bolt on me then?"

"No." But he looked dubious, and who could blame him? I'd been a dick lately. "You still think . . . okay. Hold on." I picked up my phone from where it was on the counter, and called Caitlin. The phone rang twice and I hoped my kid wasn't out partying yet. I needed her help here. (I *really* should have planned this better.)

Caitlin picked up on the third ring. "Hey, Mom!"

"Hi, honey. I'm putting you on speakerphone, okay?" I hit the button and put the phone down. Mitch and I stood, shoulder to shoulder, with the phone in front of us.

"Sure. What's up? Who's there?"

"I was thinking." I was still talking to Caitlin, but I looked straight at Mitch while I did so. "I'm planning on dating Coach Malone. That okay with you?"

Caitlin's pffft sound came through the phone loud and clear. "It's about time. Is that who's there?"

"Yeah." Mitch's voice was thick, and he coughed into his fist. "Yep, I'm here." He didn't look away from me.

"Be nice to my mom, okay?" She was trying to sound stern, but I could hear the smile in her voice.

I swiped at the tears that wouldn't go away, and when I looked over at Mitch he was blinking quickly too. "You know it." To his credit his voice sounded perfectly normal, if a little more subdued.

"Good."

After I disconnected the call I punched up Emily's number, and Mitch groaned. "Okay, you've made your point, you don't have to—"

"Hey, April! What's up?"

"Oh, not a lot," I said. "I just wanted to let you know that Mitch and I are—"

I couldn't even finish the sentence before she started cheering. "Finally! Because if I have to hear one more sad karaoke number from him, I'm gonna—"

"Bye, Emily." Mitch mashed the End button.

Once the call was disconnected and the echo of Emily's laughter faded, silence hung thick in the air between us. I'd laid it all out there, but he hadn't really said how he felt. I couldn't take it anymore. "What are you thinking?"

Mitch looked at me for a long moment, then shook his head and turned away. But before my heart could sink all the way into my stomach, he plucked the bottle opener from its place on the refrigerator door and popped open his beer. "I'm thinking we spent the better part of a week painting that living room, and you go and undo it just to prove a point." He stuck the opener back on the door and shook his head again before taking a swig of beer. His eyes danced at me as he swallowed, something I hadn't seen in far too long.

Something unfurled in my chest, and the release of tension felt a little like being drunk. "Hey," I said. "I like the blue." The ground finally felt solid under me, for the first time in weeks.

He smirked in response but didn't argue. Instead he put his beer down on the counter. "I'm thinking . . ." He turned toward me, and I caught my breath at the look in his eyes. "I'm thinking it's been about a hundred years since I've kissed you."

He tucked a lock of hair behind my ear, and "oh" was all I had time to say before his mouth brushed over mine. All the remaining tension in my body fell away; nothing in the world had ever felt more right than kissing this man in my kitchen.

His hands skimmed over my shoulders and skated down my

body to my waist, my hips, before boosting me up to sit on the kitchen island. My legs wound around his hips like they knew they'd come home, and the growl in the back of his throat told me more than any words ever could.

After a few slow, delicious minutes I pushed lightly on his chest, and he fell back a step. "Come on." I hopped down from the counter, which brought me oh so close to him. I drew a shaking breath and thought seriously about chucking the rest of my plans for the evening and taking him to bed. But I wasn't done proving myself to him yet. So I pocketed my phone and reached for my purse.

"Where to?" Mitch's expression was still a little dazed, but he took my hand in his and I knew he was ready to go anywhere with me.

"You want to go public, I can't imagine a better place to do it than Jackson's on a Friday night."

I started toward the front door, but stopped short as he refused to move. "Nah."

"What do you mean, 'nah'?" I turned around as he tugged me back to him.

"I mean, you proved your point. And I don't want to share you tonight. Not with anyone. We can hit Jackson's tomorrow night." His arms wrapped around me and he pulled me flush against him, and there went any argument I might have had.

But I still tried. "You sure about that? We don't need to stay in." My arms circled his neck, fingers playing with the hair at the nape of his neck.

"Don't need to. But maybe I want to. Two different things, remember?" He grinned, and I laid a hand on his cheek. His dimple appeared beneath my thumb and I stroked it, letting my own smile grow in response.

There was one thing I still hadn't said, and it was time to take the leap. He deserved it. "Mitch, I . . ." All the breath left my body. I hadn't said the words in so long that everything locked up. I forgot how absolutely terrifying it was to offer my heart so completely. But I needed to tell him. He deserved to know.

Mitch didn't look concerned. His expression softened and he cupped my cheek in one hand. "You got this," he said softly.

I stared up into those blue, blue eyes and took the leap. "I love you." Fresh tears spilled down my cheeks, and he dashed them away as they fell.

"There you go." His smile was small and private, not like his usual bright grin, and it was just for me. "Oh, April." He leaned down and kissed me, sweet and lingering. "I've been gone for you for months. Ever since you yelled at my grandma."

I laughed against his mouth. "I never yelled at your grandma."

He shrugged. "Maybe not technically. Now, come on." He pulled me toward the hallway. "You've got me craving those Thai noodles you like. Let's order some and play with some attachments while we wait for them to be delivered."

Damn. When he put it like that, why did anyone ever go out?

I glanced over my shoulder on the way out of the kitchen, at the flour, sugar, and vanilla tucked away in the corner of the counter. Eggs and butter were in the fridge. Book club was coming up, and you bet your ass I was bringing cupcakes.

Epilogue

I *don't know if* I can do this." My breath came hard in my chest.

"You can. I know you can." Mitch's voice came from behind me, panting practically in my ear, breathing almost as hard as I was. "Does it hurt?"

"No." But I sounded doubtful even to myself.

"We can slow down, you know. If this doesn't feel good?"

"No!" I responded a little too quickly. "You're right. I'm fine."

"That's my girl," he said. "Stubborn."

"You know it."

I was amazed at how good I felt. I thought there would be a lot more pain, but we'd trained very carefully for this. When we'd toed up at the starting line for the Thanksgiving morning 5K run, we'd agreed to take it easy. It was my first race since my accident, and I wasn't looking to set any land-speed records. That was Simon's goal; in fact, he'd probably finished the race already. That man was gunning for the podium. Me, I just wanted a nice easy jog with my boyfriend before eating our weight in Thanksgiving dinner.

My leg didn't hurt, that was the amazing part. We'd started out slow, training on the weekends. I walked for a couple of weeks before I started adding running intervals, and last weekend I'd managed two miles without stopping. But we were closing in on three miles, and now that my legs had started to go rubbery I was questioning everything.

But Mitch was just behind me, pacing me, keeping me on track to finish the race in a respectable thirty-five minutes. I had a feeling that if I'd let him run the race on his own, he'd be done by now too, and waiting at the finish line with Simon. But he'd told me he'd be there every step of the way, and he meant that literally.

"Still feel okay?"

"Yeah. Yeah, I think so." My lungs were burning and there was a definite wobble in my legs, but otherwise I was okay. I hazarded a glance over my shoulder at Mitch, and we shared a grin.

"Good," he said. He nodded in front of us. "'Cause look at that."

I faced forward again, looking up to see the finish line banner stretched over the road in front of us, not fifty feet away. Adrenaline took over and I sprinted, pumping my legs and not even caring about breathing till I'd crossed the finish, Mitch laughing a few yards behind me.

"Holy shit." My sprint turned to a jog until I slowed to a stop. I bent forward at the waist and propped my hands on my knees, sucking in air. "I did it." I straightened and turned to Mitch. "I did it!"

"You sure as hell did!" He wrapped his arms around me, lifting me off the ground, not even caring how sweaty I was. Of course, he was sweaty too, so it didn't matter. Our sweat mingled a lot lately.

"You did it!" Emily's squeal came from behind me and I turned to greet her. Simon was beside her, a smile on his face and a bottle of water and a banana in his hands. He passed them both to me.

"Good run, April," he said.

I snorted. "I don't want to hear it. You had time to go home and shower while you were waiting for me, right?"

He laughed, which for Simon was an enthusiastic exhale, but it still warmed me to see it. "Not quite. And you should absolutely be proud. How'd you do?" He addressed the question to Mitch, knowing he was the one with the stopwatch.

Mitch looked down at his wrist, a grin blooming across his face. "Thirty-four minutes, forty-seven seconds. Not bad!" He held up a hand and we high-fived. Yes, we were that kind of couple. No, I didn't care.

I turned to Emily. "How about you?" She and the puppy had done the one-mile dog jog, something that I had almost ditched my own race to see. Because dogs. Mine was safely at home asleep on the couch. Murray was the smartest of us all.

Emily laughed and shook her head. "Lord Byron here was much more interested in sniffing and peeing on things. I don't think our time was all that impressive."

While we all walked toward the parking lot, I called Caitlin. "Turkey in the oven?"

"Yep! Everything's set, Mom."

"Great. Thanks, hon." I clicked my phone off while Mitch dug his keys out of his pocket. "See y'all in a little bit?"

Emily nodded as she loaded the all-legs puppy in the back of her Jeep. "We'll be there about two. You sure you don't want me to bring anything?"

I shook my head. "It's all made. Just bring yourselves and the dog. Maybe some wine." Mitch's grandmother had emailed me her macaroni and cheese recipe, and I couldn't wait for everyone to try it.

Speaking of which . . . I turned to Mitch after settling myself in the passenger seat of his truck. "You sure it's okay we didn't do Thanksgiving with your family? I know you love your grand-parents."

"I do." He nodded as he started up his truck.

"And your cousin Lulu is great. I wouldn't mind seeing her again."

"That's good. I think you'll have a hard time getting rid of her." He cracked a smile as we got on the road. "But no. Today's great. A Willow Creek family Thanksgiving. We can save the real chaos for Christmas."

"Can't wait," I said dryly. But what he didn't know was that I was already thinking ahead to Christmas. His present was al-ready wrapped and in my sock drawer in a little white box: a tiny silver house on a key ring, with a copy of my house key. I was going to ask him to move in. He'd helped make my house even more of a home, so it was only right that he share it with me, and stop renewing his lease every February.

I sighed and took a bite of banana. "This was fun."

"Good. We'll make it a tradition."

"Except . . ." I plucked my shirt away from my body with a grimace. "I'm disgusting. And I'm pretty sure I stink."

"We'll take a shower when we get home." His grin turned wicked as he glanced over at me. "That can be a tradition too."

I raised my eyebrows. "A lot of your traditions seem to in-volve showers."

"Are you complaining, Cupcake?"

My new nickname. Now it was time for my grin to be wicked. "I am not."

Sure, there was a glimmer of Old April deep down inside, who thought, *Oh shit, Caitlin is home, abort sexy shower!* But when Mitch took my hand and drove me home, it was easy to extinguish that glimmer. She was eighteen. She could handle it.

Besides, everything I wanted, needed, and loved was either in this truck with me or waiting for me at home. And New April had no problem letting the world know it.

Acknowledgments

The majority of this book was written in the year 2020, which was unprecedented for so many reasons. It was a challenge to write a rom-com—especially a rom-com that had so! many! public gatherings!—in the middle of a pandemic. But in a lot of ways it was an escape. Spending time in Willow Creek with my characters was comforting at a time when I couldn't hang out with anyone else.

With every book, I realize anew how lucky I am to have a great group of people at my back: my agent, Taylor Haggerty, and my critique partners, Gwynne Jackson and Vivien Jackson, are basically my foundation. I would be flailing out here without you. I had a wonderful group of alpha readers who were basically the OG Mitch fan club: Annette Christie, Jenny Howe, Cass Scotka, Courtney Kaericher, and Lindsay Landgraf Hess. There is room enough in his heart for you all!

Jenny Howe, thanks for letting me borrow Murray. It helps my heart to know that he and Gambit are together in this book forever, and I hope it helps yours too.

ReLynn Vaughn, thank you for the inspo spam as always!

I cannot overstate how much fun I have working on these books with Kerry Donovan as my editor. It's a genuine pleasure to have someone love and understand my characters as much as I do! Massive thanks as usual to the rest of the Berkley team: Jessica Mangicaro, Jessica Brock, Mary Geren, Mary Baker, and Angelina Krahn. Special thanks to Colleen Reinhart for yet another adorable cover!

Additional thanks this go-round to Lyssa Kay Adams and the participants of the 30-Day Draft project, which helped me get a good portion of this book written. Thanks for all the Zoom sprints and chats! And thanks as usual to my Bs—Brighton, Ellis, Esher, Ann, Melly, Helen, Laura, Elizabeth, and Suzanne—for the morning coffee Zooms, the evening boozy Zooms, and the occasional writing Zooms. So many Zooms.

Morgan, you deserve all the beer in the fridge. There's no one I'd rather drive across the country with in a rented SUV containing three annoyed cats. I love you.

My heart goes out—and continues to go out—to the Renaissance Faires across the country that were forced to shut down during 2020 and much of 2021. Many performers and artisans lost their livelihoods and have been trying to keep it going online as much as possible. Check out digitalrenfaire.com for virtual performances and the Facebook group Faire Relief 2020 for vendors selling their crafts online. Hopefully by the time this book is published we'll be meeting up in person again. I look forward to raising a tankard with you all someday at pub sing. Huzzah!

One last fervent THANK YOU to the readers out there. So many of you have reached out to me during this crazy time and told me how these books have been an escape, a chance to attend a fictional Renaissance Faire when the real ones were closed down. I'm so touched and grateful for the chance to distract and entertain. Thank you as well to the bookstagrammers and bloggers, the bookstores and librarians who have featured my books on their platforms. These times have been so challenging, and I appreciate every single one of you. Thank you.

Keep reading for a special preview of the

next novel by Jen DeLuca

Well Traveled

I *quit my job,*" I said to my third glass of cider that morning. It didn't respond.

But Stacey did. "It's going to be okay, Lulu." She sounded like she was talking someone out of jumping off a bridge. Except I'd already jumped, and now I was spiraling down toward scary, swirling water below. It was going to hurt like hell when I landed.

"I don't see how." I shook my head and took another gulp of cider, oblivious to the revelry around me. I was in a makeshift tavern, the drink in front of me served by a barmaid in a cinched-up corset and a huge smile. Nearby a frat boy in chain-mail chugged a light beer, his friends in variously elaborate costumes cheering him on. A faint melody from faraway bagpipes floated by on the breeze. I should have been enjoying my time at the Renaissance Faire—a rare day off for me. But I had all the days off now.

Another fortifying sip of cider, and I looked at Stacey. "You don't know my family. They want . . ." My stomach clenched, and the cider threatened to come right back up. Sure, I was in my late thirties, but judgment from your parents stayed with you. They'd been so proud of my upward trajectory with the law firm. There'd always been a sense of competition between my parents and their siblings, wanting their kids to be as successful as possible. My career had never been about what would make me feel fulfilled. It was about bragging rights for my mom and dad at every family function for the rest of their lives.

"Here." Stacey took away my cider and pushed a bottle of water into my hands. "Take that and come with me. Our next show starts in a few minutes."

I followed her like an obedient child, because I was out of options and my brain was offline. We dodged costumed faire-goers and kids with fake swords, until we reached the stage and she ushered me to a bench at the back of the audience. Words echoed in my head to the rhythm of my heartbeat.

I quit my job. I quit my *job*. I quit my *job*.

It was approaching noon and the sun was high, the heat not helping things in the least. Those three ciders were hitting hard as the Dueling Kilts took the stage, so I uncapped the bottle of water and forced myself to take measured sips. Forced myself to calm down and focus on the stage in front of me.

Which . . . wasn't a bad thing, necessarily. I'd never been attracted to men in kilts—knees weren't really my thing—but the rugged good looks of the trio of kilted musicians onstage drew my attention more than their outfits. No wonder Grandma Malone had been so taken with them last summer.

Two of them looked more closely related than the third—that

odd man out played the fiddle, and he was tall and lean, with long, dark auburn hair tied back in a queue. The other two were shorter and dark haired. The one on the hand drum was boyish looking, slender with closely cropped hair, while the guitarist was more muscular, his longer hair tied carelessly back from a face that boasted sharp cheekbones and a sharper jawline. If this were a boy band from my childhood, the drummer would be the cute, non threatening lead singer, while the part in me that coveted bad boys would have gone straight for the guitar player.

Good thing I was over my bad boy phase.

The trio bantered and joked with the audience members, raising wooden tankards in toasts before, after, and even during the songs. There were only three of them up there, but their instruments and voices combined in rich harmonies and richer laughter, the music feeling greater than the sum of its parts. I leaned back on my hands, closed my eyes, and tipped my face toward the sun, practically feeling freckles pop out over the bridge of my nose. While the breeze teased strands of hair out of my ponytail and danced them across my cheek, the notes of "Whiskey in the Jar" flowed over me, carried on the air from their guitar, fiddle, and hand drum. Hard cider hummed through my bloodstream, and music surrounded me, soothed me. For a blissful few minutes nothing could touch me, and my worries slipped away, forgotten.

Then the show came to an end, and reality came crashing back, along with the beginnings of a panic attack. I took a shaky sip of water, trying to stave it off. I needed to get out of here. Out of the sun. Out of this whole damn day. But white static crept in the edges of my vision, making it hard to see. Standing up was impossible, walking out of here even more so.

I bent forward, putting my head between my knees, and breathed deeply. Tears pricked my eyes as the panic attack took hold. All my life I'd been on this path, and now the path was gone. I was alone, lost in the woods.

"Is she all right?" A man's voice spoke over my head, and I chanced a look up. The audience had mostly gone—a couple stragglers were taking pictures with the band. The man next to me was tall, dressed in black jeans and a T-shirt, a baseball cap eclipsing his vivid red hair. He wasn't dressed for a day in the sunshine, but he acted like he belonged here. His attention was on Stacey, threading her way through the maze of benches toward where I was sitting.

"She's fine." Stacey waved him off.

"Are you sure? She doesn't look so good. Do we need to call someone for her?" The redhead's eyes flicked from me to Stacey, a question in his eyes. By "someone" I had a feeling he meant "paramedics."

"I already did." Stacey brandished her phone like it had all the answers. "Here." She sat down next to me, handing me her phone. "It's for you."

"Me?" But when I looked down at the screen an almost tangible relief swept through me. "Hey, Mitch." The words were a sigh, directed at my cousin on the other end of the video call. My favorite cousin. He was five years younger, but I loved him more than my own brothers. Mostly because they were dicks.

"Hey, Lulu." He looked as happy to see me as ever. "What the hell are you doing in North Carolina? Stace says you're making a scene there at the Renaissance Faire."

"You know me," I said weakly. "Always a troublemaker." I finished off my water, and Stacey took the empty bottle from me, replacing it with a fresh one. I watched as she took the arm of the redhead, pulling him away to give me privacy. His head bent toward hers as they talked intently.

Mitch snorted. "Yeah, right. We both know that's my job." His brow furrowed, and his voice gentled. "What's going on, Lu?"

I pressed the heel of my hand to my forehead, staving off more tears. "I was here for work, and . . ."

Mitch blinked. "Who needs lawyers at a Renaissance Faire?"

The ghost of a smile tugged at my lips. "North Carolina, you weirdo. I was in North Carolina for work, and then I got one phone call too many from my boss and . . ."

"Yeah, Stacey filled me in on that part. You wanna tell me why you made your phone part of the laundry wenches' show?"

"Okay, technically the show was over." I sighed. "I'd just had enough, you know? My boss made it clear that no matter what I did, I was never going to make partner and I just . . . I'd had enough." The memory of that last phone call made my chest ache, but there was one part that had given me grim satisfaction. The part where I'd told him I quit, followed by tossing my phone in the oversized laundry tub onstage. The one that was filled with water. "Turns out phones didn't skip like stones do."

That made Mitch laugh, his boisterous laugh that always made me feel better. I glanced up again. The guy in black had his arm around Stacey—so they were a couple—and the band had joined them. They looked to be having a serious discussion, and when Stacey threw a glance my way I had the sinking feeling the discussion was about me. Probably how to get the half-drunk, unemployed lady out of the audience and on her way.

The last thing I wanted to do was overstay my welcome. "I'll be fine. I just need to get home. Regroup, you know? Get a new phone." I pushed to my feet. Time to get going. "Thanks for talking, Mitch, I really appreciate—"

"Oh no, you don't." Mitch put out a hand like he could stop me from where he was. "I know you. You're gonna go right back to work on Monday."

I had to scoff at that. "I think I burned that bridge pretty well."

"Then you'll get another job. The same shit, different office. Is that really what you want?"

"I don't . . ." My mind went blank. I had no answer for him. My goals had been just that—goals. High school valedictorian, summa cum laude at college, top percentile in law school, position with an established, high-profile firm, a partnership at said firm—they'd all been laid out in front of me like landmarks, but no one had ever asked if I'd wanted any of them.

"I love you, Lu. And I'm proud as hell of you. But when's the last time you felt really happy?"

I didn't even have to think. "Just now. Hanging out with your friend Stacey and listening to this music." My blood pressure momentarily lowered as I let myself relax into the memory, but I shook it off. "Doesn't matter. This isn't real life."

"Maybe not for you." Stacey had come back, and Mitch grinned at her through the phone.

"Damn straight. So what's the word?"

"About what?" But he wasn't addressing me, he was talking to Stacey, who nodded.

"As long as she's on board." She looked at me. "You are, aren't you?"

"On board with what?"

Stacey huffed. "You didn't tell her yet?"

"I was getting to it!" She huffed again, and he rolled his eyes before turning his attention back to me. "Lulu, we were think-ing. What if you disappeared for a little bit?"

"Disappeared?" I shook my head; he wasn't making any sense.

"Yeah. If you go home, your mom's gonna fill your head with the usual bullshit. You'll be back in that power suit, working for dickheads who don't appreciate you."

I clucked my tongue. "Don't hold back, Mitch. Tell me what you really think."

"You need a break," he shot back. "That's what I really think."

He wasn't wrong. I couldn't remember the last time I'd taken a vacation. The last time I'd had a day—weekend, holiday, didn't matter—where my phone hadn't rung or chimed with a text, with a fire at work that somehow only I could put out. I'd always told myself that when I made partner those days would end, but I'd been paying those dues for years with no return on investment.

But . . . "Let me get this straight. You're suggesting I run away and join the Renaissance Faire?" It sounded like a life plan made by a ten-year-old.

Next to me Stacey shrugged. "It worked for me," she said with a smile.

"Not forever," Mitch rushed to clarify. "You just need to clear your head. Stacey said they have room in their group, and they'll be hitting Willow Creek for our Faire in a few weeks. Hitch a ride with them, and you can come stay with April and me in July. Everything else can wait till then. Sound good?"

When he put it like that, it sounded . . . well, it sounded perfect. The thought of existing out here in the woods, not worrying about lawsuits or difficult bosses barking orders . . . it seemed too good to be true.

I glanced over at Stacey. "I don't suppose you're hiring?"

I was joking, but Stacey nodded. "We'll figure something out."

"Then it's settled." Mitch clapped his hands together. "I'll run interference with your folks, and we'll figure things out when you get here. Got it?"

"Got it." I handed the phone back to Stacey, dazed. I'd never been a "roll with it" kind of person, and I wasn't entirely sure what I'd just agreed to. But it had to be better than the life I was living.

Stacey disconnected the call with my cousin then tugged me to my feet. "Come on. We still have time before Faire closes for the day. Let's get you some garb so you'll be set up. Daniel's going to ask around tomorrow; someone always needs help with something around here." She hugged my arm. "I love this! I've been the only girl in the group for too long now. You'll have fun, I promise."

"That sounds like a threat." This was good. If I could make jokes, I was probably going to be okay.

But Stacey just laughed. "You know it! Lots of hair braiding and girl talk. Just don't let Dex flirt with you. He's bad news."

"I am not, how dare you." The voice came from behind us, a teasing growl. I turned to see one of the band members—the bad boy with the man bun. Of course. "Hey." He extended a hand to me in greeting. "Dex."

"Louisa." I slid my hand in his, giving him my best attorney handshake. Firm grip, firm eye contact, letting him know I wasn't going to take any shit.

And whoa, I needed that handshake to hide behind. Because up close Dex was a lot to take in. Strong hands, with a guitar player's calluses. That strength continued up his corded forearms, with muscles that were barely hidden by the loose lace-up shirt he wore. My firm eye contact brought me into the depths of his eyes. A dark brown that, this close, glittered with slivers of amber.

But he had to ruin it by smirking. He had to ruin it by know-ing the effect he had on women, and giving me an up-and-down appraisal.

"So you're coming along with us, huh?" A slow smile traveled over his face. "This is gonna be fun." There was no question as to what kind of fun he meant.

I took my hand back, startled. Spell broken.

Stacey whacked him on the shoulder. "What did I just say? She's not here for you." She sighed a long-suffering sigh and turned to me. "Ignore him. Come on."

I followed Stacey out to the lanes leading to the clothing ven-dors, and even though I could feel those dark eyes still on me, I didn't look back. I was well over my bad boy phase, and like Stacey said: I wasn't here for him. I had come to the Faire for me.

He just wanted a decent book to read ...

Not too much to ask, is it? It was in 1935 when Allen Lane, Managing Director of Bodley Head Publishers, stood on a platform at Exeter railway station looking for something good to read on his journey back to London. His choice was limited to popular magazines and poor-quality paperbacks – the same choice faced every day by the vast majority of readers, few of whom could afford hardbacks. Lane's disappointment and subsequent anger at the range of books generally available led him to found a company – and change the world.

'We believed in the existence in this country of a vast reading public for intelligent books at a low price, and staked everything on it'
Sir Allen Lane, 1902–1970, founder of Penguin Books

The quality paperback had arrived – and not just in bookshops. Lane was adamant that his Penguins should appear in chain stores and tobacconists, and should cost no more than a packet of cigarettes.

Reading habits (and cigarette prices) have changed since 1935, but Penguin still believes in publishing the best books for everybody to enjoy. We still believe that good design costs no more than bad design, and we still believe that quality books published passionately and responsibly make the world a better place.

So wherever you see the little bird – whether it's on a piece of prize-winning literary fiction or a celebrity autobiography, political tour de force or historical masterpiece, a serial-killer thriller, reference book, world classic or a piece of pure escapism – you can bet that it represents the very best that the genre has to offer.

Whatever you like to read – trust Penguin.